ONCE MORE TO DIE

BORGO PRESS BOOKS BY JAMES B. JOHNSON

Counterclockwise: A Science Fiction Novel
Habu: A Science Fiction Novel
Lead Me Not: A Romance of Aviation
Once More to Die: A Novel of Suspense
Trekmaster: A Science Fiction Novel
When the Pirate Prays: A Comic Crime Novel

ONCE MORE TO DIE

A NOVEL OF SUSPENSE

JAMES B. JOHNSON

THE BORGO PRESS
MMXIII

Published by Wildside Press LLC
www.wildsidebooks.com

DEDICATION

For all the Cuban families who yearned for freedom and found it in the United States. And specifically for Mayelin and Tony Llambes and their respective families whose stories helped inspire this work.

And a million thanks to friends who go over and above to help these books see the light of day, people like Kathy Houghton of Florida and Heather and Dave Datta of Massachusetts.

CONTENTS

CHAPTER ONE: HIM

When he heard the noise intrude into the background, he crouched behind a clump of leafy Brazilian pepper bushes. Tommy Atkins stuck his hand in his pocket and counted how many shotgun shells he had in his pocket.

Four and two at ready in the double-barreled shotgun he carried. The sawed-off double-barrel. Poor accuracy, and likely need plenty of ammunition.

But Atkins had lived here in the southwest Florida swamps for too many years without threat. He'd grown careless.

Today the sun was merciless; it was so hot and humid the clouds of mosquitoes had momentarily disappeared.

The noise—engine noise—reemerged and grew louder. Atkins smelled fetid swamp water and his own sweat.

Nobody ever came out here. Not ever. Not in all the years he'd lived here on and off.

So, he thought sadly. It's over. Finally. Matters not what or who's coming, it's over. Life as he knew it was slipping away as the engine noise increased. Mere minutes remained in this life.

From his vantage point he surveyed the path he'd been following. It was barely wide enough for one vehicle and vastly overgrown. He drove it maybe two or three times a month, going out for supplies. And he never fought back the jungle.

In front of him, the track widened about an acre to accommodate a towering cypress, a lone pine, and associated undergrowth. The open ground would give him a good view of who or what was coming. He broke open the shotgun and checked both barrels. He blew off imaginary dust and snapped it closed.

The engine noise became overwhelming where he went for months hearing nothing but his own pickup. The engine was low and throaty and didn't sound like any off-the-lot car or truck. Maybe a four-wheeled drive Jeep?

The camouflage nose of a military Humvee broke through the wall of vegetation, lumbered into the clearing and stopped alongside the cypress.

The Hummer was painted with jungle camo, but had no military markings.

Curiouser and curiouser. He thought regretfully of all of his books a mile back down the track, and their imminent demise.

Doors opened and six men climbed out. Like the Humvee, they were dressed in jungle camouflage. From here, they all looked Hispanic. All carried holstered pistols.

None said anything and one gestured. They dragged two figures out and dumped them on the ground. Both were bound with duct tape.

Atkins cursed to himself. He didn't need this. It wasn't his fight.

Then they dragged one of the figures—a man—off to the side and one of the men drew a handgun and shot the man in the head. The body spasmed and fell aside. What was left of his face showed a man of perhaps sixty or more wearing a distinguished moustache and white beard. Atkins begrudgingly admired the execution. A quick kill. No screwing around, no grandstanding, no speechifying, no justifying. Just do it and be done with it. Professional. The executioner, maybe six feet even, had a very sharp goatee and short, close-cropped hair,

The other bound figure exploded in action. Atkins saw it was a woman. She lashed out with her boots and took one man down. She rolled over on the soft ground and strained at her bonds. She rolled angrily toward his position, and then the two men caught her.

Well, hell. Atkins shook his head. He'd been too slow to help the man. How about the woman? Should he interfere? One man against six well armed men? And likely some kind of military or paramilitary group at that. If he did nothing, could he resume his life of the Everglades hermit?

No way on the last count. It was over. He had to leave. There'd be some kind of investigation. If not, these men might return and find him and ask questions, questions he couldn't or wouldn't answer.

The executioner looked around warily, apparently the only one alert. He had piercing eyes. He seemed to look through the brush at Atkins but then continued his search of the surrounding territory.

Two of the men laughed and, between them, ripped off the woman's fatigue jacket. Her long black hair splayed as she fought silently. Arms and legs bound and tape across her mouth.

One man cut the duct tape holding her legs. The other lifted her green T-shirt to expose her breasts. Then he fumbled at her belt for buttons and zipper.

No, they wouldn't do this. Not rape. Atkins could take almost anything, but drew the line at rape.

She bled tears of frustration and kicked and kicked until one of the men tripped her and the other held her down by the shoulders.

"Goddamnit," muttered Atkins.

He ducked back into the underbrush and slithered along until he was as close as he could get while still under cover.

They were dragging her camo pants off her now.

Atkins studied the group. Two lounged against the Hummer. Two were fighting with the woman. One stooped off to the side watching with intensity. The last one, the executioner, crouched alongside the body of the bearded man.

He waited until both rapists had dropped their pants around their ankles. They'd be at a distinct disadvantage now. The woman was bucking on the ground and making all kinds of noise even though muffled by the duct tape.

Atkins retrieved four shotgun shells and held them in his left hand. He took a deep breath, rose, and broke through the wall of the jungle disturbing dragonflies and mosquitoes like ripples.

Nobody noticed for a moment, long enough for Atkins to reach a point where the six were aligned as much as he could manage for target acquisition. Nothing he could do about the two would-be rapists. One leg of her pants was off and that was enough for the two. One man knelt between her legs and gripped her panties. The white splash of her panties made a strange juxtaposition of color in the clearing. Nothing here was of striking color other than the splattered blood from the head-shot.

The woman saw him first. Her big, brown eyes locked on him. Surprise and then dawning of hope.

The man twisted her panties in his hand and jumped when Atkins jammed the stubby shotgun against his left ear.

Her brown eyes showed no fear, but intelligence and immense curiosity. They distracted Atkins long enough so that when he looked up, the shooter had disappeared. Likely behind the Hummer.

Atkins knew his only chance was slipping away. He couldn't hold six men with a sawed-off shotgun.

Not that he wanted to.

He kicked the one between the woman's legs aside. The man rolled. Meanwhile, Atkins lifted his arm and pulled the trigger. Both men against the Hummer went down. He didn't worry whether the shot was fatal to either. Likely not, since it was a long shot and the pattern was too wide. He rotated to the single man standing aside and fired. That man flew backwards, surprise etched on his face and carnage etched upon his torso.

Atkins continued the motion and backhanded the second rapist with the barrel of the shotgun. He broke open the breach and quickly replaced the shells.

Rapist number one had recovered and was struggling with his pants to reach a handgun in a holster. Atkins shot him point blank, ripping most of his midsection out. Rapist number two was crawling off and Atkins shot him. The force of the shot so close ripped the back of his tunic off and gouged skin and gore into a pink spray. For yards around the two dead rapists, the ground had turned pink and pulpy.

Before the mist cleared, Atkins had his last two shells loaded and was zigzagging toward the Hummer. He felt large brown eyes tracking him. A shot whipped past his head like an angry mosquito and the blast told him it was likely a nine-millimeter.

He saw the head of the shooter over the hood of the Hummer and flung his arm up as if to fire. The head ducked and Atkins saved the shot.

He smelled cordite, an oddly familiar and comforting odor. The clearing was strangely quiet.

Neither of the two he'd shot first was dead, but they were peppered with shot and stunned. One of the two reached for his own weapon and Atkins stepped to him and kicked him under the chin hard. The snap of the man's neck was audible all over the clearing. The second man was lifting an automatic toward him and Atkins had to fire. The right side of that man disappeared and merged with the remnants of the Humvee's left front tire, rubber and brain matter and blood exploding simultaneously. One shot left.

Atkins scurried quickly to the rear tire to protect his legs in case the shooter was going to fire under the Hummer. He fought to control his breathing. Been a long time, he thought. He risked a quick look around the back of the vehicle. Nothing.

He grabbed the top of the Hummer and pulled it down, faking that he was climbing atop it, then dropped to the ground and swiveled him shotgun.

No sign of the shooter.

He looked around.

The woman was sitting up and screaming through her gag, pointing with her chin.

He looked where she was indicating.

The shooter was running back down the trail. Too far for his shotgun, but he fired anyway to scare the man. The shooter had somehow come up with a rifle, maybe an old M-16 from the look of it.

Atkins tore open a door and looked around inside. He found another M-16 and snatched it up. He put it on full auto, kicked off the safety, and jacked a shell into the chamber. He raised the weapon. The shooter was long gone, out of sight. He hosed off a few three-round bursts just to tell the shooter he was armed similarly. That should keep the man away.

Likewise, Atkins was constrained. If he chased the man, he'd be an easy ambush target a professional wouldn't miss. And the shooter had shown no mercy executing the man with the beard.

Atkins knew better than to leave any possible enemy alive. The only one in question was the man with the broken neck. Atkins put the M-16 to his head and fired a round. Most of the head disappeared in a spray of blood, matter, and goo.

He turned to the woman. She was staring at him in horror. She couldn't stand up, her fatigue pants bunched around her feet and her panties twisted.

Atkins reached down and pulled the knife out of his boot and swiftly cut the duct tape wound around her wrists. Then he brutally ripped the duct tape off her mouth and face.

She swore and spat.

She wobbled to her feet and Atkins caught her to steady her. She was five eight, maybe five ten.

The clearing was strangely quiet. Not even insects intruded.

She untangled her panties and straightened them. She pulled down her T-shirt, covering pert breasts. Then she struggled her fatigues up and fastened them.

Atkins was going through pockets of those he'd killed.

None had any identification, no wallets, nothing.

He found a couple of magazines for the M-16.

The woman had yet to speak. She hurried toward the bearded man, adjusting her garments. Atkins noticed she was favoring her left shoulder. Somewhere in the melee she'd been injured.

She fell to the ground beside the remains of the bearded man and wept silently.

Atkins came up behind her. "We have to go."

She looked up at him, misery boiling off her face. "Papá."

Shit, thought Atkins.

The woman's ebony hair was caked with dirt and grass, and hung loosely halfway down her back. Her light complexion highlighted scrapes and bruises.

Atkins pointed down the trail. "A mile. My place. Go. I gotta find the shooter."

"He has a radio. Probably a cell phone."

Damn. "Some cell phones don't usually work out here." He didn't have a cell phone, but he did have a prepaid wireless card for his laptop and it received a signal most of the time. With a radio, it didn't matter whether the shooter found a cell phone signal or not.

She shrugged and turned back to the body of her father.

Atkins made some lightning calculations. If the shooter had a radio, there had to be more of these guys somewhere near. He recalled the Indians telling him about Cuban anti-revolutionary group training somewhere out here in the middle of nowhere. Every month or two they came out here and played war games and shot up the landscape. Raul and Fidel were probably shaking in their boots.

His conclusion: they were out of time.

He grasped her under her left arm. She winced and jerked free of him.

"Come on, Pocahontas, we need to go. Now."

She glared at him. "I am Cuban, not Indian."

"I don't care. You gonna be dead, we don't get outa here."

Actually, she sounded American as apple pie. Only a slight Hispanic accent.

"Who are you?"

"Listen lady, it don't matter. I don't know what the fuck is going on or who the fuck you people are, but that is one dangerous son of a bitch. I can tell."

She collapsed at her father's feet.

"You were mighty tough fighting those men," Atkins pointed out.

"They killed my father."

"Let's get out of here and you can call a cop." Like hell. Not for a while, anyway. And not with him around, either. On the other hand, likely no cops within fifty miles.

She sat still.

"Look, Pocahontas, it ain't none of my business what you do. I'm leaving. I suggest strongly you get your cute ass up and in gear and join me getting the fuck out of here."

She shot him a glare, turned her head back to her father, closed her eyes, crossed herself, and rose gingerly. She favored her shoulder.

"I am not Indian. I am Cuban and proud of it."

"Where were you born?"

"Miami."

"Figgers." He headed off, walking swiftly.

What the *hell* had he gotten himself into?

She rose awkwardly and began to follow. She bent over a body and picked up a handgun. Another nine millimeter. She stuffed it in her waistline.

"Goddamn mosquitoes," she said and slapped at her arm, then winced in pain.

He continued on, taking long strides.

"Wait," she said suddenly. She turned and ran lightly, favoring her left shoulder, to the Humvee, rooted around inside, and came out with a ball cap. She pulled it on, ignoring her mess of hair, and followed him again.

He glanced back as she caught up. The cap read MIAMI DOLPHINS.

"There's hope for you yet, Pocahontas."

CHAPTER TWO: HER

"I am *not* Pocahontas. My name is María Elena Alejandrina Ximena Vásquez-Guerrero de García."

"Well, María Elena whatever. Let us expedite."

"Who are you?" she asked, steadying her left arm with her right hand, mimicking a sling.

"Nobody. That's me. Just another guy."

She spoke to his back. "An old Cuban proverb: Jovial companions make this life tolerable."

This strange man ignored her sarcasm and lengthened his pace. He'd slung the shotgun on his broad back and was carrying the M-16, combat sling wound around his wrist. He changed magazines and glanced over his shoulder, gray eyes moving quickly, searching. He was wearing jeans and a long sleeved khaki shirt.

María Elena realized he was special. This stranger was a big man, robust and muscular. He'd just killed five men on her behalf. As she watched him, wrenching at her bonds, he'd stood over her as if some colossus protecting her, coolly picking off the enemy. She'd never seen anyone move so fast. Reviewing the tableau in her mind, she saw his smooth motions all over again. He'd wasted no time, taking out the five in the quickest, most efficient manner. No extra movement, even when reloading his strange, stubby shotgun. Not any man would attack six well-armed military men with a two-shot weapon, one which was inadequate at distance. And she knew weapons; this man had not reacted to the recoil of the shotgun. He'd held it in one powerful hand steadily, and the recoil had not affected his smooth motions.

And Diego. Diego had killed Papá. Then disappeared. Don Diego was vindictive. He was a killer she now knew. María Elena thought to herself, "Papá, Diego will die for this. I promise." She crossed herself.

They were walking along in knee high scrub grass, following a dim double track of packed sand. Birds were announcing their presence again in a cacophonous uproar and the ubiquitous mosquitoes appeared from nowhere and attacked with rancor.

So who was this mystery man? When they'd thrown her and her father in the Humvee, she'd been certain of only one outcome: death. Diego was not to be trifled with.

Yet a stranger carrying an ever more strange weapon had miraculously appeared and saved her. He was not your usual inhabitant of palmetto plains and swamp and high sawgrass.

"Why are you here? Who are you?"

"Nobody, I already said. And you're welcome, Pocahontas."

"María Elena, amigo. And thank you very much. But my father…"

"Sorry for your loss. But I don't need to know."

"You are not curious? Why six men would kill an old man and his daughter?"

"I am, but I don't need to know. I don't need complications. You're a complication."

The events of the day overwhelmed her: Don Diego had killed papá. Papá had always been there for her, a grand father and a leader of men. She did not care for the world's loss, or the loss of the enslaved Cuban people. Right then, she only cared for her own loss. Yet she knew Diego would be coming for her. He needed her dead right now, especially after killing papá. She struggled to confine her grief to a section of her mind where soon she could open it and live her grief.

"As long as I am alive, Don Diego will come for me. He has a radio."

"Great. Just fucking great." He stopped and held up a hand,

turning his head as if to listen more closely to the sounds of the jungle.

They were in the open along the trail. María Elena could see the slope of a roof around a curve in the pathway.

"You ain't gonna tell me they got a chopper, too, are you?"

"Yes. Of course they do. Courtesy of the American government. Surplus." She made quote Signs with her right hand and regretted letting go of her left elbow. She grimaced. "I hear nothing."

"They or somebody got one and is heading this way."

She looked at him quizzically.

He favored her with a glance. "Back in the day, Pocahontas, I heard 'em all the time. You learn to know the sound. The mystic Mid East and points south."

"Lebanon?"

"Sure thing. And other places around there."

That made him somewhat older than her guess. She'd guessed forty, forty-five. But he was the kind who was ageless after forty. He could have been forty or sixty. That conflict had taken place when? It started during the mid-seventies? Anywhere from forty-five years ago to thirty-five years ago.

She sighed. "They will hunt me until they kill me."

"You gotta be important."

"No. I am just a blogger."

He snorted. "Hurry it up, Pocahontas, we gotta outrun a chopper."

They rounded the bend and a shack came into view. It was on short pilings. Perhaps six to eight hundred square feet, a room or two at the most. Front porch, a cistern on a tall cradle in the back. A dirty Ford F-150 pickup sat alongside the shack.

"Home sweet home," he said. "Uh oh."

He grabbed María Elena and dragged her off the path and into shallow water. He pushed her down in some sawgrass and reeds growing from the scummy water. She tasted algae. Her feet tangled momentarily in the tentacle roots of a mangrove. Noxious mud sucked at her as she settled into it.

"Keep your head down and watch out for gators and giant pythons, Pocahontas."

Gators? Giant snakes? Jesus, Joseph and Mary. "Pythons?"

"Yep. Or anacondas, I can't keep them straight. Don't worry; I've only seen a couple."

The chopper noise flowed over them as the strange man rolled onto the edge of the flat area around the house. He sprawled in a contorted, awkward position, concealing the M-16 below him. "Can you hear me?"

"I hear you."

"When you can, tell me if it's them. I'd hate to kill a bunch of tourists."

Kill? He is so confident, he is almost cocky, she thought and closed her mouth to expel a patch of slime. The thick, brackish water stank.

The chopper came into view, the old Black Hawk.

"I recognize the helicopter."

"Not me," he said, voice loud, "not familiar with this one."

"After your time," she said, raising her voice. "No weapons are installed, just only what the men carry."

"Tell me quick if they look like they're gonna shoot me."

In a moment, the helicopter swept up, and banked sideways. The mesmerizing "whompf whompf whompf" of the blades whipped gusts of wind and dirt across the open area.

"They are stabilizing. They swing sideways so those in the cabin can see you."

He didn't respond.

"Can you hear me?" she fairly shouted.

"Pipe down, Pocahontas, I hear you."

The chopper dropped altitude.

"It is maybe fifty feet off the ground." She paused. "Ten feet lower now, left hand side facing this way."

The great blades were buffeting the entire area. She dropped her head below the waterline so that only her eyes showed. But the winds blew the sawgrass aside and exposed her position.

She spit out water and gasped. "I think they see me. The door is opening and two rifles show." A plan occurred to her. "I will distract them."

"No, goddamnit. I…"

Suddenly, she stood, slimy water and mud shedding off her. She waited a moment for their attention to focus on her. Debris and dried wild grass blew past her. Her eyes dried. When they saw her, the chopper swung lower and more toward her, she raised the nine-millimeter and, with a two-hand grip while praying the weapon was not harmed by the water, she began firing calmly.

The two rifle barrels were swinging toward her and the chopper edged more her way. Sand and plant debris flew haphazardly about.

Then the stranger uncoiled like a snake aflame and came up firing his M-16. As she ran out of ammunition, she watched him fire three round bursts. The second burst found the open door and the third burst followed. He was good, shooting from the hip, like he'd done it his entire life. One of the rifles fell from above, twisting, and flew barrel first into the ground, quivering there. The next burst shot toward the cockpit and the chopper banked immediately and powered to higher altitude and staggered away.

As the engine sound faded, the stranger said, "They ain't gonna be back, not soon." He walked over and pulled on her good arm to help her out of the swamp's edge. "If they send a team from their base soon, by ground vehicle, how long will it take them to get here?"

She covered her breasts with her good arm, the automatic dangling.

"Look, Pocahontas, I already seen you topless. A wet T-shirt ain't gonna set me off any more."

She grimaced acknowledgement and dropped her arm and the weapon. No more ammo. "Maybe an hour. They have to get to the main road first, and then come this way, and finally drive all the way down this God-forsaken pathway."

"Gives us half an hour, maybe more. Another half an hour to

get to better roads where we can make different road choices."

He trotted to the shack and climbed a short flight of wooden stairs to the porch. A rocking chair and a table sat there, two books on the table. Fishing poles lay across brackets on the wall. "Come on," he commanded. He sat the M-16 on the rocking chair and opened the screen door.

Wearily, she followed him. Water and mud dripped off her. Some of the smelly mud from the edge of the swamp caked on her legs.

Inside it was neat and tidy. A bed sat alongside a far wall. A small kitchen occupied one quarter of the one-room place. An old couch and another rocker faced it. The other quarter of the room held a makeshift desk and stacks of books grew from the floor up the wall. A laptop sat centered on the desk.

From outside, a generator cranked on.

He turned to face her. "Lemme see." Lightly he traced her bad shoulder with gentle fingers. Then he went to her other shoulder, her good one, and did the same. "Shoulder separation." He grinned. "I could tell better with your shirt off, but as wet as it is, it don't matter anyway."

"What *is* your name? I have been undressed in your presence and I do not know your name?"

"All right, Pocahontas." He paused. "My name is Atkins, Tommy Atkins."

"Hello Mr. Atkins, I am María Elena—"

"I know. Listen, lie down on the floor." He eased her down and onto her back. She lay on a cheap tourist Seminole rug.

"Relax, Miss María Elena. You're safe with me." Strangely, she believed him. He grasped her left forearm. "Bend your elbow like this." Then he began pulling her forearm while twisting it. "Tell me if it pops back into position."

"Right." She tensed up.

"No, relax."

She made a visible effort and he continued to pull and rotate her arm.

She was determined not to show pain. As the pain grew, he

nodded approvingly.

He paused. "Relax, relax. Tense muscles ain't going to help."

Again she made an extraordinary effort.

He had maintained pressure and continued. He moved her forearm next to her chest and kept rotating it.

"Ahhhh." Her voice came in relief. The pain receded quickly. "Done." She knew she'd be sore for a few days.

He helped her up. "I'll get you some clothes. Outside next to the cistern barrel is a shower. It'll make you feel better. And smell better. There's a chemical toilet around back." He dug into a cupboard and handed her a towel. "Don't worry about running out of water; I don't think I'll need it any longer."

She stopped and looked up in his eyes. He was four or five inches taller than she, maybe six two, maybe six three.

"Thank you, Mister Atkins. I don't know how…"

"Never mind the bull shit, sister, just go hose off. We're in a hurry."

She gave him a faint smile and went out the door.

Around back, there was a small pallet and a PVC pipe with a showerhead. No hot water here. The plumbing connected to the barrel in the cradle. Above it, roofing gutters led to a set of filter screens on top. Rainwater shower.

Favoring her shoulder, she gingerly removed her foul clothing including the ripped panties. They'd been almost as uncomfortable as her aching shoulder. She twisted the handle and water gravity-fed onto her hair. She found a bar of soap on a ledge and soaped down quickly. After she rinsed herself, she tried to wash her hair, aware of the passage of time.

From time to time she heard unexpected noises from inside.

Who is this Tommy Atkins? And how does such a warrior come to be so far from civilization?

The water was tepid, the giant barrel having been heated by the sun.

She was soaping her legs when she heard an exclamation.

Tommy Atkins stood there stunned. "You clean up good, girl. And I thought you were scrawny under all that dirt and muck."

Shamelessly he watched her until she became self-conscious and grabbed the towel he was holding.

He put some clothes on the ledge. "Jeans and shirt from an Indian kid. Hairbrush, but don't waste time on that. You can brush in the truck."

"Indians?"

"They used to live here, and I used to rent the place from them after they moved out."

"Used to?"

"Now they got a stake in a casino and live in a million dollar condo on the beach in Lauderdale. Ain't seen 'em in five years."

Water was still running and she stepped aside on the pallet.

Atkins shook his head. "I am beginning to be impressed. You're good in a firefight. You look a lot better without clothes and mud. I betcha you got character, too."

"Thank you. I think."

"I been meaning to tell you, Pocahontas, that decoy move with the chopper was perfect. Gave me time to get the range." He set the clothes down. "We're out of time. Get dressed. No underwear to fit."

"It's okay. I'll go commando."

"If the tennis shoes are too big, there's a couple of pairs of socks and that ought to work out."

"Thank you, Mr. Atkins."

"Tommy. Mr. Atkins makes me feel old." He leered at her. "After seeing all of you, I ain't near as old as I thought I was."

Soon she was dressed. The shirt was too large so she tied it off around her waist showing a little skin.

She ran up the steps into the house. He had two small duffel bags packed. He put his laptop on them. "Take these to the truck."

She grabbed one and the laptop and went out and to the Ford. It was a few years old and she'd seen a million of these on the back roads out here.

She returned for the last duffel and found him dousing the inside of the place with gasoline from a five-gallon can. That one emptied, he picked up another and splashed gasoline on the books and bedding. He emptied the metal gas can and tossed it aside.

The fumes were gagging María Elena and she went out onto the porch.

What the hell was he doing?

He came out and went down the stairs. Under the stairs he retrieved two propane tanks. She watched as he put them inside alongside the walls. Then he turned the valves atop them and she could smell the agent they put in propane so you can smell it. The mix of gasoline and propane was deadly.

He came out and picked up the two books next to the rocker and stuffed them into the duffel she carried. "Better clear out, Pocahontas. Might be a spark someplace."

She ran down the stairs and dropped the duffel in the bed of the pickup.

He climbed in and started the truck and backed it until it was heading out. He got out and pointed for her to get in. "You drive for a minute. Put her in drive with your foot on the accelerator and the other on the brake. When I yell, drop the brake and get us the hell outa here." He looked at her expectantly.

"Wait!" She ran around the house and came back with her Miami Dolphins hat and got behind the wheel. "Ready."

He took another gas can and poured gasoline all over the porch. Then he poured a small trail of the liquid to the truck. He tossed the gas can onto the porch and climbed over the tailgate. "Ready?"

She closed the door and put her hands on the wheel and put the truck into gear.

"You betcha," she said, mocking him.

He held a large box of kitchen matches. He struck and dropped one and it went out on the way down. He cursed. Then he lighted another match. With that one he caught the whole box on fire. As all the sulfur tips began flaring, he dropped the flaming mess on the puddle of gasoline below him. It popped immediately into flames.

"Go!" He sat quickly for safety as she accelerated the truck. "Faster."

She really stood on it.

In the mirror she saw an arc of flame race across the dirt and up the stairs. The entire porch ignited at once. She felt rather than heard the whoosh. She also saw that Atkins was down in the bed of the truck, protecting himself.

She was up to forty on this terrible pathway and going faster by the second. She was afraid she was going to lose control as the Ford bounced and banged amongst the ruts.

Suddenly, the whole world went quiet, then a tremendous blast sounded and the force of it hit the truck and rocked it. She glanced over her shoulder and saw a plume of fire streak into the air two hundred feet high. "Oh my God." A quick pressure differential assaulted her ears.

The truck skidded off the pathway and she slowed quickly, trying to regain the roadway. Then Atkins was banging on the back window and she slowed to a stop.

He jumped out and went to the driver's door. "I'll take her from here."

They both looked back. Pockets of flame were burning all around where the house had been and out toward the swamp. The house was still a mass of flame, but she could see that it no longer existed. The structural integrity of the shack was gone, eight smoking pilings remaining, two at an angle, and the oils in them beginning to burn brightly.

The surroundings were eerily quiet; birds had silenced, lizards and ground animals were no longer scurrying about. The wind seemed to have been sucked away. Clumps of dry grass burned. Even the omnipresent mosquitoes had disappeared.

She smelled burned civilization. Everything this man owned, gone in a second, and by his own hand. Soon the land would reclaim the remains. Why would he do that? All he had to do was go away until things quieted down. There was only one conclusion to be drawn: not only did Tommy Atkins not want to be found, but also he did not want to exist. And apparently, he no longer did.

She had to wonder. Was he some kind of pervert hiding out in the middle of the swamps? Was he on the run? What was he hiding from? An abandoned family? A bad business? The law?

Or could he be one of those men you infrequently hear about, not hermits necessarily, but recluses, men who wanted nothing to do with society any longer. She remembered his familiarity with weapons and his quick-kill ability. She shivered. Was she safe with him?

She didn't know, but she did know he had saved her from rape and death and killed five and maybe more men on her behalf and he didn't even know her. She resolved to withhold her judgment.

Mentally, she crossed herself and scooted across the bench seat to the passenger side.

Tommy Atkins stood looking at the utter destruction for another second, sighed, then slipped behind the wheel, closed the door, and pulled the gearshift into low. Soon he was following the path again, returning the way they had fled from the scene of the gunfight.

"I want to bury Papá," she said with resolution.

He drove without answering immediately. "Would it not be better for authorities to do their CSI thing?"

She thought for a minute and said quietly, "I don't know." She dropped her head in sorrow. Then she looked at him. "By the time law gets here, animals will desecrate the bodies..."

"There's that," he allowed. "We could put him in the truck and take him to a mortician."

She sensed he did not want to do that thing. "I dunno. Don't they have to have certified death certificates and all?"

He nodded knowingly. "You can't simply drop off a body at a funeral home, not unless you already—never mind."

They rounded a turn and came into the clearing. The Humvee was there canted over like the damaged machine it was.

All six of the bodies were gone.

"Diego!" she spat.

"You betcha, sweetie. They done removed the evidence. And they will be back for the Hummer, too." He stopped and looked around. "It explains why the chopper was so easy to run off."

Through the windshield she could see back the way they had come. A column of black, oily smoke twisted angrily into the clear sky.

He saw her looking. "Gotta get going. Might be a wildlife officer want to check that out."

He reached behind the seat and rummaged around. He came out with a large square of printed cardboard. He showed her.

STEP

Save the endangered panther

He took it over and affixed it to a lone Australian pine tree. He got in and they drove off.

"Two plus two," she said. "Your own decoy."

"Smart girl, Pocahontas. Them enviro-freaks are dangerous, no?"

Eventually, they graduated to a gravel road. Which itself T-ed off on a country back road. Which eventually led to a more traveled thoroughfare. She took off her baseball cap and brushed her hair, finally parting it in the middle and gathering it in the back. She found a rubber band on his shifter and snapped it around her hair in the back.

As they slowed to turn west, María Elena saw a couple of buildings with two airboats behind in a short canal leading into the swamp.

"Get your head down," Atkins told her.

She ducked.

"Indians," he said. "They pay attention and we don't want them to tell anyone they saw an attractive young lady driving out of here." He waved at somebody. "They've seen the smoke and heard the explosion and they are curious. Jesus, it's eating at them." He laughed. "Soon as we're out of sight here, they'll be in one of those airboats heading out toward the smoke." He shook his head. "Nice guys, those Seminoles. Got my mail and picked up stuff in town for me if I wanted. This particular family didn't make it into the casino business."

The road was smoother and they accelerated. "Okay, you can get up now."

She sat upright.

"These lands, nothing is out here. I do not blame the Indians for moving to Ft. Lauderdale. If I were with them, I would too."

"Some call them 'Glades Indians,' and some of them don't want anything to do with big cities and their like. When I was growing up everything south of Lake Okeechobee and between the east and west coasts of Florida, they used to call the Everglades. Now both coasts are steel, glass, and concrete and creeping toward each other. Now they got the Big Cypress National Preserve, the Fakahatchee Strand, with the Everglades tucked in and about and below these. Sometimes you don't know where you are and you don't care: it's all the same scrub and swamp and sawgrass and palmetto plains."

They drove along for about twenty minutes.

"I don't really want to know, Pocahontas, but I can't help but noticing your father is deceased illegally and you ain't hollering for a cop."

"I don't really want to know, amigo, but I can't help but noticing you just destroyed every trace of your existence out here instead of hollering for a cop."

CHAPTER THREE: HIM

He was watching her as he drove.

"No," she said. "No, I am not afraid of you."

He shrugged.

"After what you did? What we've been through?" She touched his shoulder. "I am too exhausted to care anyway."

"Okay, then, Pocahontas, I want you to think of where you want me to drop you off. Next stop Naples." He drove west toward the coast on the ragged coral road.

She ignored him. "I suspect you have as much or more to fear from me."

"There you go." He was wondering what to do with her. Would she call law enforcement on him? Somehow, he didn't think so.

She removed her hat and began brushing her long, black hair again. It was drying out and more manageable. There was an animal scent about her, strangely reminiscent of cinnamon.

He pulled over and got the M-16 from behind the seat. He walked to the edge of a canal and tossed the weapon as far as he could.

In the truck he hid the shotgun in the seat springs under the driver's seat. He could get to it quickly if necessary.

"Awkward to have a recently fired weapon like that if a cop pulls you over."

He could see only a waft of smoke back from whence they came.

He turned onto State Road 29 and eventually they connected

with the Tamiami Trail and headed for Naples on the southwest coast.

They soon were in town.

"Gimme your hat a minute." He held out his hand and she carefully pulled it off her head, and then patted her hair down to insure it was still in place. He took it and grinned at her vanity. "Sunglasses in the glove compartment."

He put the hat on low over his eyes and she retrieved a scratched pair of sunglasses and put them on.

He went into a drive-through line at a bank and stopped at the ATM. She looked away as to not show even a profile to the mandatory camera's eye.

"Just being careful," he said. "You can never tell."

They repeated the process several more times.

"I know I shouldn't ask?"

"No problem, Pocahontas. I got a grand or two in several accounts. Raise no suspicions. And I didn't empty the account. It sits there if I ever need it again."

After the last bank, he said, "All right, María Elena. Where you want me to drop you off?"

She didn't answer and he drove through a McDonald's for drinks.

"Don't hurry with your answer," he prodded as they returned to the road.

She still didn't answer. He could see confusion on her face. It didn't matter. His own survival was at stake. He'd done his best for her. Never fucking mind the connection that had grown between them. Even as he recognized that, he dismissed it. He neither needed nor wanted complications, and he'd already helped her more than she could reasonably expect.

He headed out Pine Ridge Road for the Interstate.

"Well, Pocahontas?"

"I on't know." Her voice was quiet and meek.

"Goddamnit." He saw which lane he needed to get on I-75 north and soon they were riding in the right lane going the speed limit.

He gave her hat back and she flashed him a weak smile. "I am raggedy in these clothes," she said.

"Bullshit, Pocahontas. You look good in anything and you damn well know it. Listen, next stop Ft. Myers in less than an hour. You figure it out by then."

Once in Ft. Myers, he exited on Daniels Road and cut over on Tamiami Trail once again until he found College Parkway. He saw a big mall and pulled in the parking lot.

He parked far out for privacy. The sun was going down.

"All right, girl. What now?"

"I on't know."

"You already said that."

"I do not know what to do."

"Friends?" he asked. "Family? Johnny Law?"

"Papá was my family. He is gone."

"Friends?"

"I do not know whom to trust."

"Cops? I couldn't help but notice a murder and attempted rape and attempted murder."

She shrugged. "No proof now. And Don Diego has friends, official friends, everywhere."

"Come up with something PDQ."

"I think the best thing for me is to remain hidden for now. Until I can determine what to do. And it would confuse Don Diego."

"Jesus."

"Please? Do not blaspheme?"

"Ever since I met you, Pocahontas, I been doing that. And I ain't done yet."

She slumped in the seat and tried but failed to pout.

"Don't matter anyway," he said with finality. "Go underground, hide, find a cop, I don't care. Just do it and do it without me."

"No."

"No?"

"Where would I go? What would I do?"

Atkins leaned back and closed his eyes. "Why me, Lord?"

She shifted uncomfortably.

"Okay, girl. Here's Plan B." He fumbled in his pocket and came up with a wad of bills. "Here. Maybe a grand. Go into that mall before they close. Get some clothes, okay?"

"You'll wait for me?"

"No, I gotta make a final big withdrawal. I'll be back in an hour."

"You won't. No, you will leave me."

It was his plan, lame as it was. He was almost ashamed.

"Nah, I can't leave you, Pocahontas. I got a proprietary interest in you."

She brightened. "Promise?"

"Sure."

She looked at him with a piercing glare.

"Lookit, girl. I done killed at least five men today. So promises don't mean much to me right now. But I will come back for you."

She snatched the money out of his hand and jumped out of the truck. She slammed the door and looked at him pleadingly. She knew that he could dump her anytime and if he was going to, this was as good a place as any.

As she turned away, he called out, "Get some ibuprofen for your shoulder, too."

Her face lighted up as if he'd somehow confirmed to her satisfaction that he would in fact return for her. She headed across the parking lot to the mall.

He drove off and headed for the self-storage facility. He was angry with himself. No way he could encumber himself with her. Too much baggage. He regretted lying to her, but that's life. He'd done more for her than she could possibly expect. Actually, what he should have done was put her down. Now he was exposed. Too many years alone and hidden: not any longer. But there was something about her. He acknowledged to himself that most women would have been a ton of trouble: but she'd pulled herself together after her father's death and then made a quick choice to deal with him and not the paramilitary types. She'd performed just right when the chopper appeared, becoming the bait, the distraction to give him a better opportunity. Naah. Shame to waste a woman with those characteristics.

He spat out the window, for there was a bad taste in his mouth. She shouldn't be so trusting. Yes, let this be a "teachable moment" to her.

He found the self-storage and drove to his unit.

Parking in front of it to block any view of the door, he dialed the combination and removed the lock. After insuring no one was watching, he lifted the aluminum door, went inside, and lowered the door. He turned on the light, a simple protected bulb in the back.

The unit was almost empty. But on the bare concrete floor sat a trunk, two suitcases, and a brief case. He pulled the brief case out and opened it. Inside were dozens of business size envelopes. He sat it aside and opened the trunk. He picked up four large manila envelopes. He glanced inside and saw each was still stuffed with cash. He dropped these into the briefcase.

Next he removed a covering plastic wrap and there rested several handguns and another sawed off shotgun. Alongside these were boxes of ammunition. He got a gun cleaning kit out and oiled and disassembled and reassembled a .380 revolver. This he put into the briefcase with the money. He added a box of shells for it and a box of shotgun shells. The briefcase was over full, but he rearranged it and it fit better.

The suitcases contained clothes and he had enough from the cabin. And he did not want to be carrying around too much.

Back in his truck, he found Anderson and followed it to I-75. He took the on ramp north and settled down at sixty for in town driving. Soon he crossed the Caloosahatchee River. Dark was falling quickly, speeding from east to west. He turned on his headlights.

He tried to keep his mind off María Elena. She was a bright woman. She'd find her way. He certainly needed no complications. He had to disappear once again and find and begin a new life. He resented María Elena for causing the upheaval of his life. Intellectually, he knew it was not her fault, but still....

Ten minutes later he slowed. *"Goddamn it!"*

He took the exit, made the butterfly, and returned to I-75 heading south.

Forty-five minutes later he cruised into the empty mall parking lot. The place had shut down. "Shit."

He drove over toward the main entranceway shaking his head. Atkins hoped she would make good decisions.

He drove to the end of the parking aisle to find an exit and his headlights swept over the walkway and a forlorn figure sitting hunched over on the curb. Her silhouette was strange since her posture was usually straight as a ruler.

María Elena's face lighted up like a Christmas tree. Behind her was a suitcase on wheels and a department store plastic bag. She was wearing new slacks, a blouse, and loafers. And a new baseball cap, this one a NASCAR, #18. Kyle Busch, he knew, from Las Vegas. Natural driver with an edge. Already a star and bigger things ahead.

She jumped to her feet and lifted the suitcase into the bed of the pickup and climbed into the cab, stuffing the bag behind her seat. She beamed at him. "I knew you'd come."

He smelled a phantom cinnamon odor.

"Yeah, right," he grumbled. "I got hung up." It sounded lame even to him.

"Does not matter, you are here. I trusted you. See?"

"No. Hell, I was dumping your ass, Pocahontas. I don't need you. For that matter, you don't need me. You ain't seen trouble yet until you been with me."

"I don't believe you. God sent you to me."

He shook his head angrily. Anger at himself more than her. "Don't count on me as a guardian angel. I am no angel." He laughed out loud. "I've never seen myself as the weapon of God."

She shrugged happily. "Where to, amigo?"

"Three to four hours. International airport, Orlando."

She leaned back, her sense of relief obvious. "Wherever."

CHAPTER FOUR: HER

Two hours later she woke, fuzzy, suddenly unsure of where she was.

Then memory flooded over her. Her heart sank. Papá was dead. Diego had finally shown his true colors, a condition that had been building for years now.

Through barely open eyes, she glanced at Tommy Atkins. His face was stone, concentrating on driving. Suddenly, his right eye swiveled and found her watching him.

"Hello, Sleeping Beauty."

She sat up. "Where are we?"

They were exiting I-75.

"Tampa, outskirts thereof. Now we're getting on I-4 for Orlando."

"Orlando International Airport?"

He nodded, looked over his left shoulder, and merged onto I-4 eastbound. This time of night traffic was light and I-4 east at this point eight and then six lanes wide.

"Where are you going to fly to?"

He shook his head. "My business."

"Sorry," she said. Then she grinned. "They don't allow shotguns on airplanes these days."

"Oh, well."

She knew full well he had a knife in his boot and likely a handgun or two in his duffels—not to mention, her curiosity peaked when she'd looked around earlier and saw a new briefcase, a large one. She held her tongue. All those weapons? Not likely he was going to get on an airline flight.

"I'm hungry," she said. "I haven't eaten today."

"You should have grabbed something at the mall food court."

She glared at him. "I was in a hurry. I did not want you to have to wait on me."

A moment, then he said, "Oh."

A few minutes later he took the Thonotosassa exit, crossed over the Interstate and found a truck stop. Inside there was an Arby's and a Popeye's.

They had fried chicken, French fries and large colas.

Sitting at the table, she watched him devour four pieces of chicken.

"Eat, Pocahontas. You need some meat on those bones." He nodded. "And the energy."

"Yes, dear," she mimicked and smiled. "How domestic."

"Don't get any ideas, Miss six names."

"Seven if you count the hyphen."

"Jeez. You a English major?"

"No. Political science, international affairs."

"I knew it. A goddamn college girl."

She shrugged, self-conscious. "That was many years ago, back when I was young."

"College Girl, you *are* young."

"Too many years ago, I graduated."

"Sorry I missed the ceremony. What college?"

"Hillsdale."

"In Michigan?"

"Yes. Papá liked the place for its politics, very straight-laced, don't you know. Moral codes, written and unwritten. He thought I'd be sheltered up there."

"Were you?"

"Pretty much, Tommy. Surprisingly, I learned a bunch."

"Great for you."

"And Hillsdale is very patriotic, a trait we Cuban-Americans hold dear."

"If you say so."

She began to eat with gusto, her stomach finally making her bend to its will. After a minute, she looked up at him. "A lot of politics. Cuban people are like that. So are we expats."

"You're American. If you were born in Miami, you are an American citizen."

She nodded. "I am. But my heritage, it is Cuban. My father, my mother. They were Cuban."

"Were?"

He knew about her father. She sighed. "My father ran an anti-revolutionary group, dedicated to the downfall of Fidel and Raul, and after them, their communist legacy. It is called January 13. Or, *13 de enero*."

"Usually those kinds of dates have significant meaning," he said.

Her eyes were sad. "They do. On one January thirteen, some twenty-five years ago, they lined up my mother and her brothers and other anti-revolutionaries against a wall in Canaleta prison, in Ciego de Ávila. They shot them all down, cruelly, one by one. No one knows what they, what my mother, went through before they killed her against that foul wall."

"Jeez. A lot for a kid to handle."

"My father and I were in Miami. They always kept me there, out of harm's way, and they went to the island and organized the underground. I was five and did not understand why I would never see my mother again."

Atkins had stopped eating, eyes softening for a moment. "Yeah. Dead parents, that ain't good for a kid." His voice was reflective.

She didn't follow-up on the opening.

He drank from his large fountain cup. "You're saying the politics are keeping you from heading back home? You live in Miami?"

"I do. We did. I dunno any longer."

"This is America, College Girl. You can do whatever you want whenever you want."

"You go tell that to my father."

He sat back. "There is that."

"I am on one of those terrorist watch lists, either the original data base check list or that selectee watch list. Whatever, they run you through all kind of computer checks and extra screenings. I don't know how or when everything went to hell, but Don Diego…"

"Yes?" he prompted.

She shuttered and shook her head. "Not now, maybe later. Suffice it to say, he is a very powerful man in the exile Cuban community."

"Why did he want your father dead?"

She shrugged, indicating she didn't want to talk about it.

"Not to mention raping you. They were gonna kill you after, you know."

"Yes." She wiped her mouth. "I am no longer hungry."

"All right, enough is enough anyway. Not my business. Orlando International is less than two hours from here. It is midnight now and I don't want to get there when it is not crowded. I'd say nine in the morning would be about right. The more people, the less attention."

"Then what?"

He avoided her eyes. "I go on my way. You go your own way. We part. We're done. Finished. It's been nice, but no cards at Christmas." His voice was hard.

"I don't have anywhere to go."

"I'll give you money. Go anywhere. Hide out. Call a friend. You gotta have some."

"I don't know who is compromised."

"Don't gimme that spy talk BS."

"Not spy talk. A manner of speaking."

"There's a rest stop up the way, maybe thirty miles, I disremember. On the east side of Lakeland. We will crash there until the morning and then head for the airport."

"Whatever, Mr. Atkins. I am too tired to think right now."

An hour later they were parked in the farthest slot at the state rest stop. They washed up in the bathrooms and returned to the truck.

"It is so strange, no mosquito clouds," said Atkins.

"Other kinds of clouds."

"Okay, Pocahontas, didn't mean to cheer you up. You can try to sleep in the truck, I am going to walk around."

She climbed into the truck and watched him walk through the rest stop. Call it reconnoitering. It was like he was just walking to stretch his muscles after a long drive. Yet she saw him check out the few other cars that were here. A security car was parked at the other side of the parking lot. At the end of the sidewalk, Atkins twisted his large torso, touched his toes a couple of times and turned to come back. A weary traveler. A car drove in and parked in front of the restrooms. Atkins avoided their headlights.

He slid into the driver's side. "I don't know if they like you parking and sleeping, but that rent-a-cop doesn't seem to care. There are four others doing the same."

He slid the bench seat back and rested his head against the window. "Lock your door." He sat up and fished out the new briefcase from the back. He pulled out a revolver and an envelope. He put the revolver on the seat beside him and folded an AAA Florida map over it. He opened the envelope and sorted around inside. He handed her two credit cards. Then he removed a large manila envelope and pulled out several stacks of bills. These he dropped in her lap.

"Now you're set."

There was several thousand dollars in cash. She read the credit cards. A MasterCard and a Visa, both in different female names. "These are?"

"Credit cards, College Girl. You're a woman; don't you know what a credit card is?"

"You know the question, gringo."

"They're safe, never been used. Don't charge more than a grand at a time and you should be all right. Discard 'em after a week or two, depending on use. I had them to sell if I ever needed to."

"I am guessing there are other credit cards in those envelopes?"

"Sure, a whole bunch."

"Credit theft? Identity theft?"

"Not exactly. Got a bunch of good ones from a guy I know in Miami. Never used. I got money, but I don't have good ID. Maybe you've figured that out by now?"

She nodded.

"Anyway, I have these for emergency use only. Otherwise, I wouldn't dare think of drawing attention to myself. Sometimes credit cards are required. A lot of cash draws attention. Like airline tickets."

"I think I understand."

"Don't matter," he said. "Just be careful. If it feels wrong, leave it and walk away."

Apparently this Tommy Atkins was professional at hiding his identity and his trail. He'd planned all this out long ago. What did that mean? She was beginning to get a picture of him.

"Thank you, I think."

He settled back against the side door and closed his eyes. Soon he was asleep.

María Elena leaned back and realized he'd effectively deflected her problem. He was still going to dump her at the airport. Why there?

At nine in the morning, they pulled off 417 to 528 to the airport access.

"And I thought the traffic in Miami was bad," María Elena said.

"Lesson: consider it protective coloration. The more cars, the less you stand out."

He drove right into the south parking garage and up to the middle one. At the machine, he got the time and date parking ticket and put it in his pocket. He found a slot and stuffed all of his gear from the bed of the pickup into the cab behind the seat and covered it all with a plastic tarp.

"Let's go." He carried her suitcase rather than drag it on rollers.

Reluctantly, she followed, noting the parking row and location where he had left the truck. What was Atkins up to? Why the airport? Where was he going? Just who in the hell was Tommy Atkins? With a chill, she remembered that he had killed five men without any emotional reaction. Not your basic man-on-the-street.

More importantly, what in the world was she going to do? There was no one, not since Don Diego had gradually separated her from her group of friends. She still had Papá's contacts, but who was compromised? And, if not, could she trust them anyway? Diego had the power and people knew it.

As they got onto the elevator, she tugged her Kyle Busch hat down resolutely.

The elevator took them down to a bottom floor where they followed directions and went up an escalator.

"I'll never understand life," Atkins observed. "Sometimes you have to go down to go up."

He led her past the throngs surrounding the ticket counters. "This way." He was following some of the signs above the concourse. In a central location, he stopped. The noise level was high. The ceiling several floors up. On one side an airport hotel. Concourses led off this central location. One fed into it marked ARRIVALS, DO NOT ENTER. Another led to a very large food court. Above them starting all around the central area, grew a Hyatt hotel, rooms circling the entire central area, accessible by glassed-in elevators. They stood under the giant flight information board. Atkins looked around and nodded to himself, yet he always kept his head down. "There." He strode to a small side corridor. There sat a bank of sit-down telephones.

"All right, Pocahontas, I know you got a plan by now." He jerked a thumb over his shoulder. "Telephones. Must be one uses coins. If not, try one of those credit cards." He sat her suitcase down and telescoped open the handle, twisted it around towards her and put it in her right hand. "Buy a ticket for someplace. Go to Vegas for a couple of weeks."

She felt stricken. What was she going to do?

"Um, María Elena?"

She looked up at him. What now?

"If you could see your way to kind of forgetting you ever saw me? That thing would please me to no end. You really don't want those complications."

"Don't leave me, Tommy." She was embarrassed her voice was plaintive.

"No choice. I gotta catch a flight."

"Don't leave me, Tommy." She couldn't think of anything else to say. A passing couple glanced at her.

"You'll be fine, college girl." Gently, he took her shoulders and urged her toward the phones. He let go and patted her ass once. "Good luck, María Elena Alejandrina Ximena Vasquez-Guerrero de García."

She turned to speak and he was gone, already melting into the crowd. She felt an unaccountable sadness.

She went to the end of the row of phones and sat down. What to do? The hell with him. She could handle herself. She'd passed the big three zero; she was no longer a kid. Deciding, she fumbled around in her new purse and came up with a cell phone she'd bought at the mall in Ft. Myers.

Dialing the number from memory, she crossed her mental fingers.

"Eduardo?"

"Yes? María Elena, is it you?"

"It is, Eduardo. I need help."

"What is happening, Alejandrina?" Eduardo was her father's lawyer. And he was her Godfather. He always called María Elena by her Alejandrina name since she was named after Eduardo's late wife.

"I'm not sure—"

"Where is your father? There are rumors."

"Eduardo, he is dead."

"Dear Lord."

"Executed. Don Diego put a pistol to his head and pulled the trigger."

"Oh, Alejandrina. We've seen blood through the years, but now—"

"I'm stuck at the airport in Orlando with nowhere to go."

"Where is your father?"

"Don't know that either. They took his body."

"I will tell you, rumors are flying here at the speed of light. Don Diego has some in with the authorities."

"He must pay for killing Papá."

"We need proof. He could be on one of his secret trips to the island."

"That's what I've been thinking, Eduardo."

"I must tell you, the word is out if anyone hears from you, they are to pass the word to Don Diego."

"That means he doesn't know where I am or if I'm still a player."

"Yes. What happened? How are you alive? You were with your father."

"I escaped. I will tell you about it later."

"Well, you need to keep out of sight until I can find out what is going on and make arrangements."

"Where can I go?"

"I don't know people outside of Miami. Not much anymore. My time is past. Go somewhere and hide for a few weeks and then call in sometime and maybe I'll have some answers." He hesitated. "But keep me informed where you are and how to reach you, okay?"

Damn. María Elena was afraid of that.

"I will tell you something else, my dear. I think the Task Force could be used against you. They have resources."

"What do you mean?"

"Don't use your credit cards. Likely they have a flag set up on them by now. They will hunt you down like a dog. They can call on local FBI anywhere or local police. You should really disappear. I can send you money?"

"I have money."

"Then go and go fast for they might be monitoring my telephone."

He hung up abruptly.

It was worse than she thought.

She'd been working a thought while talking to him. No airline, no Vegas. Disregard what Atkins had said; she didn't have sufficient ID to get on an airplane. Not to mention the terrorist watch list thing.

She could, though, rent a car.

No! She had no driver's license. And if she did, it would be in her own name and that wouldn't do, not now.

Rent a car! By God, Tommy Atkins, I got you. He wasn't about to fly either. Not with lists everywhere. When he got the parking ticket, he'd absently put it in his pocket. One reason: so they wouldn't know when his truck had entered the parking garage. Thus no one would be able to guess when he'd left: whether by plane, taxi or rental car. The man was good. Where better to hide a vehicle for a long time? She admired his technique.

Where did that leave her? Taxi? Okay. To where?

She got up and walked swiftly. She followed the signs to the car rental area.

There! Atkins' large frame stood out as he talked to the agent. She stood alongside a pillar and watched. Finally, he was finished with the paperwork and headed out the door.

María Elena smiled. With shotguns and duffels and briefcases, he had one choice: pick up his rental and drive to his truck for his belongings. She turned and went down the escalator to find the elevators to go up.

She found the Ford pickup with no trouble. He wouldn't be here for a while. He had to sign for his car and wend his way around and then back up here.

She leaned against the truck and dialed her childhood friend.

"Tillie?"

"ME? Is that you?"

"It is, hon. I need help."

"Do you ever. You're hot, girl. Hot like radioactive. Like Day-Glo green. Like—"

"I got it. I still need help."

"Whatever I can do, ME. You know that…"

The word "but" hung unsaid. What could Tillie do? She was in Miami. María Elena couldn't stay with her. Tillie would be suspected anyway, even without this contact. Tillie had a husband and three young children.

"ME? A man came to the door this morning."

"Cubano?"

"He asked politely if I knew where you were."

"Oh, shit."

"He told me I had a nice home and three beautiful children and a fine husband."

"Oh, shit."

"Yeah. I—"

"Sorry I called you, hon. I won't bother you again."

"Wait, ME, I want you to know I love you."

"Me, too, Tillie. Bye." María Elena disconnected.

Depression flooded over her. Damn. She castigated herself for not figuring that out sooner. She felt like walls were closing in on her. She had no idea of whom to trust, or what to do right now, for that matter. She realized she didn't even know how to hide, not very well, not without resources, identification, and a lot of money.

"Fuck it," she said aloud. She dropped the Ford's tailgate, tossed her suitcase into the bed, and hoisted herself up to sit and wait. She had no idea what to say to Tommy Atkins. He was her one best option.

A short while later a gray Toyota SUV drove up slowly and stopped behind the pickup so that it didn't block cruising cars looking for parking.

María Elena put a grim look on her face.

CHAPTER FIVE: HIM

"I am not begging, Tommy Atkins," she told him.

"Not my problem."

She looked forlorn as he parked and got out.

He opened the pickup and retrieved some of his gear. He took it to the rear door of the Toyota and tossed it inside and returned for the rest.

"I don't have a choice."

He could see that. "No driver's license?"

She nodded. "So I can't get a car or a ticket to fly away."

"And doubtless you made a few calls."

She nodded again. "I am in deep trouble."

"Why am I not surprised? You been running with a bunch of vipers, college girl."

She shrugged self-consciously.

"So you know, Pocahontas. Go on the web, and in a few Google clicks you can be in contact with a few websites in China. You email your picture and two hundred bucks and they'll send you perfect fake ID. Like a driver's license from any state you want, including a working bar code on the back which contains the info on the front. It's almost the real thing."

He looked around and saw no one nearby, pulled the shotgun from the seat springs from behind. He held it close to his body and took it to the back seat of the SUV and put it under the floor mat behind the front passenger seat. He could lean back and grab it easily.

She stood aside resolutely.

A Lincoln edged around his car. Other cars were cruising up and down the parking aisles, echoing hollowly in the big structure, hunting empty spaces.

"You got money now, take a taxi or limo."

"I've nowhere to go. My friends have been threatened."

He didn't need her. He needed zero complications. Nada. Nothing. He did feel a proprietary interest in her. For the first time in many, many years, he felt something strange. Damn it. For too many hidden years in outback Florida he'd had no complications. Now this. What was it about her? He couldn't leave her. Maybe it was her body. Maybe it was her charm. Maybe it was her cinnamon animal scent. Maybe it was her intellect. Naah. This woman had character. Her father had just been shot to death and she was fighting hard against her attackers. She needed help and help only he could give her. There were not many people as qualified to help her as he was.

He looked at her, from head to toe. She was dejected and devoid of hope. "You look like the genesis of a great Conway Twitty song."

In the end, he'd bought in when he'd interrupted the rape and consequent murder.

He stopped in front of her and locked her eyes with his.

"One thing, Pocahontas?"

"Anything."

"You have to understand that being with me right now is perhaps more dangerous to you than a bunch of loco Cuban wanna-be soldiers."

"I trust you."

"You got a lot to learn, college girl." He grabbed her bag and tossed it in with the others, closed up the pickup and slammed the tailgate back in place. "Let us go, my dear."

Her smile was almost worth it.

They took the Florida Turnpike to the end at Wildwood, got on I-75 again, drove to the intersection of I-75 and I-10 near Lake City and headed west on I-10.

"Tallahassee is a good place to stop," he explained. "College town, lots of visitors, lots of Interstate customers for motels. We shouldn't stand out."

Among the rolling hills north of Tallahassee, they found a roadside motel. He did not park right in front of the office; instead, he found a nose-in visitor-parking place.

"If you don't have to," he said, "don't go too first class. They pay too much attention to the customers. And they might remember you. Midsize is best." He dug into his briefcase. "Here's a couple grand, keep it. I want you to go inside and register us. Tell them you want to pay cash. This place looks family owned. They'll keep the cash and not report the sale." He laughed. "If they need, give 'em a credit card number for security, but tell them you'll pay cash. Intimate you don't want your husband looking at the Visa bill. Single room, two beds. Two rooms would draw attention."

She got out of the SUV and went inside. Doubtless she had long since figured he didn't want to be seen, in person or on security camera if he could help it.

When she returned with the room key, she said, "You had to fill in type of car and tag number. I just wrote Toyota, not the make, and I scrambled the tag number so if they check it looks like a mistake, not deliberate misinformation."

"You are a quick study, college girl." He wondered how she would react to sharing a room. So far she had not objected, nor had she complained. Was she worried about her virtue? "Like a fucking movie," he laughed.

They went and found a nearby barbecue restaurant, ate quickly and quietly, and went to their room.

"221?" said Tommy. "Sherlock Holmes' street address. Baker Street. Actually, it was 221B, but we won't quibble."

She looked at him strangely as he dumped his duffle bags on the floor.

"Been a long day," he said. "Lesson four, or whatever number we're up to: RHIP."

"Okay, I give. What is RHIP?"

"The acronym for rank hath its privileges. Means I got the bathroom first," he said digging clothes out of one of his bags.

In a little while, he came out of the bathroom showered and shaved, in shorts and a T-shirt. "Next."

She went into the bathroom with her bag. Later when she came out, he was lying in bed under the covers reading. She was dressed in lacy hiphuggers and a low cut sleeveless top.

"Merde," he said, and she looked at him quizzically. He did not explain.

She went over and tilted his book so she could read the cover. "*Collapse*, by Jared Diamond." Phantom cinnamon wafted over him and another unidentifiable pheromone grabbed his attention.

"Interesting book."

"Strange book," she said, "about cultures and societies making it or dying."

"Strange?" he asked. "Because of me reading it? Or what?"

"I read the one before it, *Guns, Germs, and Steel*. Fascinating."

He looked up at her as if his eyes were focusing over the top of a pair of glasses.

"I ain't discussing theoretical history and culture with an attractive skimpily-clad young lady standing in front of me with a suggestive hip stuck out. Have you no modesty?"

"Oh." Her surprise was almost genuine. She went over to her bed and turned down a corner of the cover.

"Look here, Pocahontas, we gotta talk about boy-girl stuff."

"Um, okay, Tommy."

"What's your plan? How long you figger you gonna need to hide out?"

She shrugged, sitting down on the bed. "I don't know. Maybe until I can find some things out in Miami. Determine where I stand." She told him about her conversation with Tillie.

Atkins wondered if his special talents could be employed to help her. It certainly was not his intention. He did admit he'd been in a few wars, and not all military and patriotic. But he wasn't prepared to engage life again. He had to stay hidden.

"Sometimes," he opined, "problems work themselves out, especially big ones."

She laughed at him without mirth. "Yeah, right. Tell my father that."

"Point taken, but back to my original concern. You are a very attractive young lady. It ain't my intention of jumping your bones, I mean, ravaging you. But you gotta do your part. You can't run around like that at night—or in the day, for that matter."

She smiled impishly. "You don't like me?"

"Dumbass question, María Elena. Don't go all girly on me here. Remember I have seen your glorious naked body. Sure, it's fine and admirable. But I don't go where I ain't invited. And you goddamn well best not be playin' any games." He paused for a short grin. "Did I pass the test?" Actually, he thought she was pretty smart: get it out in the open and do it right away. Determine where they stood with each other. She had been testing the waters, whatever her intentions were. Maybe she just wanted to know if she could trust him. Or, she could want to know if he was attracted to her. Sure, she had a streak of vanity and he hadn't made a pass at her. Must have gotten to her.

"I need some frumpy jammies."

"Frumpy jammies? Yeah, that'll help."

She looked under her brows at him. "Are you gay? Or what?"

He shook his head. "Hell, no. And you might be about to find out. Lemme sleep."

"Can I use your laptop?" She wore a sly smile as if she'd just proved something to herself.

He nodded. It held absolutely nothing personal of his; just the results of his reading news, sports, and Amazon.com links. "I trust you know enough to stay away from places you can be traced? Don't sign in or otherwise identify yourself—or my computer. Use the private browsing setting."

"Yes, Tom."

"Tommy."

"Yes, Tommy."

"And tomorrow, you're going to brief me on what the hell you've gotten me into. I am not going into this mess blind."

"Yes, Tommy."

As she brought his computer to her bed, he turned out his light and rolled over facing away from her. She watched him pull his .380 out from under his pillow and place it on the bedside table.

"What was the second book?"

"The second book?"

"You brought two books."

"I have a bunch more electronical books on my Kindle machine and my laptop," he said avoiding the question. His opinion of her rose even more: it was likely she was smart enough to make some educated guesses when he told her the title of the other book he'd brought. After all, she knew the Jared Diamond books. Likely she knows this one. And Tommy Atkins wasn't ready to provide any clues to his life.

"Password?"

"VICAR. All caps."

When he woke, he opened his eyes to María Elena sitting back on only her right knee, rail straight against the wall alongside the television. Her left leg was bent behind her at the knee and was also rail straight up the wall. At least she was dressed in gym shorts now. Then she folded her right leg up behind her. Then she performed some other in-place exercises.

"A more upscale motel or hotel will have an exercise room," she pointed out, "and I wouldn't have to bother you." She waved a pair of elastic exercise resistance bands she'd apparently bought at the mall.

"Everything you do bothers me, Pocahontas."

When they finished breakfast, he sent her down Thomasville Road to find a mall and fill out her wardrobe. He gave her another big handful of twenties and fifties.

"How much money do you have?"

"I dunno. Maybe a hundred large. Maybe more."

"You *don't* know? A hundred thousand—maybe?"

He shrugged. "Also, buy a cheap wide mouth purse, a cheap wallet, a couple of handkerchiefs, some hairpins, lipstick, aspirins, and loose tampons. The usual things that fill up a woman's purse."

"A throwaway? I'm intrigued."

"Also buy one of those Swiss Army knives for your own purse."

When he didn't explain, she said, "Anything else?"

"Yes. Get enough frumpy jammies for the duration."

"How long is the duration?" she wanted to know.

"Beats me."

"All right, Tommy, whatever."

He went back to the room. She returned with an armful of shopping bags and another small suitcase. Carefully, she folded all of her new clothes and packed them.

After they loaded the Toyota, he tossed her the keys. "West on Interstate 10."

"How far?"

"We'll see."

They drove west for an hour, and then Atkins said. "Fess up, Pocahontas. It's time."

After a moment, she said, "Is this going to be reciprocal?"

He shook his head. "Nope."

"I'm not prying, Tommy. I really want to know."

"You're stalling, college girl."

She grinned. "You betcha." She thought for a minute. "Okay." She cruised past an eighteen-wheeler and settled in on the right lane.

"My father—"

"He got a name?"

"Don Carlos Vasquez."

"Everybody's a don."

"It is a title of respect. It is protocol for certain people."

"Even Don Diego, the assassin?"

"That's different. We didn't used to think he was a, a killer, but…"

"Tell the story in order."

"Stop interrupting then."

"Yes, dear."

Ignoring his sarcasm, she glanced at all mirrors, inside and driver's side and passenger side occasionally.

"My father, he has always been against Fidel. And all the other sons of bitches that ran Cuba and still do. He married my mother. She was one of his co-conspirators and twenty years younger than he. She—"

"She got a name?"

"Oh, yes, sorry. Isobel Perez Guerrero. My mother—"

"Was she as pretty as her daughter?"

María Elena glared at him. "More so. Muy hermosa. Let me tell the story."

"Go on."

She pulled out into the fast lane behind a Buick. "I hate people who go slow in the fast lane."

"Me, too, but do not draw attention to us."

"Yes, dear," she mimicked.

"Tell it, stop stalling."

She took a breath. "Alpha 66, Cuban American National Foundation—or CANF. Two Cuban exile organizations. The former more militant and the latter much less so. 13 is more like the latter but has been around longer, and is not as well known. All dedicated to the establishment of democracy in Cuba. Alpha 66 used to do violent things, blowing up stuff and hijacking and more. Papá founded 13 in memory of my mother to peacefully work for democracy. But here is the key: it was also designed to be ready and have in place plans for a peaceful transfer to democracy when Raul and Fidel and their legacy descendants are gone and the long awaited normalization takes hold."

"Maybe some general has a different idea," Tommy pointed out.

"It is possible, of course. But they are ready with money and more money. Can you imagine what will happen when Cuba opens up? Billions will flow, and not just from the United States.

No self-respecting general is going to miss out on his share."

"Point taken."

María Elena adjusted her Miami Dolphins hat so that the ponytail fit better through the opening above the snap-lock strap. This made the hat appear to sit on back of her head and the bill point more upwards. She was wearing low cut jeans and a tight top, also low cut. She was going to drive him to distraction. "Fast forward. Those days are nigh upon us. The future is here. There is a power struggle amongst even us, the Cuban community, to be the first with the most. Cuban ex-pats are drooling over the future."

"You, too? You're a full Americano, Pocahontas."

"I am, and damn proud of it. But, yes, certainly I have an overwhelming proprietary interest. My friends, my family, my family's life has been tied to this."

"Fine with all the philosophy. Gimme the facts."

"Don Diego. My father many, many years ago—"

"How long?"

"About twelve, perhaps fourteen." She avoided his gaze by checking all her mirrors. "My father brought him into the movement. He was a respected half Cuban, half Mexican."

"And?" He sensed her reluctance to talk.

"My father was becoming elderly and needed an heir." She couldn't hide the bitterness in her voice.

"Ah, now I'm beginning to understand. You were it and then you weren't."

"Latin macho paternalism," she said. Then she shrugged. "I understand it, yes; but I don't have to like it. Nowadays even more."

"Meaning?"

"I am no longer eighteen years old."

"Nowadays you'd be forceful in your own behalf."

"Correct."

"Fill in the blanks, María Elena."

She glanced annoyance at him. "I became the voice of our operation. I was an internationally known blogger—"

"You mean you are."

She paused. "Yes. I guess I still am. The cause remains."

"What remains," he said, "is why it came to murder and rape?"

"Assassination. That's what he did. He assassinated Papá."

"Why, college girl?"

"Because of me," she said bitterly. Then she went on quickly, "I discovered some things about Don Diego. He had slowly taken over the organization, of course. He was supposed to. Suddenly I noticed that many of the old guard were no longer in position or even active in the organization. Diego had all of the power positions filled with men of his own choosing."

"I'm guessing it gets worse."

"'Just how long is this panhandle of Florida?" She shook her head as a **PENSACOLA 100 MILES** sign flashed by.

"Too long," said Tommy. "I'd feel better if we were out of the state. You never know what the Florida Highway Patrol has been told to look for. Alabama is just past Pensacola and likely the alarm, if any, won't spill over."

"You're always thinking. And you know, of course, that I have no ID, specifically a driver's license."

"I am always trying to think ahead. And I don't have a license I want to show, either. If you drive carefully within the rules, we'll be okay. So what happened? It ain't hard to guess you found out some bad stuff about Don Diego."

"I did that. He now has iron control of 13. One of my jobs is to do a quick occasional informal audit of the books. I found some things didn't make sense. And began digging deeper. And asking questions under the table. What I found was probably only the tip of the iceberg. Don Diego had turned a fine and peaceful organization into a cover for his nefarious dealings."

"What nefarious dealings?"

"Human trafficking. Maybe drugs. I think it might be possible that Diego is also funneling intelligence into and out of Cuba."

"A double agent?"

"I do not know, Tommy. But he sort of bragged about it when

he grabbed Papá and me. Without specifying."

"You're saying you don't know who Diego is conniving with?"

"I do not. You have to understand the politics. It could well be he is being paid by Raul or his agents. It is equally likely that the CIA is paying him for intel. Or the CIA is paying him to be a double agent while he spies for Cuba. Or the other way around."

"My head hurts." Atkins was beginning to understand the scope of their problem. "Could be any threat to Don Diego in turn threatens some kind of pipeline he is using for the CIA. If you can get people in and out, then who'd notice a few agents going and coming?"

"Yes. They will accommodate a lot of illegalities to maintain that pipeline. Especially with an eminent transition of power. This all the condensed version. To finish, every few months, we do military training outside of Miami. But when we do certain other training, with all the so called soldiers, the government lets us use a big tract of land nearby where you live."

"Not any more."

She shook her head ruefully. "I am sorry, Tommy."

He shrugged. She was driving well: not that he was being judgmental, just that he had to know if he could trust her when and if they landed in some dangerous situation.

"Somehow Diego got wind of my informal investigation. I had told Papá and he knew. But we had no real proof and Papá did not yet know how to deal with the problem or with Don Diego."

"They grabbed you and drug you over to my area."

"Yes." She was silent, thinking, for a moment. "A real Latin coup."

"Shit. I bet it gets worse."

"Summary time: yes. It's worse. We don't know if Diego is plotting to assassinate Raul or whatever general is in charge nowadays and claim the mantle of leadership. We don't know that if and when the government of Cuba falls, that Diego might want to take over and become the next dictator. It is a position of power and authority. My father built 13 into a well-respected group. There was to be no counter-revolution. We were to bide our time and become a bridge to democracy when the time came."

"Diego must hate you."

"All the illegal activities have made him enormous amounts of money. That was the first thing he did not want jeopardized, much less his future plans. Not only had I found him out, but also I was a threat to his leadership. Since I was my father's daughter and times are now different, women can be in charge. Nor was I any longer eighteen and not yet capable of doing the job. Diego resented the status I'd earned by my blogging." "He gave you to his men before he was going to have you killed."

Her jaw clinched. "Yes. I'd come real close to thwarting his plans and an animosity had grown between us, a poison."

Tommy guessed there was more to it than that.

At that moment Tommy was thinking that her anger was spilling over to her father for not crowning her his political heir. But way down deep where he didn't use the thought process, he knew there was more to this than what she had just told him. The thought process did not take him that far because he was in the middle of realizing a massive problem.

"Okay, María Elena, calm down. Enter Tommy Atkins stage left. Now here we are." He looked at her and they shared thoughts. That scared Tommy worse than the actual thoughts. And those actual thoughts were of their death sentences.

"I'm sorry, Tommy. I didn't mean to drag you into this."

Yes, she knew all right.

"I don't usually say something which goes without saying." Tommy scratched his head. "Watch the road, Pocahontas."

"Yes, Tommy." She was very contrite.

"But I'm gonna say it to make sure it is crystal clear. One can see where this Don Diego needs you dead in the worse way."

"Yes, Tommy."

"And not only does he have his own resources, but he's got

the CIA, too."

"Yes, Tommy."

"Goddamn. Is that all?"

"Not exactly. And the FBI."

"Fuck me to tears. Why is that?"

"Quickly, the oversight of 13 by the government, and their tacit complicity, is, of course, by the CIA. However, we are inside the continental United States. The CIA is not supposed to operate therein. Thus, the FBI has an iron in that fire. It also allows the FBI to have access to us, if they want, and know what's going on. They're obviously all playing some kind of game of their own."

"Fuck me."

"I am truly sorry, Tommy. I have killed you."

"Ain't nobody done that thing yet, María Elena. Feds been on my ass for forty-eleven years. Not to mention some real professionals." Shouldn't have said that, damn it.

"Let us get to a city, maybe Mobile," she said. "Then I will go my own way. If I turn myself in, maybe they won't follow you."

"Oh, no, college girl. Put them college credits to use. Ain't no way. We spent more than five minutes together. I'm radioactive. They will hunt me down like a dog." Not to mention they'll put a forensics team on the cabin and find out just who the fuck I am.

"Oh, Tommy."

"And no way Tommy Atkins is gonna turn Pocahontas over to them. They'll gut you like a fish and you be talking sooner or later. Nobody can not talk, not when they're really serious. They'd use drugs on you so that no word of torture to the 13 blogger would leak out."

"That is reassuring."

"Look here, Pocahontas. I have been treating this not very seriously. But now we got to really go underground. It wouldn't surprise me if they didn't already have an APB out on us. The FBI is bad enough, but the CIA can pull some serious computer searches. Maybe they'll think we burned up in the fire."

She shook her head. "Do not try to sugar coat it, Tommy. I really got us behind the eight ball, no?"

"No."

"No?"

"It ain't my job to make you feel better about this. You were working for freedom for twelve million Cubans—"

"And over a million here."

"—and your intentions were good. What happened is some asshole fucked that up bad. This Diego fellow. I am beginning to take an intense dislike to him."

"Yes, Tommy. Not everybody knows the population of Cuba offhand."

"I know some shit, too, college girl. Never mind that. You understand some of the other implications, don't you?"

"We could split up. That would make it more difficult for them."

"Aye, and you'd be caught in two days and I'd have a guilty conscience for a week or so. No, this kinda marries us, don't it?"

Her look was inscrutable.

"You know the context, college girl. We're stuck together until we can straighten this all out or disappear."

"You're dreaming if you think we can take on the CIA and the FBI and a trained paramilitary group."

"I am, but I ain't stupid. Listen, we gotta start being real smart. Don't cross the state line at some obvious point on the Interstate between Mobile and Pensacola. Let us get off this obvious road out of the great state of Florida and head into the great state of Alabama on a less obvious road. The next town, we exit and head north. And no stopping until we cross the line. Every minute counts."

"They must want you very bad, Tommy."

"Shit, you don't know the half of it."

"Which is?" she prompted.

"None of your business, college girl." He grinned at her. "But nothing compared to your fair young body." He chuckled. Nothing happens for too many years, now he is on the run with more urgency than any time in his life and that not of his own doing.

They had to be fast on the way to figuring out who he was by now. Not that it mattered. He had a larger target on him now. What he was before paled in comparison to what he'd gotten himself involved with now. While they'd been taking their time wandering about Florida, the feds would have been working. And once that supertanker gets going at high speed, there was no slowing it or turning it back. And once they learned who he is, they could get others involved, like the U.S. Marshal Service and others. That would widen their net considerably. And a smart agent in the FBI, knowing who he was, would be able to track them better.

Goddamn.

"One final thing, Miss María Elena. You need to search your soul and decide what you want to get out of this."

"Me? Simple. I want justice."

"Yeah, right."

"Those who killed my father should be brought to justice." She massaged her shoulder. "I mean, ah, all except Don Diego were killed in the swamp. You know." Though the rest of his organization would be turned against her now. She wondered how Don Diego had spun her disappearance and her father's death. She shied away from thinking of what they'd done with his body.

"I am dead serious, María Elena. Think it through. We're fixing to go underground more than you can imagine. If you pop your head above water, somebody gonna be waiting to take it off."

She said cryptically, "There is a Cuban proverb which says, 'A lie runs until it is overtaken by the truth.'"

Tommy thought for a moment. "An old Bantu proverb: 'Don't flaunt the snake you have slain—the other snakes are watching.'"

María Elena looked at him askance. "Are you gonna be this enigmatic all the time?"

CHAPTER SIX:
THEM, THE BAD GIRLS

"It blew up."

"What d'you mean?"

"The girl disappeared."

The sign on her door read **SUSAN HARTFORD QUANTRELL**.

Suzie Q opened the door and went into the small office. Gray metal desk, computer, gray metal credenza with printer and a couple of books. Paper scattered over the desk and the credenza. Unused hat rack, for in Washington in the summer it was more like south Florida: hot and humid with little or no relief in sight. She carried two large coffees from Starbucks and set them down on the credenza, shuffling a few papers aside.

In fact, this office was not her real office: her real office was down south in Langley, Virginia, in Operations at CIA head-quarters. This Washington office was the location for the JTF, Joint Task Force, aka JTF 13. Joint between the CIA and the FBI. It's mission: covert and overt oversight of 13 de enero.

Suzie Q was the senior between the CIA member and the FBI member, and therefore ran the group. They had a small staff they assembled when an operation was ongoing.

Right behind her came in Linda Landover, aka Linda L. Linda Landover was the FBI rep to the JTF. Linda L was a tall willowy brunette whose model good looks always turned heads. Suzie Q was almost as tall and had short blonde hair. But not a Barbie.

Linda L said, "I walked the damn dog this morning. Then I went over to the Hoover Building to check in."

"It was your turn to walk the dog." Suzie Q sat in her swivel chair.

"Yes. But you could've since you didn't have to run through Langley before you came over here."

"I walked the dog last night because you were already in bed."

"That's because you just had to watch the movie before we got charged another day."

"Yeah, and it wasn't worth it. The girl's gone?"

"What I said, sweetie. They ain't happy over at Hoover."

"Anybody see the girl?"

Linda shook her head, her hair jerking when she did so. "Nobody's certain what happened. We interviewed some local Indians and they reported the local hermit resident driving off, and behind him a great plume of smoke. They went over to check it out and his entire backwoods cabin was gone. Torched like a professional. No sign of the girl."

"Goddamn Diego García," said Suzie Q. "Sometimes I wish we hadn't hitched our wagon to that horse." She thought for a moment, sipping on her coffee.

"We sent a team to the site at first light. We should know something soon."

"And I thought you were just walking the damn dog."

"Me and my cell phone."

"Well, I, for one, don't believe the old man simply died in a training accident. And the girl is not the heir apparent, so that is no problem—"

"For now," Linda amended. She flipped the top off her coffee and took a big gulp. "What's the count?"

"Three." Three agents buried in place in Cuba by Diego García. "Don Carlos should have played the game better. I still don't like it. García is not trustworthy, not to me. But he's our guy. I think he killed off the old man."

"And the daughter?"

"You know their attachment."

"Yeah, but 'Don Diego' would sell his mother out."

"Yes, dear. What do you think we're doing right now? We're selling out truth, justice, and the American way for a few agents to be in place awaiting the big day."

"Non-concur. We are ignoring what's right by using a slimy wannabe to further our careers. Look, Suzie. It *is in our national interest* to have people infiltrating 13 *and* the Cuban government. We cannot let García's methods blind us to success."

"Once again, sweetheart, we're earning our moniker."

"I hate being called 'The Bad Girls', I hate it."

"It has its uses. Nobody fucks with us much." Suzie Q smiled. "Diego García is ours, yours and mine. When all is said and done, he'll be high up in the new and improved government of the newly free nation of Cuba. He is a moneyman; he wants money more than power. He'll be in a trade ministry or some such. You stake your territory early and it's not a high profile admin post, you will get it without any shooting. García will do that thing, and then he will be handing out trade licenses. And he will insure they go to the right companies in the states, American companies, not the Euro-creeps or those avaricious beet-eating, vodka-swilling, ex-commie Ruskie bastards. We'll get oil leases galore, right next to the Florida waters where Florida won't allow drilling, the stupid idiots."

"And stuff," Linda added.

Suzie Q nodded. The "stuff" meaning sufficient unaccounted for funds deposited in their joint account over in Nassau. Suzie Q and Linda L would have a grand and early retirement. Then they'd truly become "Bad Girls". They were jointly known in the trade thusly because of their propensity for dirty tricks, methods that crossed the line from legal and proper, and willingness to use up people and resources. Because of that, they usually accomplished whatever they sought to, ends justifying means and all. And they weren't skimming money or anything like that. They were simply going to get their due, a thing long overdue. Suzie Q smiled at her own joke. She and Linda would retire and become, like consultants, like lobbyists. If it's good enough for ex-senators and congressmen, it was good enough for a couple of mid-level operatives. Their long, loyal service would be rewarded. And the good ole US of A would benefit big time, having grabbed all the major trade and export and import and tourism franchises over all those foreign assholes. She felt like standing and reciting the "Star Spangled Banner." Suzie Q reminded herself of Russia when Yeltsin dumped Gorbachev and the commie regime: it was like pioneer days, the start of capitalism. Russia was wide-open territory and the visionaries did not grab for political power, they cornered markets. Suzie Q dreamed almost daily of a newly open Cuba: she'd go over and buy up all the old cars and drive them onto a barge and take them to Port Everglades or the Port of Tampa and hold auctions right there on the wharfs. She'd save one '57 Chevy for herself to reclaim.

"Still, the old man's daughter is a wild card. I don't like loose ends."

"We'll find her, Suzie. Frankly, we can't have her appear and begin talking. Five others died in this aforementioned training accident. I am not sure what happened and I don't know if we'll ever find out—"

"Maybe we don't want to know? García might not be saying much if they're illegals."

"Well, he's now in charge of 13 and should be able to sell it. Wonder what he'll say about María Elena."

"That'll be the giveaway. If he says she was involved in the accident, then she's already dead. If he says nothing, that means she might turn up alive."

"I am seriously curious, Linda. Five of García's men dead? And coincidentally, this swamp hermit drives off and his place explodes and burns? What the hell?"

"We got some good forensics on the team, we should know."

"It's going to be a long day, I feel it." Suzie Q swung around to face her desk and get to work on the ubiquitous paperwork which fuels government bureaucracy at any level. She utilized the traditional technique for dealing with so much paperwork: work the one on top.

"I'll get us a chef's salad at the deli for lunch." Linda laughed. "Us Bad Girls ought to be eating raw meat and hot peppers."

They found a picnic table in the courtyard in the center of the building's U-shape. It was actually too hot to eat outside, but Linda had to have her after-lunch smoke. Even here the anti-smoking Nazi's would complain. Fuck them.

"Preliminary report," Linda said.

"Gimme."

"No sign of nothing. Cabin totally gone. Burnt and crispy shit all over. Musta been a big bad boom."

"Why would this hermit blow up his place? He wasn't even part of the deal."

"García isn't talking. But we found a sign, save the whales or panthers or something. They'd been there and gone."

"You're telling me, Linda, that some eco-freaks blew the place and ran this recluse off?"

"Nope. I'm saying that's what it looks like. Or, more specifically, that's what it's meant to look like. A bit too coincidental methinks."

"I think this hermit requires checking out."

"Roger that. And no sign of the girl. García said she was involved in the accident and is unaccounted for."

"Don't you love the passive voice?"

"That tells me she is on the run someplace, or dead and the gators are feasting upon her supple, hard-body right—"

"Look but don't touch, sweetie." Suzie Q gave Linda an admonishing glance. She forked some salad into her mouth.

"Yes, ma'am. Think about something, hon. If María Elena is actually on the run, why is that? I mean, what makes her want to take out of there all of a sudden?"

"García is lying about the accident. Something happened and he killed the old man."

"That's the way I figure it. Don Carlos must have held his

own, if García lost five men."

Suzie Q snorted. "That old fart couldn't walk across the street without a Boy Scout. No, it's something else. Could your hard-bodied babe have killed them?"

"Anything is possible. She's had some of the paramilitary training and might be capable. But I think not, Suze. Listen, follow me here. If García is smart enough to get the drop on Don Carlos, he isn't going to leave the daughter free no matter what. He had to grab her at the same time."

"Ahh, now I see why you're such a bad girl. Your leap of logic: five dead guys, give or take, not counting the old guy, one missing young lady when she shouldn't be, and one missing mystery 'Glades resident'."

"Yep. Hurry up and finish, I need a smoke."

"Three questions, Linda. One: how is García going to deal with Don Carlos' death? You need a body. And he won't want us to exhume or run it through a morgue or Miami CSI whatever it's called."

"Easy. An illegal immigrant substitute, a closed casket ceremony. Maybe shake and bake. Perhaps the evidence of murder can be obliterated. He's got the power and connections. Those Cubans are a clannish bunch, and those 13 people are almost a closed society down there."

"What's to keep the daughter from going public? She can call the press. She can expose García on the web; after all, she's a highly respected blogger. Her story would go viral on the Internet and be big news, at least in South Florida."

Linda nodded. "I am guessing here, but it wouldn't surprise me if Señor García hastened to tie up loose ends: he's got her friends and family under threat. Sorta like the Mafia used to do."

"That's how I see it." Suzie Q held up three fingers. "Three, how long before Don Diego requests assistance in locating one each María Elena and all her other names?"

"My bet, Suze, is end of business today."

"You think?"

"I'll walk the damn dog for a week if I'm wrong." Linda beamed her confidence.

At 1630 hours, Linda walked into Suzie Q's office. "It's going to be a long night."

"?"

"García requested help finding the girl. You get to walk the dog. And forensics found a couple of prints, good ones, on a shard of glass and on a CD that had blown clear of the explosion. Hopefully, the mystery man won't be such a mystery for much longer."

Suzie Q grunted. "I hope the damn dog can hold it."

CHAPTER SEVEN: HER

They found old time luxury in the Menger Hotel, Alamo Plaza, San Antonio, Texas.

María Elena checked herself in the mirror. "Lookin' good, girl," she said. Simple black sheath dress, half heels, hair loose down her back. She was reaching behind her back to zip up the dress when the door to the hotel room opened.

Tommy Atkins came in. He stopped in midstride. "Jesus, María Elena. We need to keep a low profile. Every man in the church is going to memorize you." He closed the door and walked to her.

"Thanks, I think." She turned her back to him. "Zip me up." She felt his fingers caress her back as the zipper rose. She wore no bra for the zipper to skip over the strap. Them that can, do, she thought.

He walked away shaking his head. She smiled to herself.

He went to the window and looked out at the Alamo. "There's a great deal of history here. This place was built only a few years after the Alamo fell. Presidents have stayed here. Teddy Roosevelt recruited his Rough Riders in the bar downstairs."

"It needs updating," she pointed out.

"That's why we're here. It is not a chain and nobody'd think of looking for us right on Alamo Plaza. All right, college girl, I got the new car." He tossed her the keys. "It's hot."

He'd turned in the Toyota at the airport north of downtown. His plan was to steal a replacement from long-term parking where the theft might not be discovered for many days.

"How do you have keys for it?"

"Sometimes they make it easy to steal: they hide a spare key inside a magnet box in case of emergency." He brought over a tourist map of downtown San Antonio. "Another gray Toyota SUV, parked right here." He touched a spot around the corner from the hotel and down the street. "I drew a smiley face in the dust near the rear window. Wipe it off, you don't want attention."

"Okay."

"Try to get plates from a similar vehicle or one colored the same. Preferably both. No fancy or designer tags, too easy to remember. Do the third party thing."

He meant for her to steal—exchange—a license tag from one car, put that one on a second car, and take that second car's tag for her own Toyota. Anything to confuse a computer check. They had a better chance of avoiding law enforcement if the computer search of their tag showed the same make and model, or the same color, or both.

He'd told her, "Don't steal a car with LoJack or On-Star or one of those services. And shifting tags, that's where your new floppy purse comes in. Sort of spill the personal items on the ground so as to appear like you dropped your purse and are picking stuff up. The tampons will allay suspicion because most people will be self-conscious. Then use your Swiss Army knife screwdriver blade to remove and replace the tag quickly. If you must make a run for it, maybe they'll not bother, seeing your purse lying there with the wallet out in the open. They might think they got your ID and won't know it's all fake with no contents."

Now she was going to have to do that thing. Somehow she knew that her doubts about her ability to pull this off were unfounded. She'd be good at it. After church, that is. This was Sunday and she had a lot to commune with God about.

"Wish me luck," she said as she left.

"Good luck, Pocahontas."

After church, too many people were getting in their cars and leaving; removing and replacing tags would be too obvious. Then she laughed aloud. Baptists. Their services were always an hour later than Catholic services. She stopped at a quick stop gas station, found the address of a nearby Baptist church and drove over there. The services were already in progress.

After cruising the parking lot, she parked at the end of the last line, mostly cars of those who came late. She backed into the slot as others had done. Apparently, Baptists wanted to get the hell out of church and away quickly. She lifted her own tailgate a bit and unscrewed her license tag. The intermediate tag switch was not as important as the final tag, the one that would go on their own vehicle. There was a silver Saturn Vue on the row ahead of the one in which she parked.

She slipped the license into her purse, casually looked around and walked over to it. She had the Swiss Army knife open and palmed. Even though no one was near and she was blocked from the street traffic, she was swinging her purse and it seemed to slip from her hand. She swore aloud. That ought to prove she was a Baptist. The purse tumbled behind the Saturn and she knelt and spilled most of the contents.

As she went down, she looked around for a final check. Nobody to see her. Yet she went through the motions. Quickly she unscrewed the plate and replaced it with the one she'd just taken from her Toyota. She heard a deep engine turning this way and slipped the tag into her purse quickly. It was a motorcycle and it settled into neutral as it paused alongside her. She grabbed a couple of tampons and stuffed them guiltily into her purse. Then she took her time picking up the rest of her stuff and stood, pressing her hand into her back as if to ease the pain, thus concealing a quick visual survey. A young man on a motorcycle had turned down her parking aisle and was loitering, watching her intently. Then he accelerated past and parked next to her Toyota.

Casually, she opened her driver's door and climbed in.

He was watching her as he removed his helmet. "For once I'm glad I'm late," he said. Then he grinned widely. "Finally I have proof there is a God."

María Elena smiled her thanks and relaxed. Her short dress and shapely legs had distracted him well. She pulled out her cell phone and pretended to go through the directory to find a number as he hurried inside. She could hear singing out here in the parking lot. Then she got out and swiftly put the Saturn's tag on her Toyota.

She drove up San Pedro for a few minutes looking for a mall parking lot or something similar where she might find lucky vehicle number two. A couple of false alarms and she finally found a Toyota SUV in a used car lot. It was more silver than gray and a different year, but acceptable. They were not open on Sunday morning. She parked behind an adjacent strip mall where the employees parked and walked through the sales lot as if window-shopping. After she'd taken the plate she wanted and replaced it with the Saturn's license tag, she saw a dealer's magnetized plate on one vehicle and quickly slid that into her purse, too. Just in case of emergency. You never know. The Texas Department of Motor Vehicles was going to have one heavy-duty headache.

She drove toward the Interstate 410 circumferential highway on San Pedro and found a mall with a Sears before she got to the Interstate.

She sat in the parking lot with the air conditioner running. San Antonio heat was as bad as Miami, maybe worse. She kept the SUV running and punched numbers on her cell.

"Yes?"

"Eduardo, it's me, María Elena."

"My God, girl. Where are you? I've been worried sick."

"San Antonio and I'm doing okay."

"They buried your father yesterday. It was all arranged by Don Diego."

"The bastard."

Eduardo's voice was soft. "He is the closest kin, you know. He had Carlos cremated. The padre did a very fine service. It was not advertised, so only a few were present."

María Elena crossed herself. Diego would pay.

"Do you know anything? Can you tell me anything?"

"Not much. It is as if you and he were erased from this life. I fear I am being watched, but what can they do to an old man? I have been warned, threatened subtly, but threatened nonetheless. Some people will no longer talk to me, so they have been warned."

"And if I go to the law?"

"Don't chance it."

"How can that be, Eduardo? This is the land of freedom. A place where our people have always sought sanctuary."

"Yes, Alejandrina. It is; yet some have perverted the dream. There are strange men, men likely paid by Washington, nosing around. They have been to our training camps. There are rumors of a large explosion and that you died in it."

"Not yet, I haven't."

"I am thinking that those who watch 13 have sided with Don Diego."

"I am not surprised, Eduardo. Do you know any in the press who would support us, help us?"

"I do. But the threats remain. They would attack in any way they could; against you or your friends, your loyal 13 members. Retaliation would be immediate and swift. It would come out, but at what cost?"

"My friend, I am reading between the lines. Have you been directly threatened?"

"It is difficult to tell, for men are around, asking questions, tough men."

She sighed. "I guess that's what I wanted to know."

After she hung up, she fell into a state of depression. She kept thinking on it and thinking on it and the more she thought about it, the more she found that there were no answers, at least no acceptable answers.

And here she was stuck with a stranger, a man she knew nothing about. Well, not exactly a stranger, not any more. He'd so far proved himself quite the gentleman and she was, in fact, learning from him. Admittedly, she wasn't learning academic stuff, but she was learning street smarts. She wondered if she wasn't being too trusting. Tommy wasn't talking. What did he do? What caused him to be, in essence, hiding out for years in the remote desolation of south Florida scrubland and swamps? She had no idea what the deal was with him: he could be a tax-evader or an axe-murdering cannibal. On the ninth hand, she'd be dead right now, and that death would have been long and painful, were it not for Tommy Atkins. She decided she was more confused than depressed.

So she got out of the car and went shopping. The frumpy jammies she'd gotten in Tallahassee were *too* frumpy. And she needed a few more things.

That night they ate dinner at a restaurant on the famed River Walk in the middle of downtown San Antonio. "Authentic" Mexican food accompanied by Maríachi music. As they walked back toward the hotel, rain began to fall heavily. They were soaked and she was full and content and the rain bothered her not at all. For the first time in days, she relaxed.

Suddenly, Tommy threaded his arm through hers and leaned in toward her with an amiable familiarity. Softly, he spoke into her ear. "Something's wrong. I feel it. You go on to the hotel and pack our stuff. I'll follow shortly. Be ready to head out." His arm was rigid against her.

"Umm, okay."

"Smart girl, Pocahontas." He brushed his lips on her cheek, disengaged his arm, and patted her on the butt. "I'll get us a bottle," he said loudly. She was almost convinced herself.

She pushed rain off her forehead with her palm and realized he was gone. He'd disappeared.

Goddamn it, she thought. Don't get comfortable, Emmy, she told herself.

Maybe it was nothing. How could anyone know they were in downtown San Antone?

She worried the problem as she skirted the front of the

Alamo, deserted at this time of night in the downpour. A taxi slowed as it passed her. How nice, she thought. The driver didn't want to splash her. Not that it made any difference, since she was soaked anyway.

Then the taxi stopped altogether.

"Uh oh," she said aloud.

And then it was too late. The rear door opened and a man jumped out, grabbed her, and dragged her into the taxi.

She fought him, but was off balance going into the backseat where another man waited. The first guy pushed her, and she sprawled across the seat. He climbed in behind her and the taxi sped away. Her sore shoulder started complaining.

María Elena struggled to a sitting position and used her elbow on the seated man. As she pummeled him, she spun around, freed her feet and began kicking the first guy.

Until someone in the front seat jammed the barrel of a revolver into her right eye.

CHAPTER EIGHT: THEM

"I walked your damn dog before I left," said Linda L.

"Thank you, dear."

"Stuff starting to shake out."

"Gimme my coffee first."

"Listen, Suze. We ran the phone records on that old lawyer guy, down in South Florida. Señor Eduardo they call him. Two calls unaccounted for. One from Orlando International and one from somewhere near the center of San Antonio, Texas, home of Lonestar and Pearl beers. Same cell made the calls."

"Good work. Reckon it's your hard-bodied hot babe?"

"It's all we got."

"What's up with the prints? Did we find out who our hermit is?"

Linda took the lid off her coffee and sipped carefully. "More interesting now. In fact, it's past interesting into the intriguing territory."

"Doubtless you're gonna tell me any hour now."

"NCIC has a block on the info—if they got anything they won't tell."

"National security bull shit as usual?"

"Uh uh. I got the distinct impression that was not the case. Quite the contrary. But we stirred up a hornet's nest."

"Those folks over at the National Crime Info Center aren't supposed to play favorites."

"Sometimes any federal bureaucrat can get caught up in something when people higher on the food chain get involved."

"That's supposed to be us," said Suzie Q.

"I turned up the flame. Maybe we get something soon."

"Another thing. This aforementioned cell phone?"

"Already on it, Suze. We should know something soon."

"And then?"

"Um. And then? Yeah, sure. Decision time. Do we use the local FBI office?"

"What with our involvement and all, I dunno."

"Your call, Ms. Quantrell. You're in the chair. If we do, we might blow the whole operation. Expose agents in place and maybe their contacts."

"Tell me about it, Linda. You and I both know that those Cubans are famous for networking; they'll have ignored all protocols and not maintained the integrity of their cells."

"You're saying exposure results in our failure."

"I am. Damn it, we got too many years tied up here."

"Concur. Listen, Suze, why don't we, um, ah, sort of leak the location of the cell phone to good ole' Don Diego and see what happens?"

"We don't have much choice, Linda. If we don't, we drop out of the loop and lose any control we have."

"It jeopardizes the old man's daughter."

"More than likely it does more than jeopardize her." Suzie Q snapped a pencil in half. "Sometimes I don't like this shit. Sometimes I don't like myself."

"We don't know what he'll do, Susan. We suspect. But we've done worse to protect the mission."

"I need to call Personnel and find out how long before I can retire."

"You got too many years to go, hon. But if you want, I can support us." Linda patted Suzie Q's hand.

"You're too good for me. You know I wouldn't do that to you."

"It's okay," said Linda.

"Fuck it. Alert Don Diego and as soon as we isolate a location or two, tell him we'll let them know."

"Done, hon. And I'll keep working on our mystery man."

"All right. But Linda? I have a bad feeling about this guy. Something stinks. Which leads me to say, we need an exit plan or two."

"Jesus. Suze? Is this one of your famous extrasensory leaps of logic?"

"I dunno. Just a feeling."

"Exit strategy is defined as? The Project, and our official involvement? Or you and me from the scene?"

"Yes."

CHAPTER NINE: HIM

South Texas downpours could be mistaken for monsoon storms.

They were returning to the Menger from eating dinner on the Riverwalk. María Elena dressed the part, wearing an open sleeved Mexican peasant blouse with colorful flames and embroidery.

Tommy Atkins had felt it. The rust was coming off, but maybe not fast enough. As soon as his sixth sense told him something bad was wrong, he acted. They were within sight of the hotel—were it not raining. Momentarily, they walked between blurry pools of light. He whispered to María Elena and patted her on the ass and faded into the shadows.

He didn't want to use María Elena as bait, but had no choice. If they were lucky, she'd make it to the hotel and follow his instructions to get ready to leave.

Someone was watching, he felt it. When they saw María Elena alone, they'd wonder. But she would show no signs of panic and that would throw them off. She was learning and learning fast. He was close to being proud of her. He the mentor to her, the student. He distracted himself for a moment finding the humor in that thought. Him? The ultimate loner? Yeah, right.

And that second of distraction was enough for him to blow it.

He was far enough behind her now to start trailing her. Shadowing her in the night and the rain wouldn't be difficult. She'd make it to the hotel then he'd go on a search and destroy mission. Just like old times.

But the momentary lapse cost him. He watched helplessly as the taxi pulled up beside her, stopped, and someone dragged her inside. He couldn't chance a shot without the possibility of hitting her. Nor could he run that distance in time.

Then it was too late; they were skidding off into the rainy night.

He cursed under his breath. He thought about the timing. The taxi had to have been on the way before he faded off; there was no other way. Probably their plan was to shoot him and take her or kill them both; but when the only target was María Elena, they had to take her without killing her. It would be the only way to get him, too. Bait.

All this meant they had to have a spotter and he was still around. Doubtless the spotter knew Atkins had dropped out of sight and was in touch with those in the taxi by radio or cell phone.

Tommy Atkins had one chance and one chance only to make this end right. Otherwise he'd have to leave her and disappear or allow them to bring him in for an ostensible trade, or some such. His opportunity was now. Find the spotter.

Moving a bit behind a corner, he surveyed the area. The rain proved friendly then: it precluded the spotter from being inside or on top of a building; anywhere the rain would ruin his vision. Atkins picked out a likely place for the spotter on the far side of the Alamo. If this guy were professional, he'd be there; the secondary position would be back fifty yards under an awning in a recessed doorway. Once the spotter figured out things, he'd be on the move, likely from the primary to the secondary. With no further waste of time, Atkins slinked down a side street and hustled to where he could observe the secondary. Then he determined where the spotter would go after that, the safest escape route. He went along into a doorway and waited.

The spotter was more professional than Atkins gave him credit for. He skipped the secondary and was walking swiftly along the likely escape route. No doubt it was the right man, a purposeful walk, maybe a businessman going home. But Atkins could tell the spotter had an immediate awareness of all around him. He wasn't missing a trick.

For a change, fortune smiled on Tommy Atkins. The spotter was staying close to the street, away from the walls of the buildings. But walking toward the man was a pod of four tourists, umbrellas and all. Perfect cover.

Atkins faded in behind them, urgency overcoming his caution.

The spotter barely spared the tourists a glance, but by then it was too late.

As they passed him, Atkins swung behind the man and jammed his weapon into the small of the man's back.

"Into the doorway."

The spotter froze for a second, and then his professionalism took over. He walked straight into the recessed doorway. Atkins didn't even bother checking what the place was; whatever it was, it was closed. He pushed the spotter against the locked door, the top of the door glass.

"All right, where are they taking her?"

"Please, Sir, take my wallet and let me live." The voice was of an older man, maybe seventy.

"Five."

"What is going on? I have done nothing wrong."

"Four," said Atkins. The man had a Mexican accent.

"I have grandchildren," he said. "I am but a retired laborer."

"Three."

"Madre de Dios! Vicar? It cannot be."

"Two."

"It must be. Vicar, I thought you were dead."

"That's what everybody thinks." Atkins scoured his mind.

"I meant you no harm," said the old man, scrunching up away from the barrel of the gun without luck.

Then he knew. Somebody that professional and capable. Only one man. Juan Pablo, no last name. The assassin from Sonora. "Juan Pablo?"

"Sí. Mi amigo. I am retired, down in the valley, raising horses and playing with my grandchildren."

"In Texas?"

"In Texas. My own country is too dangerous for raising a family. Certainly in the provinces from which I operated."

"You a citizen?"

"No, but my application is in. My grandchildren and other family are citizens."

"The girl you took, Juan Pablo, she is my only family."

"I searched for you for years. You disappeared."

"Your people were after me. The fucking feds were after me." Never mind what happened, he added to himself.

"It is why I could not retire in Arizona," admitted Juan Pablo. "It is why I couldn't resist the big money they pay me today for a day's work. I told you I was retired and I am." He crossed himself, a difficult thing as he was lodged against the door. "I would like to continue that endeavor."

"How did you know we were here? And where to find us?"

"Cell phone. Many cell towers nearby."

"Shit." Atkins had never had a cell phone, but had read a little and knew they could find one through the GPS or some kind of triangulation between cell towers. That meant María Elena had bought a cell phone and had used it, and recently. Not for the first time did he realize things he'd been missing for twenty plus years. The first day in the 'Glades with María Elena had triggered a growing resentment at himself for his circumstances. Circumstances that prevented him from enjoying what life had to offer. And he wasn't referring to cell phones. While, of necessity, he'd been all business, he could see the other side of life. He began to resent himself for being on the run from every organization, legal and illegal, in the country—or so it seemed.

"Vicar? I am not a rapist coyote or mule. I do not want to die."

"Where's the girl?"

"In a house, south of here, in the barrio—if they have made it that far yet in this rain."

"Take me there. Now."

"I will, but you will kill me anyway. We both know that."

"You don't know that, Juan Pablo. The longer you stay alive, the better your chances."

"We must have a deal first."

"No."

"Then kill me now, for I have no leverage and you will kill me anyway."

"Listen to my voice, Juan Pablo. Remember those grandchildren of yours in the valley? I swear upon your dead body I will kill as many as I can. And their parents. You have my word."

The Mexican Assassin from Sonora dropped his head. "Sometimes I talk too much."

It occurred to Tommy Atkins that Juan Pablo was a high-end hire. It showed the importance of María Elena. More so, it showed the importance of her enemies. "Who hired you?"

"I know not, Vicar. An old contact. Easy money, I could not refuse. I was closest real talent—not some gangbanger. I was a fool. I should have subcontracted out the job. Instead I hired some of those gangbangers. Zetas."

"The kill orders?"

"The woman, we know her name. And some hombre with her, nobody knows who that man is. She was primary."

"You told your men to hold her so you could use her as bait if necessary?"

"I did."

Atkins thought about it. Somebody had enough power to isolate one cell phone and chase it down. Enough power and money to buy the best assassin, even if he was retired.

Tommy recalled the forlorn, trusting figure hunched over on the curb at the mall in Ft. Myers.

"All right, Juan Pablo. Here's the deal: you and I go and retrieve the girl. If she is hurt in anyway, I will kill all of your family. You got that?"

"There is utter certainty in your voice. I would believe you even if you were not the Vicar."

"Think little children bleeding on the grass, staining their toys. Think their parents running to their aid and not knowing they're running to their own deaths."

"Vicar, I feel the cold. I believe you. My van is near." He paused. "But it is not like you. Not like the old days. You do not war upon women and children. The contrary."

"Now you know how important the woman is to me. Let us go, then, Juan Pablo. I will let you remain armed, for I will kill you if you even make a false move toward the weapon."

"Yes, Vicar."

They drove in an old van, Juan Pablo driving and Tommy Atkins sitting directly behind him with the barrel of his gun in the assassin's neck.

By instruction, Juan Pablo pulled up directly in front of the ramshackle house. The torrential rain kept a veil over them and Atkins couldn't see any neighbors.

"A moment," said Juan Pablo as he turned off the ignition. He dropped his head and murmured. Then he crossed himself. "I have made peace. Now I am ready."

It had not escaped Tommy's attention that if someone had hired Juan Pablo and located a burner cell phone the hard way, that this whole thing was a much larger deal than it appeared on the surface.

They hurried up the walkway, as planned, with Juan Pablo behind Tommy Atkins. Tommy's gun was in his hand lodged against the sidewall of Juan Pablo's lungs. It gave every impression of Juan Pablo bringing in a prisoner. Tommy had figured that the Mexican had hired local talent because of the short lead-time. He hoped he was right.

At the front door, Tommy pulled the screen door aside with his left hand. He edged Juan Pablo in front of him. "Take out your weapon. When we go in, shoot the first man you see."

Juan Pablo hesitated. "I have your word you will let my family live?"

"You do. If the woman is okay."

"Thank you, Vicar." The Mexican assassin sounded like he

knew he was going to die.

"Go," commanded Tommy.

Juan Pablo hesitated no longer. He knocked briefly on the door, three quick raps, turned the knob and went in quickly. A man with a wide broom of a mustache was standing in front of the opening door. Juan Pablo shot him in the center of the chest.

Tommy Atkins, now the Vicar, killed the most dangerous man in the room. He shot Juan Pablo in the back of the head, just as Juan Pablo had known he would. Yet the old man kept his bargain, going to his death to protect the children.

Atkins swept the room and two men were scrambling off a couch. Atkins shot them quickly, one at a time with body shots. He didn't want to chance missing with headshots. Three down.

Nobody else in the front room.

"Tommy!" María Elena screamed. "Back here. One man."

Without stopping, Atkins reflected that María Elena was keeping her head about her. He'd be proud of her later if they got out of here alive.

Tommy lifted the man Juan Pablo had shot and ran toward the only hallway leading from the front room. It emptied upon a typical kitchen with scarred and chipped linoleum on the floor. Tommy held the mustache man in front of him.

Number four was a balding punk with no shirt on and gang-banger tats all over his torso. He stood behind María Elena with a gun to her head. She was sitting taped to a chair behind the kitchen table.

Number four shifted his revolver toward the door and fired immediately. The sound was as if he were hitting one of the hanging pots and pans with a wooden spoon.

Tommy launched the body toward the kitchen table as the punk continued to fire into the body.

María Elena's eyes were as big as saucers when she saw Tommy throw the dead man. But she retained her senses and banged her head back into tattoo guy to spoil his aim, and then she ducked away from him, tilting her chair, trying to tip it over.

This gave Tommy the time and angle he needed. As the man

swung his weapon unable to decide between shooting Tommy or the girl, Tommy triggered three shots into him. Number four jitterbugged backwards into the refrigerator and slid down it to the floor, smearing blood all over the brand new icebox, dead before he hit the floor.

Without wasting a movement, Tommy ejected the magazine and slammed another home. "Lesson number five. Always reload immediately. Is there anyone else here?"

María Elena's eyes were still enlarged and she was desperately trying to remain upright now. Finally, she stabilized herself.

Tommy had turned and was scanning the hallway.

"Three others, far as I know," she said.

"Not any longer." Tommy pulled his knife out of his boot and sliced her bonds. "We gotta get the fuck outa here, Pocahontas, pronto."

"If you're waiting on me, you're backing up," she said, yet her voice quivered.

Tommy took the time to search the men swiftly for money and weapons. They all had five crisp hundred-dollar bills and no ID. He picked up a throwaway .32 auto and a couple of clips for María Elena and gave it to her.

"You know how to use this?"

"You betcha, Mr. Atkins."

"Let's go."

"Tommy?" She was trying to hold it together. He could see the emotions race across her face. She moved toward him, as if for support, then stopped.

"What?"

"Thanks. Again." She shook her head. "Damn, I gotta pee bad."

"Any time, college girl. My pleasure." He felt a proprietary pride. She'd been through a lot and was holding it together well. Not many women—or men, for that matter—would have showed the presence of mind that she had. And none of them were as professional at this business as he was.

He retrieved his magazine and wiped her prints from the metal on the chair and the surface of the table.

CHAPTER TEN: THEM

"Five more dead?"

"The local FBI office says the local cops are calling it a charnel house. The main guy is called 'The Mexican Assassin', for what it's worth."

Suzie Q pondered. "That wouldn't be Juan Pablo from Sonora?"

"You know him?"

"Not personally, Linda. I've heard of him. Jesus. This is getting bad. That idiot Don Diego hired Juan Pablo? This is high profile shit."

Linda shrugged. "What did you expect? You play with the devil; somebody's hands are going to get burned."

"You are speculating this girl, María Elena, and her phantom friend, done all that?"

"It looks that way, Suze. I suggest we rethink what the fuck we're doing and how the fuck we're doing it."

"No word on who the shooter is?"

"Actually, yes. The local Indians down there in the Everglades admit his name is Tom Atkins. That's all they know. He's been a hermit back in there for years."

The secretary buzzed, three rings: priority.

Suzie Q answered. "Yes."

She said nothing, then after a moment, "Okay. We don't have a choice." She slammed the phone into its cradle. "Oh, shit."

Linda leaned across the desk. "What now?"

"The US Marshal Service and some assistant muckety muck

from the Attorney General's office are on the way to talk to us."

"About?"

"Tommy Atkins."

Linda sat back. "When it rains, it pours."

Suzie Q looked directly at Linda L. "I do not think it is necessary to share the extent of the blood bath we've got going on."

"Concur, hon. But listen, I ain't altogether certain that all those dead guys is a bad thing. In fact, the world might be better off for their unlamented passing."

"We don't know that, Linda. Even if you're right, we face criticism from the PC crowd around here. You can't just be involved in ten plus deaths in this day and age. In fact, I'd think we'd be in extreme jeopardy."

"Oh."

Suzie thought some more, and then went on. "Keep in mind they're hanging other CIA operatives for a little persuasive questioning. And they're court-martialing Navy SEALS for slapping a known terrorist and killer around. I could go on—"

"Please don't," Linda said. "I don't want to think about it. In fact, I need a smoke."

"Are the geeks making progress on the surveillance recordings from Orlando International?"

"I'll check. I don't trust that facial recognition software all that much, but we have the exact time of the cell phone call which simplifies matters."

Suzie Q smelled the cigarette smoke on Linda L's flowery yellow dress and once again regretted quitting herself. Unfortunately, it was one of Suzie Q's favorite dresses on Linda and now they'd have to add it to the dry cleaning load.

They sat in a basic government conference room, Linda and her on one side of the rectangular table and the two men on the other side. Each position had an official government yellow ruled tablet and official government pen. One of Linda's attractive aides was at the foot of the table ready to work the computer and the large screen. Linda did not allow ugly women to work in her office. Plus they were all so very competent, which spoke well for Linda's own competence. Hire good people, get good results. It was just that, did they all have to be so damn good looking? On the ninth hand, Linda herself was the most attractive person in the room.

The balding guy was the rep from the U.S. Marshall Service named Eisenberg. Suzie Q didn't know whether to call him officer, agent, deputy or what. She settled on mister. The other guy, a third assistant Attorney General, she dismissed as a political flack. They sensed something was up and wanted in on it to share the credit if something good came out of this. Which led her to speculate that whoever this Tommy Atkins was, he had some importance. The assistant AG was, in real life before the political storm caught him up, a professor of law. BFD, thought Suzie. But this guy, Henderson, went by the professorial moniker of doctor.

Henderson opened the meeting. He went on about interagency cooperation and the importance of what they were doing.

Finally, Suzie Q had enough. "Fine Doctor Henderson, how can we help?"

Henderson paused, gathered himself, and pointed to Eisenberg. "Mallory Eisenberg is charge of our cold case JTF." And that's all he said as if it was supposed to floor them and put them in their place. Eisenberg had been openly looking at Linda, apparently working hard to keep from staring.

Eisenberg spoke, his voice a low base. "We're responding to your NCIC inquiry."

Suzie Q waited and nobody said anything. So, she said, "Okay, go ahead and respond."

"So where did you get the prints? Is this man alive? Where is he?"

"Why do you want to know?" asked Linda.

Both men switched their eyes to Linda, not a hard thing to do, as Linda L was gorgeous. Her voice was whiskey-like, probably from all that smoking thought Suzie Q.

The two men exchanged a look. "We have nothing to hide, so

we'll lay our cards on the table."

To Suzie's jaundiced view of government bureaucrats, this meant they weren't going to lay out all their cards and they did have something to hide.

Suzie glanced at Linda who was watching her, telling Suzie that Linda suspected the same thing Suzie was thinking. Then Suzie saw the marshal guy Eisenberg had been paying attention and was aware of the exchange between the two women. Uh oh, this guy was sharper than he let on. The AAG was the traditional political appointee idiot, but not the man with the star.

Eisenberg cleared his throat. "The info I'm going to tell you we do not know exactly, but we are pretty sure it is correct. If the prints are the same person, he is an escaped federal and state of Florida convict. One we long thought dead. From what I can tell, this man Atkins has also been known to us variously as John Doe, Sam Adams, The Vicar, and a few other minor aliases. It is thought his birth name is Evan Longboat, but we don't know that for sure."

"What in the world did he do?" asked Linda.

"Ms. Landover, the question should be, what didn't he do?" Eisenberg said.

"He's a shooter," said Linda, trying already to be inane, but Eisenberg apparently wasn't buying her act.

"Well, this Tom Atkins, he was at one time or another, a numbers runner, a U.S. Marine, a hitman, an outlaw biker, a mobster, and, we're pretty sure, a French Foreign Legionnaire." He shook his head. "The French are notorious about their legion and security and privacy. If we think it's really important, perhaps higher authority can pressure them?" Eisenberg looked directly at Henderson.

Henderson shifted uncomfortably.

Eisenberg turned his attention back to the other side of the conference table. "Why is it the FBI search did not find a print match?"

"I'd like to know that also," Linda admitted. "I'll check with my superiors."

"Ah, ahem," started Henderson."

"Yes, Doctor?" said Suzie Q.

"Ah, there is a minute possibility that it was, ah, blocked, in order to flag some higher authority or, ah, security program."

Obfuscation, thought Suzie Q. This proved she was right about the AG US involvement. Or some other high political appointee or even elected official.

"What was he doing federal time for?" asked Linda.

"Ah, RICO."

Racketeering, thought Suzie Q. She spoke while she thought. "Why is it that a hitman and all those other nasty things he was, ends up in the slammer for RICO?"

"We should be concentrating on what we're going to do," said Doctor Henderson, obviously trying to change the subject.

Linda smiled openly. Suzie Q knew they had something.

"If we had a visual on this guy," said Eisenberg, "we could confirm the partial prints and know who and what we're dealing with."

"*We* are not dealing with anything," Suzie Q said with iron authority. "JTF 13 is working an ongoing operation; one, I might add, with a high national security priority." She was sending a message that what these two clowns wanted wasn't as important as her mission and that she is in charge and would accept no interference.

"Ah," said Dr. Henderson, "the Marshall Service has a Fugitive Joint Task Force in operation to recover this fugitive."

"You're telling us," Suzie Q said slowly, "that if Atkins is captured, you get first dibs?"

"Ah, yes, so to speak."

"Look," interrupted Eisenberg. "We just want to work together. We're all in the same boat, working for the taxpayer."

Linda chortled.

Suzie Q said, "Bull shit."

Eisenberg grinned. "Now that we understand each other, shall we proceed?"

Suzie returned his smile, knowing the battle wasn't over.

"Yes," she lied, "let us work together then when and if we catch this guy, we can fight over him." If he lives, she thought. And we don't even know if we want him—which we didn't until now.

Eisenberg held her eyes. "Yes, we seem to agree here." That told Suzie, in the world of government bureaucrats that he had his own agenda and would do what it would take. Eisenberg glanced at Henderson then back to Suzie Q. Suzie guessed that meant that the political hacks would rather Atkins not come out of this alive. Unfortunately, this might be closer to what she wanted in the end, rather than recapturing Atkins for Eisenberg. Too many people were pissing in the same pot.

"Proceed, Sandy." Linda pointed at her attractive assistant and the lights dimmed.

A security camera digital recording of an airport concourse leapt onto the large screen.

"Orlando International," said Sandy. "To one side are the departure gates, the other side, the arrival gates. And, see offset there are a bank of phones." A laser pointer indicated the areas she was addressing. "This is five minutes before the phone call." Sandy fast-forwarded the video. "Now, from the lobby, it's crowded, but you'll see a man and a woman. She's pulling a suitcase on wheels after he gives it to her."

Suzie Q saw the laser indicate the couple. A big guy. And the girl, they already knew well. The big guy was wearing a hat and sunglasses. Smart, thought Suzie. Not to mention arriving while the crowds were the largest.

On the screen, they stopped under the giant flight schedule board. The two talked for a moment, then the big guy patted her ass, left and the woman went over near the phones so she could be out of the way. She pulled out a cell phone.

"That has to be our call," said Sandy. "Times are exact."

"That's it?" asked Henderson.

"We just chased the next video down," Sandy said. "Ms. Landover, shall I show it?"

"Go ahead."

Sandy was sharp; she didn't want to give anything away unless Linda okayed it. Suzie prized loyalty. Suzie decided Sandy needed a great performance report.

"The best we can see is this shot; we've a few of him weaving through crowds and using escalators, but we managed to follow him to the rental car area." Sandy's laser pointed to the big guy threading his way to the rental car counter. He usually kept his head down, seemingly aware of the possibility of cameras.

Once, he looked backwards as if searching for someone, but apparently saw nothing worth his attention. Then he walked out, pocketing paperwork.

"We just found this. Since we have an exact time, our team will soon determine who rented what car and under what circumstances, what driver's license, and what credit card."

"Good work, Sandy," said Linda.

Eisenberg scribbled on his official tablet with his official government pen. He pushed the paper down to Sandy. "Can you call that up?"

Sandy began typing onto her keyboard and nodded. "Just a sec."

"It's a couple of official photographs, booking photos," said Eisenberg to the others.

"So how'd Mister Atkins escape federal custody?" asked Suzie Q coyly.

Eisenberg shrugged.

Henderson cleared his throat. "Ah, um, we don't know."

Linda shook her head. "You don't know how somebody escaped from prison?"

"Not exactly. One day he was there and the next roll call or head count or whatever they do in the slammer he was nowhere to be found."

A mystery indeed, thought Suzie. But not likely germane to this current effort.

"Got it," said Sandy.

"Isolate the shot of him," said Eisenberg, "looking back over his shoulder, then superimpose the booking photo or put 'em side by side."

Sandy clicked and dragged for a moment. "There."

"We can check dates later," said Eisenberg, "but remember this photo is at least twenty years ago."

"Hard to tell," said Linda. "I wish he hadn't worn the sunglasses and hat."

"Look at the line of his jaw," said Suzie. "The edge of his lips."

"Ms. Quantrell?" said Sandy.

"Yes, Sandy."

"I'll just run a subprogram of facial recognition."

"Oh. Good idea."

Sandy typed some more and clicked her mouse and scrolled.

A small word flashed at the bottom of the screen. MATCH.

"So," said Suzie, thinking furiously. "Whom was Atkins a hitman for? Whom did he kill? How many did he kill? Why is he now involved? And who the fuck is this Vicar guy?"

Eisenberg said, "I'll put out an APB for our guys across the land."

Henderson said, "We better add Border Patrol to that APB. They'd be smart to head for the border and disappear."

Suzie Q said, "Fine. I trust you all will notify us should something come up?"

"Yes, certainly," said Henderson.

Eisenberg nodded agreement.

Somehow Suzie Q didn't believe them.

Henderson got up to leave.

"Go ahead, Doctor, I'll make it back later." Eisenberg waved.

Henderson nodded, seemingly distracted.

Linda and Suzie Q were gathering their stuff when Eisenberg settled back. "Now maybe we can do some business?"

Linda grimaced and sat back down.

Suzie saw they'd not fooled the deputy marshal. "Go ahead, Sandy; let's find out what flight our girl boarded."

Linda shook her head. "She didn't. Go back to the rental counter, Sandy."

"Yes, ma'am." The shot isolated with Atkins beginning to walk away.

"She's just barely in the shot," Linda said, "over there behind that group of tall college kids."

"I see her." Suzie Q hadn't caught it, but Linda had. "Follow her," she told Sandy.

A few more clicks of the mouse and they watched María Elena walk toward the escalator, the exit for baggage pickup and the parking garage, and points near.

"So they split up," said Eisenberg.

"I dunno," Linda replied. "Could be a feint, making it look as such. Trying to throw off pursuit."

"Why's she spying on him, then?" asked the marshal.

Suzie Q said, "Something is going on we can't understand, Linda. Otherwise he wouldn't have dropped her at the phone bank."

Eisenberg shook his head. "Maybe he didn't drop her. Maybe he dumped her."

Linda smiled. "All them U. S. Marshals ain't all that stupid, are they?"

"She's following him," said Suzie Q.

"They went out different exits," said Linda.

"Shit," said Suzie Q.

"So why was it that he patted her ass?" asked Suzie.

CHAPTER ELEVEN: HER

Sudden violence. Immediate and overwhelming force. Death and destruction.

María Elena drove and wondered what tiger she had by the tail. She'd grown up in a paramilitary environment, shielded though she was. And she had gone through some of their training. But nothing she had ever encountered prepared her for this, this enigma that was Tommy Atkins. Big, quiet, lethal. And boy, did she feel good about it right now. Perhaps he was proof that God does in fact exist. Why else would she be here, alive and well, after two episodes of certain death?

Skirt the border on Interstate 10. El Paso. Las Cruces, Deming, Lordsburg, New Mexico. Arizona. Tucson.

She sensed he was becoming comfortable with her, trusting her to do most of the driving. She recalled fondly what he said as they drove away from the barrio house in Juan Pablo's old van. "You done good, Pocahontas." He'd briefed her on Juan Pablo, the Sonoran assassin, the famous retired gunman. When she asked how he knew all this, he merely shrugged her question off. But she had wondered aloud how he'd found her so quickly. He merely shrugged. "I know my way around," he told her.

Her cell phone, still on, was currently en route to Dallas and Chicago on a bus. One day soon, some cleaning guy would find it and put it to good use.

Tommy would read real books or books on his laptop, occasionally checking traffic. "Highway patrol. It's more difficult for him to check tags if you're in traffic when he's around. He's gotta watch the traffic and other vehicles and run his radar. Too much for him to do. But if you're alone and he's tooling along, he might have nothing to do but run a tag, just for the hell of it. And if you're in front of somebody else, it's hard for him to read a tag when he drives by."

"Fine. Where are we going?"

"First to Tucson."

"Why?"

"See a guy."

"Why?" She settled in front of an eighteen-wheeler and the cop went around the pack which had built because nobody wanted to speed when a cop was around. Cops had to love that.

He looked up from his book, now taking her seriously. "I don't mean to not be forthcoming, I'm just feeling my way."

"Tommy, it's not that I'm ungrateful, I sure am. But…"

He gave her a shy smile. "We need to go underground for a while and regroup. We need new ID. We need a safe hiding place. We need to think."

Was he saying he wanted to be done with her? "You've done plenty, Tommy. I don't want to get you hurt." Her words were impulsive and she regretted the implication they made.

"Shit, college girl. I got an investment in you now. A proprietary interest, if you will. I ain't scheming to run off on your cute ass."

"Oh." Her eyes roamed ahead and checked each of the three mirrors. "Yet my point remains. I'd be long dead without you. But I have no…um…"

"Cards on the table, María Elena etcetera. I been out of sight for too long. I got my reasons and they're good ones. I need a project to keep me busy and in the game. I pick you."

"Oh."

"While your womanly charms are many, it ain't them neither. I am not one for introspection—in fact, fuck that shit. But, maybe I see something going on needs my attention for a while. And your situation kind of parallels mine: we both need to get under the radar and find out what's going on. Then take whatever action we can to disengage cleanly." Something flared in his eyes.

She could tell he had not clearly articulated what he was thinking even to himself or he would've said it more plainly. Some trick of her mind saw and heard the call of distant drums to the warrior. She shook off the feeling. She saw he was uncomfortable and so, too, was she with the conversation. All she knew is she had to stay alive. "My goal is to expose Don Diego. I would see Don Diego dead." She surprised herself.

"I concur that he needs to die. It occurs to me that to get you back into society, he needs to be dead bad. But we can't just get a rifle and pop him long distance. That won't solve anything."

"Yes, Tommy."

"We get some ID, hide out for a while until the smoke clears and these feds and gunmen give up, then we surface and take care of business."

His "taking care of business" likely means sudden overwhelming violence. Death and destruction.

"Yes, Tommy."

"And do you not forget that we're married in this endeavor. Sort of like we have no choice. You need me for my, ah, abilities, and I need you to navigate us through this mess." He colored slightly.

"Yes, Tommy." Was he embarrassed at the marriage line? Or the need each other line?

"Lemme look at the map. Tucson is ahead and I don't want to Google an address because that leaves an electronic footprint." No telltale GPS for them.

"Where did you get all those credit cards? Don't they run at least a quick double check on you when you sign up?"

He smiled at her. "Ah, if you have social security number, date and place of birth, stuff like that, it's easy. I don't do it myself, just to be safe. I trade info for credit cards and ID. Then, sometimes if I open accounts like you saw in Florida, I put my own money in them. Just to hide it and not use my own name. I traded a guy in Miami some social security numbers and birth dates, etc, for the ID or the credit cards. He does the work with legit info and I share with him."

"Where in the world do you get the info? Do you dumpster-dive for it?"

He looked at her strangely. "I worked in the medical office in prison, college girl. I had access to all the records upon which appeared all the aforementioned information. I recorded it for my own benefit later. Lots of it. Especially the data from dead guys, guys who died in there. Makes it cleaner if they can't object."

"Oh. I wasn't prying."

"Sure you were. Now you know what a badass motherfucker I am."

She set her jaw. "Not to me." But his point settled between them. He was quick with a gun and almost indiscriminate about shooting. Suddenly, she said, "I'm glad I'm on *your* side." Unconsciously, she reached over and patted his hand.

His quick smile told her she'd said the right thing. She thought about her training days in how to negotiate minefields. This was a bit trickier.

"Sometimes you network," Tommy said. "There's a guy in Tucson who can come up with identity documents. I figure we might need a couple of passports, too."

"And am I to extrapolate correctly that I found you ensconced as an Everglades hermit because of?"

"Yeah, that. I sort of failed to get their concurrence about my release from joint federal and state custody."

"I think it was preordained. Somebody in the Planning Department up in Heaven was doing their job." She turned to him and batted her eyelashes in an exaggerated manner.

"And, you found me?"

"Sure I did, Tommy. It was fate." Her smile was disarming and he shrugged. "An old Cuban proverb says 'Even a leaf does not flutter on the tree without the will of God.'"

"Jesus save me."

"I hope so; I will pray for it."

The guy in Tucson wasn't happy to see them. He lived in middle class house in a middle class neighborhood quite near the mammoth Davis Monthan Air Force Base. There were children playing in the streets and rocks in the yards and some grass. And lots of flies. María Elena reflected that your basic Everglades mosquitoes could eat these flies alive.

"You are not supposed to come to my house," he told them.

Tommy shrugged and handed him a package of money. The guy's eyes lighted up. Tommy handed him a flash drive. "Money and on the flash drive you'll find a lot of clean names, numbers, data. I want three full sets of ID for each of us, including electronic passports and those new passport cards you can use for nearby border travel."

The guy couldn't keep his eyes off María Elena. She was wearing a tight tank top. She felt creepy. "Gimme a week. I'll call you."

"We don't have a phone. We'll be back in a week."

María Elena changed into a more respectable top and he took proper passport photos and they left. She marveled at Tommy for he was always clean shaven, and he didn't have to shave for the pictures.

"See," Tommy told her, "now he's aware we know where he and his family live. That comes under the column titled 'insurance' for us. He's less likely to give anyone info on us and, conversely, more likely to produce high quality documents."

"Good thing you know of people like him."

Tommy shrugged. "You can get excellent ID by ordering direct from Chinese websites. Good RFID chips, too. Problem is, in my line of, ah, work, you don't want to leave an electronic trail. Doubtless the feds have somebody or program monitoring who can break secure transactions and email. If I were them, I'd keep a list and have a computer program to run the names periodically to see what comes up for current or future reference. I don't want to be included, but I'm jealous all you gotta do is send 'em a credit card payment and picture, and you got new ID. Mail order."

Then they found a couple of used bookstores downtown and near the University of Arizona. Tommy bought a couple of hundred books, mostly paperbacks of classics. He simply shrugged at her questioning look.

"Find me a mall," María Elena told him. "My wardrobe sucks."

Tommy grinned. "To quote me: 'Vanity, thy name is María Elena.'"

She favored him with a thawed glare then stuck her tongue out at him.

Then they went to a grocery store where they bought a great deal of food. "Get what you like and what you're comfortable with," he told her. At her further look, he said, "We don't want to shop anyplace near where we're going to hole up. No patterns, no trace, no nothing."

She was beginning to understand his cryptic personality. "Yes, dear," she said sarcastically.

Interstate 19 south to Nogales on the border. And she'd always thought south Florida was hot.

"Lesson eight or whatever," Tommy said as she drove. Heat shimmered off the roadway and adjacent scrub land. "Always pay attention. Situational awareness. Know exits of anywhere you enter, eyeball them immediately. Paying attention, soon you'll notice people or things out of place, odd stuff going on you might not ordinarily notice. Like triggers, clues, and soon that stuff will shout 'beware' to you. You develop a sixth sense after a while, and pretty soon it becomes automatic."

Almost to the border town of Nogales, Atkins directed her to drive off I-19 onto Algeria Road. They took it to the end. "Looks like Algeria all right," María Elena muttered as the SUV rocked and bounced.

"'Don't worry about it," he told her, "this car's not going much farther."

Way down Algeria Road they turned on a faint double track outline. Tommy pointed and she turned onto it. Half a dozen miles later, they teed off that gravel road onto another, less obvious trail.

"Line's are blurry here," Atkins said, "Coronado National Forest property interspersed with state land and private property all over hereabouts. Both sides of the Interstate. Few people come back this far."

The terrain was rough, hardpan and gravel on the trail. Sometimes they drove through small canyons with sheer or sculpted rock. "Some of these arroyos you don't want to be in when a storm comes," he continued. She was surprised at the underbrush. Probably meant there was sufficient water here. Not exactly desert. Mesquite. Big, round skeletal bushes she guessed were sage, which dried up and blew through ghost towns in Western movies. Saguaro cacti were the large ones, and scattered small cacti, round or Mickey Mouse-eared.

A flock of turkey vultures scattered and leapt into the air. Just like vultures on road kill in the 'Glades.

Then she recognized it: it was the same as Tommy Atkins' hideout in the Everglades: hidden, almost inaccessible, inhospitable. She drove on with determination, finally garnering his plan.

They rounded a turn and dipped into a greener valley of a few acres, towered over by rock face. Dust which had followed settled behind them.

Tucked under a cliff overhang was an adobe house. It looked almost cool in the shadows. Alongside it sat a brand new Jeep.

"We need a four-wheel drive next, Pocahontas. A safe ride. A vehicle that can navigate this God-forsaken land if we have to go off the road."

"Off the road?" she asked rhetorically.

"Don't get too close. Kill the engine and stay in the vehicle." Tommy leaned into the back seat and retrieved a briefcase. He pulled out one of the envelopes of money. "Twenty-five ought to do it." He climbed out and María Elena triggered her window down before she shut off the engine.

He went around to the back of the SUV and took two boxes

of books out and carried them toward the adobe house. About fifty feet away from the house he dropped the books at his feet and stood waiting. "Charley?"

"The fuck you want?" came a voice from an open window.

"It's Atkins. From Florida. How about we talk for a minute."

"What's in the boxes?"

"Books."

"No shit?"

"No shit."

"What's that in your hand?" The voice was reedy now, peeved at the intrusion.

"An envelope with twenty-five grand in it."

"No shit?"

"No shit."

"What's it for?"

"Your vacation in Vegas. Four weeks paid vacation. Rent money for your place for that four weeks."

"The books?"

"I read your reviews on Amazon and know what you like. They're my bonefides." Tommy opened his arms innocently. "How long since you been outa here, Charley?"

"Too fuckin' long, Tom. Too fuckin' long."

"We all need to get away once in a while."

"Ain't that right." A tall, scrawny man with a beard came out the front door, rifle cradled in his arms. He peered at the SUV and then back to Tommy. "You on the run?"

"There was a little trouble down in south Florida."

"You ain't alone."

"Nope."

Charley scratched under his beard. "I could use a professional shave. Lissen, lemme do the math. Thirty days expenses, that'd be maybe fifteen K. I feel like doing some gambling; I like the women and the shows, and some 21. Generous, that would cost maybe ten K a week. So, you got another twenty?"

"Yeah, I got it, Charley."

Charley laughed, almost a loud cough. "What do you bet

that's not as much as the reward."

"I don't know reward, Charley." Tommy's voice became dangerous.

Charley shook his head. "You got me wrong, Atkins. This old vet ain't gonna look it up. We don't operate thataway. Just pulling your leg. Gimme the extra twenty and I'll leave right fucking now. If I get lucky, maybe I won't come back. I been out here a long time. This shit gets old. Fuck being a recluse. I signed out during Vietnam and ain't regretted it. Well, not often."

"Charley, show me your generator, water pump, and systems. Then you can go. And Charley? I need you to lay out what weapons you got. I won't take 'em, but I gotta know what's here and what's not."

"You start a fuckin' war, Atkins, and we're all fucked."

"Yeah, I know the drill. Boy Scout motto."

Charley grinned. "Me, too. Always. Be prepared."

María Elena stayed in the SUV for twenty minutes while the two went inside.

She wondered how many veterans were peppered across the land, playing the recluse. She'd heard of them in places like Montana and Alaska. But not here or the Everglades.

She wondered if there were a website for hermits where you registered and then you could network amongst each other. Tommy was certainly knowledgeable. On the other hand, Tommy paid attention to everything. He would cultivate these kinds of distant friends. Maybe it was a hermit-guy thing.

Then Charley came out with a bag, climbed in his Jeep and pulled out. Tommy got another package of money and handed it to the man as he drove up.

Charley eyed María Elena with surprise. "Goddamn," he told Tommy. "You dog, you." He grinned and gunned the Jeep out of the shadows.

Tommy led her into the house. "Home sweet home," he said.

"What's with him?" she asked.

"Charley, he's an old mob guy. Ran afoul of the feds and

this is the mob's version of the Witness Protection Program. He could have been set up in a city, but he prefers to hide out here. He's an old vet."

One bedroom, of course. One open central room. In the corner, a kitchenette. Book cases on the walls. Television and desk with computer. Fireplace on the outside wall. Small bathroom, no shower. Meticulous housekeeping. Maybe all these hermits took the same class in hermiting.

"He's got satellite dishes on top of that cliff. Television and Internet, too. Something called WildBlue Satellite System. On top of this house is what they call a swamp cooler. Big fan sucks air in through filters which have water pumped over them all the time it's on."

"It's plenty cool in here."

"He also has got a whole house fan. Sucker blows some air. Generator and water pump. Septic with a good field way away from the water source. Outside shower, tough in the winter, okay now."

"Just your basic hermitage?"

"So to speak." He pointed at a back door. "Deep rock pool out there, fed from a seep. You can swim in it if you take short strokes."

Tommy slept on the couch. She got up at dawn, put her hair in a pony tail and went for a run back down the track to get familiar with the lay of the land. She jogged two miles getting the kinks out; it had been a long time. Then she ran back at double the speed.

When she rounded the curve and came to a stop at the house, Tommy was sitting in a lawn chair sipping a cup of coffee. Next to him atop an upside down bucket was his .380.

"Hi honey, I'm home," she said.

He smiled. "I put soap and towels at the shower out back. The setup is just like my old shower in the Everglades, this one with a pump from the pool to the overhead barrel. Or you can hop in the rock pool." At her look, he said, "Don't worry. I'm already familiar with your fair young unclad body." He grinned. "And I admit it is an attractive one, even though your hips are a shade wide."

"My hips?"

"I think they're very attractive that way."

Her breathing was returning to normal. She took his coffee cup and drank deeply. "My hips are too wide?" She missed good, thick Cuban coffee.

"Don't worry about it, Pocahontas. You'll get plenty of exercise here."

"My hips?" He grinned.

She stuck her tongue out at him and returned his coffee and went to take a shower.

While showering, she realized she was comfortable for the first time in a very long time. She found their situation was almost domestic and tranquil. Strange: here in the middle of nowhere living with a professional killer, she liked what she was doing. She realized then that she was very fond of Tommy. Sure, he'd saved her life a few times, but he wasn't an overwhelming presence, a demanding person. In fact he was very easy to get along with. She recognized she'd been learning, in essence, a new lifestyle from him. Even if she returned to Miami, she'd never be the same again; her perspective had changed significantly. And she was intellectually engaged with him and she could not deny they had a gut level attachment which was growing every day.

After all the violence and running and hiding, she almost hoped they could stay here and ignore the rest of the world.

In a week, they drove back to Tucson. They picked up the passports and other ID's. From there, they went to a self-storage facility off Speedway. In a small unit, she watched as he rolled up the door. Against a far wall sat a small suitcase.

"Let me guess," she said. "Money."

"Yep. Another hundred grand."

"You must be rich."

"Now that I have you I am."

"Wow."

"Shit," he said regretfully and his face grew red. "Sorry, Pocahontas, that one just slipped out."

"It kind of makes me feel good, Tommy."

"I mean, now I enjoy the wealth of your company and all that other shit, I have an abundance of riches."

"Yes, dear."

"I always stash money. Well, I used to. Don't have an income any longer which produces so much money." He cleared his throat self-consciously.

They went to a seedy used car lot and bought a four-wheel drive Jeep. For an extra couple of hundred dollars, the salesman took care of their lack of insurance and found them an untraceable license. "Give me a week, and I'll have the real tag from the state." He said it like he knew they wouldn't be back.

"Can you drive a floor-shift?" Tommy asked.

"I can drive anything. I drove Jeeps and four-wheel trucks with those giant tires and motorcycles, too, all on the 13 training ground outside of Miami. There were mud pits and bogs and little hills we made with backhoes and front-end loaders for training."

Back at Charley's cabin, Tommy parked the SUV in front and directed her to park the Jeep in a shadowy overhang of the mesa above some quarter of a mile on the far side of the cabin opposite the approach road.

"If we need it," he told her, "we can hop in and go across country since there is only one so-called roadway in and out of here." He put some canned food and bottled water in a bag and dumped that in the back seat. He wrapped a .22 rifle, two .38 revolvers, and ammunition in towels and covered them up on the floor of the back seat.

"I know," she said, "Boy Scout motto."

That night, she fixed arroz con pollo. "Cuban yellow rice and chicken," she explained. Even she thought it was very good.

But he barely ate his, just picking at it.

"You don't like it?" she asked.

"It's good, it really is. I'm just not hungry."

"You're always hungry, like a growing boy."

"Not tonight. I feel like I got the flu."

In an hour he was feverish. He did not complain, but she could tell he had nausea. He vomited in the bathroom. He took a cold shower outside.

When he came in from that, he looked pale.

María Elena was becoming concerned. "That bug took hold quickly."

"Stay away from me, you might catch it."

"No, I don't get sick. Here, lie down." She led him to the bed she'd been sleeping in.

He collapsed on it and began shivering violently.

"Tommy? This doesn't appear to be the flu." She tucked sheets and a blanket around him.

"I'm freezing." His teeth chattered. He was sweating profusely.

She found another blanket in a closet. He continued to shiver. She felt his forehead and he was cool, very cool. Maybe the body sweats, she thought, when temperature falls.

His eyes bled misery and his body shook. He curled up on his side in a fetal position.

She thought a moment and then pulled her shirt over her head and stripped off her jeans. She stood for a second watching him.

María Elena climbed into bed and got under the covers with him. His back to her, she spooned with him and wrapped her arms around him.

She held him tightly as he continued to shake with chills.

"God, you…feel…good," he said, voice plaintive. "I…am… soooo…cold."

His muscles trembled. She could only hold him.

"S'not flu," he gasped. He squirmed back into her.

"Not good, Tommy," she said into the back of his neck.

"N…nope. Malaria…. relapse."

"Jesus, Mary and Joseph," she said, voice muffled against his shoulder as his whole body shook. She felt a puckered scar etch into her cheek.

He gasped, which she thought was an attempt at laughing.

"Where did you get malaria?"

"F...fucking Angola. Or the fucking Congo. Some fucking place." Suddenly, he rolled over on his back and pulled her on top of him. Even incapacitated, he was so very strong. He was shaking badly, but it did not even mimic sex as she would've thought. "So nice...warm." His breath was sour, his skin clammy.

"Angola? In Africa?" What was he doing?

"Is...there...another...?"

"What were you doing in Angola, Tommy?" He did not appear excited, so maybe he wasn't looking for sex. But he wrapped his arms around her and held her tighter. He still shivered uncontrollably.

He laughed again through clinched and chattering teeth. "Killing...Cubans."

CHAPTER TWELVE: HER

Shortly, Tommy stopped shaking and began breathing deeply, as if in a fast sleep. He didn't seem inclined to move her off of him, but she felt that he was warming. This fact gave her some chills of her own. "Chills and fever" were a term commonly used. She slipped off of him and rearranged the blankets over him.

She took the opportunity to hustle to the laptop. She went on the Internet to look up malaria.

"Oh, shit." She'd known they were in trouble, but until now she hadn't admitted it to herself. He needed hospitalization. And sooner rather than later.

She read on and found possible things that could happen without treatment: liver and kidney failure, dehydration of course, fluid in the lungs, and something about an enlarged spleen. She didn't exactly know what the hell a spleen was and what function it performed in the body, but she didn't look it up, either.

Maybe they'd be lucky and it would be a minor episode. But one look at him negated that thought. He was sweating again, and threw off his bedclothes. She felt his forehead again, and touched his shoulders and chest. He was burning up.

Though she searched, she found no thermometer or first aid kit. She did find some aspirin and forced them into his mouth. He choked them down with water she virtually poured into his mouth. She continued giving him water as long as he tolerated it—not long at all. His eyes opened infrequently. Sometimes he seemed to know who she was and what was going on, other times it was as if he were in a coma. She bathed his head with a wet cloth, and then his chest and legs. It seemed to cool him a bit, but he continued to have a high fever. His skin felt hot to her touch.

Then he fell into what she thought was a coma, though in fairness she knew nothing about medicine or comas. He became unresponsive about five hours into the attack. His temperature stayed high and he was sweating again, though not as much. She thought this might be due to dehydration. She continued to bathe him. She got all the ice from the freezer and chilled water with it and bathed him again.

María Elena became intimately familiar with the cicatrix of scars on his body. His thigh had what she thought was a bullet wound scar. There was a long slash on his left side. Another bullet hole on the shoulder she had felt hours ago. Two other areas where she could tell where he'd gotten stitches—not very professional jobs, either, as the scars remained.

At two in the morning, his fever seemed to reach a new and higher plateau and she became more scared than she had in a long time. She didn't want to lose this man.

"God damn it, Tommy!" She shook him and his eyes opened, rolled up, then returned and focused.

"Pocahontas…"

"Tommy. We gotta get you up, right now. C'mon." She dragged on his arm and snaked under it and put her other arm around his torso. "Get up. Now, damn it."

"Don't wanna."

"I am going to put you under the shower."

"'Kay."

Shakily, he got his feet under him and sat upright on the bed. María Elena squatted and lifted him with her legs.

"Good thing I'm in shape," she said aloud to herself.

"Damn sure are," Tommy mumbled.

She half dragged him out the back door. They stumbled to the shower. The only clothes he still wore were his underwear.

They were sweat-soaked anyway. She held him up against the wall and turned on the shower. The nighttime air was much cooler. She directed the showerhead at him and he grumbled. Soon they were both soaked. She found herself very cold, but she held him there. His temperature was moderating somewhat, according to the newly calibrated palm of her hand. She ought to rent herself out to hospitals and save them money from buying all those fancy thermometers.

As usual, she wondered at the skies. Here in the clear air of Arizona, you could see millions more stars than you could in Florida. She guessed that was because of humidity diminishing your view rather than Arizona skies having vastly more stars than Florida. Real good, college girl. Next time take more science courses.

After maybe ten minutes, he seemed to revive slightly. "Son of a bitch." He looked at her in the spill of light from the back door. "We showering together?" His voice was groggy.

She realized she was still dressed only in panties and a bra. "Sort of."

"Goddamn.... just my...luck." He put his other arm on her shoulder and pulled her closer. His knees began to buckle.

"Back to bed." She leaned him against the wall and grabbed a towel off the rack and dried him. She stripped his shorts off resolutely. He didn't seem to notice.

She laughed harshly. "After all your jabs about seeing my nude body in the shower, now it's my turn." Somehow, it was not satisfying to make the point. He wore a chain around his neck with an intricate silver cross, a fact she found strange about him.

She dragged him back inside and put him in a chair. Quickly, she changed the sheets and managed to get him back in bed. He fell asleep immediately.

She went back outside and dried off. In the bedroom, she dug out her stuff and dressed.

She looked at his sleeping body and asked, "What in the fuck am I gonna do?" She shrugged to herself. "You're not gonna die off on me, Tommy Atkins."

After a while, he began tossing and turning and she felt his temperature rising again. "Damn it."

Again she bathed him with cold, wet cloths. She got him to drink water infrequently. She found that if he was awake, he was more responsive and she could get more water down his throat. She couldn't quantify how much he sweat out, but it was plenty. Dehydration was going to be a problem. She opened the front door and the back door and turned on the whole-house fan and created a nice cooling breeze. That wasn't going to work during the day.

She continued to try to keep him aware so he could rehydrate. During one of these times, she asked about medicine.

"The prison doctor gave me chloroquine or some fuckin' thing."

She'd found a bottle of Gatorade and made him drink it for the electrolytes and sugar, in addition to the liquid. If football players drank it during the games, she reasoned it would work on malaria.

He pushed the drink away and started to slump down.

"Not yet. Drink more."

"Don't wanna. Gotta sleep."

"In a few minutes, drink this."

"'Kay."

She had to keep him awake so she could get liquids into him.

"Tell me about Angola, Tommy. What were you doing there?"

"Killing Cubans, nothing personal."

"Tell me."

"'Kay. We were assigned to the Congo, shit, I dunno, it was Zaire or Republic of or some goddamn name at the time."

"We? Who are we?"

"My unit."

"Army?"

"Hell, no."

"Marines?"

"I was in the Marines before this. Then I mustered out."

"Mercenary? Here, drink some more."

"Sure thing, college girl." He sounded like himself, but he wasn't. Suddenly, he grinned, a fierce and deadly thing. "Tough motherfuckers we were."

"Who, Tommy?"

"Us. The Légion étrangère."

"The Foreign Legion? The French Foreign Legion?"

He coughed and spewed water all over them both. She put the glass to his lips again. "Drink."

Over the next hours, she coaxed the story out of him. He was very much like an innocent child, not hesitant about answering questions or shading answers.

Apparently, when Tommy was a very young man, somewhere in his early teens, he was a bolita runner in Tampa. Bolita was a Cuban game brought to Florida in the 1880's and run out of Ybor City, a part of Tampa. Bolita being a numbers game operated by the mob. It was like the lottery, they drew numbered balls out and paid off those who had those numbers. Tommy brought the betting numbers sheets in with the money. Or he collected, depending on the middleman. Of course, law enforcement finally caught a couple of the middlemen, not the big bosses. Tommy, being a juvenile, was by then eighteen and the judge kindly gave him a choice: jail or the United States military. He chose the latter and wound up in the Marines. The Vietnam War was over by then, but he served overseas in various locations. When his enlistment was up, he mustered out from his post in Germany and took a train to Paris where he took another train to Marseille and then a taxi to Aubagne nearby—where the Foreign Legion's headquarters were. The training was easy for a recent Marine; the hardest part was learning enough French to get by with until he became more fluent. Fortunately, his English sufficed, as there were recruits from all over the world.

Eventually, his unit was posted to the Congo, Zaire, whatever it was called at that time. Kolwezi, a city in the mineral rich Katanga Province of Zaire. Rebels and Cuban "mercenaries" instigated a take-over attempt. Murder, rape, kidnapping and hostage taking ensued. The Legion parachuted in and saved over two thousand Europeans and maybe three thousand Africans. They remained after the battle and quietly went on patrols and action against the Cubans; and that included the neighboring Angola. María Elena knew full well that at the time Castro was renting out soldiers, whole armies, to foreign powers. It wasn't as catchall as it sounded: Castro's troops were bought and paid for by the Soviets who, in turn, wanted to install Marxist regimes throughout Africa in the global chess board that was the cold war.

After due consideration, María Elena decided that Tommy Atkins had decided to help her for reasons other than to make up for "killing Cubans" in Angola and Zaire. He certainly had no remorse, for they, and their allies, were "a rag-tag bunch of rapists who came and raped and killed in the name of freedom fighters."

But certainly a fascinating résumé was emerging.

A couple of hours after dawn, his delirium disappeared in exhaustion and so did his talkativeness. She still had not found out why he was in prison. She thought that he'd sleep for at least a couple of hours.

Making up her mind immediately, she liberated a pocketful of cash and jumped in the SUV.

CHAPTER THIRTEEN: HER

From the Internet, she knew there were pharmacies in downtown Nogales. She parked off the road in a safe place near a McDonald's and walked several blocks. She'd learned from Tommy to not park near where you're going to be unless you need a quick getaway.

María Elena skipped national pharmacies and chose a rundown looking one near the border. She went in and asked the girl at the counter if she could talk to the pharmacist.

The pharmacist was a balding, short man.

"I've somebody I can't move," she told him. "He has a bad relapse of malaria and says he's taken something called chloroquine in the past to combat it."

"Do you have a prescription?" he asked.

"No, sir, frankly I don't. I can't get him to a doctor. He's too big for me to move." Well, sort of, anyway.

"Call an ambulance."

She shook her head sadly. "We're way off the beaten path, without real roads out there. No 911 service can help."

"The Sheriff's office will be glad to help."

"Do you have the medicine?"

"I do, young lady, but you need a prescription."

Jesus. What's it going to take to get through to him? She turned on the charm. "Sir? Is there any way I can simply get a supply of chloroquine without a lot of formality?"

He shook his head. "Sorry."

She took a deep breath. "I have plenty of money."

He eyed her warily. "I sympathize. But let me tell you what. The state would pull my license in a nanosecond. I can't, even if I wanted to." He shook his head and went back behind the counter.

Dammit. Wouldn't you know it, an honest man.

The girl behind the counter sidled over. "Señorita? Right over the border, there are many farmacias. They can help you."

"Thank you." She'd already figured that out, but wanted to try the American side first. She hadn't wanted to go through a formal border crossing, even with her new ID. She had an idea. "Could maybe you go over there for me? You work in the business and know what I need and can talk intelligently to them."

"Yes, ma'am, I could. But, if the border officers find me bringing prescription medicine, I might lose my green card. I cannot do it."

"Thanks anyway."

She walked out the front door and observed a pod of young men walking toward the border. "In for a penny, in for a pound. Not an old Cuban proverb." She turned and followed them.

She was acutely aware of the time. Tommy would probably be out for another hour or two. Her sense of urgency clamored. While she'd left him a note and a couple of bottles of water next to the bed, she wasn't confident he'd wake up with any clarity of mind. Most likely, he'd slip back into delirium or coma or worse. No matter what, she would not let him down.

The south Arizona heat pounded down on her as she followed the marked walk through the customs and border security. High chain link fences loomed over her; concrete walls crowded her. Border security officers were lackadaisical, but paying attention nonetheless. Going into Mexico from the U.S. was not a problem. She walked through and under a building, a great structure over her head spanning the road and the pedestrian walkway. She guessed there were offices and walkways above. The young men laughed and pushed on through customs. The security merely waved them on, and along with them, María Elena. Others were following them. María Elena stretched her neck studying the officers and their procedures; however, this wasn't the re-entry passage so it didn't matter. Though it did appear that people were walking through freely with no waiting like you'd think of in an airport security checkpoint. The Mexican entry was even less formal. Following the example of others, she waved her newly acquired RFID passport card.

Soon she was walking down the street in Nogales, Sonora. The young men she'd followed headed off one way, punching each other in the arms and making jokes. Doubtless, they were headed for Boys' Town, the area where the most bars and whore houses were located.

The northern Mexican sun pounded down upon her equally merciless as the south Arizona sun.

María Elena looked around as she walked. Nogales, Sonora, at this point was much like Nogales, Arizona. Off in the distance, she saw the city climb up nearby hills. It was hot and dusty. Not far into the city, she found a street where several pharmacies were located. She passed the first couple on the general principle that the first ones would be tourist traps. Most of the pharmacies had large, English printing on their windows that proclaimed: PHARMACY. Only in small print did she see: FARMACIA.

At the third pharmacy she had little trouble. It appeared to be a mom and pop operation. She explained about the malaria and symptoms and the heavyset woman pharmacist nodded and spoke good English. "Yes, chloroquine. That's what you want. What does the patient weigh? The dosage depends on weight." He looked serious. "Overdosing is very bad."

María Elena did not know. However, she'd half carried him in and out of the cabin. "I'm guessing two hundred pounds, maybe two twenty." Not much fat either, she thought. And, apparently, better to underestimate to prevent overdosing.

Behind the counter were hundreds if not thousands of bottle and vials and boxes. The pharmacist rummaged around and scooped some tablets into a large vial and put them in a paper bag.

María Elena went to pay her, and the pharmacist asked, "Would you like a prescription for those?"

"I have the meds, why would I need a prescription?"

The lady shrugged. "Border security may search you and question these. It has a label, but you never know. For ten dollars more I can consult a doctor and get a prescription."

María Elena sighed. You can't fight city hall no matter where you are. "Okay." She noted a pharmacy school graduation certificate from someplace in Phoenix. That would also explain the pharmacist's excellent English. María Elena had determined not to use her Spanish in case she might learn something unexpected.

The pharmacist went through a door in the back and was back in a few minutes with a printed piece of paper which assured the world that this was a legitimate prescription for chloroquine, with specific patient dosage information. "Please, do not overdose. It is difficult to do; you'd have to take most or all of these tablets."

María Elena remembered her last period. It had been a painful one and she had none of her own stuff from Florida. She addressed this with the pharmacist and the pharmacist smiled knowingly and dug around in the back and gave her a three month supply of birth control pills. She smiled when she handed María Elena the package. "Now you will be safe."

"You don't understand—ah, never mind. And, I wish, but it ain't happening." She'd offered herself half-heartedly to Tommy, but he had the grace to decline. While that part was a relief at the time, she wondered if anything was wrong with him, despite his denials. And now she was happy, since her last period had been no fun at all. After being on the pill to regulate her period and minimize the cramps, her first one off the medicine was memorable.

Soon María Elena was approaching the border crossing. To facilitate her trip through customs, she opened the top two buttons of her shirt suggestively. It worked as she breezed through the Mexican side, merely showing her passport card.

She suspected you could get through locally with only a driver's license, but what the heck. Her trick worked as they paid more attention to her breasts than her documentation.

She walked behind a couple across no-man's land toward the U.S. side.

Right in the middle, somehow she knew that right now Tommy Atkins would be pausing. She glanced around. Above and in front of her loomed the runway with glass windows. Either they were super reflective and she could see nothing inside or they were tinted. She fancied a flash of light or reflectivity that in her paranoid mind screamed that someone was watching her with binoculars.

The couple ahead slowed and María Elena saw that there was a long pedestrian line waiting to get to the customs area. Strange. It hadn't been there when she crossed an hour or so ago.

"First time in a long time," the woman told the man ahead of her.

"Bureaucrats," he replied.

What had Tommy said? Beware. The sixth sense. Something here wasn't right. It might well not be about her. But it well might be solely about her.

Immediately, María Elena made a decision. A quick glance showed her a few more uniformed border guards checking all the cars. And the traffic was beginning to back up.

"Dammit!" said María Elena, snapping her fingers.

The couple turned to look at her.

María Elena touched her Kyle Busch hat. "I'd forget my hat if it wasn't stuck on top of my head," she told them. She turned and walked back to Mexican customs. She waved at them. "Forgot something, be right back." They merely watched her and she insured that her walk was sexy.

Soon she was back into the city. Was she being paranoid? Maybe. Why would they have changed from lackadaisical to focused and thorough within an hour? A tip about a drug runner? Could be. But her dealings with the federal government told her that they had facial recognition software. Or it could be that someone belatedly remembered her picture or description. After all, she was on the terrorist watch list or some similar list up there in Washington. So, too, had been her father. He'd speculated that it was the CIA or FBI's way of being able to track them when they went out of the country or tried to fly somewhere.

Whatever, she couldn't afford to take the chance. Even if the alert were not for her, she might well get caught up in the net. And then what would happen to Tommy? She clutched the bag of chloroquine tightly and walked faster.

Her sense of urgency was growing. Already she'd been gone longer than she'd budgeted for. Tommy needed her.

And another thing. "Sorry, Kyle." She took off her Kyle Busch #18 M & M's hat. There was a box of trash outside a small clothing store and she dropped it in.

Traffic drove along beside her. Where to go? She headed the way the young men had earlier. Some of the slabs of sidewalk were cracked and others broken. Most of the pedestrians were Americans. Boys' Town. Whatever she ended up doing would be illegal and that would be the place for illegality. Tommy would already have a plan forming. But she had no idea. The only thing she could come up with was to find the bus station and follow people who were carrying their belongings. Maybe they'd lead her to an illegal border crossing. There were plenty of downsides to that one, including time. That would likely take a couple of days. And might well lead to confrontation with border guards who were well armed. Or worse, drug dealers, she'd read, usually accompanied groups of folk trying to cross the border illegally.

On her walk, she noted that traffic in this country was just as bad as she'd encountered in the U.S. Oh, well, a virus we've given them, she thought, though she knew heavy traffic was not an American exclusive event. Some of the border fence she saw was constructed of old corrugated tin sheets like they used to put together Quonset huts. More people ignored the traffic and crossed the road. Sometimes men, women, or children hit her up for money or tried to sell her small items such as cigarettes, matches, cigars, chewing gum by the stick, prophylactics. There was a central municipal area that held several metal statues, one of which looked like Neptune with a spear through his head. She did not take the time to figure that one out.

Finally, since she was almost lost, she grabbed a taxi. An ancient Ford and told the driver to take her to Boys' Town. She doubted it was far, but didn't have the time. Negotiating with the driver, they finally settled on five dollars, which told her it wasn't far at all.

He looked at her speculatively, shrugged and drove her there. Carefully, she mapped the route. He drove like most taxi drivers across the world.

Beer and tequila signs told her where she was. She handed the driver the five and escaped. She walked along slowly, trying to think, keenly aware of the passage of time. Again, many parts of the sidewalk were broken. How would Tommy go about this? He was a good problem solver, but most of the time it involved hitting the problem head-on with sudden violence and great force—which was not something she was equipped to do versus the United States government.

Men watched her as she passed bars or restaurants. There was something about the area where many of the drinking establishments had men standing or sitting in their doorways or loitering outside. Maybe pimps? There was a thriving sex business here she knew. And she'd seen many news stories about drug gangs and violence.

More Americans drifted in and out of bars. It was early yet, the crowds would come later and in the evening. She thought it worth of remark that many people were smoking.

She had an overwhelming desire to go into a cool bar and drink a couple of cold beers. She shook that off. She became acutely aware of the passage of time. A couple of the men approached her questioningly, assuring her they had "what she wanted." It took her a few minutes to figure out they thought she, as a single woman, was looking for female love. A couple of others watched her openly. She began to worry. It was like the word had traveled up and down the street preceding her. She turned down one street that was less traveled and cars packed alongside the street as if parking were at a premium hereabouts.

Soon a noise permeated her mind. It was one she'd been hearing for the last few minutes and ignored. Casually looking around like a tourist, she saw a man trailing her on what she guessed was a Yamaha motorcycle. He had an expensive helmet, but it hung from the handlebars. Yeah, show how cool you are.

Immediately, it occurred to her that she'd be a nice target for so-called "human-trafficking", not the kind where you guide or take people from one nation to another illegally, but the kind where you kidnap and drug young females and sell them into sex slavery. She shook her head. Surely not. But…her experience in that thing told her how prevalent the practice was, only most people did not know about it.

Well, she wasn't inviting his attention, but her behavior sure was. A woman alone trolling along in Boys' Town? While she did not feel overly attractive, she knew damn well she was and she recognized her effect on men. That was one of the things that intrigued her about Tommy Atkins. He knew how good-looking she was, but ignored it.

She sure as hell didn't want to be kidnapped and sold into slavery or a whorehouse in some flea bit town. Or sold to some sheik. On the other hand, she might well be imagining things.

Breathing deeply, she increased her pace. The Yamaha kept behind her and matched her pace. He could maneuver through the little traffic on this street since he was on two wheels—a decided advantage. One she'd surely like to have. Now he was on a cell phone. That she didn't like. He could be talking to his mother or calling in help.

She had to do something and do it quick, not to mention that time was speeding by. Tommy could be dying for all she knew. She did know that he needed her and she wanted to be there when he needed her. She realized she hadn't slept for almost two full days and tiredness crept over her.

On her right was an even quieter street, not paved, but gravel and hardpan. She turned down the so-called street. The Yamaha followed. Buildings here were all in need of fresh paint. A few tired small, sun-bleached warehouses lined up down the block.

A space between buildings was open with no parked cars. She walked into it and looked around. An old mangy yellow dog rose slowly and walked away. She stepped to the lip of the hardpan and stopped. The Yamaha slowed, not knowing what to do.

María Elena pointedly looked at her wrist. She acted angry she didn't see a watch. She looked around and appeared to see the motorcyclist for the first time. She looked around again, then shrugged, and waved at him to come over and stop. Her movements were commanding. Was she not Papá's daughter? Was she not the beautiful María Elena appealing to masculinity?

The motorcycle approached and pulled up alongside her, kicking the machine into neutral. The man leered.

She tapped her wrist imperiously. "Time?" She used English on the principle that if the enemy didn't know she spoke Spanish, she had an advantage.

He took the bait and flipped open his cell phone.

María Elena took a quick look to the right and left and saw no undue attention. Not that it mattered anyway. While the man was trying to read the time in the glare of the sun, she struck him in the throat with the knuckles of her right hand, just as she'd be trained to do. He fell off the street side of the Yamaha coughing and gasping and choking.

She grabbed his phone out of his hand as he went down, with her other hand, she held the motorcycle upright. She dropped the cell phone into the bag with the chloroquine, threw her left leg over the seat, kicked the machine into gear and sped off.

She checked the mirror and he was still rolling on the ground holding his throat.

The Tommy Atkins School of Planning was working so far.

Quickly, she made her way out of Boys' Town and headed

back the way the taxi had driven. She put on the helmet for safety and so it would decrease the recognition factor. She stuffed the pharmacy bag into her shirt. She had two choices: go along the border fence and look for a break that would fit the motorcycle. Or she could go through the official border crossing. Perhaps they wouldn't be looking for her on a motorcycle. Besides, they hadn't seen her passport card close enough to read it. Border fences near the international crossing and in town had to be very effective and likely under surveillance. Not to mention she didn't want to encounter any professional pistoleros.

What would Tommy do? He'd have a Plan B if Plan A didn't work, of course.

Well, shit. She didn't need his phantom presence to figure out what to do. After all, she was María Elena. Downtown again, she stopped and went into a small clothing shop.

She bought a large, bulky denim jacket and several scarves. She put the jacket on. Maybe they wouldn't profile her so well now. She tied two of the pretty scarves around her neck. She didn't look the same, not with the helmet on.

She found a street vendor, a boy in raggedy clothing, and bought a pack of cigarettes and butane lighter.

She drove over to the border crossing all the while checking for attention, both official and unofficial. Apparently, the motorcycle guy hadn't turned her in yet, or the authorities were slow on the uptake.

She idled on a spur to the border-crossing road. After about ten minutes, she was becoming concerned that she wouldn't find what she was looking for. Additionally, her sense of urgency to get back to Tommy was clamoring like a fire alarm. It also occurred to her that the longer she dallied the more likely the Mexican authorities would be looking for a female motorcyle-jacker. Maybe the guy was too much of a bad guy and wouldn't resort to law enforcement. This, when she thought about it, was much more likely.

Finally, what she was looking for cruised by heading for the border. She pulled out behind the van. There were two young men in it, and they were playing hard rock music at lethal decibels. The van was ratty and brown and the color hid much abuse. And she could smell the residual of them smoking weed or hash or something. Didn't they know the border security would search them big time? Maybe they did and they didn't care; they smoked everything already and were not afraid.

She stayed right behind them and offset to the right side as all the traffic slowed for the border. She looked ahead. Yep, still backed up. So they were searching everyone, meaning they'd check all ID's and especially scrutinize anyone who fit their profile. Probably the exact profile of one María Elena Alejandrina Ximena Vasquez-Guerrero de García.

Again, on the Mexican customs side, they virtually ignored her and her passport card, still laughing about the "two idiot Americans" in front of her. They were anticipating the U.S. Border Patrol in stopping them and stripping the van.

The line of vehicles was a couple wide and they were nearing the checkpoint.

María Elena was starting to cough from the van's fumes. It needed a tune-up badly.

She watched the driver and the passenger talking. She could also see the right side mirror and saw they weren't paying attention. Casually, she untied one of the scarves as they sat unmoving. Surreptitiously, she dipped one corner of the scarf into the gas tank of the motorcycle, the bulk of the scarf and her body concealing her movements. She draped the scarf over the handlebars carelessly.

The traffic inched forward. She saw a large number of Border Patrol officers standing around and checking each vehicle's occupants, checking ID's and looking in back seats and trunks. There were several pullovers, or insets in the traffic islands in which cars or trucks were pulled over and parked for thorough searches. They were under the cover of the runway above now and the traffic continued in an orderly fashion, though slowly.

It was time for the sudden violence and great force part of her plan.

There was no doubt that if they were in fact looking for her, they'd nail her. Soon as she showed her passport card, they'd recognize her picture or decide she fit the profile. She wasn't going to bluff this one out. The hardest part was being patient--and breathing the foul emissions from the van. She began to hate that van and the occupants. Which was a good thing, according to her plan. Their music continued to rock the van, throbbing weird echoes in the underbelly of the runway.

The traffic inched ahead two more car lengths and María Elena saw her opportunity. She wanted to do this before she was scrutinized. And she was close enough to map out a pathway. Quickly, she looked around determining who'd be in jeopardy. Another thing that training with 13 gave her some familiarity: explosions.

She edged closer to the van, watching the right passenger side mirror. The men were busy accompanying the music and talking to each other. Her body blocking view of the gas tank on the van, she pulled off the gas cap and then stuffed the scarf in as far as she could, leaving at least a foot's length hanging out—including the gasoline soaked corner.

Casually, she leaned back on the Yamaha and pulled out a cigarette. She lighted it with her butane lighter, took a fake puff, and blew it out, working around the face shield of her helmet. The lighter was in her left hand and she flicked it and the gasoline soaked corner of the scarf blazed up. Flames ate a large hibiscus.

María Elena turned to the car behind her and saw them watching her with horror. She pointed at them imperiously and shouted, "Run!" Since they were locked in a line of unmoving vehicles, they did so. Two middle aged women, one returned quickly for her purse and a package. Then they sprinted back along the line of cars yelling at others. Good, nothing like a fine panic to generate a little chaos.

The scarf was beginning to burn up toward the gas tank opening and she moved her motorcycle alongside the passenger side window. "Hey!" she shouted over the beat of the music.

They ignored her and she flipped the cigarette at the driver. He quickly brushed it off onto the floor of the van. "Listen, you stupid bastards, your gas tank is on fire and this van is going to explode any second. You better bail." She grinned at them. "Next time turn your music down, assholes." As she released the clutch to take off, she saw the passenger looking out and back and watched his face blanch. He didn't say anything to the driver, he simply slammed open the door and ran. The driver got the idea and did the same, running forward shouting "Fire!"

Other drivers were getting out of their cars and looking around curiously. Somehow the word traveled and within thirty seconds full panic enveloped the entire traffic line to the customs check point.

María Elena was already accelerating. She weaved around the van and behind the car in front of the van and bumped over a traffic island into another lane. As she did, she felt more than heard, a giant whoosh as the gas fumes in the filler neck of the gas tank ignited. She envisioned a plume of flame shooting out to the side and hoped no one got hurt. Then there was a smaller explosion.

Cars were jumping lines and going everywhere, filling every empty hole they could find and trying to get out of there.

A smaller explosion than she expected came quickly. It echoed well amongst all the honking of horns and metal crushing of smaller vehicle crashes.

María Elena continued accelerating, avoiding a couple of officers running toward the center of the storm. There was no way they could respond to the emergency and contain all the people trying to get out of the way. Already a few of the cars that were at the front of the various lines were speeding away. Border Patrol tried to stop some of them without success. María Elena followed a pickup truck that appeared to have no intention of stopping for any reason. He made it to the exit highway and screeched through the stoplight. She turned at the traffic light, wanting to get out of the line of sight of the border crossing as quickly as possible. She weaved around in town for a few minutes to discourage anyone who might have been following her. She didn't want to waste much more time for two reasons: Tommy was waiting and her sense of urgency was clamoring like a fire truck; and, secondly, she wanted to ditch the motorcycle before the local police could be alerted for a BOLO and begin searching for her.

Soon, she found what she was looking for: the large McDonalds. She wheeled into a parking slot between a black SUV and an electrician's service truck. She left the key in the ignition. Maybe someone would have the common courtesy to steal it and further confuse the police.

She walked inside and slowly began to remove her helmet. She didn't want anyone to think she was there to rob the damn place. So she took the helmet off slowly and made it into the ladies' room before she completely removed it. She went into the handicapped stall for privacy. She took the top off the waste can and stuffed the shiny black helmet as far down as she could, and then the same with the bulky denim jacket. As she was doing so, she felt the overwhelming pressure on her bladder. What is it about stress? When she left the rest room, she was quite a bit lighter and was wearing a scarf to conceal her face. She hoped she looked totally different. She went out the side door and crossed the street immediately. She heard many sirens zeroing in on the border crossing station. Sorry about that. She grinned. Tommy would be proud of her.

Soon she found her own parked SUV. Even though her sense of urgency was clamoring loudly, she drove slowly, observing meticulously all traffic regulations. Even then her eyes were glued to her mirrors, searching for any sign of pursuit. Or even undercover tailing. All the driving Tommy had her do was paying off in caution.

Even on Algeria Road, she took an early turn and followed a gravel road up a hill and around several turns. She stopped and waited for ten minutes, and then she slowly returned to Algeria Road watching for any other vehicles. She even stopped and got out and scanned the sky for aircraft or choppers. She'd teach

Tommy a few things about paranoia. Soon she was back on Algeria Road headed towards the end. When she came to their turn-off, again she stopped, got out and climbed onto the top of the SUV so she'd have a better and longer view. Again, nothing. She jumped back in and sped toward the cabin.

Was Tommy all right?

CHAPTER FOURTEEN: THEM

"Suze, you need to come into operations to see this." Linda gestured for her to hurry.

Suzie Q rounded her desk and followed Linda into their operations center. Screens flickered and people worked their computers. Linda led her to the central station where Sandy hunched over her keyboard.

"I knew we couldn't trust them," Linda said.

"Doubtless you're going to explain it before midnight?" Suzie Q's voice was dry and Sandy glanced over her shoulder.

Linda pointed and Sandy returned to her task. "That AAG and that marshal guy ain't sharing. Sandy has been trolling and lookit she found."

The wide screen showed a security camera shot of many abandoned cars and trucks and whatever surrounding a burning van. The action appeared to be taking place half inside and half outside of some kind of drive-through building.

"Sandy caught it first, some kind of priority alert from a border station down in Nogales."

"Arizona or Mexico?"

"The former," Linda said. "From what we can extrapolate, their facial recognition software caught our disappeared Cuban blogger. She was headed into Nogales, Sonora, clearing the U.S. checkpoint easily. It took a few minutes for it to matriculate through the system and trigger the alert. By then she was long gone."

"Surely you're going to get to the conflagration part eventually."

"Somebody got up on the wrong side of the bed," said Linda, giving her a fake pout.

"Now I'm gonna have to fight that stupid AAG asshole. And maybe the U.S. Marshal Service, too. And now throw in the motherforping Border Patrol." Suzie Q paused. "Sometimes this job sucks. I trained to go overseas and speak all kinds of foreign languages and shoot spies and steal secrets and other stuff. But hell no, here I am trying to apprehend some Byronic hero guy and this hot babe, neither of whom probably did anything to merit our attention. Yet half the federal government is chasing them and the other half wants me to report on chasing them."

Sandy hunched farther over her keyboard than seemed possible.

Linda said, "I'm sure you'll out maneuver them all, Suzie, you always do. Anyway, so the Border Patrol and Customs slaps on a red alert after the young lady in question had cleared both sides of the border."

"I feel a lot more secure with them in charge," Suzie said.

"To continue," Linda said, ignoring her sarcasm, "a couple of hours later, and maybe only coincidentally, the vehicle entry area of the U.S. border. All hell erupts. This is the current feed."

Several officers were standing aside with spent fire extinguishers and three firemen were spraying foam on a burning van in the center of a sea of vehicles, all empty and stopped. Obviously, the fire truck couldn't get any closer because of the stalled cars and Suzie could see no fire truck. Somehow oddly this disappointed her. She'd always loved fire trucks and their machinations. Whoever figured out the internal plumbing and workings was a genius—though she suspected, like many other things modern, that the contemporary fire truck was merely the tip of the evolution of that particular animal.

"Now run it back, Sandy," Linda told her. The scene unfolded backwards too fast to follow as the feed reversed.

Then they watched as traffic inched forward innocently.

Finally, a van she recognized came into view.

"Watch the motorcycle operator, not the van."

Fascinated, Suzie Q observed a figure in a bulky denim jacket and helmet with a full-darkened faceplate. As the line of cars moved jerkily, she guessed the rider was female from her motions. "You're saying that's María Elena?"

"I'm pretty sure."

"How can you tell?"

"Oh, believe me, I can tell," said Linda.

"I don't know if I like that," said Suzie Q.

"Put your guns away, Suze, it's okay."

"Sandy," Suzie asked, "do you think that's our girl?"

"I can't tell, Ms. Quantrell."

"I'm sure," said Linda. "Watch."

The camera angle was such that they couldn't see what the rider was doing, but she lighted a cigarette and Linda sighed jealously. María Elena's arms and hands moved and Suzie noticed the hanging scarf was gone. "Back it up until that scarf appears on the handlebars," she ordered.

Obediently, Sandy did so. "She's dipping it into her gas tank,"

Linda glanced appreciatively at Suzie. "You still got it."

Suzie knew when she was being schmoozed. "Back to the cigarette part."

Sandy fast-forwarded until they returned. They watched her move a little and light the scarf. They watched her warn the occupants of nearby vehicles. They watched her pull even with the van and flip the cigarette into it. The watched her weave her motorcycle in front of the van and do a wheelie to jump a traffic island and speed out of the picture. They watched the flames shoot out of the gas tank opening. They watched the occupants run. They watched panic ensue. They watched the explosion. They watched until the scene returned to a live feed.

"You know that's our girl? For sure?" Suzie asked Linda.

"I do."

"How?"

"It ain't easy since she's sitting in these pictures and you gotta ignore above the waist on accounta the jacket, but I recall the Orlando airport video. Ankles the same. Great legs, even in jeans. Hips. The way she holds her head high. The precise movements. And, most of all, in Orlando she was favoring her left shoulder from some kind of injury. In the current video, you can tell her shoulder has mended, but she still faintly and subconsciously favors it."

"What's it mean?" Suzie asked.

"Means she, at least, was last seen in Nogales, Arizona on this day."

"Why is she there?"

"Dunno, Suze. I expect she's found a place to hide out."

"I concur," said Suzie. "So why is she tempting fate by crossing the border and returning? She knows they have her on all kinds of lists so we can track her. It's a big risk." She paused and thought. "Okay, how often does a high profile fugitive cross the border and then return shortly thereafter?"

"Drugs?" asked Sandy.

"Yep," replied Suzie Q. "Legal or illegal. That would explain the fireworks. She could have thought they would search her and diverted attention." She considered for another moment. "In reality, it could be anything. She could be meeting someone; buying ID; arranging something; looking for information. Anything."

"I think she has a sixth sense," Linda said. "She knew they'd be on the lookout for her in particular."

"And why is she hiding from us, too? She knows about JTF 13, though you and I've never met her. We've dealt with the old man and now Don Diego."

"I'd have liked to meet her," said Linda.

"The day's already bad enough and here you go pining after María Elena?"

"Not really. I simply find her attractive."

"Humpf."

"But Suze, this is where you earn your big bucks. What do we do? What do we do if we find her? What do we do if someone else finds her? Like those marshal guys or Border Patrol or anybody?"

"Don't know, Linda. We'll interrogate her and find out exactly what the hell is going on."

"I fear we're gonna have to do something before that event, if it does happen."

"Yeah. I'm working on that," Suzie said. "You have the full resources of the Arizona branch of the FBI working on this?"

"We do, and they're not happy. They're overwhelmed these days with drug stuff and murders and kidnappings. Phoenix is the second highest kidnap frequency after Mexico City nowadays."

Suzie turned to go back to her office.

"Ms. Quantrell?" said Sandy.

"Yes?"

"What's a Byronic hero?"

Suzie smiled, the first time today. "It's from Lord Byron and his writings. The dark character is mysterious, he's flawed, he's cunning, he's an outlaw of sorts, he hates people who have power over him, yet he's world-weary."

"Mr. Atkins is all those things?"

Suzie Q shrugged. "Beats me. I suspect he's some or all of those things and more. We don't know anything about him—other than he's killed maybe nine or ten people since all this started, even though those people likely needed killing a lot. Usually by the end of the piece, this Byronic hero has a good heart. There's stuff about sexual dominance and bipolar crap, Freudian stuff, which don't really fit in this modern world."

"If he's even in the game any longer," Linda said. "Last guess, he was in San Antone."

Sandy said, "He sounds like a real hero."

"Not if he's dead," said Suzie Q.

CHAPTER FIFTEEN: HER

María Elena sped toward the hidden cabin. She had to force herself to slow down since she was raising a small dust trail. As Tommy had taught her, when she was within a mile, she stopped and turned off her engine and got out to listen.

Nothing, just hot wind.

She resumed driving and drove past the cabin looking hard, then turned around and returned to the cabin, parking so that the SUV was pointed outward. No use in a quick escape if you had to back out of where you parked.

For a moment she breathed deeply. Her body cried for sleep. She got the hideout revolver from under the front seat.

Wearily, she dismounted and walked around the outside of the house. She peaked inside and saw nothing out of place. She slipped inside the back door. It would be difficult to hide someone in the one bedroom cabin. As she'd learned, the first thing she did was return to the SUV and hid the pistol under the seat again. Then she went back inside using the front door. This constant paranoia was almost to the point of obsession. But, she observed, it had kept Tommy alive and well for years and even this day, it had to have saved her ass. God, she was tired.

Tommy was still in bed, tossing and turning, and the fever had not broken. She got some water and forced him to drink and swallow the first tablets. Ordinarily, she could figure the number of milligrams of chloroquine per kilogram of weight, but she relied on the lady pharmacist. The first couple of days were the most important. She forced him to drink the entire glass of water. That woke him somewhat and she dragged him into the bathroom and then back outside to the shower. While his fever was still going, she had to keep cooling him off.

She stripped down to her bra and panties again and held him under the water. Then she dried them both off again and took him back inside. She reflected she was going to have a lot of laundry to do. She changed into her pajamas and sat on the bed alongside him and bathed his forehead and chest with a cool, wet rag.

She awoke with a start. She was sitting beside Tommy on the bed with a wet rag in her hand and she was oh, so tired. Her eyes were crossing and she felt nauseous. Malaria was mosquito carried and therefore was not contagious. She told herself that and repeated it. She realized she was at the end of her rope. She elbowed Tommy aside a little, and fell alongside of him. In thirty seconds, she was asleep.

In six hours, she woke because Tommy was tossing and turning and had laid his left forearm under her breasts and was gripping her rib cage. She checked the time. Strangely, she felt refreshed. She heated up some broth and fed it to him. He was conscious, but not completely aware.

Finally, he slumped back. His eyes roved and clouded over and he fell back asleep.

María Elena rummaged around for something to read. She glanced at Tommy guiltily. She'd known this moment would come since he refused to tell her about the book in his duffel. The stuff from his duffel was stacked neatly on a side table. She found the book and brought it to the chair she'd put beside the bed.

Kipling? *The Portable Kipling*? He was concealing a book of stories and poems by Rudyard Kipling? Tommy did some strange things, but this was weird. Why the secrecy? Maybe he was screwing with her? She wouldn't put it past him, not at all. "Gunga Din" had always been one of her favorites. She sat back and read it. She'd always liked Kipling, his words rolled off your tongue. When she was done, she started thumbing through the book, but not far. In fact, the poem just before "Gunga Din" was called "Tommy". Uh, oh, this was too much of a coincidence. And in the space below the poem, there was some handwriting.

She started reading the poem, but it was so mesmerizing, she started over and read it aloud.

I went into a public-'ouse to get a pint o' beer,
The publican 'e up an' sez, "We serve no red-coats here."
The girls be'ind the bar they laughed an' giggled fit to
    die,
I outs into the street again an' to myself sez I:

O it's Tommy this, an' Tommy that, an' "Tommy, go away";
But it's "Thank you, Mister Atkins", when the band begins
    to play,
The band begins to play, my boys, the band begins to
    play,
O it's "Thank you, Mister Atkins", when the band begins to
    play.

I went into a theatre as sober as could be,
They gave a drunk civilian room, but 'adn't none for me;
They sent me to the gallery or round the music-'alls,
But when it comes to fightin', Lord! they'll shove me in the
    stalls!

For it's Tommy this, an' Tommy that, an' "Tommy, wait
    outside";
But it's "Special train for Atkins" when the trooper's on
    the tide,
The troopship's on the tide, my boys, the troopship's on the
    tide,
O it's "Special train for Atkins" when the trooper's on the
    tide.

Yes, makin' mock o' uniforms that guard you while you sleep
Is cheaper than them uniforms, an' they're starvation
    cheap;

An' hustlin' drunken soldiers when they're goin' large a
*   bit*
Is five times better business than paradin' in full kit.

Then it's Tommy this, an' Tommy that, an' "Tommy, 'ow's yer
*   soul?"*
But it's "Thin red line of 'eroes" when the drums begin to
*   roll,*
The drums begin to roll, my boys, the drums begin to roll,
O it's "Thin red line of 'eroes" when the drums begin to
*   roll.*

We aren't no thin red 'eroes, nor we aren't no blackguards too,
But single men in barricks, most remarkable like you;
An' if sometimes our conduck isn't all your fancy paints,
Why, single men in barricks don't grow into plaster
*   saints;*

While it's Tommy this, an' Tommy that, an' "Tommy, fall
*   be'ind",*
But it's "Please to walk in front, Sir", when there's trouble
*   in the wind,*
There's trouble in the wind, my boys, there's trouble in the
*   wind,*
O it's "Please to walk in front, Sir", when there's trouble in
*   the wind.*

You talk o' better food for us, an' schools, an' fires, an' all:
We'll wait for extry rations if you treat us rational.
Don't mess about the cook-room slops, but prove it to our
*   face*
The Widow's Uniform is not the soldier-man's disgrace.

For it's Tommy this, an' Tommy that, an' "Chuck him out, the
*   brute!"*
But it's "Saviour of 'is country" when the guns begin to
*   shoot;*
An' it's Tommy this, an' Tommy that, an' anything you

please;
An' Tommy ain't a bloomin' fool—you bet that Tommy
   sees!

And written by hand in bold black ink immediately below the body of the poem:

But it don't matter, when the shootin' begins,
They send us out once more to die,
They send us out once more to die.
Kill this one they tell me,
Kill that one they tell me,
But I ain't never killed nobody,
Nobody who didn't need killin'.
They send me out once more to die,
They send me out once more to die.

T. Atkins
The Everglades
2012 AD

"You read beautifully, college girl." He was lying on his side, eyes open, watching her intently.

For a moment she couldn't speak. What was wrong with her? Well, maybe, she told herself, you are not used to staring into the open soul of a killer. Could it be that he had been secretive about this Kipling because it reflected his own soul? She decided that maybe now she was beginning to understand the man.

"It's...wonderful...and touching."

"It's a fucking poem."

"That's what Kipling's Tommy would say. Could this be the genesis of one Tommy Atkins in this room right now?"

"If that's what you want to believe."

She handed him the ever-ready glass of water. "Drink."

She didn't want to become emotional over this discovery. But it showed where he thought he fit in the world. The every-man soldier, military or civilian, it didn't matter. Or maybe that was just what he was comfortable with.

She mused on the theme. "You're not just another trooper, Tommy. You're special. You're unique. You are not just any soldier in any war. Certainly not in this day and age. You don't fit the world very well, but that surely was and is to my advantage." She realized she was talking from her own viewpoint; this was starting to make her uncomfortable. Jesus and Joseph, get over the philosophy queen crap.

"You went to college too long," he told her and rolled over on his back. He held out the empty glass for her to take from him. "Here. It's not an everyday glass, it's unique and special."

"Yes, Tommy." She took the glass.

"Read it again, Florence." He popped his right eye open and looked at her. "Please?"

She did so softly and he was asleep before she finished.

As she watched Tommy snore lightly, she reflected that it had been a good thing they were here, alone and in the middle of Nowhere, Arizona when he had his malaria relapse. Suppose they'd been running from motel to hotel, stealing cars and switching tags? She wasn't sure she could have handled that.

María Elena almost wished they could stay here forever. She didn't want to face the future. It seemed all elements were aligned against the two of them, including earth, wind and fire. She smiled to herself when she thought that there was nobody left, no agency, no people, and no group, which wasn't searching for them with lethal intentions.

But right now none of that mattered. The only thing significant in her world was that Tommy had begun to recover. A strange feeling washed over her as she realized how really scared she'd been.

She leaned forward and took his hand and wrapped both of hers around it. She sat there for a long time without moving.

CHAPTER FIFTEEN: HIM

A week later, Tommy was on his feet and well rested. But he continued to be weak.

They sat at the kitchen table eating chicken cooked over a mesquite fire outside.

"For a man, you cook well," said María Elena.

"For a woman, you sure eat well," said Tommy.

She favored him with a smile.

"I been on my own my whole life. I cook, clean, do laundry."

"You'd be a real catch for some woman."

"You betcha, Florence Nightingale. You proposing?"

"Well, what's in it for me?"

He grinned. "A life of leisure and entertainment."

"I must say since I met you, Tommy Atkins, I have been entertained to death almost daily. Only in the last few days have I encountered the leisure part. I've even learned stuff from you." She wiped her mouth daintily, then grabbed another piece of chicken and took a big bite.

"So, what have you learned?"

"How to drive, how to live in the mirror when I drive, how to think in a crisis, stuff like that."

"So, Florence, how'd you come up with the chloroquine?"

"So, Tommy, how'd you, ah, liberate yourself from federal custody?"

"The chloroquine connection?"

"Yep. You gotta tell me first."

"Sure thing, Flo. I was stuck in the pen for a long time. It was a state penitentiary outside of Tampa while I was waiting for police investigation and trial. Feds already tried and convicted me. I think the feds didn't mind since they were overcrowded and would've had to pay a lot of back and forth transportation. Florida was making money housing federal prisoners. Then I had a malaria relapse. They sent me to the infirmary, sort of a mini-hospital there. A year or so later, it happened again. Remember, my work assignment was there in the medical unit. It's amazing if you keep your nose clean and you got any kind of intelligence, you can get an easy job. Anyway, I had one of the screws primed. I had already told him the combination of one of the self-storage units and he'd gone there and was a hundred grand richer. He helped me."

"He could have run out on you or not honored your agreement."

Tommy ate some rice. "Nope. All I had to do was tell the warden and that guard would go away to another prison, only as an inmate. He had to keep the deal."

"So? How'd you do it?"

Tommy pulled out his cross on a necklace. It was ornate and a silver cross and Jesus dangled.

"I've wondered about that."

Tommy twisted and pulled. The necklace came apart. He held up a section. "Standard handcuff key." He performed the operation in reverse and replaced the necklace. "It was hard waiting for the right time and I had to fake being in a coma for a day longer as I got well. But one evening, the local mortuary came by for a couple of bodies of prisoners who'd died. Working there, I'd already prepared dummy paperwork for a body. They had me handcuffed to the bed that night as their manning was short. I used the key, made my way to the back room of the infirmary and the guard had a body bag waiting. I got in it on a gurney next to the others and the screw annotated the paperwork for the mortician. He made sure they loaded me first to make it more difficult for the gate guards if they wanted to check. The morticians dumped the bodies at their mortuary and went home for the night."

"That's it? Didn't they notice the difference between two bodies and three bodies when they returned in the morning."

"I took care of that."

"And?"

"You want to hear? This ain't a Sunday school story."

"Yes."

"I borrowed a hearse. They kept the keys right there in the 'incoming' room. I drove to Tampa, hid the hearse, and found the son of a bitch who turned me in. Then I put him in the hearse and drove back. The funeral parlor guys probably didn't check very closely as the prison doctor had allegedly already generated a death certificate, including mine. Since I worked in the infirmary, I simply got an empty death certificate and filled it in on a typewriter; then I faked his signature. I had it hidden in a fake file in a filing cabinet. So all the funeral home guys had to do was shake and bake. I made sure not to mark up the body I switched with me too much."

"Oh." Her voice was small.

"Your turn, Ms. Nightingale."

She told him as he finished eating and they washed the dishes.

"Not bad for an amateur," he opined. "The explosion was a nice touch, distracting supposedly alert and professional border guards. Had you jumped the line and took off on the rice rocket, you'd likely have made it, but cops and border security would have been after you."

"That was my reasoning."

"And the collateral damage to bystanders?"

"I minimized it as much as possible. It was a calculated decision and I don't think anyone was hurt. I really did want to blow up the van and its annoying loud music. And the jacket and helmet and scarves might have been enough to disguise me for any of those grainy security cameras."

"You done good, Pocahontas. Thank you for saving my ass."

"Anything for you, Tommy." She had a strange gleam in her eye.

"I'll be up to speed in a week and Charley is due about then."

"He'll just show up?"

"That's it. When he runs out of money, he will save enough for gas and come home. If he wins money, he'll stay until he loses it all."

"You hermits have weird habits."

"Not me, sweetie. I'm a reader."

"You're pretty domestic for a tough guy," she said.

"No comment."

As was their custom, he went outside and took the first shower, so that he could read in bed for a while.

As he was soaping down, María Elena came out and left the door open for the light. She pulled up a plastic chair and sat down.

Tommy continued and began to rinse the soap off. "I guess this means we're not going to shower together again?"

She simply looked at him.

"You can bet I remember that part. Hell, I thought I was out of my mind—or died and went to heaven. I wish I could remember it more and better."

"More than once," she told him.

"Just my luck." He turned modestly.

"Don't worry," she mimicked him. "I've already seen your glorious naked body."

"You ain't here to look at my body," he said. "What's up?"

"To the contrary, I am. I want you to tell me about all those scars." She pointed.

"Have I no privacy?"

"Tell me."

He fingered his side. "In Tampa. This one was just a graze, didn't hit anything vital. Good thing since it came from a 1911."

"What's that?"

"A forty-five."

"What happened to the shooter?"

"He's deceased."

"I guess I'm not surprised. And that one? The shoulder?"

"AK-47, I think. Never saw the guy. Shooting from the jungle. We were in a firefight. And as you can see, the exit wound is worse than the entry wound."

"How about that scarred mess on your left side?"

"Ah, that was a machete if I remember right. The local troops that the Cuban merks were supporting. Ambush."

"He's deceased, too?"

"Oh, yes. Tenacious bastard, though. I'll give him that." He shook his head at the memory. "Had to sew that one up myself and walk twenty-five miles back to base—well, back to where I stole a truck and drove another twenty-five to base."

"The slice mark on your back?"

"Shrapnel. When I was a Marine. Semper Fi. Lebanon or someplace over there."

"How about that big patch on the outside of your left thigh?"

"I dumped my chopper doing eighty."

"Motorcycle?"

"Yes, Pocahontas. Hog, Harley. With the high handlebars. Not no rice rocket."

"You are some kind of guy, Tommy Atkins."

"Sure thing, Florence Nightingale." He turned off the water. "Gimme that towel, will you?"

She went inside and after he dried off and pulled on his shorts, he went inside and she edged sideways past him. "Next." She wouldn't look at him.

"I'll wash the sheets tomorrow," he told her, "and then you can have the bed back."

"Whatever."

She was acting strangely. But he'd never really understood women, so he dismissed it.

He covered himself with a sheet and began reading a Kipling poem. For some reason, he had an urge to read Kipling. It was now a comfortable feeling. He recalled María Elena curled up against his back. And he had a gossamer memory of her wrapping herself around him when the coldness of body chills had overwhelmed him.

María Elena came in freshly showered, toweling her long, black hair. She shook it out. Then was when Tommy saw what she was wearing. No unisex pajamas tonight. She wore the hip huggers and the low cut sleeveless top she had on the first night they'd spent together in a motel.

He whistled his appreciation. "No fair, Pocahontas."

She hung up her towel and came over to him. "Nothing's fair, Tommy." She bent over him and tousled his curly hair. She kissed him on the forehead.

Her animal cinnamon scent sank down on him; now it had a raw edge. And it accompanied a wave of body heat.

He looked into her eyes and saw them change to the deepest brown.

Her top dropped down and gave him a full view of her breasts. Her nipples were already hard. He felt himself responding.

Her lips brushed his and then pressed down for a demanding kiss. His eyes opened wide.

He tried to push her away. "No."

"This is what *I* want, Tommy."

"I don't want to want what I can't have."

"Sure you can. Here I am. Let's." Her hunger was overwhelming them both.

Suddenly, he felt all his pent-up passion for her break through his iron will. He pulled her down against his body and kissed her deeply. He cupped her butt cheeks and breasts and she squirmed frantically on top of him, the heat of her loins burning into him. She moved rhythmically atop him and breathed hoarsely and moaned against him. Her hair cascaded all over him. Their tongues danced.

She pulled the sheet off him and then, with more urgency, his shorts.

She lowered herself on top of him. He ran his hands all over her back, under her hiphuggers and under her top, searching, demanding. Her skin was dry and smooth to the touch and he ached for more. She ground into him. Their kiss was full of passion and need. Then she broke off the kiss and sat up on his hips, straddling him. She pulled her top off and freed herself. His hands roamed her breasts and body. She looked down on him for a moment. Then he tore off her panties and tossed them aside.

After a moment, she said, "Oh, my God!" She arched her back and her body began demanding.

Later, they nestled together regaining their breathing. His hands roamed, gaining tactile memory of every inch of her body. He tested her bad shoulder with good results.

"Wow," she said into his neck.

His hands moved more demandingly.

"Do you still think my hips are too wide?"

"Hell, no. And I never did." His hands continued to work.

"Again?" she asked.

"Again," he said.

Much later, he said, "God, you taste good."

"I didn't know it could be like this," she said.

"Me, neither," he said, and realized how special it really was.

CHAPTER SIXTEEN: HER

In the morning they showered together and ended up in bed again before they'd dried off.

Finally, they stood side by side at the stove: Tommy was cooking four eggs straight up in the bacon grease from the pound of bacon he'd fried. She was stirring a pot of oatmeal. Their silence was comfortable. María Elena wondered, "What next, Lord?" Life had been full of surprises lately.

Soon they were sitting across from each other. Tommy had a slice of bread he was mopping up egg yolk with. María Elena had finished her oatmeal and was eyeing his food hungrily.

"We got to talk, Pocahontas," Tommy said.

"About our love life or our situation?" Her voice was coy.

He grunted and grinned. "Actually, both, now you mention it."

She took a slice of his bacon. It was soft, not crunchy at all.

"I like it chewy," he read her mind.

"Me, too," she lied.

"Charley's likely to return soon," he continued.

She took another slice of bacon. She hadn't been this hungry in a long time. Especially, she was hungry for protein. "You can go, Tommy. There's no reason for you to be involved any longer."

"Do you seriously think I'd desert your cute ass right now?"

"Thank you, Tommy."

"Maybe we get organized and set up; we go after this Don Diego. The other option is to take out that JTF 13 thing. They're in this up to their necks." He was obviously referring to the cell phone tracking and the border crossing quick reaction.

"Neither one will be easy."

"Love conquers all," he said, and then sat back realizing what he'd said.

She reached across the table to the plate with the bacon on a paper towel and took another piece.

The silence stretched out and became awkward.

She took another piece of bacon and ate it.

Finally, he said, "Are you gonna be hung up with emotional baggage about us? Or am I just a one night stand, a man when you need one?"

"That's not fair," she said.

"I ain't feeling charitable right now. Remember, I'm the one who didn't want to get involved. I didn't want to be attached to you. Sex like that is a commitment to me. I don't want to be hurt. Like I said, I don't want to want what I can't have."

"I'm not sure I like the term 'emotional baggage,' Tommy."

"Well, goddamn it, Pocahontas, this ain't a subject I'm real articulate at or I got a lot of practice at. I got no fancy words. I only know what I feel and what I'm afraid of." He paused. "And I know that my life started all over the minute I saw you fighting those men in the Everglades." He fixed his eyes steadily on her. "So you know, while you are smokin' hot, I was able to fight that part off. But the more we were together, the more your character unfolded in front of me. If it was just your looks, I wouldn't have fought against it so long." He leered at her and then became serious. "See? It's as if you were the north pole and I was a compass arrow."

She smiled broadly and grabbed his hand. "Okay. It's enough to know how you feel, anyway. I've been growing fonder of you every day. And I want to be with you for a long time." She used her other hand and picked up one of the last slices of bacon. She chewed it enthusiastically. "You've been there for me and I've been there for you."

"Longtemps. Ensemble."

"French?"

"It's been too long, I've forgotten my grammar and many words. Means 'a long time,' and then, 'together.'"

"That's so sweet." She looked into his eyes. "We're proving we were made for each other. We just found out later rather than sooner."

He let her hand go and grabbed the last piece of bacon and broke it in half. He handed her the big half. "I've been alone a long time, María Elena. After all this time together, I think without you I'd be more alone than I've ever been."

She ate the last of the bacon and wiped her hand on a paper napkin. "Another real nice thing to say. I want to be with you, Tommy. For a long time."

"What about when I get a lot older, maybe fifteen, twenty years?"

"I'll stay with you like I did this last week." She beamed at him. "Cubans say cheese, wine and a friend must be old to be good."

"And when I die and you're still young enough?"

She shrugged. "Beats me. I'll mourn you and find somebody else. Or nobody. Nobody can replace you. I don't want to talk about this stuff."

"You need to think about it before you get in too deep."

"That's your job." She grinned.

"Somebody's gonna kill me anyway." He smiled. "Who ate all the bacon?"

Her return smile was coy.

He held up his hand. "Just to be clear, I am not a father figure to you? You ain't missing your old man? You gotta be certain about this."

"Stupid question," she said angrily.

She saw he realized he'd hit a sore spot.

"You were pretty torn up when they killed your father."

"Of course! He was my father. He was my mother's husband."

"Sorry I hit a nerve," Tommy said, sitting back.

"No, damn it all, I do not have a father fixation." She steamed inordinately. "I was obedient to him like any Cuban daughter would be to her father. I did not like a lot of what he did to me, but he was a great Cuban patriot."

"Did to you? Did he abuse you?"

"Not like you'd think." She stood and paced. "Hell no, his abuse was the Latin machismo patriarch bull shit. Just for political purposes, he fucked up and married me off when I was eighteen...." She shut up when she saw the look on his face.

"You're *married*?" He stood abruptly, pushing the chair back.

She couldn't meet his eyes and stared at the floor. She nodded her head.

"Son of a bitch. I figgered you were hiding something. But this...."

"I'm sorry, Tommy." Her voice was very low.

"Shit, now I know why you didn't want to talk about us. All that stuff you just told me was just bull shit."

"No, Tommy, I....I'm sorry. I still..."

"You said you were married. That lets out that you're divorced or widowed?"

"Yes, Tommy. I can explain..."

"It don't fucking matter, María Elena, it don't fucking matter." He sat down again. "Jesus shit, here I am pouring my fuckin' heart out for the first motherfucking time in my whole goddamn life and you're fucking married?"

"I'm sorry, Tommy." She sat back down.

"You coulda told me."

"Yes, Tommy."

"I never knew what love was, I didn't. Now I thought I was in love and I was so fucking happy—even though you're pretty young for me. I'd do anything for you. Like kill bunches of fucking people and I did that thing. I knew you were special back in the 'Glades when you were fighting those assholes. I knew you were my kind of woman when you jumped up and made yourself a diversion for that fucking helicopter and then I saw you under my shower. Hell, I even called you Pocahontas because you were a fucking princess out of nowhere. And princesses are always beautiful. Make that smokin' hot in your case. Then when I went back to that mall to pick you up, my heart fucking melted. When you chased me down and braced me at the airport in Orlando, I fucking knew you were the one I didn't fucking know I been waiting for all my life. I wanted you bad, but didn't want to break something fragile. I just didn't fucking know that fragile thing would be my fucking heart." He glared at her. "And more important, I've respected you every goddamn minute since the first time I saw you."

"I'm sorry, Tommy." She admitted that he'd always been a gentleman to her.

"After all these years, I finally found a woman I could love. My heart opened for the first time ever. And that lasted a full fucking ten hours." He wiped his nose with a forearm. "When we had sex, were you just scratching an itch?"

"Tommy, I..."

"Well, I wasn't. I thought we were making love, not screwing."

"I didn't..."

He took a deep breath and sighed, the most heart-breaking sound she'd ever heard.

"Well, where the fuck is this limp-dick son of a bitch? And why ain't *he* rescuing your perfect ass? Is he in jail? In the military? Out of the country?"

"No, Tommy."

"What the fuck, María Elena?" He looked up at her, stricken, and her heart broke.

"Papá made me marry Don Diego."

Tommy stared from under lowered brows. "Fuck me to tears."

Tommy Atkins stood and stormed out, tearing one hinge off the front door.

Suddenly, he reappeared at the door. "Alexander Dumas once said something about all human wisdom is contained in two words: Wait and Hope. Well, I waited and I hoped. I guess it wasn't so fucking wise, was it?" Then he was gone.

María Elena Alejandrina Ximena Vásquez-Guerrero de García slumped into her chair and put her face in her hands.

CHAPTER SEVENTEEN: HER

Head in her hands, María Elena heard the door to the SUV slam shut.

She heard the SUV start. She heard it spin tires. She heard the engine wind up as it headed away. Finally, the engine sound faded and she was alone.

Empty, she didn't know what to do. So she cleaned. She did all the laundry. She tried to read. She tried to watch satellite television. Nothing worked. She tried to nap and, surprisingly, that worked for a couple of hours. It had been a long night.

Her stomach began cramping occasionally, apparently her period kicked off early by stress.

The sun was almost down now. She sat outside the front door in a lawn chair and waited. Nothing. Tommy did not return. She did not hear the tell-tale engine sounds of the Toyota.

She thought about taking the jeep and going off looking for him.

She thought about packing her stuff and taking the jeep and heading back to Florida. At least in Florida you could feel the air you were breathing.

The sun dropped below the mesa and shadows grew long.

No Tommy.

What could she have said? What should she have said?

Well, maybe she should have leveled with him from the beginning. She knew now that to be the case. The confession would have taken a lot of guts and stripped some of her pride. It had been so much easier to put it off. So when was she going to tell him anyway? She didn't know any answers. She felt worse.

Maybe Tommy had left for good?

No, he was thorough if nothing else. He'd have taken money and clothing. She didn't admit it to herself, but she hoped he wouldn't have left her--although the evidence to the contrary was growing.

Later, María Elena made herself a small meal and didn't eat most of it. She drank a glass of wine and that didn't help. She spent an energetic half an hour with her resistance bands.

Eventually, she gave up her vigil and went to bed. She chose the couch so that when—and if—he returned, there were be no questions of who sleeps where.

She slept desultorily. When she did sleep, she slept fitfully.

At a quarter after three, she heard an engine approach. Not taking any chances, she got a pistol and looked out the front window.

The Toyota slewed up in front and slammed to a stop. Tommy almost fell out comically, outlined in starlight and moonlight. He staggered to his feet and stumbled toward the door.

María Elena quickly returned to the couch, dropped down, and covered herself with a blanket. Not knowing what else to do, she feigned sleep.

He walked in, ignoring the fact that she'd fixed the hinge on the front door. He didn't try to be silent, but he didn't make much noise anyway. That was Tommy. When he moved, he was quiet and economical.

Through slatted eyes, she watched him.

He raised a bottle of mescal to his lips and drained the remainder. He stopped above her for a moment. She felt his eyes on her. Then he lurched toward the back and fell into the bed. The empty bottle of mescal dropped to the floor.

Soon he was snoring, seriously snoring.

María Elena tried to return to sleep. No luck.

What she needed was a nice long run.

At four thirty, she got up and quietly dressed in her running outfit.

Outside, the predawn sky darkened and began to turn light far in the east. She performed her stretching exercises and felt some of the tension drain. She looked forward to her run. She started out, running down their hardpan lane toward Algeria road. She could run five miles that way without getting to the spur which led to Algeria Road. One thing she liked about running here was that the terrain was not level. She went up and down hills and inclines and around canyons. Florida was flat and level. And Florida did not have a whole bunch of ravines and canyons and arroyos, dry storm beds, boulders, cliffs and cacti. None of that stuff. She decided she was born to be a flatlander.

She violated their rule about going armed everywhere you went. She never carried a gun while running. She might need it for snakes, but wouldn't use it for the gunshot might draw attention. But she did adhere to Tommy's advice: always carry your Swiss Army knife. How do you carry a weapon if you wear only a pair of nylon running shorts with a mesh tank top? The latter was risqué, but she knew she wouldn't see anyone out here well before dawn. Or any time, for that matter.

On mile three she was warmed up and increased her pace to maybe a six or six and a half mile pace.

The more she ran, the angrier she became. It wasn't her fault Diego had turned out to be scum. What could she have done? Papá had been insistent and sold her on Don Diego. He'd painted a glorious future for them. Diego had been nothing but a gentleman and she respected him—at the time. She had even understood the necessity of the union. Her stride was into a fine rhythm by now. At the five mile point she turned around and headed home. She reflected that there was more rock right here than in the entire state of Florida.

At four miles out, she heard it. The sound was low but steady and was getting louder.

"Uh oh," she said aloud and increased her pace. Even over her own breathing she heard the motor. She ran faster and realized she was at a dead run, after six and a half miles, she was running a sub-six. She knew she could hide in one of the small canyons or draws which fed off their path and not be found. But Tommy was back at the cabin, likely in a drunken stupor, and he'd never be able to protect himself. Certainly he was still in his REM sleep and wouldn't hear any vehicle. Whoever it was, if they were looking for Tommy and her, could walk right in and arrest him or shoot him.

"Damn." She concentrated on running and breathing. She didn't need to be caught short of breath. Again she wished for Florida humidity so she could tell if she were getting enough oxygen right away. Often she glanced over her shoulder.

Then she saw light stabbing through the disappearing darkness behind her. She veered off the gravel pathway and raced down a short arroyo, slowing to avoid obstacles now becoming visible in the growing light. Abruptly, she stopped and slid behind a rock outcropping. She gulped air to make up for not running or walking a cool down half mile. Twin beams pooling together in front of the vehicle announced its presence. The motor growled, being driven slowly in a low gear. They were either going slow to negotiate unfamiliar territory or to avoid warning Tommy or her.

She picked the latter option as she saw the headlights had been taped over, showing only two slits primarily focused on the ground in front of the vehicle. It was a large SUV, probably a Yukon. Maybe seat six or seven? She couldn't see inside the Yukon, and all the instrument lights had been turned off.

Not good, she thought as her mind raced. Trying to run silent and masked headlights? An attack. They knew where they were going, too. While she wondered about that thing, she pushed the worry aside. The prime thing she had to do was to warn Tommy. She had to do something. And even though the Yukon was driving maybe ten or fifteen miles an hour, there was no way she could outrun it. But as the SUV rounded a bend ahead, she resumed her run trailing behind it and losing ground. When she caught sight of it again, she realized they had disabled the brake lights and now turned off the taped headlights, trusting to the murk of dawn. She knew that hereabouts when dawn came, it would come suddenly. At that time, she would become vulnerable if the driver were to check his rearview mirror.

From running the hardpan to and from the cabin daily, she knew the distances. At this point she was a shade closer than three miles away.

María Elena ran faster. At least since they were not driving fast, they weren't raising much dust for her to breathe. Too eager, she stumbled once and fought to regain her balance, cursing the waste of time. She was at her top speed. She usually ran mile seven at a good clip; but now she was running in a killer sprint, even faster than what her routine was when finishing up the last mile. Her arms pumped and she concentrated on proper breathing, her eyes scouring the earth in front of her.

Even though Tommy had exploded against her, she knew she had no choice. Sure, she could save herself, but that wasn't in her character. And, by God, Tommy had never hesitated to save her time after time, and they hadn't known each other that well then.

Her body was failing her, she couldn't sustain the pace with the oxygen she was taking in. She had to slow down from a sprint to a hard run, realizing she had a couple of miles to go and wanted to be able to make it. She was thankful that pre-dawn is almost cold compared to the daily highs over 100.

As she eased up, she smelled burned fuel and saw the outline of the Yukon ahead of her. Veering off the beaten path, she slipped behind a large Saguaro cactus. It took her a moment to regain her breathing as she fought against the urge to gulp in great gobs of air. Soon, her lungs stopped complaining and she released the iron control she had imposed on her breathing.

She caught sight of a slight movement at the front of the SUV. The shadow of a man leaning against the grill exposed him. There had to be others. No. They'd gone ahead, not wanting to take the noisy vehicle any further. They were sneaking up on Tommy. She didn't know how far they had gone, but she estimated this location to be perhaps a mile and a half from the cabin. The one man here would be the rear guard, securing their transportation and watching the only roadway. Good tactics. You gotta bet the rent they left only one man, she thought. What to do now? Sneak past him? Okay, then what? Likely with their head start they'd beat her to the cabin. And she wasn't armed, except for her Swiss Army knife she usually carried. What was she going to do? Threaten them with a bottle opener? The only answer was to attack the only enemy she could right now.

María Elena moved laterally so that the Yukon remained between her and the sentry. She moved her feet close to the ground so she could feel any impediment which might give her away. She edged around some loose rocks and picked one up. It was the size of a grapefruit and had plenty of planes and corners and indentations to where she found a very comfortable grip.

On another hand, Florida comparisons: Rocks? Hereabouts, it was as if they grew rocks like weeds in Florida. Humongous rocks, fist-sized, boulders, odd shapes, well-rounded large and small. In Florida, you're talking mostly coral and gravel and limestone.

She arrived at the rear of the vehicle with no plan. Fortunately, it was large enough to conceal her. She glanced inside to insure no one remained and the dawn's early light showed her empty seats. It could seat seven comfortably she saw. They wouldn't have come all this way with only two or three men, but she didn't know. She had to find out.

María Elena crept around the right side toward the front. She picked up another rock and tossed it like Kareem shooting his patented sky hook for the Lakers back in the day. It thunked and rolled not far on the other side of the Yukon. Immediately, the rear guard guy straightened and dragged a Glock from under a windbreaker. As he shuffled his feet and turned to face the possible threat, María Elena scooted silently around the front right quarter panel of the SUV, her arm already winding up. She was behind him before he felt her presence and her arm shot down from overhead and the rock smashed into the side of his head. He froze, and then slid to the ground as if he had no bones.

She snatched his weapon from his hand and stuck it into his eye. But the man was unconscious. She couldn't have that. Swiftly, she removed his belt and tied his hands behind him and then attached the belt to his feet in a loop. That would be difficult to escape from, she hoped. Then she searched the car for more weapons but to no avail. She found a couple of unopened plastic bottles of water. She drank deeply then poured one over the unconscious man's face. He didn't respond, so she doused him with the other one. He seemed to gain a degree of consciousness, but still wasn't fully conscious. She pulled down his pants and found he wore no underwear. Then she began slapping his face. His breathing pattern told her he was coming around. This wasn't working out like it did the movies. She noted his head was bleeding profusely, though she knew that head wounds bled a lot. She twisted one of the water bottles and jammed it into his mouth so he couldn't yell.

Finally he came around, eyes opening and darting about it panic. He jerked his arms and they tugged his feet and then he tried to move his feet and they stretched his arms in pain, so he stopped and began trying to shout through the water bottle. She jammed the barrel of his automatic into his left eye. "Quiet."

He mumbled for another few seconds and she pushed the weapon deeper until she could feel him react in pain. He fell back and held still.

"Can you hear me?"

He nodded with hesitation.

She took his gun and jammed it into his scrotum. He winced in pain, now aware he was naked below the waist.

"I'm going to say this one time, and one time only. When I ask a question, you will answer it in a low voice and truthfully. If you don't, I will cut off your genitals with my Swiss Army knife. Understand?"

Nervously, he nodded again.

She removed the automatic and pulled out her knife, flicked open the largest blade, and showed it to him. "Sorry, it's not very sharp. I'm going to free your mouth. If you yell or try to, I will saw off those little things down there." She was conscious of the swift passage of time. She had to do something quickly. But she had to do it right and that would take a little more time.

As she twisted the water bottle to get it free from his teeth, she began talking in a low voice. "You got me at the wrong time in my life," she said, thinking of what happened between her and Tommy yesterday. Was it yesterday? It felt like an eternity. "And it's the wrong fucking time of the month for me, too." She paused again. "Not only am I pissed, I'm past being pissed. I'm coldly furious. Right now you represent all men and it would give me great pleasure to saw off your private parts." The plastic bottle popped out of his mouth. He smacked his mouth in appreciation. "How many are you?"

He hesitated and she immediately jammed the water bottle partway back in, and stabbed his scrotum with the blade. His body bucked and she withdrew the knife.

"Last chance," she said and he heard the conviction in her words. He nodded violently. She pulled the water bottle out again. "How many?"

"Six." His voice was harsh and dry.

"Why are you here?"

He hesitated until she moved the water bottle toward his face again. "Take out Atkins."

"Why?"

"Orders. And reward."

"Whose orders?"

"The boss."

"One more chance. Who, what, when and where? Tell it all right now." She flipped his penis with the blade of the knife.

"Jesus, lady. Gimme a break. Owwww! Our boss got a tip about him, somebody wanted the outstanding reward. He checked with Florida and confirmed it. He sent us down here."

"Names?"

"He'll have me killed."

"I will kill you—after I castrate you."

"Okay. Jesus. His name is Hamilton."

"Where?"

"Vegas."

"How long ago did the other five leave."

"Shit, maybe five minutes, maybe more, before you clob-bered me."

"How are they armed?"

"Handguns. One shotgun. One auto, a Mac-10 or something I think. My head hurts."

"Did they have a plan?"

"Deploy when they get there and see the layout."

She knew she was out of time. She jammed the water bottle back into his mouth. His eyes were fearful and she drew back with the rock once again. "Sorry, I don't have a choice," she said conversationally. She had intended to clip him on the other side of his head from the former wound, but he tried to dodge the blow and the rock slammed into his forehead.

She wondered if he had died. It wasn't her intention, but if so, so what? Turning killer wasn't a large step from what she'd come to be, anyway. And Tommy's safety was paramount. When this all gets over, she told herself, you'll have time to feel remorse.

Was it too late to warn Tommy? Even as the thought appeared, the answer leapt into her mind. She jacked a shell into the chamber, saw that the safety was off, and fired five shots into the air. The night seemed quieter when the sound faded. If it got his attention, then he'd wonder why five rounds. As soon as his mind settled that she might be the origin—and why not?—he'd figure it out and be prepared for that many attackers--if it wasn't already too late.

María Elena searched the body and found two more maga-zines. She dropped the half empty one and slid a replacement into the slot. Her hearing was returning quickly to normal. She'd shot Glocks at their training range before.

Now what?

Again, the answer formed immediately in her mind. This reaction must be from exposure to Tommy Atkins, shooter, tactician, and strategist.

She jumped into the Yukon and sat in the driver's seat. Like any good getaway car, the key was in the ignition even though the buzzer had been disabled. She started the engine and slammed the vehicle into gear. She accelerated quickly, not worrying about sound. Let them wonder, just as her five shots would confuse them. Unless they had a smart guy with them who'd figured out the significance of the five shots. The SUV slid in four wheel drifts as she powered forward and around tight turns.

María Elena had the windows open to hear gunfire if and when it occurred and the wind whipped through the Yukon, blowing her hair every which way. She wished she had a NASCAR ball cap to hold it in.

With no idea what she'd do when she reached the cabin, she pressed forward and downshifted for better control when she rounded the final bend.

A man stood up and stepped toward the road, his face quizzical. He carried some kind of automatic weapon. She let her foot off the gas pedal to decoy him and slowed down as if to talk. When she was close enough for him to see her and begin to react, she floored the accelerator and smashed into him. For a moment he hung on the right \side of the grill, then he fell away and the Yukon rolled over him, bouncing off the wheels momentarily. She heard nothing for a few seconds, and then shots began.

She straightened the wheels and kept accelerating. Another man dived behind a large rock in front of the cabin. María Elena swerved, clipped the rock with a crescendo of screeches and ran over his legs as he tried to crawl aside.

Two down. To avoid gunfire, she switched back to the hardpan, spewing sand and dirt behind her. She swerved right then left then right again, zigzagging to confuse her as a target. It occurred to her without seeming to count, that she was receiving fire from one handgun and a shotgun. The shotgun had peppered the side of the Yukon and some of the pellets flew through open windows. One gouged her bad shoulder and stung. Oh, well, it figured.

To further confuse them, she performed a high speed U-turn. "Beat that, Kyle Busch," she said through clenched teeth.

Once she passed the cabin, she saw one of the attackers crouched in the shadows behind the cabin. She slewed the Yukon to the right and braked hard. Another shotgun blast scarred the back of the vehicle and shattered glass. She leaned out with the Glock and carefully aimed at the guy behind the cabin. He didn't wait to aim, and he started firing a revolver. His haste cost him as she put two rounds in his torso and he flew backwards.

She smelled gun oil and smoke from her Glock. "Tommy!" she yelled and her words sounded more like a panicked shriek, but she went on. "Two out front. One shotgun."

Another couple of shots came from in front of the cabin and sounded like a kid beating on a pan. She dropped the brake and accelerated at max, heading straight into the fray. She saw the two remaining hoods stand to take more certain firing positions and aim at her.

"Oh, shit," she said aloud.

Then out of the corner of her eye, she saw the front door to the cabin slam open and Tommy burst out. He wore only jeans and had a pistol in each hand. The two bad guys saw him immediately and swiveled to target him. But he kept running—straight at them firing from his hip. Before María Elena could realign the Yukon, Tommy stopped and took up the classic shooting position, side on to the target and emptied one of his guns into the shotgun wielder. So she aimed at the remaining shooter and floored the Yukon again.

But he'd learned from experience and ran at a cross-angle she couldn't compensate for. However, it didn't matter, because he jerked and stopped and jerked again as Tommy shot him three times. He tried to run again and Tommy shot him again with another pistol he'd pulled from his waist. The last man standing tumbled askew, limbs flying and flopping in ways they shouldn't.

She stopped the Yukon and jumped out. She ran to Tommy. She flung her arms around his neck. His breath was foul, thank you mescal bender.

"Good work, Pocahontas." His voice was raw and he shook his head to clear it.

Then she pushed him away strongly. "Outa my way, buster, I gotta pee bad."

When she returned from the bathroom, she was coming down from the adrenalin high. And weariness washed over her. She'd never run that fast that long before in her life.

She heard a gunshot and rushed out. Tommy was coming across the open space from the rocks where she'd used the Yukon as a weapon.

"Don't ask," he said. "Brief me."

Quickly she summarized what had happened, including what the getaway driver had told her. "Somebody named Hamilton," she finished.

"Looks like you done just fine, college girl." He grinned. "Your learning curve is going up more steeply every day." He held up a hand with five fingers straight out. "It did wake me up and it took about five seconds to figure out what the five shots meant." He surveyed the carnage and eyed her. "Maybe I shouldn't oughta piss you off."

"You betcha." She slapped her final magazine into the Glock.

"Not sure I can do without you," he mumbled. His eyes admired her beneath the mesh tank top.

She looked at him, eyes up and quizzical. She regretted not putting on her sports bra.

He stared down at the ground. "Hard to break in new talent at this late date."

"Tommy? We got dead people lying all over the goddamn place. Maybe we can have this conversation later?"

"All right. First we rob these guys of guns and ammo and their wallets. We'll use the money and maybe the ID, if they got any. I suspect they do. They're mob guys, sloppy and cocky.

They wouldn't have taken precautions. Then I'll take the Yukon and check on the guy back up the trail. You grab the money and documents and our armament, throw it in the jeep and when I get back, we'll eddios this fucking place."

"Revision," María Elena said. "You do that stuff and I'll take a shower. I go nowhere without taking a shower."

"Déjà vu," he said.

She granted him a smile. "And when you come back, you take a long shower and brush your teeth."

Tommy cocked an eye at her. "That bad?"

"Roadkill bad." Usually she liked his smell a great deal and subconsciously knew that his pheromones were one of the things which had attracted her to him.

"Okay. We might have time. Their protocol approximated something like they called their contact or boss as they were incoming, starting the operation. And likely they were supposed to call in upon completion. But this is way out and their cell phones might be out of range, I dunno. We could check, but I don't want to know." He paused and scratched his chest with a revolver. "When they don't check in, maybe their boss sends backup. Maybe somebody local heard the shooting, a hiker or another hermit, or a friggin' game warden, whatever. Maybe the feds are trailing them. We need to pack up and leave real quick."

"After our showers."

"Maybe we'll load up the bodies and dump them in the desert, hide 'em. That will confuse matters."

"Tommy? How did they find us? Nobody knows we're here."

"One person knows."

"Charley."

"Yep. He's an ex-mob guy. Served in Vietnam back in the day. Went to work for them. Finally, he went through that stress thing and they couldn't trust him to do the job right, so he and they parted ways. Maybe he got drunk up in Vegas and talked to the wrong people. Maybe he turned us in for the reward."

"Hold on. Reward?"

"The mob has a long standing reward out for me."

"Oh? So *you've* been holding out on *me*?"

"Um, I didn't want you to think ill of me."

She put her hands on her hips and got in his face. "Goddamn, Tommy! I finally start to fall in love for the first real time in my fucking life and find out you're holding out on me? Son of a bitch. I figured you were hiding something, but this?"

"I didn't think it was any of your business, not at the time."

She fumed. "First time I saw you, you were standing over me like an NFL linebacker, powerful and mean and going in for the kill. You were smooth, bang bang bang and it was over. What a wonderful sight and sound. Then I think you dumped me and I was dying inside and it was dark and gloomy and you drive up at that mall and I feel like a million dollars. So when it came to Orlando, it was only natural to figure out what you were going to do and very easy to appeal to you. Then it was becoming an 'us'. I did sort of offer myself to you that night, I was willing to sleep with you for what you did and I was okay with that, too, not just feeling obligated, even though I'd never done anything like that in my life. In San Antonio, you didn't have to come after me—that was too much to ask. But in my heart of hearts, I knew you'd find a way, I knew you'd come in with guns blazing, I knew the next gunshots I heard would herald your arrival and I was so confident over that thing. Everything that happened between you and me pointed us in one direction, and I was so happy over that. When you got sick, I fought the malaria devil with everything I had because I simply had to. As long as I had something to say about it, we were going to fight the disease with all our energy as if it were bad guys trying to kill us. Like all these dead guys here right fucking now, nothing was going to come between us; nobody was going to harm you if I had to kill every Goddamn one of them. All that damn buildup and after what we shared? You could well have confided in me."

"I'm sorry." He hung his head.

"I hear you."

"I need you bad." He studied the gun in his hand.

"Are you married, too?" she demanded.

"No." He was obviously flummoxed.

"Have you ever been married?"

"No. Listen, María Elena. We need to get moving real soon."

"I want you to squirm, damn it all."

"I am. I'm truly sorry."

"I thought we were kind of a couple, a loving couple, but now after a mere twenty-four hours, it's shot in the ass." Maybe she should have mercy on him. What had her mom told her once long ago? "You have to train them early, or it might not ever get done."

"Look here, Florence Nightingale, I know what you're trying to do now. But really, really, if we want to live through this day, we need to hit the road fast."

She shook her whole body. "You're right, Tommy. We can talk later." She'd mimicked his declaration of love and angst and anger—was it just twenty-four hours ago? It felt like an eternity.

He hopped in the Yukon and brushed some glass out of the way. Soon he was heading up the dirt road. María Elena packed quickly and efficiently. It occurred to her that they had extra stuff now, a result of putting down roots, albeit temporary roots. As a conciliatory gesture, she stacked all his stuff on the bed and put his duffle next to it. She gathered guns and ammo. Then she went outside and, against her will, searched bodies. The one she'd hit directly with the SUV was pretty messed up and she managed to fish out a wallet. The machine gun was smashed past use. She surveyed the dead men. She was growing tougher. Well, screw them; they shouldn't have tried to kill Tommy and her. She knew she should feel some remorse, but was too hyper to feel it. She suspected she would never feel remorse for soldiers like this. Had Tommy been one of them at one time? She shook her head not wanting to know. She stripped her running clothes and stepped under the shower. It seemed so long ago she had started out on her run. Finally the adrenalin high was leveling off.

She heard the Yukon return and in a minute Tommy came out the back door with a mouthful of toothpaste and a toothbrush scrubbing away. He stripped off his jeans and stepped into the shower with her. She saw the question in his eyes and pushed him aside.

"Bad timing," she told him. It could mean anything.

"Hold still," he told her and held her shoulder wound under the water.

"Just a scratch."

"It's more than that, María Elena. But a little alcohol and a Band-Aid and you'll live."

"Sure." They were standing under the running water face to face.

His hands began to roam.

"No, Tommy." She noticed he was beginning to respond to her.

"There was a guy with no pants and a Swiss army knife jammed through his nuts. I guess when you say something, you mean it." He grinned at her and cupped her butt cheek once quickly and then let go and stepped back. "I brought your knife back."

She grabbed a towel and went inside to change.

When he came in, he was all business. "We have no time left to play games with the bodies. Our problem is that our fingerprints are all over this place. We could blow it up and they'd still find prints."

"Burn it like your cabin," she said. "I want to get even with your good buddy Charley." She held up her hand. "Yeah, yeah, I know. Rock and adobe don't burn well."

Tommy grinned for the first time in a long time. "Here's what we'll do. Write a note to him. I'll write 'Thanks for the cabin, Charley. Will look you up here again real soon.'" He nodded to himself. "He won't return and stay here as long as he knows we're still alive."

"If authorities find this place, they'll take the note for evidence," she said. "Let me send him an email. Surely he's checking his account from his hotel in Vegas?"

"There's hope for you yet, sweetie."

She eyed him. "We've yet to determine that thing." She went to Charley's desktop and powered it up. While she was waiting on the mail program, Tommy packed his duffle. Then she wrote the email, plain and simple just as Tommy had said with no signature block, and hit send.

Soon they were outside and finished loading the Jeep.

"I'm going to take the Toyota and dump it in the middle of the wilderness, another decoy," Tommy said. "Maybe it'll lead them to believe we walked away and perished out there."

"They ought to know better by now. All of them."

"Could be, Florence. But we have to try everything."

She followed him and they headed out. They climbed onto the desert plateau and eventually he turned off, flagged her to wait, and drove up a canyon. She turned off her engine and waited. Eventually, the sound of the Toyota receded and half an hour later Tommy came walking out. She reversed direction and headed back. They didn't stop when they passed the cabin, but she sensed the growing presence of swarms of flies on the bodies. Carrion buzzards floated above in a cliché formation. When they reached the area where she attacked the Yukon guard, she saw that flies had settled in here, too, and a couple of vultures were circling overhead. It was chilling.

Five minutes later, Tommy grabbed her arm and pointed. "Over there, quickly."

"Over there" was a draw under a couple of scraggly mesquite trees on the incline above it. María Elena knew not to ask, but to act quickly, and she did so.

"Kill it," he said and rummaged around in the back. He came up with an old GI blanket, and got out and spread it over the hood and windshield, roughed it up, and got back inside. "Best I can do."

Then she heard it, the overhead buzzing of a helicopter. "Too much coincidence," she said.

He dug into the weapons cache in the back and came up with a twenty-two rifle, bolt action. "Not much help."

The heat built in the vehicle. The sounds of the helicopter

circling the area came and went, and then suddenly disappeared. Two of the vultures fled overhead. María Elena smelled
heat. She continued to sweat wondering why she'd bothered to
shower earlier.

Tommy saw her discomfort. "You smell good either way,
Pocahontas."

She stuck her tongue out at him.

"He landed. If they're the law, they're going to be on the radio
to every cop in Arizona." Tommy retrieved the blanket and she
backed out of the draw avoiding a few prickly cacti, turned and
headed out toward Algeria Road.

"Somebody's dead serious," Tommy said.

"The question is," said María Elena, "are they after me or
you?"

He grinned at her. "Don't fucking matter."

CHAPTER EIGHTEEN: THEM

When Linda came into the office, Suzie Q reflected that Linda always lighted up any room. Suzie could tell Linda had her requisite smoke on the way here from Hoover.

Linda's wide smile said that she'd learned something important. She came into Suzie's office and shut the door.

"Where's the coffee?" asked Suzie Q.

"No time. Something's come up and we need to address it."

"Speak now, my dear, or forever hold your peace." Suzie settled back in her chair and thought about sending out for coffee. Maybe she'd fold and get some from their office coffeepot in the break room. That might suffice in an emergency.

Linda sat on the edge of a visitor's chair and crossed her long and shapely legs. "ORG CRIME over at the home office in Hoover has an undercover op in the mob. Get this: Vegas."

"Surprise surprise surprise. And this affects us how?"

Linda held up her hand for patience. "Okay, one of 'em. Anyway, this guy reported they got a tip about somebody named Tommy Atkins—"

"Now I begin to understand."

"The way I understand it, Suze, is that this sub-boss, name of Ralph Hamilton, got the tip. He did some research, or his informant did, and found a longstanding reward from some mob guy in Florida, Tampa to be specific. Different name, of course, but they added two and two and figured out this was their guy. Apparently they had a description and the circumstances fit and this Atkins was their guy. Reward has been out for years."

"So where is Atkins?"

"Southern Arizona, outside of Nogales." Linda paused dramatically. "There's a beautiful woman, unnamed, with him, too."

"Did they have a specific location?"

"GPS coordinates."

"So this guy Hamilton knows them, too. What'd he do?"

"Dispatched a hit team."

"When?"

"Two days ago."

Suzie Q twirled her chair around and thought. "Organized Crime passed this on to us because?"

"They thought it worthy of note and we had a red, immediate flag in the system for Atkins and the woman."

"Perhaps Hamilton and his hit team will do the job for us?"

Linda pulled a pack of Marlboros out of a hidden pocket, snapped open the hard pack, took a deep sniff, and closed it back up. "Not as good as Luckys," she said.

"Lemme ask, Linda, what is the job we want done?"

"I have been wondering that myself, Suze. First all we knew was somebody killed some of 13 de enero soldiers. Even though our guy Don Diego has not been very forthcoming. The old man's gone. Then young Miss María Elena disappears—García's wife. Then the Orlando International episode we witnessed. Then she and this Atkins guy are in Olde San Antone and we locate them and pass along the info and all of a sudden, you got five more dead guys."

"Exactly."

"So, whose side are we on?" Linda asked.

Suzie Q smiled. "The red, white, and blue. Don Diego is running 13 and has some agents in place on Cuban soil for us, Linda, for you and me, for this 13 JTF."

"JTF 13," corrected Linda. "To be fair, we have received some innocuous reports from these agents in-place."

"Proving nothing."

"Sufficient, Suze, to continue our funding."

"There's that."

"To be fair," Linda pointed out, "we, you and I and this office, didn't know what Don Diego was going to do with the info we gave them from San Antonio."

"We still don't know."

"We posit he sent a hit team to kill them and the tables got turned."

"Now it's happening out of Vegas," said Suzie. "Lots of people want the woman and the guy dead."

"I don't care about him, but it would be a waste for her to die so young and stunningly beautiful."

Suzie shook her head. "There's that. But we got no stake in her death. Something stinks here. Since we've now figured out people want to kill her, we might have a stake in keeping her alive."

"You figure we've been used?"

"We are always being used. It's our job to turn that around and use them while letting them think they're using us."

Linda gave a wide smile. "I even understand what you just said. Not only that, but I concur. It might be in our best interest to keep her alive until we can determine just exactly what the fuck is going on."

"And how we can use it." Suzie leaned back thinking. "Although I will admit this Atkins fellow is doing a mighty fine job of it on his own."

"Don't forget cover our ass, bureaucratically speaking." Linda reached over and patted Suzie's hand. "Put your Machiavellian mind to task, sweetie, and solve this shit. I kind of like our autonomy here; I'm not certain I can go back to either a desk job or being a field agent again."

"Yes, dear. My aforementioned giant intellect asks me if we can scare up a chopper, send it to those GPS coordinates and report back to us."

"Can do. We have the authority. Dunno if we got one available in Nogales, but I'll dispatch a team from there if so. Likely can get one out of Tucson quicker."

"How far from Tucson?"

"Beats me. Maybe sixty miles. Won't take long."

"Do it now. It's very early their time."

"Yes, ma'am!" Linda left in a swirl of a long skirt.

Susan Quantrell worked on obligatory paperwork for an hour then Linda returned smelling like she'd just had a smoke outside.

"We should hear something soon."

"Project review," said Suzie Q proudly.

"Okay. Why?"

Suzie pushed back in her chair and smiled. "We need to cover our ass. We need to reassess our goals, the reason for our existence. We need to insure we're doing what we need to in accordance with our regulations and procedures."

"Bureaucratic horse shit," said Linda.

"Sure. Look, we suspect stuff we don't have control over is going on which might or might not be antithetical to our mission. Not to mention your and my careers. Therefore, we perform a Program Review in which we actually review and document our findings and make recommendations."

"No kidding?" said Linda. "That's brilliant, and covers our aforementioned ass." She applauded lightly with her hands. "So, who performs this review?"

"We do."

"Prince Machiavelli, stand aside."

"So whatever we do is covered," Suzie said. "And we document. What's our mission? Originally, we monitor and provide assistance within the law, ahem, to 13 de enero and, secondarily, acquire intel from the island of Cuba. Anything to put a thorn in those Castro sides. But now that they're on the fast track out, the military option is dying. Our review must encompass these upcoming changes. Not only does it cover our ass and give us motive for doing what we're gonna do, whatever that is, it allows us to change the mission and thus provide job security for me and you and your crew of pirates out there in the ops room."

Linda excitedly took up the thread. "If we can modify our mission to include getting in on the ground floor or having some control over international trade out of Cuba, we'd become instant legends."

"I'd see it as simply doing our jobs."

Sandy knocked on the door and stuck her head in. "Tucson agent on line two, radio relay as his cell doesn't work down by Nogales."

Linda spun the phone around and hit line two and the speaker function. "Landover."

Static then the carrier wave with background noise of wind and people talking in the background. "Linda, this is Smitty. Listen, it ain't pretty here. Over."

"What do you have, Smitty, over."

"A cabin tucked under a mesa overhang, deserted, nobody home. Oh, except for six bodies. Over."

Linda took a deep breath. "Have you seen the bodies, Smitty?"

"Unfortunately. Over."

"I need to know if any of the six matches two descriptions. One, female, thirty years old, highly attractive, long black hair. Two, male Caucasian, don't know much, but a big guy, curly hair, maybe six two. Over."

Suzie held up her hand and crossed her fingers.

"Linda, that's a negative. All white males, all shot to death— well, a couple look like they were smashed with a car and another had his head bashed in. We can tell there was a huge gunfight here, but there are no weapons and the dearly departed have no identification. Over."

"All right, thanks, Smitty. Call me if you turn up anything interesting. Over."

"Hard to get all worked up about a mob hit team," said Smitty. "I'll copy you on my report. This is gonna look good on my record. Over."

"You're welcome, Smitty. Over."

"Linda, you ain't gonna believe this one. Guess who's landing a chopper here right now and right alongside ours? The U.S. Marshal Service."

"Surprise, surprise," said Linda. "Over and out."

"Okay, Linda, thanks again. I'd be very pleased to buy you dinner next time I'm up there in Never Never land. Out."

"Is he married?" asked Suzie.

"Yeah, but that fact ain't never bothered him yet." Linda killed the speaker and the line and swiveled the phone back toward Suzie Q.

Suzie surprised herself by asking, "Does everybody hit on you?"

"Pretty much."

"Another thing or two. How come Atkins and María Elena are still together?"

Linda shook her head. "Convenience? True love? Money?" She paused. "Some variation of the Stockholm Syndrome." She shrugged. "My insight on this one ain't, Suze." She thought for a moment. "We can safely rule out that he's some kind of agent in place, not with that record. A hidden ally? An illicit lover? We need a clue and I don't have one." She laughed, the sound of smoky whisky. "Maybe it's Reverse Stockholm Syndrome: he's following her around like a puppy."

"Me neither." Suzie applied Occam's Razor, the principle that the answer lies with the solution which has the fewest assumptions. "We're gonna go with coincidence. Maybe he was a bystander and got caught up in this mess."

"Complicates things to a degree," said Linda. "I note that immediately upon his entry onto the scene we have a plethora of dead people."

"Why does Hamilton guy want Atkins killed? What reward and from whom?"

"I'll try to get an enquiry through to the undercover guy. Might be touchy."

"Naah, it's his job and he loves this kind of shit. Gets his name out there as the premier undercover op; it sets him apart."

"And we want to know why, Suze?"

"My read of Mr. Atkins is that he doesn't take kindly to people trying to kill him or the girl. My further guess is Mr. Hamilton and whatever that mob guy's name is in Florida, is they're now in jeopardy."

"Oh." Linda sat back, obviously impressed.

"And, if we need, that's where we'll find Atkins and your cute girl, and pretty soon at that." Suzie Q had a long-developed sixth sense from administrative in-fighting and bureaucratic wrangling. Something odd was going on here. "And why are the marshals going independent on us?"

CHAPTER NINETEEN: HIM

Tommy drove the lonely desert road.

María Elena drowsed. They were somewhere northwest of Nogales, but not to the California border. Both knew it was time they talked. She shook her head and sat up. She popped the seat belt and turned and leaned into the back seat. "Soda?"

"A sip."

She retrieved a diet Coke and buckled herself back in. She twisted the top off the plastic bottle and drank deeply. She handed it to Tommy and he drank some.

María Elena sipped again and settled back. "See, here it is in a nutshell. I was eighteen. My father needed help running 13 and this half Mexican half Cubano had helped out before with men sometimes and info, inside info from Cuba. He was some kind of landowner in southern Mexico but headquartered in Miami. Papá decided he had the political moxie and connections. My father's sometimes partner was too involved in politics and earning money and was not as involved as he had been. I don't know—now—if I was part of the deal or just to cement the deal or an anointment of Don Diego to establish his credibility with the men and women of 13. Perhaps I was there to maintain Papá's linkage when he got too old and had to relinquish control. I think Papá envisioned 13 would go on long after his passing." She shook her head sadly. "Some would call it an 'arranged' marriage."

"Well, he's dead now." He glanced at her. "Sorry, don't mean to be insensitive."

She shook her head, distracted. "I am not addressing the politics right now, just me personally. We stayed together for maybe five years. During that time he was gone a lot, Mexico, Cuba, elsewhere. He used me as a toy—no, a trophy would better describe it. Our marriage gave him instant credibility and he reveled in that. Then he became more and more involved in 13 and spent a lot of his time and political capital gaining trust and control. Much of the time he ignored me. After the first few years, he was playing around with other women—or he did that at the start of our marriage and I didn't realize it."

"Sounds like a circus."

"Sort of, Tommy. I was eighteen, twenty, what did I know about life? Papá protected me and I was not world-wise—"

"You're getting a lot better."

"In fact, during the first few years of our marriage, I went to college. Remember Hillsdale?"

"Sure thing, college girl."

"I spent a lot of time up in Michigan. They're pretty strict up there and I was married, so my party life was non-existent. Consequently, I studied all the time and my grades reflected it." She thought for a moment. "That could have caused a schism in our marriage, now that I think of it."

Tommy shook his head and checked mirrors and the speedometer. "The man was using you and, through you, your father. If he had cared, he would have encouraged you go attend the University of Miami or someplace much closer."

María Elena shot him a grin. "Maybe that was me finding an escape."

"You're pretty bright today, college girl, I guess it follows you might have had some semblance of intelligence even back then."

"Gee, thanks. Anyway, after five years of that, we no longer lived together nor did we maintain the traditional husband and wife relationship."

"So, you been estranged for seven years?"

"More or less."

"That's a long time, María Elena. Why not divorce?"

"Religion. Tradition. Papá."

"Bull shit, Pocahontas. You and Papá were afraid divorce would split 13 or diminish it. Or some damn thing. Diego obviously wanted to keep the veneer of marriage as that was much of his power base."

"Pretty close. The apple cart was safe." She shook her head. "Papá was getting too old to be operational all the time, and Don Diego was inheriting the leadership propped up by marriage to me."

"Fast forward, María Elena. You discovered a new layer to Diego's duplicity. You found out he was doing illegal stuff."

She took up the story once again. "They were doing military exercises in that big area near where your cabin was. We've another where we are based, a couple of thousand acres the government lets us use, closer to Miami, but still in the boondocks. But this area is larger and you can live fire and use equipment and so on. I went to look up my father and brief him on what'd I'd discovered. Somehow Diego ferreted it out and here we are."

"By then he'd consolidated his hold on 13 so that he didn't need you or your father."

"Exactly. It even wouldn't surprise me if he were a big time drug dealer out of Mexico."

"More likely, María Elena, he *wanted* to be or wanted to be rich."

"Which would happen if the Castro regime disappeared."

"But Don Diego didn't know when that thing would occur."

She finished the diet Coke. "Exactly."

"Where does the government fit in all this?"

"A lot," she said. "They provided the land, and some equipment, and training—not so much training any more as their money has been cut." She twisted the cap onto the bottle and set it in a garbage bag.

"Most of that's obvious. Why would they help Don Diego?"

María Elena shook her head sadly. "He's the formal head of

13, the operations officer, too. Papá has been marginalized."

"They have to know 13 isn't going to attack Cuba itself and take over." He tweaked the steering wheel to miss a dead buzzard in the road. A motorcycle came up behind them and blew past them, the Doppler noise reverberating within the Jeep. Tommy was driving 75. At least that was an encouraging sign for their destination.

"Very good, Tommy. There's a watchdog agency up in Washington called JTF 13. Joint Task Force. Half CIA and half FBI. Their mission has evolved from strictly oversight into one of being able to take advantage for the U.S. when the Castro regime is gone. Nowadays, that means trade. Don Diego has sold them on that tantalizing goal. So they support 13 in the hopes of having major influence in the forthcoming new Cuban government."

"Well," said Tommy, "it keeps them busy and maintains their budget. Are these bureaucrats aware Don Diego is trying his best to kill you? That he killed your father?"

"I doubt it. How could they unless he tells them?"

"So they've been inadvertently helping him find us to kill you?"

"It could be, Tommy. Or, advertently. The CIA has backed plenty of bad guys, killers, whatever, to get what it wants. I think they think they own the 13 members who are underground in Cuba right now and do not want to jeopardize any of that."

"Still...real people, Americans, don't want to contribute to murder and rape and whatever else Diego is doing."

"He is making a giant profit. But no, we don't know what these faceless bureaucrats are up to."

"Do you know them personally? Have you met them?"

"No. Papá refused to let me get involved in that end of 13. He was only trying to protect me. I didn't protest because I had other things to do and had been excluded from the leadership of 13. Frankly, I was angry over this macho male oriented culture which Papá was part of, and which kept me out of leadership and operations."

"So you don't have a clue who these Washington guys are?"

"Nope. Would they believe us anyway?"

"I don't know, Pocahontas. I'm only looking for a way out. It looks like we might have to do it the hard way." He sighed. "And I guess this JTF doesn't know about rape, pillage, murder, plunder. Which brings me to this: I can see why Diego wants you dead. Fine. But what's with the gang rape bit?"

"Several things, but mostly the last seven or eight years, I've refused to submit to him. He has built up a lot of animus toward me because of that. It hurt his Latin macho pride and somewhat diminished his authority and his credibility. But mostly, it was to get even for me and my research causing things to come crashing down, likely pushing him to make his move earlier than he'd anticipated. Mother Mary, he was angry with me."

Tommy sat back. The road was straight. Heat boiled off the surface. Tiny mirages danced in the distance.

"Here's what I think, María Elena. If we need to, you can call up this JTF. They'll take your call and we can meet with them someplace safe. But that would almost certainly prevent us from killing Diego, which needs to be done. They'd either protect him or scare him off. Not to mention, I got a major allergy towards feds of any kind or any kind of law enforcement whatsoever. That means we gotta solve our own problem."

She reached over and patted him on the knee and he liked her touch. "Nice transition, Mr. Atkins. Your turn: 'fess up. Prison, hiding out, mob reward for your death. Nice résumé."

"It's embarrassing. It's awkward."

"Try me."

Tommy watched another Harley catch up with them and go around passing. The driver slowed and rode alongside them for a moment, looking in the Jeep and checking them out. Tommy nodded to him amiably. Then the rider pulled away with a throaty roar. Tommy swallowed hard and savored the disappearing thunder. His palms atavistically spasmed and clutched around the steering wheel as if it were the handle bars of a Harley-Davidson.

"I was working for the mob in Tampa. Guys like Santana, some independent contracting."

"Doing what?" she asked sweetly.

Tommy squirmed. "Whatever they wanted. I was a fixit man."

"With a gun?"

"Goddamnit, yes. With a gun. But I never killed anybody who didn't need killing."

"Tommy," she said with a soft voice, "I am not being judgmental. Look what you and your guns have done for me?"

"Don't mean to be touchy."

"Go on," she told him.

"One day, one of the Santana bunch, their son, young, maybe twenty, raped and beat up the daughter of another guy in the leadership. He, um, contracted me to discontinue this young man. Since I knew the girl, I was eager. She was actually very nice. She could cook anything anytime anywhere. Brunette, full of life. Ah, shit, I don't wanna remember. So I took the mother fucker out clean. Fine. But I got a thing against rape big time. Maybe you noticed?"

"I'll say."

"I'll tell you about it one day. So, anyway, turns out this asshole rapist kid had done it before and brutally. Back in the day you could buy a judge. So the Santanas bought a judge and the kid got off. Well, I was much younger and anger burned like a long fuse so, um, ah, I took out the judge for free."

"An equal opportunity contractor."

"That's me. It worked well since I used the same gun I used for the kid and therefore the bullets matched. I figured that would divert suspicion onto the victim's family—not to add to their misery, but I knew they'd probably appreciate the whole thing anyway, the perp and the accomplice judge going down. Since they were innocent, they couldn't possibly be nailed for the double deed because they didn't do it. The whole thing worked on several levels and it was one of my happier professional—ah, accomplishments."

"Professional accomplishments?" He could tell she was trying to keep emotion off her face. He wasn't sure if he liked that or not. Oh, well, she wanted to know, let it be on her.

Tommy smiled. "Well, needless to say, that pissed off law enforcement, including the feds. Turned out that judge was popular. He mentored young lawyers and raised money for scholarships to law schools. Probably a cover to get good local PR. He looked a lot better with a hole in his forehead. An informant tipped 'em off and they couldn't pin either hit on me, but they got me on RICO. From some federal laws called like Racketeer Influenced and Corrupt Organizations Act. I was in the business and they linked stuff to me; it wasn't difficult."

"This informant would have been your substitute in the body bag?"

"You betcha, María Elena. Maybe it was a good thing they sent me to prison because Santana wanted me dead. They too suspected, but didn't know and couldn't prove I done it. But that don't matter to the mob. In prison I was safer from them because where I went, most of 'em hated Santana and I was friends with the brothers and Hispanics and especially bikers. They were all tight knit and kept my back covered."

"Now we know the origin of the reward. Must be big."

"They'd take me out anyway as a favor to their counterparts. Vegas, Chicago, Tampa and Miami. Peas in a pod. They all got unwritten reciprocal agreements, professional courtesy. Anyway, this Santana is old and when he's gone, the memory is gone. It ain't institutional, since that whole mob out of Tampa has been whittled down by the locals and the feds."

Another two Harleys approached in the other lane, these going more slowly—maybe seventy. As he flew past them at a combined speed of probably 140 plus miles per hour, he guessed they were maybe twenty minutes out. He was uncomfortable talking about himself and his past. He did realize that he'd just confessed two murders to María Elena. While that might be deemed hearsay, still he trusted her with his life. And she was smart enough to realize that.

She must have sensed his sudden silence. "I don't know anything, Tommy. Um, I consider that stuff well done as it became practice for your skills which in turn saved me a few times." She touched his cheek. "I know this is a different world—hell, a different universe than the one in which I used to exist. You've trusted me with these damning experiences of yours; I should have trusted you with the fact I was married, and married to Don Diego García."

"Yeah, you should have. Listen, María Elena. I should have trusted you. Hell, I do trust you, that's obvious. I just didn't feel it was the right time to lay out my whole life in front of you. Some of it wasn't pretty. I been stumbling around in the dark. I don't even know how to go about a relationship. It ain't something I ever did. When I reacted to you being married? I should have remembered you saying not long before that about staying with me until we're both old, even though I'll beat you there by a mile."

"Thank you, Tommy." She smiled gently. "That's all you need to say. There is an old Cuban proverb, 'A love that lasts forever takes but a second to come about.'"

"Well, Pocahontas, I don't even know what the fuck love is. All I know is I am very comfortable around you and that's where I want to be for a long, long time."

"Tommy, that's the nicest thing anybody ever said to me."

His smile was crooked.

She reached over and ran her hand through his hair. "Not a spot of gray. You'll be around forever."

The intersection of two long roads in the middle of nowhere came up on their horizon. He could see a couple of buildings. It was just as he remembered it.

Glad to change the subject, he said, "I was going to ask you to play arm candy, but I think your intelligence can guide you through this if you take your cues from me or just use your brain. Otherwise, one misstep and we're in bad trouble." He pointed at her chest. "Undo the top two buttons. Got to show some more skin. And yours looks outstanding." He grinned at his pun.

The buildings grew and one became a gas station and quick stop and the other became a sprawling biker bar. Maybe thirty Harleys sat out front, all nosed out. Tommy backed the Jeep in and parked on the far end of the row of choppers. He eyed the line of hogs admiringly. Extended front forks, saddlebags, odd paint, lots of chrome.

"Let us go in," he said, "and commence going on the offense."

CHAPTER TWENTY: HER

They walked through a pair of doors with frosted glass. Inside the first set of doors was another, two batwing doors. They pushed through alongside each other. She was wearing what Tommy had dictated for this: Daisy Duke cutoffs and a shirt tied in a knot in front exposing plenty of her flat stomach below and cleavage above.

Tommy paused and they waited for their eyes to adjust from bright overwhelming sunlight to the traditional dim environs of a bar. On the far side several pool tables were in use. The bar was horseshoe shaped and surrounded by many tables with traditional red and white checked plastic table cloths. The whole establishment shouted cliché. An old fashioned jukebox played old country favorites. Right now, Patsy Cline was falling to pieces.

María Elena looked around. It was obvious that Tommy was counting people and assessing. Every one of thirty bikers had stopped what they were doing and were watching the two newcomers. Two guys in mechanic coveralls were obviously from the gas station across the road. Half a dozen women were scattered about. Tommy led her to an empty table alongside a wall. She felt sixty or so eyes on them, most undressing her. Well, she told herself grimly, if you got it, strut it.

As they sat, the waitress came over, nervous. She looked her question.

"Two Bud drafts," Tommy told her. María Elena recognized it as protocol, even though she didn't want a beer.

Life slowly returned to normal in the bar, though most of them looked their way frequently.

The waitress brought two icy mugs of Budweiser and set them down. She backed away. María Elena nodded her thanks and the woman looked back at her strangely. Maybe people didn't thank the wait staff in bars like this.

Johnny Cash walked the line.

Tommy held his beer in front of her. "To us, María Elena," he said quietly.

"Me, too," she replied and they clinked glasses. The beer was cold and good.

Occasionally, bikers would walk by or stop and look and go back to the bar or their tables. María Elena smelled the cigarette smoke which hung in the air. She was surprised this bar was clean and neat. Smokers used ashtrays. They belied the stereotype biker.

Eventually, a grizzled bear of a man walked over and sat down. "Welcome, strangers." His hair was brown and tumbled down his neck and he wore a heavy three-day growth on his face. María Elena categorized his eyes as mean and intelligent. He drank some of his own beer. "I'm Bear."

María Elena noticed the noise level in the bar had dropped perceptively and that most of the patrons were watching the three at the table now.

"Been around long?" the Bear asked.

"No, passin' through," said Tommy.

"Any reason you're stopping in here?"

Tommy nodded. "Looking to score some hardware, you don't mind. Maybe trade, maybe cash."

"You don't fuck around," said the Bear.

"Not today, not ever," said Tommy.

The Bear looked at María Elena speculatively. "I can tell you're carrying already."

"Call a cop," said Tommy.

"Trade for the hardware?" asked the Bear, leaning forward, interested.

"Cash and maybe some assorted handguns, a rifle, a shotgun, stuff we don't need right now. And some credit cards." He was referring to the credit cards of the late six hoods from near Nogales.

The Bear looked hard at María Elena again and undressed her with his eyes. "Get a lot for her."

Somebody killed the jukebox as Marty Robbins died in El Paso.

María Elena was becoming more uncomfortable by the minute, but she followed what Tommy had tasked her with. She favored the Bear with a bored smile.

"You don't need that kind of trouble," Tommy told him.

The biker looked at María Elena again and shook his head grinning. "Babe like that, you could get a lot for her." His repetition was making his point.

She was squirming inside. She had to remind herself to trust Tommy and play along.

"Not interested."

A series of smoke rings arced toward a lazy ceiling fan.

"She'd bring maybe a good bike, a blonde chick slightly used, and any two of three weapons."

Tommy shook his head slowly as to not offend. "Thanks anyway."

"I had a score yesterday. Toss in a couple grand." He grinned. "And a pound of weed."

"Nope."

The Bear began to look angry. María Elena saw everybody in the bar was watching now. He checked around the bar and turned back to Tommy. "I got thirty of us, you got one of you. Maybe we take her anyway."

Tommy froze him with a wary eye. "Nope. Two points: First, she's worth six of your guys easy. She proved that very recently. Second, it don't matter. The real count is one of you: you. One of us: me."

A murmur ran through the bar.

María Elena was proud that Tommy said she was so good.

Tommy had given her instant street cred.

The Bear sat back in his chair and scratched his large belly. "Shit, I like that." He eyed María Elena with new appreciation. She gave him her best "Aw shucks, me?" look.

"We do business or not?" Tommy asked mildly. María Elena noted that he'd been using his left hand to drink and his right lay on the table near his waist, so that if necessary he could get to his gun faster. Then she watched the Bear and saw he was doing the same.

The Bear said, "Not that you scare me shitless, but what can I help you find?"

"A couple of AK's or AR-15's if you can find some, full auto model. No knock-offs. Something auto with power anyway. A long range rifle with a good scope if no AR-15's. Ammo. Some nine mike ammo."

"You starting a war?" asked Bear.

"Just a little sports hunting and target practice." Tommy smiled thinly.

"How I know you ain't the feds?"

Tommy shrugged. "You don't."

Jesus and Mary, he had balls, thought María Elena.

"Got any bona fides?" asked the Bear.

"Used to did, not anymore, I don't think."

"They were?" The Bear emptied his beer and held up three fingers on his left hand.

Tommy thought for a moment, his eyes far away. "Big Bobby. Downtown Brown. Partly Sonny. Chains. Sensitive Sammy. The Sarge. Cookies Galore."

"No shit? Way back in the day. Jesus, I only heard of them guys."

"Mostly dead and gone," said Tommy.

"Yeah, it happens, don't it?"

"To the best."

"You got a name?"

"Atkins."

The Bear thumbed toward María Elena. "She got a name?"

"Yep."

The Bear waited and Tommy said nothing else. María Elena gave the Bear a sly grin.

"Jesus," said the Bear.

The bartender, not the waitress, brought three mugs of beer. As he put them on the table he stared at María Elena's cleavage. He was a brother, and he was much older than Tommy. He wore a long, gray ponytail. His eyes flickered to Tommy and returned to her, then he stood upright abruptly and peered at Tommy. "Christ on a crutch."

"Hello, Phil," said Tommy. "How you been?"

Phil shook his head. "Been saving. Fixin' to retire. Lookin' to sell this joint." Phil turned to the Bear. "Don't fuck with this guy. Goddamn, Bear, he's the fucking Vicar." He looked at Tommy again. "You're different now. Was young and raw back in the day. Same guy, older, but you don't look much older like I do." His gaze switched back to Bear. "He's a motherfucking legend."

The Vicar?

"Well fuck a duck," said the Bear. "The Vicar. Whatever happened to you?"

Tommy shrugged. "I went away, did some other stuff. The feds got me eventually."

"And here you are in the flesh." The Bear shook his head. "A fuckin' legend, no? You don't look that old."

Tommy nodded at María Elena. "She don't think so either."

María Elena gave her now-obligatory half-smile.

"Goddamn, looking at you, I'm inclined to believe you."

"Those are my credentials."

"What you been doing since your hard time."

"This and that. South Flordia. Lately around Nogales."

The Bear squinted. "We got rampant rumors today about six dead hitmen down there. Know anything about it?"

"I don't kiss and tell. Nobody in his right mind would own up to something like that." Tommy shrugged.

"No connection between her and my six guys and your

mention of six guys a minute ago?"

Tommy smiled thinly without comment.

The Bear nodded and was more respectful. He pointed at María Elena. "One last time, seein's as you're the Vicar. I can up my offer. Change the blonde to a redhead you wouldn't believe. And guaranteed she ain't been rode hard and put away wet. Up the ante five, six thousand and a new bike, less than a grand on it."

María Elena guessed he meant thousand miles. Her grin told the Bear, "Thanks for the offer, I'm flattered, but I'm with him, the living legend," and was demure all at the same time.

"Tempting, Bear, I'll pass this time," said Tommy.

Phil the barkeep said, "Probably be advised to drop it, Bear. Be safer anyway."

The Bear looked like he didn't want to take that advice, so María Elena said, "That was flattering, Mr. Bear, thank you very much." She favored him with a grateful smile. "That must be short for Teddy Bear."

The Bear sighed and sat back and the situation was defused. His intelligent eyes belied the stereotype he was portraying.

The Bear and Tommy went off to make the trade. María Elena felt conspicuous in the biker bar, a woman alone. But she knew she was covered by the umbrella of the Vicar, Tommy in another one of his guises, and the Bear. Mostly, the bikers ignored her, but several watched her openly or obliquely and she didn't know whether to be flattered again or take offense.

She went to the bar and talked to the bar tender.

"Mr. Phil, can you tell me something?"

"And that is?"

"Tell me where this Vicar thing came from?"

"You mean the origin of the term?" He leaned forward on his elbows. "Those were the days. Wild and crazy. Nobody knew the Vicar when he showed up. I disremember what name he used, but it was something French sounding."

María Elena nodded. That fit with his tour in the French Foreign Legion.

"Pretty soon the Mexican mules—drug runners and such, the Vicar was terrorizing them big time, not to mention the human traffickers, the so called guides and coyotes who got paid to bring illegals in, were all scared to death of him. He was getting a reputation. Some wiseass biker called him the Vicar, since he brought the wrath of God down upon them. And he put the fear of God in all of them." Phil laughed, his pony tail bouncing. "And he sure did."

"He terrorized them?"

"Constantly."

"Why?" she wanted to know.

"Money, honey. They brought drugs into this country for money. The bikers at the time, especially the Vicar, made a living off them, and a good one at that. Tipped me big time, they did, I was able to buy this place. Pickings been slim since that crew been gone. They'd take the money off the drug runners, or they'd take the drugs and resell 'em wholesale. Mostly it was easier to get them on the way out with their money than to have to resell the stuff. And the human traffickers. They mostly carried the money they made with them, since most of them got partway into the desert and told the people they were guiding they needed more money to finish the trip and make sure the INS didn't catch them." Phil shook his head. "It was almost as if he had something personal involved."

María Elena began to understand how it came about that Tommy had money stashed seemingly all over the place.

"It was funny," continued Phil, "the Vicar was so effective that the Mexicans ganged up and went after him. They set up ambushes, sent gangs of them all trying to kill him off. This was their territory and other Mexicans claimed other territory so they couldn't just move elsewhere. A lot of 'em didn't make it back to Old Mexico. They even sent a known killer after him, a gunfighter out of Sonora. Top of the pyramid guy. The two played hide and seek and never resolved it between them."

"Juan Pablo?"

Phil looked at her in surprise. "You know of him?"

She nodded.

"One tough fucking Mexicano," said Phil.

"Not anymore," she said.

He cocked his head at her in question, but she thought maybe she shouldn't have said anything. Tommy was seldom if ever forthcoming. So she did not explain further.

Not wanting to drink, she wandered outside and went over to the gas station. It was stocked inside like a mini-food store. She looked around a found a rack full of baseball caps. She picked three, a #88: Dale Earnhardt, jr.; another 18: Kyle Busch; and an old #15: Tim Tebow. NASCAR and NFL, a neutral balance. She also bought a biker's lady skull cap and a leather pony tail holder. She decided she liked pony tails and this would help.

As she put her purchases in their jeep, the Bear and Tommy returned out of the desert in an old pickup. They pulled up next to the jeep and Tommy got out with a blanket covering several long packages. He moved into the lee provided by their Jeep. "Never know when the feds got their glasses on you."

Another lesson. She nodded.

Soon they were heading north on the north/south crossroad splitting the bar and the service station quick stop.

Ten miles to the north, Tommy pulled off onto a faint desert trail and drove for about two miles. He stopped in a clearing devoid of brush and cacti. María Elena wondered why they called this desert land when it wasn't all mountains of sand like in the movies. In the clearing sat an old picnic table.

Tommy spread a blanket over the picnic table and spread out the weapons he'd bought. There was enough ammunition for an army at war, she thought.

About two hundred yards out was an embankment. Tommy produced a silhouette human target and she took it and affixed it to the embankment.

When she got back, Tommy had the AR-15's loaded and ready. They fired about a hundred rounds each to get used to the weapon and the recoil, and one full auto load each. Tommy sighted in one of them with the scope.

"Never really liked sniper work," he said, "not even in Africa, though I did more than my share. We had guys there who could really shoot and they took out the enemy one by one from a distance time and time again, but they kept on coming. It makes a different war when the enemy doesn't care whether they live or die. Kinda like the terrorists nowadays. Onliest thing you can do is kill 'em and keep killing them."

María Elena felt a chill. This wasn't "her" Tommy talking, this was a killer, born or self-made, it didn't matter, but a killer, cold and professional none the less. This thinking scared her for she'd known what she was getting into: after all, had Tommy not killed a bunch of them chasing after her? But in the light of day, she began to understand a professional killer. She'd kind of known that, but she hadn't put it in those terms. She'd been thinking, sure he'd killed plenty before, but that was more of a byproduct of his situation than the focus of that situation. She began to understand she was dealing with a real hitman here. Is he a mass murderer? Shit, scary thought. Rephrase that to a mass killer. That didn't sound right, either. Make that a wholesale hitman. Better yet: an upgraded "Tommy this and Tommy that". All she knows is what she's seen; he's been tough, murderous even, but on her side: a good guy. This is what she chooses to believe. Maybe he was right; he never killed anybody who didn't need killing.

She crossed herself. Jesus, Mary, and Joseph. And she also began to understand that the odds against them were no longer overwhelming, not with Tommy. They were sort of even now. Should she take comfort in this? Suddenly, she was no longer pessimistic about the future.

Out here in the middle of nowhere, the shots did not reverberate or echo as much as the movies seemed to show. The sound was not as dramatic as it was in south Florida, likely a function of very low humidity here. And she was getting used to the hot desert sun, even though she was wearing her new #88 Dale, jr. hat.

Tommy was sitting at the table watching her curiously. "You

okay there, Florence?"

She sighed. She wasn't going to solve anything here today. "Yeah, sure. Just wondering." She sat down opposite him and unscrewed the top of the can of gun oil.

Tommy was breaking down his scoped AR-15. "That session back there at the biker bar got you thinking."

She started to disassemble her own AR-15. "Make that wondering."

"I got some stuff I don't need you to know worse than I don't need you to know some other stuff. But we established no secrets between us back at the cabin."

She doused a rag with gun oil. "Phil the barkeep told me some things and got me wondering. One was I'm thinking about going with a pony tail some."

Tommy nodded. "You look good in anything, Pocahontas."

"Thank you. The other thing is the drug runner mule war that you had going on back in the day."

Tommy screwed on the extension rod to the barrel cleaning brush and pushed it in and out. "We get done cleaning these, we should oughta clean our handguns, too. 'Bout time."

"Yes, Tommy. Go on, please." She went to the Jeep and got their handguns, most secreted inside the Jeep in various hide-outs. She brought them back and carefully set them on the side of the blanket. She removed the rounds from the cylinders of the revolvers and magazines from the automatics, checking the chambers, too.

"First of all, you note those bikers back there? Even in my day we didn't use a so called gang name or whatever. Not that Hell's Angels kind of stuff. We didn't want people to know anything about us. It was a money making enterprise, and apparently still is. We were entrepreneurs. By the same token, we never named the bar. Called it the 'No Name Bar.' My thing was robbing mules, drug runners so to speak. Some of them ran drugs while they were leading in families or groups of Mexicans and Guatemalans and Hondurans and others. They were fat with money. I never really hurt them; I just stuck them up and took their money, their stuff—the mules and guides, not the regular folk."

María Elena began to wipe down the handguns and oil the moving parts.

"One day," Tommy continued, reassembling his AR-15, "I knew the trail and ambushed these three guys. Just held them up. They had plenty of money and a backpack full of marijuana. I took their weapons and money and pot and let them go. They were all acting sort of weird, so I stopped and wondered." He shook his head sadly. "I back-tracked them. I had a trail bike I used for running out there near the border." He stopped as if remembering. He checked the magazine for the AR-15, loaded it, put it in the weapon and jacked a shell into the chamber. He pulled the magazine out and replaced the one round and rein-serted the magazine. He set the weapon down and leaned back. "You know I ain't fond of rape."

"I do."

"Soon, I found the family that those three hombres had led across the border and then deserted. One father, one mother, one teenage daughter, and one younger daughter, I don't know ages real well, but the kid was maybe seven or eight. They were all lying under an old, dead mesquite tree. The wife and daugh-ters had been brutally raped, um, front and back, and killed. The father was wounded but tied up and made to watch the rape and murder. He had to go to hell to get better. The funny thing? The three rapist and killers had tossed the women's underwear into the bare branches of the tree like some kind of fucking flag. Now they call it a 'rape tree.' Jesus fucking Christ, what a scene. Me, I been to war in Africa and seen rape and pillage and plunder, but that day took the cake. Fuck. The old man, he was in purgatory. I went over with my knife and began sawing through his bonds. His eyes begged me."

Tommy stopped talking.

María Elena moved to his side. "You don't have to finish."

"Yes, I do, hon. Jesus, I do. He said, 'Señor? Por favor?' Well, I fucking knew what he wanted and didn't waste any time. As

I brought my pistol up his eyes turned grateful. Then I put a bullet in the poor bastard's head." He shook his own head and wiped sweat from his forehead with his arm.

"That wasn't the end of it, was it?" she asked.

"No. Right then, I heard a whimper and saw the young girl move. I wrapped her own shirt around the wound and hopped on my bike and carried her off. I was going to the nearest hospital, come hell or high water." He took a deep breath. "Her hair was long and black and her eyes pleaded with me, but she didn't know what for. She flat didn't understand what the world was all about right then. It was awkward carrying her and negotiating draws and hills and cactus and rocks and what all. I flew over that terrain, jumping sand hills and ravines and wheeling like an off-road biker—which, in essence I was. Then she bled out and died before I got a couple of miles." He sighed again. "I took her back to be with her family. I dropped her off and chased down those three rapists and killers. Caught up with 'em at a road where another guy in a pickup was waiting for them." Tommy grinned. "You should have seen the look on their faces. Nobody had a weapon showing except the new truck driver. He had a small automatic and I shot him from afar. The three started running in different directions and I chased each one down and killed them." He shook his head. "I drove the truck with the bodies in it back to the mesquite tree. There was a shovel in the truck and I buried the family. The four dead guys I left for the vultures. But apparently some other mules came upon the remains first and the word got out."

María Elena collected the weapons and put them in the jeep. She brought back a couple of bottled waters from the cooler. "That would explain a lot. Soon you were at war."

He grinned. "A good one, too. After that, I took no prisoners. The downside was that they started crossing the border elsewhere. My income took a big hit. But enough of them came across to keep me going. The Border Patrol should have paid me. Soon they were sending hit teams and gangs to get me, and the other guys liked that for a while as it made for good sport for them. That's when old Juan Pablo showed up. We accidentally met at a bar one day in some town, maybe around Yuma or more toward the border. Neither one of us wanted to alert the law so nothing came of the encounter. We even shared a drink. I told him what had happened; he understood and told me he was a family man, too. But he'd already taken their money and his family was in jeopardy if he didn't pursue me. We left from different exits and played tag for about three months."

"What happened?"

"Well, my income was down, and there were too many hit teams looking for me and it made the whole area nuclear hot. My guys, the other bikers, were feeling the heat, too. So I packed it in and headed for Tampa and became an independent contractor there."

María Elena ticked off on her fingers. "Correct me if I'm wrong. Running the numbers as a kid in Tampa. Judge sent you off to join the Marines. In the Middle East when your time was up, you mustered out and joined the French Foreign Legion. When that was done, you wound up in southern Arizona in a biker gang. After that you were a hitman—I mean, contractor—"

"It wasn't all shooting work," Tommy said.

"Okay, contractor. Eventually, the feds and the staties nailed you and you went away to hard time and escaped and finished up in the Everglades."

"And here I am, just your luck, Pocahontas."

"It is my luck, sweetie," she said.

"We done talking about me? Never mind, we are." He began reloading. "Lately you've shown a rather lethal turn. What I'm saying is, is you done good at the cabin, you done good saving my ass, and you done good down in Nogales."

"A lethal turn?" She frowned. "I didn't think of it that way."

"You would not; that's why I'm bringing it up. I think you showed incredible acumen in both instances without having to learn the rules beforehand—sort of like I did."

"Rules? Rules for what? Lethality?" She helped finish reloading weapons and magazines.

"You betcha, Florence. That dustup at the cabin was instructional in a lot of ways. For instance, shoot what you can. And keep doing it until something or someone else appears. Then shoot them. You done that at the cabin. And you want to win, not be honorable. In a gunfight do whatever it takes: like running over them with your vehicle. Ain't fair, but they're dead and we are not. Keep shooting until everybody's dead or you're out of ammo. And speaking of that, given the opportunity, always reload. If you ain't pulling the trigger, feed shells into the cylinder if it's a revolver, change mags or snap rounds into the magazine. Know how many shots you have and how many you fired. If possible, always be on the move. It keeps 'em guessing and you safer. And it scares them good. Moving targets are harder to hit. When you're shooting, you don't have to do it in a hurry unless you're very good at it. More important to hit the target than to scare them." He smiled. "Although upon infrequent occasion, it is beneficial to scare them and it keeps their heads down while you flank them." He paused for breath. "And go for the kill, otherwise what's the point? Make your kills clean and quick, for seldom is there any reason to draw it out; and you never know if they will recover enough to shoot you while you're screwing around or reinforcements or cops will show up."

"Yes, professor." She began carrying weapons to the Jeep.

"You're pretty bright, college girl. Point is, use your head to maximize your advantage and ability to live through it all." He grinned at her. "Now that I think about it, I ain't seen you panic yet, and you've been a couple of places where you ought to have panicked."

"Thank you, Tommy."

"I guess that means I've been a good influence on you."

"Yes, Tommy." She stuck her tongue out at him. But as they finished loading, she admitted to herself that he was right: she'd learned a great deal from him. And not all of it had to do with killing people or shooting guns.

Before they left, he found a broken board lying around, one

which had held targets. He went off through the desert scrub out of sight and returned in five minutes. He brushed the sand off of a plastic bag and opened it. Inside she saw rolls of bills. Another stash.

A ten-foot high dust devil followed him out of the desert and they ran for the Jeep.

CHAPTER TWENTY-ONE: HIM

They came into Las Vegas heading south on U.S. 95. They'd been staying in Pahrump and today came into Vegas from the north. On one side of the road, they passed a lonely prison surrounded by rows of barbed wire and guard towers. It was so isolated and locked up it gave Tommy chills. Some miles later, on the other side of the road they drove past Creech Air Force Base where they fly the Predator drones all over the world.

The police car began to shadow them almost immediately when they drove into town.

"The rule of thumb I've established is: do it efficiently, cold, quick and clean. No layers of complexity. The more complicated you make it, the more chance for mistakes for it to go wrong, and for you to leave traces of yourself. Do it simply, and then get out and away. Leave 'em guessing." He smiled grimly. "That's my professional opinion."

Tommy saw the cop eye them from another lane. You'd think law enforcement would have more important things to do early on Friday evening. He wondered if this wasn't a bad luck omen.

"I see him," said María Elena. "We're going a bit faster than the speed limit, but we're running with the traffic."

"Problem is," said Tommy, "we don't know whether the guy who sold us this Jeep actually processed the paperwork." The guy had obviously known the two were not street legal or they wouldn't have bought the Jeep for cash as they did. Not to mention the fact that they'd paid him to fake insurance. "Our ID will hold up, but you never know about the registration."

They were already in Vegas, heading south. They passed a sign for W. Cheyenne Ave., a hospital, and another for Cheyenne Village. The cop slotted in behind them.

"Jeez, if this traffic isn't enough," said María Elena.

She whipped into the exit lane. The cop followed down the exit ramp.

"Sort of slump over to the right," she told him.

"You got a plan?" he asked as he tilted to his right and leaned against the window.

"I do. But maybe he'll peel off."

The cop stayed behind them as they hit the light on green.

"We might be able to outrun him, but they got lots of cops and radios. We got one Jeep."

"He's up on the steering wheel," said Tommy watching from his side mirror. "He's gonna pull us over."

"Did you know Kyle Busch is from Las Vegas?" she asked and whipped her own steering wheel to the right.

MOUNTAINVIEW HOSPITAL

She followed the signs to the emergency room and pulled up in front.

"Play sick," she said. "If he asks you have an episode of malaria coming on, you're cold and clammy, and you need to get treatment quick. I'll be right back."

As the cop came up behind them, she opened her door and ran inside. Tommy knew their weapons were well concealed, but they could afford no scrutiny. He saw the cop get out of his car and watch María Elena run inside. Christ, Vegas was hot as Nogales, maybe more so, even on an early Friday night. The cop hesitated, not certain what to do. That meant he hadn't run the tags yet or that the results were inconclusive.

The thing he did notice was María Elena. She was dressed in her black pullover dress, showing a lot of leg and a lot of cleavage. And her hair was piled atop her head in some kind of fancy formal affair he couldn't name if he had to. She looked good.

In twenty seconds, she came hurrying out with a wheel-chair, bent over it and showing a lot of breast. She threw the cop a beleaguered look and sort of shrugged her shoulders. She opened Tommy's door and snapped off his seatbelt. "Lean on me," she said. He did and collapsed into the wheelchair. She spun him around and headed into the emergency room. It was crowded, a definite sign of good luck. She kept pushing him until they were out of the line of sight from the pneumatic doors.

Tommy looked at the signs and ignored them. It looked like maybe they were supposed to check in at a triage desk maybe— or the finance desk first if you could, he didn't know. But they were efficient and very busy. They'd seen it all before. He wheeled himself alongside a chair where he could see a corner of the pavement outside the entrance. María Elena was getting into the Jeep and held up a finger to the cop, telling him to wait a second while she got out of the way and parked. The cop waved her off and got in his own vehicle and followed her through. Tommy saw him cut back to the way they came in and drive off. Moments later, María Elena came in and went over to Tommy.

"Jeez, I gotta pee again."

"Good exit strategy," he said quietly. "Me, too." An old lady had been watching them. Tommy asked her, "Where are the restrooms?" His voice was louder so that people would know that's where they were headed. The old lady pointed to a promi-nent sign. Tommy gave her a sheepish grin. "Thanks."

María Elena wheeled him toward the rest rooms. Of course they were wheelchair accessible. Afterwards, she pushed him farther down the corridor and toward the main entrance to the hospital, acting totally natural. Next to an unmanned courtesy desk were several wheelchairs for visitors and patients alike. The lobby was large and airy. She pushed him outside and past a row of palms and he climbed out gingerly and sat on a bench. While no one was particularly watching them, you still don't want to do something out of character. She wheeled the chair back inside to the wheelchair corral and came out and went into the parking lot. In two more minutes, she pulled up out front and he climbed in to the Jeep.

She didn't exit the hospital parking lot the way they'd come in, she went out the back and drove around and soon they found themselves on something called Peak Drive. Smart; don't give the cop another glimpse of them in case he was parked nearby doing paperwork or checking them out on the computer.

"See," said Tommy, "the really good thing about that hospital was if anybody recognized us or wanted to nail us, we had plenty of exits, and any hospital is a maze to locate people in. Doors on all sides of the hospital and cars all over you can steal and get away in a couple of minutes. Did you plan it that way?"

She gave him a half smile. "Yes and no. No because it was our only hope to dodge the cop and his questions. Yes, because I did remember your lesson about when you go into any building, always figure an alternate way out immediately. So, when I ran inside, I eyeballed other corridors and exits from the emergency room and knew we could run for it if we had to. Problem is that he saw us."

"Sort of. I kept my head down and he was busy looking at your tits."

"So were you." .

"Well, yeah, and with pleasure."

"Thank you, I think."

"And you in that killer dress gave credibility to an emergency room visit as if we were doing something else, something formal, and you had to bring me here. Also, your physical movements carried a sense of urgency. You done good, Pocahontas." He winked at her. "Now I know why I never suggested a bra holster for you. Don't want to ruin that fine profile."

She smiled acknowledgement at his praise.

"And another thing. It appears you've already learned the lesson: situational awareness. You go in a house, an office, a store, the first thing you do is figure out where the exits are. Boy Scout motto."

"And, in my case, the bathrooms," she said.

"Now we go hunting," he said.

CHAPTER TWENTY-TWO: HER

They drove to the strip and into the parking lot behind Caesars Palace. She dropped Tommy off and drove away. She went to the Luxor Hotel and parked as far out from the building as she could. When she was sure no one was watching, she slipped the dealer magnet plate she'd stolen in San Antonio onto the rear tag of the Jeep. Just in case they were looking for the tag the cop had seen. In a few minutes, she saw Tommy cruising up and down parking isles in a Buick.

She got out of the Jeep and flagged him down. He pulled up to block the Jeep and she moved the stuff wrapped in a blanket into the Buick. From there they went to Caesars Palace and María Elena moved into the driver's seat of the Buick and he got out. Later, she was sitting in the Buick at the crowded Mandalay Bay when he called on their recently purchased pre-paid phones. "Some kind of green Ford F-150 pickup," he said and disconnected.

Ten minutes later he stopped in front of her in the pickup. She waited for two cars to navigate around them and got out and slid the long blanket wrapped package through his open door. He slammed the door and accelerated away.

Now it was all up to her.

Having plenty of time, she drove slowly. Flamingo to Durango to Alta Drive and then she was on Rampart Boulevard and pulling into the Rampart Casino. She drove close to the front guessing that's where the Maybach would be parked and she was right. She parked nose out on the Marriott side where she could exit to Canyon Rim Drive quicker than the exit for the Maybach on North Rampart just like it had two nights ago. She peeled off her fancy gloves and put them in her purse—right alongside her pistol. She thought about but was certain she had left no prints; nor had Tommy when he'd stolen the Buick. The ignition lock was a mess, though. Shortly, that wouldn't matter.

She went inside and wandered through the casino. It certainly was more sedate than the casinos way over on the strip. The Rampart was tucked right into the Red Rock section of western Las Vegas. As a matter of fact, it sat at the foot of Charleston Mountain, part of the range between Vegas and Pahrump where they were staying. Just on the far side of Pahrump, Death Valley sweltered.

The Rampart Casino had much less smoke than other casinos. Maybe they had better air handlers. This thought gave her an idea. She went and bought a pack of cigarettes and got a pack of matches to go with it. Cigarettes sometimes provide a good cover.

She found Hamilton in a semi-private area playing poker. She'd found his picture online on Facebook and she and Tommy had followed him on and off for a week. She was still sort of jealous about the Maybach 62 he was using as a limo. An Internet search told her that car started around five hundred K. While she was wondering how people lived like that, she coincidentally wondered at living like that herself. She decided that if she had that kind of money, she'd be more than willing to spend it—though not necessarily in such a flashy manner. Yeah, right, like that dream would ever happen. Although, she admitted, Tommy did keep coming up with bags of one hundred thousand dollars.

She searched for the chauffeur and found him sitting off to the side like a spectator watching the action. She memorized what each was wearing and then went outside the front entrance as if to take a break and have a smoke. She was awkward trying to smoke the cigarette since she had never done so in the past.

She wandered off to the side to be out of the way, but also so she could keep an eye on the Maybach.

After that, she went to a bar from where she could see the exit to watch for Hamilton and the chauffeur and drank two glasses of tonic water.

Four men hit on her with varying degrees of seriousness.

She continuously checked her watch and looked over at the entrance.

The bald bartender eventually stopped in front of her. "Look, lady, you're obviously not a hooker or you wouldn't have turned those men down. But management here might not know that. We kind of discourage soliciting here."

She gave him a wry smile. "I ought to be, the last guy offered me a grand for two hours." She shook her head and looked at her watch again. "It looks like I've been stood up."

"Jesus. What incredible dumbass would stand you up?"

She shrugged. "He won't do it again." She stood off the bar stool. "What a worthless son of a bitch."

"If you want to get even with him...?" he asked with raised eyebrows.

"No, but thanks for listening." She left an appropriate tip not wanting to over tip and be remembered. But, she thought, a little late for that. Her plans were such that she didn't think that the police would think they had to review all of the obligatory camera footage. They couldn't have enough manpower, even if they connected her with the deed.

But she left anyway. Outside, she dialed Tommy's cell. "They're beginning to notice me—"

"No, shit?"

"Never mind the sarcasm, Tommy. Do you have line of sight on the Maybach?"

"I do."

"I'll wait in the Buick then, until you call."

"Done, Pocahontas. Good luck."

"Yes, dear. You too."

Before she stepped into the Buick, she pulled a rodeo vest

out of the back seat. Tommy had bought it. It was designed for bull riders, bronco riders, clowns, others. It was built to absorb shock and blows and protect from other direct trauma. It was made of high density foam and layers of fiber and resins. This one had an outer cover of leather. María Elena zippered and Velcroed herself into the thing, grateful that Tommy had made her try it on earlier.

At one thirty in the morning, María Elena was bored out of her mind. She was thinking about smoking a cigarette for real just to stave off the boredom. Her cell rang twice and stopped.

This was it.

She reviewed what she had to do in steps. She checked to see if she had what she needed in her purse. For the third time. She started the Buick.

The last time they'd followed Hamilton, the Maybach had left by the Rampart Casino entrance/exit onto North Rampart Boulevard and turned right, driving south alongside Angel Park golf course and past Canyon Run Drive.

The phone rang again and this time she picked it up. "They're on the move. Must be nice to have parking up front."

"I'm on my way, Tommy." She put the phone on speaker and sat it beside her. She drove out the Marriot exit toward Canyon Run.

Timing was everything. She tried to go slow and hoped there weren't any cameras to identify her. She'd parked in the most remote place she could find and departed the car and approached the car later in a circuitous route with her head down, and then slid in the more protected passenger's side. Theoretically, it shouldn't matter.

"I'm going slowly and there's no traffic right now," she said, surprised her voice was so calm.

"I think the timing is about right," Tommy told her. "That's what dry runs and watches are for."

"Okay. I'm turning onto Canyon Rim right now."

"You're doing fine, college girl. There they come. Nice damn car."

"Yeah, too bad."

"We hope. Okay," Tommy said, "his blinker is on to turn right onto Rampart and you still got no traffic. Nice of them to accommodate us at such an accommodating time."

"Are you okay, Tommy?"

His voice turned cold. "Don't worry about me. Do your part. I'm professional at this."

"Okay, I was just…okay."

"They're accelerating toward the light and the intersection with you. They have a green and no other traffic to trigger a change if that's the way it works. Go ahead and accelerate."

She did so, the intersection of Rampart and Canyon Rim right ahead. According to plan, she killed the phone as soon as she spotted the Maybach. She stuffed it into her purse and tugged her gloves a little tighter. She sped up because she could always slow down before the collision, which in fact was her intention so the impact wouldn't affect her as much.

The red light ahead seemed to glow with a special fury.

The Maybach entered the intersection, and she had to goose the accelerator.

She shot into the intersection, touched the brake, swung the wheel to hit with her front left quarter panel, and slammed on the gas again.

The Buick slewed into a four-wheel drift and when she accelerated, the car straightened out and smashed into the right rear door of the Maybach. The collision was a grating cacophony of metal on metal and tires screeching, reminiscent of a NASCAR wreck at Talladega.

"Good thing I'm an excellent driver," she said aloud.

The airbag deployed immediately, banged her back into the seat, and she felt like she was suffocating. She'd wanted to disable that function, but Tommy had nixed the idea in favor of her safety. For some reason she could not explain, some kind of smoke or gas came out and blew out the window. Maybe CO_2 spillage? Dust? Propellant? She found she had no idea what inflates airbags. Even as the cars continued to spin in their macabre dance, she pulled out her Swiss Army knife which was stuck open into the passenger seat, half buried for quick access of the largest blade. She jammed the knife into the airbag quickly several times and it began to deflate. She pushed it in to hurry the process as she folded the knife back and dropped it into her purse. When she got out, she didn't want to have to return to the car for any belongings.

Suddenly, there was an eerie silence. Her driver's door still worked, but she'd left all the windows open in case she had to crawl out, not to mention it minimized the danger of flying glass. In the silence she reflected appreciation for what bull riders went through.

She started to climb out of the Buick and her left side complained. She remembered the airbag hitting her. Maybe she was turned in the seat wrong. She remembered her head bouncing around but without whiplash. If it hadn't been choreographed safely like it was, Tommy wouldn't have gone with this plan. But it was so much easier to get to Hamilton without a bunch of goons around. She pushed the limp airbag aside.

She got out shrugging her purse over her left shoulder. She made sure she went around to the Maybach's left side where Hamilton and the driver would get out. The choreography had been specifically designed for Hamilton, if he were able, to get out. If the wreck had involved a male or several males, he would likely have remained locked in the car while the body-guard checked out the situation. Their plan hinged on Hamilton exiting the Maybach—or else María Elena was going to have to smoke him out or kill him herself. Tommy didn't want that. He'd insisted she do no killing other than in self-protection. She'd been willing, but he was adamant. Maybe this was better. On the other hand, she was bait, and a willing accomplice in the eyes of the law.

She staggered around as if dizzy and disoriented. As she did so, she checked both directions on Rampart and back down Canyon Rim. She saw no other cars yet, though there was some activity in the Rampart parking lot if she could tell by moving lights.

The burly driver/bodyguard was pushing himself out of the Maybach shaking his head.

No activity came from the back seat, so María Elena banged on the window and shouted, "Are you all right in there?" They'd already decided Hamilton would not get out of the car should there be one or more men involved.

The door rattled and began to open. Good, the impact hadn't affected this side of the automobile as much. The door did screech as if out of alignment.

Hamilton's left hand was atop the door frame pulling himself up and out.

María Elena stepped toward the driver, ignoring Hamilton. "Can you understand me?"

He looked at her strangely. It was not a question he expected. His eyes catalogued her fancy short black dress and the tight bull riding vest above her waist. The discontinuity seemed to stop him in his tracks.

She spared a glance toward the dark golf course lining the intersection. She could see nothing in the dark shadows. "Do you hear me?" she asked again, tensing her shoulders. Her right hand snaked into her purse to seek the butt of her gun.

"Yeah," said the bodyguard, her move to her purse alerting him to something. This guy was sharper than she would have thought.

Out of the corner of her eye, she saw Hamilton coming around the back door toward them.

"It's going down," she said, trying hard to keep her voice level. "If you move at all, you will die. Discipline yourself."

The nearby blast of a high powered rifle came simultaneously with Hamilton slamming up against the car, pushing the door closed with force against it. Another shot and his midsection exploded and she fancied she could hear the bullet plow through him and prang against the metal of the door. Hamilton slid down to the pavement already dead.

The driver was frozen.

"Very good," she said to him, his eyes still staring at Hamilton. As much death as she'd seen lately, up close and personal it still wasn't pretty. She thought she smelled blood.

The driver sort of lifted his arms as if in a holdup.

María Elena pulled out an envelope and handed it to him.

"What the fuck's that?" he asked, voice harsh.

"Look inside," she told him.

He did so. "Son of a bitch. I know them. Six of the guys. Their drivers' licenses. All dead in Arizona."

"You got it," María Elena said, knowing time was flying. "Here's the deal. Paybacks are hell. Got that? You tell that to whoever controls Hamilton. We know he acted alone in that hit attempt, but this is a warning. Anybody else wants in, they end up the same. Got that?"

"Jesus. Yes, ma'am."

"What's your name?" she demanded.

"Tony Caputo."

"Give me your wallet."

He dug into his rear pocket.

"Slowly."

He pulled out his wallet and handed it to her.

"Face the golf course and don't move."

He did so, and she could tell he knew full well he was facing the shooter.

"Remove your handgun, please. Slowly."

His right hand went beneath his jacket and brought out an automatic.

"Hold it upright behind your head."

He did so. María Elena saw a car coming down the casino exit. She continued by the numbers. She took the weapon and stuffed it inside her vest. Better safe than sorry.

"All right, Tony, here's your wallet back." She slipped it into his back pocket under the jacket. "Here's the deal. I have your license and I know where to find you. Do not, I repeat, do not describe me, either to the police or to your friends. Understand?"

"Yes, ma'am."

"You are the messenger. All you know is that some man crashed the car and you heard gunshots and then it was all over. The cops don't need to know about the licenses, but your friends do. We have a source or we wouldn't have been able to pull this off." The lie came easily. "I say again, you describe me and you will die. Get back in the car."

The car at the Rampart casino exit turned away from them, but now a jobber's box truck was headed their way.

Caputo started to climb into the wrecked Maybach and she hurried into the brush alongside the road. María Elena didn't take the time to check the cross arms from which the traffic control lights hung; had there been a traffic-cam, Tommy would have taken it out with a silenced shot before the action began. She walked up a small dune covered with grass and started down the other side when a flashlight blinked once. She was grateful for clear skies and bright stars. She could see well enough. Soon she climbed into the golf cart and Tommy sped off.

"How you doing there, María Elena?"

"I'm okay. It was a bit unsettling." She shifted the AR-15 to accommodate her legs.

"Your first real operation and you handled it perfectly. Do you think the bodyguard will do what you told him?"

"I don't know, Tommy. He's a tough guy. The crash and then Hamilton dying didn't seem to bother him much."

"That's good," Tommy said. "That means he's really professional and we can probably trust him to figure the odds and act properly."

Without lights, they sped along a cart path, and then cut across a fairway. María Elena was becoming confused of their location. After three minutes she heard sirens. She wasn't certain she could get used to this world. Then she thought about Diego and her father and what had happened to her and Tommy since that fateful day. So be it, she thought. She knew she was much safer with him than on her own or with somebody else.

"Stop the cart."

He slowed and stopped. "We got no time to waste."

"I don't care." She hopped out and, pulling up her dress and pulling down her panties to her knees and squatted alongside a palm tree. When she finished, she stood and adjusted her clothing and took off the vest as quickly as she could.

When she climbed back into the golf cart feeling much better, Tommy said, "In poetry or song, they'd call that a refrain."

She leaned against him and dropped her head to his shoulder for a moment and felt much better.

Shortly, they returned the golf cart to the cart barn where no one would know they ever used it. They headed into a dark parking lot sticking to the shadows in case of any security cameras. In the pickup, soon they were on their way.

They drove back and ditched the pickup and got in their Jeep and drove down Interstate 15 to San Bernardino in California.

They stayed the following night in a roadside motel.

When they finished making love, María Elena said, "It gets better and better."

"You are pumped up on adrenalin and need to burn it off."

"Okay, let's burn off some more."

Later, he said, "I knew there was something wrong the first time. You were favoring your side. You got sore ribs, maybe a broken one." He traced the bullet scar on her shoulder, too. "You have bad luck on this side. Dislocation, bullet wound, now a busted rib."

"It's okay, Tommy."

"No, it's not. Doctor Atkins will fix it first thing tomorrow."

"Good, I'm busy tonight." She snuggled against him. "Querido."

* * * *

In the morning he taped her ribs. "Can you imagine had you not worn the vest?"

"Thank you, Tommy."

They bought a newer and more comfortable Ford Explorer and traded in their Jeep. Tommy explained this might leave a slight trail if anybody could pick it up and point them heading consistently west.

Then they headed east on Interstate 10.

It was coming to a head, she thought. They were going to finish it.

CHAPTER TWENTY-THREE: THEM

"Don Diego?"

"*Sí?*

"Susan Quantrell calling for you. Confirm with your caller ID."

"Yes, of course. It checks."

"Standby, I'll put her on, sir."

Sandy nodded to Susan and Susan picked up the handset. She punched the lighted button and said, "Don Diego, good of you to take my call. We've been trying to contact you."

"I have been out of the country."

"There should be several voice mails for you to call and some emails, also."

"Forgive me, Ms. Quantrell, for my inattention to detail. I've been so busy, you understand?"

"Quite frankly, no." Suzie Q emphasized the no part.

Linda, listening on a headset, gave her thumbs up.

Suzie smiled an acknowledgement. "I understand Don Carlos Vasquez passed away?"

"He did, Ms. Quantrell. We buried his ashes."

Okay, Suzie thought. No CSI stuff, no pathology report.

"And his daughter?" Suzie thought how he answered this one would be telling.

He paused. "I'm sorry, Ms. Quantrell. What business is it of yours and your joint task force?"

Got him. "It is the reason for this telephone call. We haven't received the annual manpower report from you." Suzie had long ago figured out you can baffle 'em with bureaucratic bull shit. People tend to believe administrative details.

Don Diego García said, "What has that to do with my wife?"

"The last half dozen years or so, she's been the one who submits all the requisite reports."

"I do not know these things."

"A good leader takes care of details," she chided.

He did not answer.

She had to hit him harder. "There are also rumors, Don Diego, of her demise. She's an officer in 13 de enero. I was just checking to see before I check with Miami-Dade police."

Linda leaned forward in her usual visitor's chair.

"Ah, this is quite embarrassing."

"How's that?"

"I do not know her whereabouts."

Suzie grinned. "Your own wife? That is somewhat odd."

"It is something for which I am ashamed, no? Let me explain. We have been estranged for many years. Lately our relationship has turned worse, I do not know why, but I suspect another man. In fact, I've been trying to hide my humiliation since I think she ran off with that man." His voice trailed off. He didn't sound too ashamed to Suzie. He went on, "We do not need her services any longer. Frankly, I cannot get along with her and we will not coexist in 13 de enero." He paused. "Are you being polite? Perhaps you know something considering all of your resources?"

Linda nodded her appreciation for Don Diego's ability to turn things around.

"No, nothing at all," Suzie lied glibly. "We follow 13 and update info as things change. We have a proprietary interest in 13 de enero."

"I don't have to report to you, Ms. Quantrell."

"Don't be counter-productive, García. We get reports from you for our investment in 13. Additionally, we get intel, and that's as far as I go on a non-secure phone."

"Madame, the United States government has not given us—or any group like ours—any money for a long time."

"Quite the contrary. You are equipped with our surplus equipment and weapons. Also, your organization exists on our land." Suzie let some anger into her voice. "True, they stopped funding your groups, but my JTF contributes by paying plenty of money for, ah, assets in place." Translation: We're supporting your spies in Havana and in the government of Cuba.

"Ah, yes, Ms. Quantrell. We thank you for your largesse. We are surrogates for America on the front lines and I am supposed to thank you?"

"No," she said emphatically. "Thank the American taxpayer." She left it at that.

"Then we have nothing else to discuss, madam."

She was going to get nothing further from him. "Please submit the required reports in a more timely manner, Don Diego."

"Of course. And if you will give the most beautiful Ms. Landover my regards?"

Suzie raised her eyebrows and punched the button then hung up the handset. "What did that mean?"

Linda frowned. "If I didn't know better, I'd think it was a shot across our bow."

"Should we extrapolate something is going down and he won't be involved with 13 de enero any longer?" Suzie sat back pondering. "They have good political connections."

"It could mean anything." Linda stood. "I need a smoke."

"One might be able to read between the lines that he is threatening me, us, through you." Suzie checked her coffee and it was cold.

"What's our next move?" asked Linda.

"It is time for the mighty hammer of the entire weight of the United States government to come down hard. Tell Sandy to schedule us an aircraft for in the morning. Full weapons issue. Alert the Miami office of the FBI for on-call assistance, if necessary."

"And Mr. Atkins and Miss María Elena?"

"I don't know yet, Linda. But they are not integral to our mission—that we know of. We have to go our own way and get involved now. Things are not working correctly and we must fix same. It'll also fit in our mission review."

"I'm interested in why this mobster in Vegas wanted them or him dead. And reward? How much was it and why for starters. This wildcard shit doesn't fit well." Linda stood.

"Perhaps check with Org Crime and see if they have anything new?" Suzie didn't trust anyone nowadays.

Ten minutes later, Linda was back. "They hadn't relayed the info, Suzie. The mob guy in Vegas—Hamilton—was gunned down last night." Linda explained the circumstances. She finished up, "And the bodyguard, one each Tony Caputo, said he saw nothing, some guy in the dark crashed into them and then ran away. After that came immediate gunshots. Hamilton becomes another good mob guy, dead."

"More tears to shed," said Suzie.

"Not much evidence," Linda continued. "The local cops suspect a hitman concealed in a nearby golf course. But no signs of nothing, nowhere."

"More extrapolation. We know the guy's name in Tampa who put out the reward, we go find him and set up surveillance and along will come Atkins and the girl."

"For what good that does us," Linda said. "Though admittedly he is a federal fugitive."

"Why didn't we know right away from our flag in that vaunted FBI system?"

Linda looked triumphant. "Nobody would talk, but I know plenty of people. It was shortstopped by the assistant Attorney General."

Suzie said, "The AAG? Why?"

"Dunno, but the U.S. Marshal Service was part of the notification."

"Curiouser and curiouser, said the cat."

"Which reminds me, we gotta get a dog sitter for the damn

dog," Linda said pointedly. "If we can."

Sandy came in and cleared her throat.

Suzie and Linda stopped and looked at her.

"Something strange," Sandy said. "I coordinated for the aircraft and got it scheduled and everything. I was finishing up some details and the phone rang. That Deputy U.S. Marshal named Eisenberg wanted to know who it was for and the destination."

"I'll be dipped in spit," said Suzie.

Sandy went on. "I told him I was just following orders and if needed to know anything, he should talk to you."

"Very good," said Suzie. "He wants us to call him."

"Not exactly," said Sandy, "he's waiting on hold, line three."

"Ah. And how long has he been on hold?"

"During your alleged meeting while I waited for an opportunity to break in. Maybe five minutes."

"Good move, Sandy. Linda, give her a raise."

"Tell that to HR and payroll," said Linda.

"Yeah, right." Suzie swung her swivel chair and picked up the phone, punching line three.

She put on her sugary voice. "This is Susan Quantrell."

"Hey, Quantrell, your raiders won't tell me what I want to know."

"Deputy Marshal Eisenberg?"

"You already know that." His voice was controlled anger.

"Oh, yes, that's right." Voice still sickeningly sweet.

"Where are you going tomorrow?"

"That's classified, Deputy Eisenberg."

"I'm cleared."

"This isn't a secure line. Besides, need to know rules apply."

"The AAG says I need to know and, by extension, the AG."

"Is that a threat?" Suzie asked, voice going from soft to steel. She could play these bureaucrat infighting games all day.

"Okay. Gloves off. Here's the official message: Hands off Atkins."

"This JTF doesn't take orders from you."

"You'll have confirmation through the deputy director of the FBI and the deputy director of the CIA."

"My, my, you throw your weight around, Mr. Eisenberg."

She could imagine him rethinking. "Ah, be advised, Ms. Quantrell, that these orders come from the AAG."

"Not you?"

"I do what I'm told."

Suzie turned to Linda and spoke so Eisenberg could hear. "He's throwing his weight around but covering his ass and grabbing your basic deniability."

Linda just nodded, knowing the comment was for him, not her.

"Okay, Deputy Eisenberg. Noted." She hung up the phone.

"Jeez," said Linda.

"We're proscribed from contact with one each Tommy Atkins, and involvement with him in any fashion."

Sandy scratched her head. "That ties our hands."

Linda smiled and shook her head. "Nope. Suzie said nothing about María Elena. She belongs to our portfolio. It might just be coincidence that Atkins is along with her. But we'll do what we need to."

"Right," said Suzie Q. "We're on the same page."

"All systems go," said Linda.

They were perched on the top step to the wooden porch. Two Brentwood rockers sat on the wrap-around porch circled by vintage wooden railing, but the two eschewed the comfort. The Virginia night was clear. The dog was sniffing every tree and bush like it was his first time out in the back yard.

Suzie Q had a giant mug of coffee laced with cheap brandy; her reasoning for the cheap brandy was if you put it in coffee, what difference did that make?

Linda L sipped on a Tanqueray martini, more of which she had in a shaker sitting next to her on the porch. "The update after you left is that I talked to a friend in Interpol. The French Foreign Legion is legendary in their personnel security; it's one of the things which make Legion service attractive. The way I heard it is that when you join, you select a name and that becomes your Legion name. Nobody knows your real name."

"So what difference does that make?" Suzie asked, swirling the dregs of her coffee and brandy.

"Maybe it's more traditional nowadays," said Linda. "Back in the pre-information and computer age, it might have been important to remain anonymous—or to hide your past more so. In essence, a man could flat out disappear that way."

"Consequently," said Suzie, "our man Tommy Atkins took a name."

"Yep. And their military record of service is unavailable, another guarantee of privacy for the same reasons. They are jealous of that security and privacy. That being said, my friend in Interpol did me a favor. He somehow got access to those records. But the records of that era have not been digitalized so he had to read them. He wasn't allowed to copy information or bring the records out."

Suzie upended her cup over the side of the stairs. Fluffy chased a firefly quietly. Were Fluffy a barking dog, Fluffy would not be a part of their family. "That's a long way to get there, Linda. So he gave an oral report of Atkins' Legion service?"

Linda nodded. She sipped her martini. "He gave me an oral summary. And, I might add, he was suitably impressed."

"Well, he's French, isn't he?"

"He is."

"There you go." Suzie unscrewed the martini shaker and poured some into her mug.

"Our Mr. Atkins—"

"Was that his Legion name?"

"No. He used Dumas, Alexander Dumas. He was a scout and a sniper. Did the Kolwezi thing and then operations in Zaire and neighboring Angola against the mercenary Cubans and the Popular Movement for the Liberation of Angola guerrilla group, the MPLA."

"I've read about that conflict," Suzie said. "Those Angolan

MPLA were badass mofos and the Cubans played the game with them against the West backed UNITA. The Cubans and the MPLA were backed by the Soviets."

"According to my friend, after Atkins there were a lot less MPLA and Cubans running around cluttering the landscape. When he was a sniper he had seventy-six confirmed kills, even though that wasn't his normal position. When on patrol or a mission, he was a scout and spent a lot of time hunting them alone, out in the jungle or more appropriately in the areas they roamed through all that dry brush and rock and plains. Not certain, but I'd think Mr. Atkins counted for more than a hundred one on one dead, likely more in firefights. Back in the day they took no prisoners. Those MPLA liked to rape and apparently our boy Tommy took exception to same."

"Good for him." Suzie upended her cup, draining the martini. "Not much has changed in that part of Africa after all these years," she said, shaking her head sadly. She poured more for herself and offered some to Linda. "I know a guy in French Intel. I'll check with him, too."

"No, thanks. Still nursing this one. It occurs to me, Suze, that our Miss María Elena has unleashed a plague upon the land—"

"Define plague."

"Your point is taken. So far we're down upwards of twenty scumbags…"

Suzie said, "And the Hamilton hit?"

"An important man in the mob, but not top level. Close, though. Be interesting what happens to what's his name who offered the reward?" Linda tapped a cigarette out of a Marlboro hard pack and lighted it. "Hard to find Lucky Strikes anymore."

"Santana. An old man. Tampa mob. He's retired to Sarasota now and probably senile."

"We won't know. The AAG and the AG warned us off."

"That's not a bad thing for us, Linda. If there's any consistency or synchronicity, Santana will be dead in the week."

"The Marshal Service has set up surveillance. I think they think they're gonna get Atkins and the woman."

"Right now I got my money on the two. Wonder if they're a couple now? Adversity has a way of dictating those kinds of things."

"Boy does it ever." Linda grinned and drained the martini shaker into her glass.

"Makes you wonder, too," said Suzie looking up at the stars, "what is a killer, nay, a hitman, a mob guy, a Legionnaire, an escaped convict, and hell, an outlaw biker doing running around using the name 'Tommy'?"

"Ain't something I've been worrying about," Linda pointed out.

"The name's not imposing. But did you ever read Kipling?"

"Doesn't everybody?" asked Linda.

"Nope, and that is a sad thing."

"Got it." Linda snapped her fingers. "Tommy this and Tommy that, and Tommy do some shit again, I can't remember all of which."

"That's the one. Kind of literary, isn't it?"

"If you say so, Suze. Are you trying to say we got us a literary hitman on our hands?" Linda inhaled and blew a smoke ring.

"I dunno, Linda, Maybe it simply falls under the heading that everybody's different."

"Yeah, right. Different."

"I'm beginning to think we need to talk to this one man and one woman wrecking crew."

"Well, the jet awaits in the morning. I hereby claim tonight formally fulfills my turn to walk the damn dog. Your turn next."

Suzie whistled. "Here, Fluffy. Time to go in." She stood. "And Linda? A point of all of this? I'm warning you to caution. You're good, probably the best we've got. But I'm not sure even you can take down Mr. Atkins."

Linda flicked the burning end of the cigarette into the yard and field stripped the remainder. She smiled a challenge at Suzie. "Oh?"

CHAPTER TWENTY-FOUR: HIM

It all started out so normal, but then became too complicated, and turned into a comedy of errors.

Tommy Atkins slid through the night. Rusty night-operation skills he hadn't used since the biker days in Arizona and before that in Angola and Zaire kicked in. While he could use rain as a cover, the Sarasota skies held no clouds.

He and María Elena had stolen an eighteen foot fishing boat docked at a dark house on the mainland. They'd paddled out into Sarasota Bay and started the outboard. In a little while, they were paddling again to a secluded cove on Longboat Key. They beached the boat and gathered their gear. They walked past a few mangroves along a lip of a beach and up a path onto the private and secure grounds of "CAPTIVA BAYSIDE, AN EXCLUSIVE BAYSIDE CONDOMINIUM RESIDENCE." A set of docks housed a dozen cabin cruisers and yachts. Another leg of the dock berthed smaller boats, pleasure and deep sea fishing boats, for the residents. Less than a half mile to the west sat the Gulf of Mexico. The same company had built a similar condominium tower on the Gulf.

They circled the single tower building avoiding security lighting. Around to the side, they found a dark place in a clump of Australian pine. Tommy set the special gear down.

María Elena was already dressed in an expensive pair of light blue silk pajamas and matching robe with matching slippers. She waved a few mosquitoes away. They didn't bother Tommy who was used to clouds of the damn things in the Glades.

Tommy picked up some road flares and a crowbar. He nodded to María Elena and reached out and ruffled her hair. "Bed hair," he said.

She gave him a big, wide smile of confidence as he melted into the dark.

He took his time and soon was at the delivery end of the condominium. A loading dock was lighted with a bracketed lamp, and in the pool of light on the dock Tommy saw the now-ubiquitous camera perched in the corner above the door.

Using long forgotten skills, he maneuvered to just outside the pool of light, where a dumpster carelessly left askew on the dock blocked the camera angle. He checked the area again. The rent-a-cop security hadn't shown a propensity for cruising around back here during their preliminary surveillance, but you always check.

Tommy double-checked his equipment and pulled out a twenty-two with a silencer—not that you'd need one way back here, but you always err on the side of caution. His first shot pranged loudly off the light's cage, but the second shattered it. Swiftly Tommy scrambled up the stairs alongside the dock, keeping along the forward wall just in case the spillover light was good enough to make him out. He slunk behind the dumpster hugging the wall until he reached the door. He stretched up with the crowbar and smashed the camera.

It didn't matter if that triggered a security response, because they'd be heading this way soon anyway.

Tommy smashed the door lock with the crowbar and jammed the crowbar between the door and the doorframe. It popped immediately with little complaint—cheap construction. Probably the contractor's brother-in-law. Tommy went inside and hurried down a large corridor to a double door marked GARBAGE. This was the same in most condominiums. The garbage chutes drop garbage to one room on the bottom floor into a dumpster. When that gets full, the maintenance staff rolls it aside and slides another into its place. Then they push the full ones outside on garbage day for waste management to come and empty. In the garbage room, Tommy found two full dumpsters. He snapped two road flares and tossed them into the first dumpster and repeated with the second. The most important dumpster was the one under the garbage chute, and it was half full. He lighted two more flares and insured they caught the contents on fire. The smoke would rise up the garbage chute and invade all the floors above. Tommy propped the double-doors open and went down the hall and opened another door exposing stairs upward. The stairwell would serve as a good flue. Using the crowbar, he crushed the arms of the pneumatic door opener so it would swing free and remain open. He ran up two flights and found the garbage rooms in the second and third floors, propped the doors open along with the garbage chute doors to insure the smoke would flood at least part of the building. He hurried back down the stairs. Fortunately no one was about at this late hour.

While this plan was mostly María Elena's and designed to minimize bloodshed, he disliked it for its complexity; he did like it more though, because it kept him from attacking an upstairs condo which would be guarded by professionals, thus decreasing the risk big time.

On the wall outside the garbage room a red CO_2 bottle hung from a bracket. He snatched it off the wall, broke the safety wire, and pulled the safety pin. Then he set the fire bottle down against the opposite wall.

Smoke was beginning to fill the corridor. He found another door leading toward the front of the building. He insured that door would not close. He hurried down another corridor and found community rooms and an exercise room full of aerobic and strength training equipment. He ignored these. He located the main door to the front lobby of the building and peeked out. A security guard sat at a reception desk.

Tommy turned and made his way back. The corridors were full of smoke. He thought about lighting more flares in some of the community rooms to set off insulation to generate more smoke, but he didn't want to burn the damn building down and kill a bunch of people. A couple of dumpster fires ought to do what he wanted without indiscriminate killing. He started coughing.

Suddenly, the alarm went off. Finally. Then the sprinklers kicked in and soaked him, which wasn't what he wanted. He retrieved the CO_2 bottle. On the landing, he dropped another flare into the waiting dumpster.

He made his way back to the concealed spot where they had parted. Above him, lights were coming on up and down the floors. He smiled at the inconvenience all the residents would endure because of what he was doing. María Elena was already gone. Upon reflection, he decided those pajamas were definitely her. She had a knack for picking out the right clothing and wearing it well. He slaked water off himself and picked up his other gear from the ground.

He was already wearing black work boots, so that went with the firefighter's overcoat and hardhat. He put them on and immediately began sweating. He moved back toward the water and flung the crowbar as far as he could into the bay. Then he returned to a vantage point at the edge of the pines.

Already he could hear sirens. He sweated more. He checked his weapons. He moved silently through the brush and pines around to the side where he could observe the parking lot. Most of the building was alight now. People were beginning to stream out the front doors and into the parking lot.

A fire engine and an ambulance swung into the circle approach to the condo and stopped next to a fire hydrant and firefighters swarmed and began dragging equipment and hoses.

Another fire truck, this one with the long ladders whipped in and parked, too.

On the other side of the circle two private security cars were already there, yellow lights rotating, and doors open. One Longboat police car was in a clump with the two.

Tommy saw amongst the people and vehicles that a team of firefighters was making its way toward the entrance to the building. And right in front of them came two hard cases and a nurse pushing an old man in a wheelchair. An indecently clad young lady scurried next to the wheelchair.

Tommy hoped they hurried. It wouldn't take the entry team long to determine the extent of the fires and the cause.

People were milling about in the grass beside the parking lot and throughout the parking lot. Firefighters and a cop were herding people away from the building that way.

Many were coughing. Soon somebody would make a distinction between the odor of burning building and that of burning garbage.

Tommy came out of the dark on the fringe of all this activity and joined the large, moving group. Right in front of him an elderly lady in a housecoat limped along. He sidled up beside her and took her arm. "Here, let me help you ma'am." He swung the fire extinguisher into his other hand.

She glanced her thanks at him acknowledging his help that wasn't necessary. He maneuvered the two of them toward the largest group gathering. "Why do you need those red lights to keep flashing?" she asked. "Everybody can see a big ol' truck."

"Safety regulations, ma'am." He didn't need her to remember him. He kept the hard hat brim tilted toward her. When they made it to the main group, he parked the old woman next to a pickup truck. He dropped the tailgate. "Sit here if you want."

"Why thank you, young man."

Tommy moved quickly, threading through the parking lot to the far side where he saw the wheelchair and accompanying bodyguards, nurse, and hot babe. People were talking amongst themselves, some wet and some dry. He wondered idly at the sprinkler system. Did they only go off where there was smoke and fire? Or did the entire system trigger at once? He shrugged mentally and continued through the chaos. He could see smoke pouring out of the front entrance. The firefighters must have opened the access to the garbage section to get their hoses through. This meant time compressibility to him. He was running out of time.

Finally he made it to the small group around the wheelchair.

He dropped the fire extinguisher even though it would continue to give him good cover, for he needed his hands. He stepped in front of them and pulled out his automatic.

"You want to die, you go for your guns," he told the body-guards. They were two surprised gents. Tommy's fire gear obscured the rest of the milling crowd from seeing his gun and watching him make his play. He tipped his hat up and looked at the old man.

The man in the wheelchair had eyes burning with intelligence, even though he was handicapped and over eighty years old. "You!" he said, spittle flying out of his mouth.

"Tell your goons to drop their weapons," Tommy told him.

"Fuck you. You killed my kid."

Tommy wasn't going to admit anything in front of witnesses. He nodded at the two goons. "You can drop your guns now, or I will kill Santana. Right fucking now."

One of them said, "Boss, is this the guy who aced six over in Arizona?"

"And a lot of others, too, back in the day," spat Santana. "And maybe Hamilton."

The woman was blonde and wore only a diaphanous wrap. Her eyes were wide. She was no threat.

Tommy pulled out the silenced twenty-two with his left hand and shot Santana in the left leg. "Drop your weapons. Or don't and go for them."

Santana, to his credit, only grasped his leg in pain. He grabbed it and hugged it with his hand.

The two hastened to do his bidding.

A family huddled next to a nearby van was watching in horror at the sudden violence and the husband hustled them away, fear on his face. Tommy judged he had less than two minutes before the situation became untenable.

He turned to Santana. "Your son was a serial rapist. You would never have allowed that if he was one of your men. He deserved to die." Tommy pulled out a tight roll of paper the size of a poster. He handed it to the woman. "Blondie, unroll this and hold it up to Santana." He observed she had very large breasts. While she did so, he turned back to the two bodyguards. "Sit down and cross your legs. Push your guns this way."

They did so and he bent and picked up the guns and pocketed them in the firefighter's overcoat. Thank goodness for large pockets.

He was down to maybe one minute.

Sirens and the sounds of vehicles permeated the area.

The blonde had the paper unrolled and was holding it against Santana.

His face went ashen.

The unfurled was a paper target with a human outline. It was designed to attach to a downrange bracket for target practice. On it, Tommy had drawn the outline of a scope picture with the crosshairs on the head of the target. Above that he had written in bold letter, SANTANA.

"You can thank a certain young lady for me not killing you. There's been enough killing. She did suggest that you've lived with that pain for all these years, and that is real punishment. Here's the deal: You withdraw the standing reward immediately. If not, I got a sniper rifle and a super scope with your name on it." He looked at the two bodyguards. "That proves my intent. You are not in jeopardy unless you try to follow me or whatever. Understand?"

Both nodded.

"I have an accomplice in a tree with that particular rifle trained on us right now. So you know."

They both nodded.

Santana started to say something when three men materialized from behind the van.

The leader was a balding man who pointed a government issue nine millimeter at him. "Freeze, Atkins. U.S. Marshals. You're under arrest."

Shit. Tommy thought furiously. He had to hold on and draw them closer.

"I got no beef with you, marshal. Only Santana."

"Drop your weapon, Atkins."

"I got these people covered with my weapon, marshal. You want the innocents caught in the middle of a firefight?" Damn it. He'd waited too long, played around too much. And he'd been caught. Somehow, the Marshal Service must have heard about Hamilton in Vegas and deduced that Santana would be next. Tommy shook his head mentally at himself for failing to game this one out properly. He could blame his error on lack of practice lately, but that didn't cut it when he was caught flat footed.

They were moving closer, coming up from behind Santana and his crew.

Tommy looked a warning at the two bodyguards. They were bewildered. Tommy smelled burning garbage. It was not pleasant.

"Stand aside, lady," the balding marshal told Blondie. Her tits jiggled as she moved away from Santana. Santana glared at her defection.

"Marshal," Tommy said, "no need for gunfire with all these innocent people around."

The three kept moving and clustered closer together as a necessity. They walked abreast, mimicking Wyatt Earp and all at the OK corral. Tommy knew he had a chance with them. As soon as your opponents start playing games or become too arrogant, they lose an edge.

Out of nowhere, a shapely blue-robed figure appeared behind the three. She stepped right up to Baldy in the center and put the muzzle of her automatic to the back of his head.

Baldy froze and the other two took another step until they realized something was wrong. They turned toward him. This gave Tommy the split second he needed. He stepped aside and grabbed Blondie. He put his gun to her head.

"Who dies first?" he said. "If you want nobody to die, drop your guns. Or start shooting."

The three marshals didn't move. The two flankers looked to Baldy for guidance. He swallowed painfully, careful to avoid triggering the gun jammed into the back of his head.

Tommy knew he had to do something. Pretty soon someone was going to go get the cops who were gathered in front of the tall condo. "Listen, Mr. Marshal. You know I have nothing to lose. You do. There are too many people standing around out here for you to chance a gunfight. I like this woman. Shame to harm a lady with such fine tits. So that's a trade off. Here's what we'll do: You all will drop your weapons. I know you travel with handcuffs. You will remove them and cuff yourselves to each other. And you will give my associate three keys to those handcuffs."

"No way," said Baldy, swallowing again.

Tommy thought the man ought to control his swallowing. It gave him away. "And you will do so in the next sixty seconds. If you don't, I will shoot the young lady in a shoulder or something non-lethal. The incident review will result in your firing. You cannot ever justify civilians being harmed when you can prevent it. Not to mention Santana bleeding to death while you dallied."

Baldy thought for a moment and his two fellow marshals fidgeted.

"Forty-five seconds," Tommy said. To María Elena, he said, "If he fucks up, kill him." She wouldn't of course, but Baldy didn't know that.

"A bonus," Tommy told him. "You can have the two weapons from the body guards which likely aren't registered. That should give you grounds for a warrant to search Santana's suite. Never know what you'll find. Thirty seconds."

"I'm dropping my gun," said Baldy, squatting to put it on the ground. His fellows did the same.

"Better hurry," Tommy said. Twenty seconds."

They fumbled out and awkwardly snapped handcuffs. They ran over the one minute limit. But Tommy was satisfied. He glanced around. People quickly dressed in night clothes or shorts were staring at the tableau. He tried to spot the cops over near the fire trucks but couldn't, and that was not a good thing. He pocketed the .22 and fished out the bodyguards' guns. He ejected the magazines and kicked them aside.

"Lie down on the ground, face down, right now." He tossed the two automatics at the feet of the lawmen. He patted the blonde on the ass and whispered in her ear, "Thanks for being a good sport."

Her eyes were grateful even though her face showed fear. Tommy guessed he still had the look.

"Santana, next time no talk. Just one shot from afar." He motioned to María Elena. "Go ahead to the car, we gotta be off this key before they close the bridge on us." He doubted they'd buy the misdirection for long.

María Elena disappeared behind an SUV. Tommy surveyed his immediate surroundings. He waved his handgun and watchers ducked. Immediately, he faded behind the SUV.

The smell of burning garbage permeated the air.

María Elena was waiting for him inside the pine tree line. Tommy threw his firefighter gear over a bush hoping the silhouette would buy them a few more minutes.

They wound their way through the mangroves and soon were at the boat.

The pushed it into the water and María Elena jumped in. He ran a few more feet, shoved hard, and swung aboard. They both paddled swiftly.

"Don't you have to pee bad?" Tommy asked quietly.

"Yes, but I'll hold it."

"What a fucking circus," Tommy said.

"You have a good rifle," she said coyly. "Next time why don't you just shoot the son of a bitch?"

"Blood thirsty wench." Tommy sighed. Women. He stumbled over a couple of fishing rods and stepped to the console. He started the engine and swung toward the mainland. "You're probably right," he said, swinging the wheel. "The best plans are the simplest. That one had too many elements which could go wrong. Not to mention too many people around. That's dangerous in itself."

"I admire the way you barely looked at that woman's

breasts," María Elena said. She dropped her robe and removed the pajamas. She started dressing in her jeans and sweatshirt.

"Sarcasm does not fit you well," he said, admiring her body, what he could see in the dark.

"Tommy? Don't hit that channel marker."

He swung left thinking they were taking a chance running without lights.

"Look," she said and pointed up and toward the north. A helicopter sporting a spotlight was coming out over the water. "It'll be here in a minute."

"Two choices," he said as he pulled back the throttle. "We can strip and show them we're out here for a little boat sex or we can pretend to night fish."

"Fishing," she chose immediate. "If it's sex, they might hover to watch and we don't want the extra attention."

She handed him a pole and found an empty beer can on the floor. Quickly she took off her sweat shirt and grabbed the beer can again. She did not need a bra

Tommy recognized that a little risqué was better than blatant. He grinned his appreciation. Small waves slapped at the hull.

The light hit them and centered them. Tommy hoped their wake had dissipated. He held the fishing pole over the side. They both shaded their eyes and María Elena held up the beer can to them invitingly and opened her arms showing off her breasts. Party girl. The chopper moved on almost reluctantly.

Tommy dropped the pole and advanced the throttle. They needed to get out of town fast. The marshals had somehow identified them, or him, and predicted after the Hamilton hit that he would go after Santana next. And they were right. He hated to be predictable. He was smarter than that. And he regretted the ostentatious mess he'd created tonight. There were too many opportunities for it to go wrong. And way too many witnesses.

And why the hell had he worried about the cameras earlier? Here he was in the middle of a bunch of evacuees and wandering around like they're lost. And firefighters and police not a hundred yards away. And then he was identified by name by the U.S. Marshal Service. What sense did that make? Not that his position with the law wasn't totally untenable, but they'd just compounded it. The Marshal Service apparently had a long institutional memory; and this episode was going to refresh it and boost their enthusiasm for hunting down one each Tommy Atkins.

And he should have considered that Santana might be under surveillance, not just because of him, but because of who the old man was. They probably had his condo wired. Tommy cursed himself for so blindly walking into a trap. But he didn't regret not killing the old guy; hell, he'd worked for Santana for a while. The guy had been a decent boss and paid well. And the reward was only natural; any man would do the same when someone killed his son. Not to mention he'd chosen his bimbo of the week well: that girl had spunk.

María Elena moved back and stood beside him. She linked her arm in his. "What's up with U. S. Marshals?"

He shook his head. "It makes little sense. FBI sure. But U.S. Marshal Service? It's unlikely they're even authorized to place surveillance on Santana. So it follows they were after us—or me."

María Elena wrapped her arms around his left arm. "We've graduated from Mexican assassins and gangbangers to mob hitmen to U.S. Marshals. So, what's next?"

He pulled her closer. "It's gonna take more than a few marshals to figure what we're up to. Have to be someone smarter than those three." But he wondered. It didn't matter though. They were going to do this. María Elena performed her part very well. And she had improvised when it counted, and followed his lead. He'd never expected to get a proficient partner out of all this. He hoped they hadn't seen her well enough to identify her. It was probably against the law to interfere with U.S. Marshals doing their official duty and sticking a gun against their head. His eyes became distracted. "You might want to put your sweat-shirt back on before we hit land."

"Yes, dear."

"Upon further consideration, this operation, as fucked up as it was, served an additional purpose. While our intention was to clear the decks of major obstacles to our living happily ever after, it also might well send a confusing message to whoever or whatever agency is managing the search and destroy mission against us. They might now think that we're just playing get even with my enemies and therefore fail to prepare for us down in Miami. Hopefully, they won't send your soon-to-be late husband a warning."

"Yes, Tommy. I gotta pee bad."

CHAPTER TWENTY-FIVE: HER

The Tamiami Trail used to be the major route from Tampa to Naples and then across Florida to Miami, all via U.S. Highway 41. Nowadays, U.S. 41 from Tampa to Naples is one traffic signal after another, one fast food restaurant after another, one car dealer after another. Concrete, steel, asphalt. Then 41 runs to Miami, a two-lane rough road nicknamed "Alligator Alley." To get to Miami nowadays, you take I-75 south to Naples whereupon I-75 turns from a north-south corridor to an east-west corridor. An eighty mile stretch called the Everglades Parkway. Outside of Naples heading east toward Miami, the Florida panther roams and you can see black bear and deer. The Interstate skirts through the Everglades and the Big Cypress Swamp, both of which are mostly the same, only with different names. It is a lonesome road, except for cars and trucks and SUV's flying across the state with their air conditioning on high.

María Elena was driving a Nissan 4X4 pickup, a tough vehicle she liked immediately.

She was worrying about Miami. She checked her speed and kept it on 70, the maximum, so as to not attract attention. Back when she lived in Miami, she drove around the area, Miami, Ft. Lauderdale, Key West, wherever, at higher speeds: everybody did so. If you went too slowly, they'd run over you. Unless the traffic was gridlocked, this circumstance occurred seemingly half the time. Upon reflection, she was glad she'd spent a lot of time in the swamps and uninhabited areas of Dade

County driving anything with two or more wheels. This skill had certainly come in handy. Big wheel trucks, four-wheel drive Jeeps, and three and four wheel ATV's splashing through swamps and mud and through dusty fields. She even drove most of the military vehicles during her weapons training at 13's expansive training grounds. She grinned to herself deciding that she didn't know back then that she needed to get a life. Well, now she had one, God help her.

"What are we going to do to Don Diego?" she asked, already knowing the answer, but needing a way to address it.

"Kill him dead," said Tommy matter-of-factly. He was reading *Guns, Germs, and Steel*. He didn't look up.

"While I've seen a lot of blood lately, necessary blood I admit, I'm not fully comfortable with killing Diego."

"You know the answer, college girl. He threw you to the wolves, rape and murder. He killed your father. He stole 13 de enero. He engaged in human trafficking, from what you've said. Selling people for debts? For wanting to come to this country and freedom? Add to that laundry list drugs. More..."

"Yes, but..."

"Don't worry, Emmy, I'll take care of him. I have been antic-ipating that very thing. I can almost taste it." He smacked his lips and looked at her. "We cannot continue with him still alive. It's also a travesty what he's doing."

"I know you're right, we have to do it. It's just, well, I've tried and can't think of another way."

"You ain't gonna, either." He closed the book. María Elena knew he did not turn the corner of a page down to mark his place; he simply remembered the page number. "That Santana thing in Sarasota was a frigging circus and I don't want to repeat that."

She looked to the south. Somewhere out there was where Tommy had spent years of his life secluded—until she had come along. She smiled at him. "You could still be sitting out there among the mosquitoes and snakes and gators minding your own business."

"My whole life, hon, it built towards this, towards here and now. So, it don't matter what went before, just that it led me here."

"That's sweet. Thank you, dear."

He winked at her. "The road's in front of us."

She switched her eyes forward. "Since this all started, I've been through a bloodbath. Make that 'we'. I didn't know the world was anything like this. Except I knew horror from stories of Castro's prisons and torture chambers."

"This is the real world, college girl."

"I know...but still..."

"You're not saying we done wrong here? We've produced too much blood on your behalf?"

"No," she said, tongue tied. "I don't know, Tommy."

"It matters not, María Elena, for I am going to kill that motherfucker anyway."

"That might be easier said than done."

"Let me quote an old Bantu proverb: He who has caused thee to shed tears, cause him to shed blood."

"I was thinking out loud, Tommy, not challenging your abilities or manhood."

"Well, okay. But don't you worry about blood, that's my department. And I do like a challenge." He laughed softly. "Though I must point out that lately you have done your share of shedding blood."

She reached over and patted his arm. "Yes, dear. I'm learning from the best." She wondered whatever happened to that happy-go-lucky blogger girl with the fine heritage and promising future. She'd matured in a way she would never have envisioned. She stole a look at Tommy who was obviously still smiling at the memory of her shedding blood. She thought, I gotta admit I'm happier right now than I can remember being; and I am so happy I've fallen for this crusty guy twenty-some years older than I am. "I'm horny," she said, surprising herself, too.

"We'll stop at Weston, just outside of Ft. Lauderdale. All the major roads intersect there. Small town hosting a dozen specialty hospitals and clinics and they're used to strangers. We'll fit right in. We can take the edge off of your horniness."

"I was thinking of pole dancing for you."

"Knock me over with a feather. What brought that on?"

"I never had a reason before. I do now." She looked at him with bedroom eyes.

"Well, thank you, dear." He scratched his head. "There's a bar in Miami near the Cuban section where they have amateur pole dancing on Wednesday nights. Called 'Rosey's.'"

"I think I remember it, over near Little Havana." She lifted an eyelash. "And you know this how?"

"I get around. Pole dancing is an art, if you do it right."

"Well I know that, sweetie."

"You're not saying?" he asked wonderingly.

"I am. I admit I do it for exercise and I try to do it aerobically. My friend Margarita is an instructor and I've taken her classes. I've even substituted running her class upon occasion. It helps me tremendously with flexibility."

He grinned at her. "I'll say."

"I didn't do it for sexual reasons. Exercise and flexibility."

"Everything you do is sexy."

She dimpled. "Just for you, Tommy." She paused. "It's why I'm pretty well trimmed. As if you hadn't noticed." She smiled fondly.

"I wasn't going to ask," he said.

"I also teach Zumba. That keeps me limber, too." At his blank look, she added, "A workout routine to Latin music."

"My dear, they ought to change your name to Constance Surprise."

"Thank you, I think."

"You shoot well, you drive like Kyle Busch, and pole dance." He leered at her. "I like the limber part, too."

"I'm a woman of many talents," she teased.

He ignored her. "We're early for check-in. Head for Hollywood."

They flew past Weston and the intersection of more major

highways than should be legal. Hollywood is a town ensconced in between the metropolis of Miami and the metropolis of Ft. Lauderdale.

They wound up at another self-storage facility, "U-Plenty Self-storage." The gates were open and they drove in behind another car. Tommy directed her to unit 408, the fourth one in a row of ten buildings.

Tommy got out and went to the door of the small unit. María Elena joined him.

He scratched his head. "I always put a combo lock on these and I always use the same combination." He held up a large key padlock.

"Uh, oh," she said.

He let the padlock go. "Actually, I'm surprised of all of them only one's gone. Let's go to the office."

They drove back out of the storage yard to the office. It was air-conditioned, of course. A middle-aged woman sat at a counter chewing on a pencil. "Help you?"

Tommy nodded. "My unit is 408 and that's not my lock."

"Are you sure?"

"I am. I paid for ten years in advance and I have seven to go."

"Lemme check." She rolled her chair to her computer and grabbed the mouse. "408 is rented to a Boy Scout troop for their camping gear."

"I'm not mistaken about the number," Tommy said. "I don't confuse that way."

She looked up at him. "No, I don't reckon you do." She glanced at María Elena curiously. She shrugged. "I saw them unloading into 408 last weekend after a camping trip to the keys." She turned back to the computer. "What's your name? Maybe I have something on it."

"Atkins."

She typed in a search window. "Nothing."

María Elena stepped forward. "Check your spreadsheets or accounting program for statements or a paid receipt, something."

A few more clicks of the mouse and a couple of searches. "Got it. It was in there, scanned from before this program was installed. I don't understand. There's no evidence of you in the operations program." She ran her finger down the monitor's screen. "Yep. Paid in full in advance." She rolled back. "Mister Atkins, I don't know what to tell you."

"There can be only one answer," he said.

"I know, but I don't have it. My husband and I bought this place last year--well, us and the bank, and those Boy Scouts were already in 408. I assure you, we didn't steal the contents. Just a minute." She went back to the computer for a moment. "Nothing under abandoned or auctioned."

"I need those contents now. Who'd you buy this from?"

"McAllister. He put it on the Internet and we saw it and came down from Atlanta to start over."

"You got his address?"

"That's private info."

Tommy smiled a disarming smile. "Look, lady. I don't want trouble. But you got it. If he robbed me, likely he robbed others, and your insurance can't handle that. Nor can the county or the city who issues you a business license. Nor can the law."

María Elena knew he was pressuring her for he certainly couldn't go to the police.

"I might add," said Tommy, "that this person whose privacy you're protecting has trick-fucked you and me both and got you in trouble. Lawyers cost a lot and insurance companies don't pay off when there's fraud."

The woman sighed and her shoulders slumped. She clicked the mouse again and moved it around. Then she wrote on a sticky-note. "Here's McAllister's address. It's off Ninth Avenue in Ft. Lauderdale. The bum told me he was tired of working and was gonna retire."

"Thank you," Tommy said. He stared at her and she shifted uncomfortably in her chair. "Do not think about calling him about this. Am I clear?"

"Yessir."

"If it works out, you might not hear from me again and you don't have legal problems or insurance problems."

"Yessir."

"Then you forget this conversation."

"Yessir."

As María Elena drove out of the parking lot, she said, "I know the area. Want to go there now?"

"Why not."

"What was in 408."

"Same ole. Getaway suitcase with clothes. Maybe a hundred grand. A couple of handguns and ammo. Damn it, I wanted this. We're not running low on cash—nowhere near broke, you understand, but I wanted to clean this out since I doubt we'll have time to return here later and I likely don't want to ever revisit this area."

The house was modern, maybe a three bedroom, two baths. It had a circular gravel driveway eating up most of the front yard. The garage door was open revealing a Lexus SUV and an expensive looking boat, skewed slightly sideways to fit in the garage. Alongside the front door and in the U made for the circular drive were children's toys, including two small bicycles and a big wheel for a toddler.

On the driveway lip of the garage sat a strange contraption: to María Elena it looked like a Harley with a metal or plastic case affixed upright which had the shape of a golf bag.

"What in the world?" she asked.

"Pretty," said Tommy. "It's called an Autolinx case. It's centered on the back of the bike for weight and balance and is positioned so it doesn't interfere with your mirror vision. You can carry anything in it, but most people, golfers that is, put their golf bag and clubs in it so they can show off their Harley to their golfing buddies. It's a status thing. But if you go on a cross country trip, you can take a lot more stuff. It's made of high density polyethylene and you can even use it to carry your golf clubs on airlines."

María Elena pulled in the circular drive and continued around until the Nissan was facing the road, just short of the sidewalk. A lesson she'd learned from Tommy: always park so you can leave in a hurry.

"Stay in the truck," said Tommy. "I don't want anybody to be able to identify you later."

He climbed out and closed the door.

Just then a big Chevy pickup pulled in behind them. A large man got out, a questioning look on his face.

"McAllister," said Tommy through the open window. Tommy walked around the back of the Nissan and McAllister came forward. They stopped together at the left rear corner of the 4X4. María Elena had a good view in both the inside mirror and the driver's mirror.

McAllister wore a ragged Fu-Manchu and a wife-beater tank top. His face was rugged and he was maybe six five. "The fuck are you and the fuck you want?" His size made him aggressive and not careful.

"408," said Tommy.

"The fuck is a 408?" His voice was rough, but María Elena could see comprehension dawning on his face.

"McAllister, you robbed my unit. I paid ahead ten years. I want my money and, ah, equipment."

McAllister glanced at the garage with the boat and Lexus SUV. "Shit, I didn't hear from you annually, so I confiscated the contents of your unit."

"Even though I paid you plenty in advance?"

"Look, Jack, I don't know who the fuck you are, but them guns was prolly illegal. And all that money and guns, all bein' hid out for ten years? Yeah, right, go call a fucking cop."

"Am I to understand you are not cooperating?"

"Fuck off. Get off my property." McAllister turned to walk toward the house.

That was when Tommy hit him with two short jabs to the abdomen. McAllister folded immediately and vomited. Tommy straightened the man out and slapped him hard.

María Elena saw that Tommy had chosen the protected space

between the two trucks so that their altercation was not visible to much of the street or the front of the house. A glance told her no neighbors were out and watching.

Tommy slapped McAllister again, whipping his head around. "I spent it all, man. Nothing I can do."

"And my guns?"

"I sold them. Don't want no guns around with young kids."

Tommy slapped him again with the other hand, and McAllister's head whipped the other way. "Shit, man." He raised his hands to protect his face. Tommy jabbed him in the kidney. McAllister went white and bile spewed from his mouth. Tommy ducked aside. María Elena once again marveled at how fast Tommy moved. "Please?" McAllister mumbled. Tommy pulled the man's right hand down from his face and snapped his thumb. The digit stuck out at an obscene right angle. "Fuck!" McAllister's voice was shrill now.

María Elena was amazed such a big man could be transformed into a whimpering idiot so quickly. Suddenly, she was so glad Tommy was on her side. Don Diego, start looking over your shoulder.

"I spent most of it, man. I thought I'd never see you again!" Tears were rolling out his eyes.

Tommy pointed at the garage. "The boat. The Lexus. Sell them. Withdraw whatever you have in the bank. I'll be back tomorrow."

"Ain't no way can I do that, man." He held his right wrist with his left hand staring down at them."

"Sure you can," Tommy said. "And no cops, understand?"

McAllister looked thoughtful.

Tommy leaned down and picked up the big wheel. The plastic was bright red. Causally, he spread the forks around the front wheel and pulled the front wheel off. He spun it out onto the road. Then he tore off the steering handle and tossed it aside.

The south Florida sun beat down on the silent tableau. María Elena wiped a drop of perspiration from her brow. She almost felt sorry for McAllister. But she'd known a few real punks in her life and this one was no different. He understood only strength.

"Am I clear?"

"Yeah, man, fuck. Leave my family out of this."

"Your choice, McAllister. Have the money tomorrow by noon."

"Shit. Fuck."

Tommy shoved the man headfirst into the front of his Chevy truck and walked to the Nissan and got in beside María Elena. "Let's go."

CHAPTER TWENTY-SIX: HIM

Tommy drove, threading through the bothersome Miami traffic. He didn't know this part of the city. It was on the bay and there were numerous so called "islands" and "peninsulas", manmade, sitting right off a winding bayside road. All contained multi-million dollar homes. Some of the islands were small, others large. Some had only a few homes, others twenty, thirty, more.

Their night at the Westin hotel had been memorable. There was no pole in the room to dance around, but María Elena had managed to make the night into—Tommy shook his head to clear it. No time for this now. Time for business.

"This one," said María Elena and he turned right onto the entry road to the island. He slowed to a stop at a guard house where a uniformed rent-a-cop stepped out.

María Elena leaned forward and waved at the man. "Hey, Elmer."

"Miss María Elena! Long time no see."

"Has Eduardo left yet this morning?"

Elmer leaned in to talk to her and saw Tommy and straightened immediately. "No ma'am, not unless he took his boat."

"All right, thanks, Elmer."

"I'll tell him you're on the way in," Elmer said.

"Fine. See you."

Elmer hit a button and the gate arm rose. Tommy accelerated away from the gate. They climbed a small bridge, more of a decoration than a functional structure.

Eduardo's circular driveway was not gravel: it was comprised of variously colored pavers. The house was on the water with lots of lawn. It sat two stories high with a crow's nest atop the second floor. Tommy knew little about homes these days, but he did know this was one expensive place. As he pulled into the driveway, the angle showed him a cabin cruiser docked behind the house, gently rocking from the wake of a passing boat.

He drove through the circular driveway until he was facing out. In his outside mirror he could see the back half of the boat and part of the bay. Tommy didn't like the fact that the security guard had called ahead. He didn't like anyone having a few minutes warning, if that were to be the case.

"You go ahead on in," he told María Elena. "I'll stay out here for a while and pay attention." He didn't say he didn't trust this Eduardo Quinones. He did not know the man which, therefore, put Quinones in the do not trust category. Even if the man was María Elena's godfather and an original founder of 13 de enero, and her father's oldest friend.

She nodded and stepped out of the 4X4 pickup. He watched the inside mirror as she approached the ornate front door. It opened and an elderly man with a fancy moustache rushed out. "Alejandrina," he called.

They embraced and he ushered her inside. After a few minutes a likely servant opened the front door and peered out at Tommy and the truck. Tommy thought it odd that anybody would have on a long-sleeve dress shirt and a short cut jacket in the Miami heat this early in the day. After a minute, the servant went away. Tommy turned in his seat and studied the house. Just another Miami mansion. He hoped María Elena would learn enough for them to formulate a detailed plan. If not, she intended to find out Don Diego García's location and particulars.

Tommy fiddled with the radio then turned it off. He wanted no distractions. A fancy Mercedes drove past and pulled in the mansion at the end of the cul de sac. He figured that was on the outer tip of the island where it jutted into the bay.

A few more minutes passed. In the right side exterior mirror, Tommy watched two crewmen jump onto the cabin cruiser. Shortly, the engine started. Tommy wished he could see the front of the boat where the boarding ladder was. One of the crewmen, dressed smartly in white pants and a white pullover shirt, moved through his line of vision quickly and reached out to free the rear tie down rope. He certainly showed a sense of urgency.

"Oh, fuck." Tommy slammed his door open and ran to the front door. The damn thing was locked. He drew his gun and shot twice into the lock. The doors swung open. Tommy rushed in. The jacketed servant was running toward him down a long hallway, his right hand pulling an automatic from under his left armpit.

Tommy shot him midsection, knowing that he might need the man alive, but couldn't take the time to be certain to only wound him and take him out of the action. The servant slammed sideways into a wall, dislodging a fancy beach painting.

Tommy kept running, spilling into a great room with an enormous plate glass window overlooking the dock and the bay.

"María Elena!" he screamed.

Nothing. Maybe running feet upstairs.

Outside through the plate glass window he watched the cabin cruiser swing away from the dock. The pilot must have applied a lot of power for the boat surged ahead. Tommy knew little about boats and boating in the bay, but he did know that you don't power up immediately; usually there is a no wake zone, especially around residential areas.

He saw a door off to the side of the room and ran out of it to the dock. The cabin cruiser was moving out quickly. He read the name on the transom: CUBAN BEAUTY.

He smelled fuel, likely diesel. The engines sounded like they were going full throttle. Someone on the boat saw him then, one of the crew, shouted and extended his arm pointing at Tommy.

The tanned guy with a mustache stepped through a doorway and stared at him

"Goddamn it!" Tommy raised his automatic and fired the rest of the magazine at the man. The sound of the shots seemed small in the embrace of the bay. He ejected that clip and slapped another in. CUBAN BEAUTY was still accelerating, which wasn't yet very fast as it was a large boat.

Tommy spun and sprinted around the house and leapt into the truck, glad he'd left the driver's door open. He cranked the engine without closing the door and slammed the shifter into gear with the gas pedal to the floor. Tires spun and caught and the truck took off, fairly leaping into the air. He guided it to the left and headed toward the end of the street where the island peaked. The door whipped closed. He fishtailed up the street driving with one hand. With his right, he reached behind the seats and grabbed the heavy duffle. He threw the duffle on the passenger seat and unbuckled it, helping to steer with his knees.

Immediately, he reached the last house on the street, the fancy super-mansion. He jumped the curb still accelerating. The Nissan's tires ate up fancy lawn and spewed it out behind. The engine was screaming in protest, the RPM's already past the redline on the tachometer. He clipped the edge of an aluminum patio pool cage sending most of the cage crashing against the mansion. The truck plowed over shrubs and out onto the grass of the final spit of land. He downshifted and hit the brakes and the throttle at the same time, going into a four-wheel slide to the right.

As the truck slowed, he dragged an AR-15 out of the duffle and opened the door simultaneously. He jumped out not caring about the truck whether it continued going into the bay or not. The truck was going too fast, and he went over, tucking into a paratrooper's roll, ducking his shoulder and protecting the rifle. He continued the roll and converted the energy into powering himself back on his feet.

Tommy jacked a shell into the chamber and tucked the weapon into his shoulder steadying on the CUBAN BEAUTY. He didn't know where to aim, so he aimed at the cockpit beneath the fly bridge. He selected full auto and loosed a three-round burst. He couldn't tell if he hit it or not, but it seemed he was close for the boat veered to the left and then the right. A moving target, he fired another three-round salvo. Then another. The boat continued to slew right and left. Tommy finished the magazine knowing it was fruitless and he wasn't going to stop the boat.

People were coming out of nearby houses. A woman still dressed up came out the back of the mansion and stared at him through crushed screen. At once they seemed to realize he was probably an armed madman and ducked back inside.

Tommy was castigating himself for his failure and ignored them. Then a thought occurred to him. He searched the docks nearby. A couple of boats, bigger if anything than CUBAN BEAUTY. It would be impossible to hijack one and catch up. Not now. And he certainly didn't know enough to crew and pilot one all by himself.

Time slowed and he realized this place would be full of cops really quickly. Not only was he wanted, probably dead or alive, but he couldn't talk his way out of this one. He looked around for the Nissan. Thirty feet to his right the 4X4 had stalled out, nudging onto the sea wall. He trotted over and climbed in. The truck started and he slammed it into reverse.

Think! he told himself. The truck slewed back toward the street kicking up more grass and dirt, plowing through a flower bed. He jumped the curb back onto the street.

He realized it was imperative he send a message; he needed to do something to keep them from harming María Elena. He screeched up the street, the truck complaining all the way. Into Quinones' driveway once again, he skidded to a stop. He pushed the AR-15 aside and grabbed his automatic.

As he stepped out, Elmer the security guard, on a golf cart drove quickly into the driveway. Elmer was fearless.

Tommy stepped to him quickly and stuck his gun into Elmer's throat.

"Elmer, they took María Elena. You gotta talk to the cops, but likely some other people will question you, too, not good guys. I have a message for you to deliver to them. You tell these other guys to not touch her and they can expect me. Understand? If they kill her, I have nothing to lose and I will hunt them down and kill them. Then I will find their families and kill each one of them, too. Understand?"

"Yes, sir, I do." His face was scrunched up and head stretched backward to avoid the pressure of the gun sight and barrel. "What do you mean somebody took María Elena?"

"Guns, kidnapping. They're going to kill her."

"No!" squawked Elmer. "Move your gun, please."

Tommy did so and Elmer sat up. "What happened to Mr. Quinones?"

"I don't fucking know. They're all gone and I'm wasting time."

"If I can help."

"Cops ought to be on the way. Stall them."

Elmer gulped. "If I can."

Tommy saw the beginning of disbelief crawling across his face. "All right, now get out of here."

Tommy pushed the man back onto his golf cart and turned and ran through the ruined front door. He needed to send a message in case they didn't grill Elmer. Something to tell them Tommy Atkins was on their ass and they better hedge their bets and cover their ass until they dealt with him.

Nobody was stirring downstairs and he didn't have time to search upstairs. The body of the "servant" he'd shot was still where he'd fallen. That the servant/body guard had attempted to shoot Tommy and impede him finding María Elena told Tommy that somehow Quinones was involved. He didn't know but his anger boiled over.

Tommy found himself in a large library office. Bookshelves were lined with law books and another section contained history books, hundreds of them. He saw a fancy wet bar and looked behind it and saw dozens of bottles of liquor.

Off in the distance through all the doors he'd left open, he heard sirens approaching. He didn't have much time.

Making an instant decision, he tore dozens of books off the

shelves onto the floor in a flurry of action. The desk drawer and desk surface provided handfuls of paper. Then he went to the bar and began smashing liquor bottles. High end booze, Makers' Mark and single malt scotches and expensive vodkas, all earned a regretful smash against the desk and poured over the accumulated books and papers. The 100 proof stuff would be the best.

Sirens were closing in on the island.

Tommy tossed the contents of the drawers in the bar itself and found what any good man would keep there: matches, whether you needed them or not, every man should have matches handy for emergency. Just like a church key.

Soon a blue blaze ripped across the spilled alcohol and onto the curtains and fabric of the furniture.

Tommy was satisfied it would burn the house down. The outside of the house was stucco over concrete block and the roof was Spanish style red barrel tile. The insides would burn fine and ignite all the rafters, plywood, and likely the underlying tar paper. It would make a fine conflagration.

He hurried outside and hustled into the truck. He jammed it into gear and powered out of the drive and down the road. The transmission or something was protesting all the abuse, but Tommy kept the tach over the redline.

Approaching the turn for the road off the island, he saw police paralleling him on the access causeway. Tommy slowed, trying to look normal. He turned onto the exit lane to the bridge and drove at moderate speed over the bridge. Elmer's golf cart was nudged askew against the butt of the guardhouse.

Two police cars were slowing to a stop.

Tommy glimpsed a tendril of smoke in his right outside mirror.

He didn't know if the exit gate would open on demand or if Elmer had to actuate it. He drove sedately toward it, slowed almost to a stop and it rose as if by magic.

Thanks, Elmer, he thought.

Elmer was standing in the sentry position at the door of the guardhouse gesticulating wildly and yelling at the cops. Sirens were silenced but the lights on the light bars were still going strong. Tommy averted his gaze and put his left arm up through the open window to obscure a view of him and his profile. Then he realized that would be singular in itself: anybody who didn't look would become immediately suspect. So he turned and stared, hoping they weren't watching.

On the other hand, he didn't care. He had to find María Elena and do so quickly. The only other person he knew about who was involved in this thing was Don Diego García. The son of a bitch wouldn't be in the phone book.

Tommy turned right on the causeway since it was easier than waiting for traffic to turn left. A nice column of smoke had begun rising behind stately queen palms lining the island. With cell phones and instant communication, they'd start digging and find out what was happening and soon formulate a plan. This, Tommy admitted, was better than he had.

He needed information. He needed a starting point. And he knew he had maybe less than a day. It could be that all this unwanted attention would drive García and his cronies out of hiding and perhaps scare them out of the country. If so, that action would issue a death sentence to María Elena. Briefly he cursed himself for allowing her to go in to the house alone. But Eduardo Quinones had been a long time associate of her father's and he was María Elena's godfather. Tommy decided he wasn't going to solve these questions by himself right now. He had to press on, to take the offense.

An hour later, midday, he pulled into the small parking lot next to ROSEY'S BAR. The outside of the building was grubby and it was on the edges of the Little Havana district in Miami. As he walked away from the truck, he saw fluid leaking beneath it. Not much, but it would get worse. He'd blown a seal somewhere along the way.

The old fashioned glass door was propped open and Tommy walked out of the daylight into the dark. There was a small wood dance floor centered in the room.

Just past the dance floor rose a small stage where a band played sometimes; and on that stage to one side stretched a stainless steel pole from floor to ceiling; it looked more like aluminum and should be in a fire station. On the opposite side of the room ran a bar the entire length of that wall. A couple of dozen tables were peppered about.

Apparently, the place had just opened as none of the usual noon crowd was here yet. The empty bar fueled an atmosphere of mustiness and smoke which would air out from the breeze through the open door. This was one of the few places which took the hit from the law: most places in Florida were, by law, smoke free. Only some with outside venues were exempt.

His eyes now accustomed to the dark, found Rosey at the pass-through of the bar against the far wall. Raven haired, tall at maybe six one, busty, big wide smile, forty-something, bright red lipstick. She was talking on her cell phone standing in a pool of light from a Budweiser lamp hanging from the ceiling.

Rosey saw him, clicked off, and yelled, "Tommy!" She rushed over and gave him a big hug and a kiss. He was a reluctant participant. She linked an arm through his and walked him to the bar under the Bud light.

"How's it going, Rosey?"

She eyed him. "Lookin' good, hon. Long time no see. How about a quickie?"

"I can't right now," said Tommy and averted his eyes. He felt crimson creeping up his neck.

Rosey clapped her hands and chanted, "Tommy's in love, Tommy's in love!"

Tommy shrugged self-consciously.

"Who is she? She must be beautiful?"

"Well, um, she is."

"Oh, Tommy, you cad."

"It ain't like that, Rosey. Listen, I need to find Don Diego García."

She pursed her full lips. "He's one mean son of a bitch, Tommy. You don't want anything to do with him."

"Oh, but I do." He couldn't hide the vehemence in his voice.

"Oh, shit. Not her? The old man's daughter?"

Tommy shrugged. "It's about her, Rosey. I gotta find her. He's got her and he'll kill her."

"Damn, Tommy, it must be real love."

"Help me find him, Rosey."

"I don't know where he is, he doesn't check with me. I heard he has a big condo up in Lauderdale on the beach someplace."

"Ft. Lauderdale? Let me use your phone for a minute."

She slid the cell phone toward him on the bar.

Tommy punched in a number.

A deep male voice answered. "This is Pat Tanyan."

"Hello, Pat. It's Atkins."

"Tommy?"

"Yeah. Listen, I'm real sorry about your cabin burning down."

"You disappeared. They saw you drive away."

"I had to. A bunch of militia guys were trying to kill me."

"The cabin is no loss. We did not even want rent money from you anymore. But trying to kill a man such as you..."

"They were. A group called 13 de enero." Tommy watched Rosey visibly flinch. "A Cuban anti-revolutionary group taken over by thugs."

"I don't know them." Tanyan sighed and Tommy envisioned him tapping tobacco into a pipe. "When you left, they told me all hell broke loose. Soon there were helicopters and volunteer fire teams, and game wardens, and likely some school crossing guards, too. Oh, and more feds than feathers on a chief's head-dress."

Uh, oh. "You ever heard of Don Diego García?" He tried to keep the anxiety out of his voice.

Pat thought a moment. "No. He ain't no Seminole."

"He's supposed to live in a fancy condo on Lauderdale beach."

"That narrows it down to a few thousand units."

Tommy shook his head. "Thought I'd give it a shot, Pat.

Thanks anyway. About the cabin?"

"I didn't say I couldn't find him," Tanyan said. "I just said I ain't ever heard of him."

"What do you mean, Pat?"

"Having little else to do, I am the president of the board of the condo owners' association in this building, Tommy. As such, I've contact with other condo associations up and down the beach, a kind of informal thing. We have an online data base of tenants for many of the different condominiums. Just a second, I'm cranking up my desktop." Tanyan whistled a tune Tommy knew as something called "The Tomahawk Chop." "Here you go. Got him. Jeez, that's top end."

"What do you mean?"

"That condo and those in that building are more expensive than this one. That's very heavy hitting. It has an Olympic size pool, security at a reception desk, marble in a fancy lobby, that kind of stuff."

"Great. Let me grab a pen." He slid onto a barstool.

Rosey slid a bar Bic toward him and turned over a Budweiser napkin for him.

Tommy wrote as Pat read off the details. It was a thread to María Elena. It might not pan out, but it was all he had. He didn't have time to cruise the Cuban section, a stranger asking questions. "Thanks a million, Pat. You don't know what this means to me."

"Anything for you, Tommy, anytime. Don't forget, you owe me a cabin."

"Sure, I—"

"Did you say militia? And you are going looking for this García guy? You are not telling me you are going hunting?"

"I'm not saying anything specific, Pat. But be advised this guy is why your cabin got burned down." Not admitting he did it, but what he said was true. Technically, Don Diego was at fault.

"You best be careful, my friend. Alice would never forgive me if anything happened to you on my watch."

"Give her my best, Pat. Thanks again."

Tommy closed the cell and handed it back to Rosey.

She'd been listening to his side of the conversation. "It's nice to know people," she said. "It is your intention to take on Don Diego and his minions?"

He nodded. "I got no choice."

"Tommy maybe you need to reassess. Stay with me tonight. Stay alive."

"I can't." He slipped off the barstool. "Gotta go. Thanks for your help."

"I'll never see you again, will I?"

Tommy grinned. "You'll get over it."

She smiled back. "Damn straight. Don't mean I gotta like it." She grabbed him and hugged him hard. "Take care, Tommy. You're too good a man to lose."

"Thank you, dear." He unpeeled her arms and turned and went down the bar and out the door.

An hour later, he wheeled the Nissan into McAllister's circular drive once again. The transmission had been slipping.

The Lexus and the boat were missing from the double garage. The Harley with the Autolinx kit and the pickup were occupying the space. McAllister must have been waiting for him or heard him pull into the driveway. He stepped out of the front door and said something to somebody inside and closed the door.

As Tommy got out of the Nissan, McAllister said, "You're late."

"Give me the money."

"I couldn't raise it all," McAllister said nervously.

Tommy moved so that the big man was between him and the house. "If you have a friend inside with a weapon, you need to know that I will kill you first, then him next." He stared at the big man. "Your move."

"I, um, sold the Lexus at a big loss. Couldn't find a buyer for the boat, so I used it as collateral for a loan." He looked down at his bandaged and splinted right thumb.

"You got a savings account? Checking?"

"Naw, I'm kind of cash strapped right now."

"Give me what you got, McAllister."

McAllister handed Tommy a folded over grocery bag from Publix Supermarket. "Forty grand."

"Less than half."

"Best I can do."

"You still got a Harley and a pickup. And I know you held out on me. You should have sold the other vehicles."

"I need something for my family."

Tommy spoke as the thought struck him. "You should also have plenty of money from the sale of the business."

"No, I don't, mister. I ain't a good money manager and I barely covered what I owed."

Tommy held out his hand. "You're lying." A man like McAllister would never turn loose of all the cash right away. But Tommy had no time to screw with him. "Give me the keys to your motorcycle."

Surprise etched across McAllister's face. "I can't do that, I..."

Tommy took a step closer and McAllister saw the edge of Tommy's boiling rage escape from his eyes. McAllister stepped back and dug into his pocket. He handed Tommy keys on a ring.

Tommy wheeled the motorcycle alongside the Nissan, which put the 4X4 between them and the street. He gave McAllister the keys. "Get me the rest of the money; I'll be back. When you get the money, I want you to take it all down to the Rape Crisis Center and give it to them. Get a signed letter of receipt. When I return, I want to see that letter. And if you're smart, you'll dump this pickup and make sure there's no link to you, understand?"

"It's hot?" He was bewildered trying to understand Tommy.

"Cops will know you didn't buy it or just find it. I'm being nice to you because you're a family man."

Tommy removed the top of the Autolinx carrier and pulled out a golf bag full of clubs. He tossed that aside and opened the door to the Nissan. He uncovered his weapons and stuck them into the vertical carrier.

McAllister's eyes went wide. "You gonna start a war?"

"Something like that." He put the cash and a couple of hand-guns in a saddlebag.

"Jesus."

Tommy found a helmet in the garage. Florida laws allowed motorcyclists to ride without a helmet; however, the real smart guys wore them. He'd read somewhere that the largest source of organ donations came from motorcyclists. He also didn't want to be recognized. There was a brand new leather jacket hanging off the mirror of McAllister's pickup. Tommy pulled that on; doubtless he'd paid for the damn thing anyway. And it would help conceal some handguns here shortly.

He pulled the helmet on and dropped the sun shield. Without another word, he gunned the motorcycle and burned out of the driveway and down the road. He had to know the capabilities of the bike. Then he slowed back to the speed limit. No need to attract any local traffic cops.

He'd already studied maps and knew where Don Diego García's condominium was. He drove straight there. It was an imposing building with three towers. Apparently residents parked on an enclosed bottom floor, and guest parking was in a large parking lot in front of the building. It had a circular driveway running under a portico. Hoity toidy, thought Tommy.

The more he looked the more convinced he became that María Elena wouldn't be here. But this was his only lead, at least locally. If he could find García, he could use the man as a hostage to get her back. The only other place he could think to look was the 13 training acreage, somewhere to the west out in the swamps and palmetto plains.

One thing at a time. He parked out on the street, facing out, behind a van. Relatively concealed, he slid his automatic under his new jacket and another automatic into a jacket pocket. He took a couple of extra magazines, just in case. Most of the time he only needed one weapon and a lot of extra ammo. Often it was easier to drop a magazine and slap another in than drag out another handgun, which, of course, had different shooting characteristics.

He walked into the parking lot and saw a couple go in. They slid a key card through a scanner. Well, he could follow someone in. To stall, he bent to tie his shoe behind a BMW. This time he had a shoe to fake tying; he wasn't wearing his usual boots, but light Nikes. If you might have to move quickly, heavy boots aren't the right footwear. And while Nikes didn't kick as well as heavy boots, he could make up for that by being faster with his feet.

A UPS truck pulled up through the entranceway with plenty of clearance.

Tommy stood up and walked quickly toward the door. The brown uniformed lady was waving to someone inside and the door opened and she walked in and the door closed before Tommy could get there without running. Maybe he could have another opportunity when the UPS driver left. But, Tommy saw the lady disappear down a corridor.

Then he stopped to tie his shoe again. He was violating all his hard-learned training. He should have scouted around the building and the neighborhood for a couple of hours until he knew all of the roads and the nuances of the area. However, his sense of urgency was overwhelming. He shook his head physically. As soon as you get an emotional involvement, your professionalism goes away. God damn it! He'd always avoided personal attachments. He smiled grimly to himself. Oh, well, she was worth it. Hell, she was worth anything. Once he'd embarked on this journey, he'd given up, without articulating it exactly, any hope of living through this. That was a major reason he had tried to not become involved with María Elena; for once he'd scoped out what was going on, he saw a huge need for his talents and as a compliment, likely his own untimely death.

Once more to die, Tommy Atkins, once more to die.

However, it was his full intention to live through this to get María Elena out of trouble. Except now, he had another couple of reasons to live: there were at least two people who needed to die, and Tommy vowed to be the instrument of their demise. And hopefully, sooner rather than later.

Two attractive women were walking under the overhang heading for the door. He cursed himself for failure to pay attention. Pay attention, Atkins, he told himself. This is not the time for your mind to wander.

Quickly he got to his feet a second time and wandered slowly toward the door. From behind, the two women were well worth following.

CHAPTER TWENTY-SEVEN: HER

María Elena hurried across the driveway and was enveloped in Eduardo's comforting arms.

"Come in, my child." The old man glanced at Tommy in the truck.

She didn't say anything, but allowed Eduardo to usher her inside. He seemed older than she remembered. A classic patrician moustache and long gray hair, Eduardo Quinones presented a formidable appearance. And he was as a well known barrister and Cuban-exile advocate, he'd become a local legend. Her father, mother, and Eduardo had been the original members of 13 de enero. And Eduardo had naturally become her godfather. She knew that back in his day, he'd been tall and handsome, not that he was no longer such, just that then he'd been dashing and always around. His wife had died years ago; thus one of her own names, Alejandrina.

Eduardo continued to usher her down the hallway. "Who's that man in the truck? Where have you been? Do you know what kind of trouble you're in?"

This did not match his words during their brief phone conversation when she'd called from Orlando International. She wondered what had changed. Should she have checked in sooner?

They emerged in a great room with the entire dockside wall made of one giant plate glass window. Eduardo urged her toward the door. "I was just getting ready to go out."

She saw white-dressed crewmen swarming over the boat, preparing to cast off. "I need to talk to you, Eduardo." They went through the door where two more crewmen waited.

"I would like to show you my new toy," he told her. They walked down a sidewalk toward the cabin cruiser. "CUBAN BEAUTY?" asked María Elena.

Eduardo nodded. "I named it after your mother?"

Something struck María Elena as odd. "Okay. Why?"

He took her arm. "Come for a ride with me, my dear."

"I can't, Eduardo." She stopped and he tugged her arm. "I need to know some things."

"But I don't have time," Eduardo said. He nodded at the two crewmen behind them and they stepped forward.

María Elena had developed a sixth sense in the last couple of months. She dodged aside, but it was too late. One grabbed her by the arms; the other slapped a strip of duct tape across her mouth. As she struggled, he wrapped duct tape around her arms and torso pinning her arms. The two men lifted her by the arms and carried her toward the boat.

She screamed fruitlessly into the tape and kicked out. She connected to one knee and the man went down. The other ignored him and dragged her across the dock and up the gangplank. The second man limped after them.

Eduard Quinones was already on board. "Cast off."

The limping man jumped aboard and disconnected the gangplank. Another crewman cast off the last line from the cleat on the dock and jumped aboard.

The engine was already idling.

"Go," Eduardo commanded. "Get her out of sight."

They dragged her kicking down into the salon and sat her on a couch. Beneath her, the boat surged ahead. One of them searched her roughly and, while he found her hideout gun, he surprised her by not feeling her up any at all. So she cooperated a little instead of fighting against her bonds and her captors.

Her thoughts were bitter. Was there no end to treachery and treason? The one person in the whole world whom she'd counted on.

In a minute, there came a shout from above and glass shattered. Immediately thereafter, she heard the sound of a gunshot.

Tommy!

Quinones tumbled down the stairs into the cabin.

Another shot, then a series of three. CUBAN BEAUTY zigzagged. Quinones cursed.

"That must be the man I've been hearing about." He shot her a piercing gaze. "Well, it matters not, for he'll be dead in a few minutes."

María Elena mumbled into the tape.

Eduardo made his way over and gently pried the tape loose. "What did you want to say?"

"I was trying to say you've just signed your own death warrant."

He laughed. "You do not sound like my old Alejandrina. Now, you are so much more like your mother."

She spat at him. "Diego bought you off. You are a traitor to my family and to Cuba."

"Such is not the case," Eduardo said.

More gunshots, now father away and yet María Elena heard the plunk of rounds striking expensive wood. "He will hunt you down and kill you."

Eduardo shrugged. "It's not me, my dear. It's your husband he must negotiate."

"All those years, all those people counting on you."

Eduardo went to a sideboard. "It is not of my concern."

She had an epiphany. "You. You're the one who introduced Diego García to Papá. You brought him in."

Eduardo smiled. "I did that. Yes, my dear. It was my pleasure." His smile went away and his voice hardened. "He was to be my puppet. But this puppet master lost his touch. The puppet took control." He pulled a bottle out of a slot and poured himself a glass of vodka. "I learned to drink this from the Russians." He held up the glass to her. "Cheers." He drank. "Yes, my protégé took the reins and took control. But I had other business; I was into politics and power and it was okay since García's goals were close to mine." He paused. "Now we are uneasy partners. But I do make an embarrassing amount of money."

"Why? For God's sake, Eduardo, why? It was always you and Papá against the world and against Castro and his minions. Why?"

He walked to her. He cupped her chin and she tried to pull back.

"Because of you."

"Me? I don't understand." He'd never shown anything but a grandfatherly interest in her, a favorite uncle.

"The name of this fine piece of boat? *CUBAN BEAUTY.*" He sighed and sat next to her. She fidgeted away from him. "Your mother. You. The whole point is that you could have been mine—my child. Your father stole her from me. It was the three of us in Cuba. Those were exciting times." He stopped and seemed to be remembering.

The boat had straightened out and was powering along in the bay. Tommy had failed.

"I don't know what your game is, Eduardo, but you need to know something."

He looked the question at her and drank some vodka.

"To keep you or even Diego from a horrible death, you should know Tommy will hunt you down and kill you slowly— if I'm harmed. The only chance you have is to keep me alive and whole and trade me for your life."

Pain was in his eyes. "Brave words, but I care not." He shrugged. "I have died slowly a thousand times. And sometimes I regret what I have done, for I should roast in hell."

"What are you talking about?"

"Your mother. I held such resentment against her choosing your father over me. I had someone turn her in to the Revolutionary authorities on one of her trips to Cuba. They took her into that prison and misused her and put her against the wall and killed her."

"No." Her mind spun. "It can't be."

"Do you not think I have lived in hell ever since? The only thing I have done is prolong my worthless life to atone." He sighed once more. "But I am weak and I have become accustomed to this life, the money and the power. I do not wish to give it up."

María Elena sank back. Her entire world had just collapsed. She could not even think about what her mother had gone through. And Eduardo was responsible for Diego García. In turn, Eduardo was responsible for her father's murder. He was responsible for the demise of 13 de enero and the rise of something hideous in its place.

María Elena didn't know what to think; she didn't know what to do. All she wanted to do was get away from this craziness.

Another and worse thought struck her: Tommy. Tommy Atkins would find her. Nothing would stop him, of that she was certain. But he would be arrayed against unknown forces, thugs, military, and gang members. He'd rush in and become a sitting duck. All of her bluster: she should have said nothing; she should not have warned them Tommy would come for her no matter what. Damn. Why hadn't she thought it all through?

She understood that now Tommy had become her steel; she relied on him being there for her. She was thankful she had known him and loved him. It was all she had left.

And she had just committed him to die violently.

CHAPTER TWENTY-EIGHT: HIM

He was timing it so they'd reach the entrance before him. One had a key card out. As he neared, he saw through the glass alongside the double doors that in the lobby and off to the side was a security guard behind a counter. He had a couple of computer monitors on his desk, obviously for review of security cameras. Great, just fucking great. Tommy did note that the rent-a-cop had the same uniform as Elmer down in Miami. That private security company was making a lot of money.

One of the women was scanning a card and the door unlocked just as Tommy arrived. The other woman stubbed out a cigarette in the courtesy stand. He extended his arm for the two and held the door. They barely paid any attention to him. Unusual, since often he rated a speculative look. Tommy followed them through the doors and toward the elevators. The guard nodded at the women and his eyes questioned Tommy.

"Hey," Tommy said, "Elmer says hello."

The guy shook his head and then recognized what Tommy was saying. "That old goat?"

"He's got an outside job, you got air conditioning." Tommy sped up toward the elevators. Apparently, that held the guard and precluded a challenge.

Three elevators, three towers he realized. He was looking for 502. A sign regarding all three guided him. All the 01's were the first tower and the left elevator, the 02's the center tower and center elevator, and the 03's the right tower.

The women were standing at the center elevator and Tommy went that way. One of them was holding a little white dog in her arms. Tommy thought idly that dogs in a condo were not an easy thing logistically speaking. You had to walk them or something. Not his problem.

The door opened and he dallied so he could take an elevator alone. The tall, super attractive brunette held the door open for him expectantly. He realized it would be very awkward if he stayed standing around in the lobby; so he hurried onto the elevator and turned around, his back to the wall.

The blonde with short hair and white dog said, "What floor?"

"Five," he decided. When in doubt, go in fast and go in strong. Surprise is your best weapon.

The brunette pushed five for him and then six for them.

The little white dog eyed him coldly.

The tall brunette adjusted her striking sun dress, showing plenty of cleavage. Even as his mind was occupied with whatever was coming next, he realized she was one hell of a good-looking woman. She smelled faintly of smoke.

Upon further scrutiny, the blonde was highly attractive, too. She had an ass to die for. She scratched the dog's head and he absorbed the attention haughtily. "Nice dog, Fluffy. You're so cute," the blonde crooned. She was dressed in a traditional women's business gray pantsuit.

Tommy's eyes couldn't help but scan back to the brunette's cleavage. Her dress seemed even lower than when he'd first looked at her. He tried to not appear to be looking down her dress, though doubtless she was used to it.

The elevator passed three.

It was a sun-yellow south Florida sun dress and did little to conceal her shapely hips.

She caught him looking and gave him a speculative glance.

He colored slightly, caught like a teenager.

The blonde was still cooing to the dog, nuzzling into its neck.

The elevator chimed at five, and Tommy waited as the doors opened.

Back on task, he scanned the landing before he walked out. Fancy. Only one door and that was directly opposite the elevator. Nobody was on the landing. It was a damn fine condo unit, your own floor in the center tower.

"Have a nice day," the blonde said.

Tommy glanced at the brunette once more, letting his eyes flow up her body past her jutting breasts to her finely sculpted face. She smiled knowingly at him. Was there an invitation hidden in her glance?

He shook his head, more to get back in focus than to ignore her.

"Thanks," he mumbled and stepped to the door of the elevator.

As his foot went over onto the fifth floor landing, the brunette's arm moved aside and her purse struck the wall of the elevator with a definitive thunk.

It took Tommy a split second to come to realization. "Oh, shit," he said aloud and turned toward her. He'd heard that kind of noise before. A gun in her purse striking the fake wooden wall.

The brunette had a sly smile on her face.

The door pinged angrily at him to move so it could close automatically and go up to six.

Tommy reached for his gun.

"Ahem," said the blonde.

Tommy glanced at her as his arm streaked inside his leather jacket.

The muzzle of an automatic gaped at him from beneath the damn dog Fluffy.

Tommy's shoulders slumped. By the time he looked back at the brunette she had her gun out from somewhere.

He shook his head at the trap. "Jeez. You're the best. I've never been had like that before." Clever they were; and they must have co-opted the security guard.

The blonde smiled amiably. "Step off the elevator, Mr. Atkins."

Two automatics tracked him. The blonde had her weapon

arm through the elevator door to stall the auto-close mechanism. They stepped out behind him, neither gun wavering from its target.

In seconds they were standing on the fifth floor landing.

"What now?" asked Tommy. He eyed the brunette. Usually he was immune to hot babes, but this one—If I wasn't smitten with someone else, I'd chase you around the office, he thought to himself.

"Me, too, maybe," the brunette said, interpreting his look. "Hands behind your head, you know the position."

He clasped his hands behind his head while she removed his weapons. The blonde kept her gun at his head.

Tommy was scanning through his mental files and they fit no profile involved in this. Could they be part of Don Diego's cabal? No, there was something about them, something— "Feds," he accused.

"Guilty," said the blonde. "I'm CIA and she's FBI."

And there could only be one kind of fed associated with this whole mess. "JTF 13?" If so, they were on Don Diego García's side as far as he could extrapolate.

The blonde looked under attractive eyebrows at him. "You know us?"

He shook his head. "I wish."

"I'm the Good Fairy and I'm granting your wish," she said.

The brunette laughed, the sound intriguing and one you want to hear in the bedroom.

"I am Susan Quantrell and she is Linda Landover."

"Doubtless it's Suzie Q and Linda L," Tommy said. He castigated himself for being too garrulous; you don't learn anything when you're talking. And if nothing else, you certainly don't want an opponent to know how smart or how stupid you are.

"Inside," Suzie Q motioned with her handgun.

Tommy went that way, biding his time. Would García be here? He surely hoped so. But he did admit grudgingly that the newfound Linda L would be a dangerous adversary and he'd have to plan his move carefully. Her eyes did not telegraph; most times people's eyes telegraph when they are holding weapons on you. Not hers. But they followed him unblinkingly, and he could tell she was plotting each step he took as if she were doing that thing. So she'd no doubt identify anything he could use against them just as or before he did.

The blonde opened the unlocked door and nodded for him to precede them. He walked into a short entry hall past a very roomy kitchen into a large open family room. Dark wood paneling. Expensive furniture obviously done by a professional decorator. Several large sliding glass doors opened onto a wide patio overlooking the Atlantic. Tommy saw the requisite sailboats and small boats all the way to the horizon. He felt pangs when he saw a similar cabin cruiser to CUBAN BEAUTY. He wondered where that boat had gone. The condo was empty around him; his sixth sense told him no one else was here. He was surprised that the place looked tossed. If García was allied with JTF 13, then they weren't treating him well. There was more going on around here than he was aware of. The hell with that, he decided, that's their problem. His problem, his focus was María Elena and her safe return.

The brunette set his weapons down on a sideboard next to a laptop computer. The evidence was telling him they'd already been here, obviously looking for something, maybe even Diego García.

He looked around for a weapon he could stand close to and perhaps use it when the time came.

Fluffy trotted over to him and sniffed his Nikes.

Two automatics were still trained on him. Linda dropped a set of handcuffs on an end table. "Put them on, please."

He considered not doing so, but one look and he knew she'd kneecap him or something similar. He hurried to seemingly comply, because he wanted to cuff his arms in front, not behind. He put them on and clicked them onto the first détente.

"More," directed Landover.

Two more clicks.

This time she shrugged. She'd seen his hands and knew he

wouldn't be able to escape. "Sit down, please."

Tommy moved quickly to a hard chair next to a window overlooking another condominium next door. He could get up easier and even if the sun was setting now the window would provide a background glare which might give him a slight edge. He placed his feet directly under him for a quick launch.

But they stayed far enough away to negate an escape attempt with any chance of success.

They stood in front of him, neither weapon straying.

"Mr. Atkins," said Suzie Q. "We've got you making your first kill at sixteen in Tampa."

They were going to try to intimidate him with their knowledge. He could tell from Quantrell's eyes and demeanor that she was the boss here.

"He deserved it," Tommy said.

"You were described as a thug"

"I prefer 'roughneck.' Ah, the folly of youth."

"Granted," she continued. "Your name at the time was Longboat. Admittedly, we don't know what all went down back then. After that you volunteered and enlisted in the Marines. Based in Lebanon mainly. I got into some super secret CIA archives about your unit and their operations in the Middle East, and those missions were way, way off the books."

She must be CIA for sure, then.

"Yes ma'am. That President Reagan and Director Casey were pretty cagey. Nobody ever knew."

"We do not know what your participation amounted to."

Tommy said nothing.

"Interpol knows of you; we have reports to that effect. I have a contact in the *Direction du Renseignment Militaire*." The French Directorate of Military Intelligence. CIA's French was better than his. "Quite illegally my contact accessed personnel records of the Légion étrangére. You enlisted under the name Alexander Dumas. Quite literary, I might add."

Tommy shrugged.

"Conservatively, they have you killing maybe a couple of

hundred Cubans and MPLA guerillas."

"I was a soldier; I did what I was ordered to do. MPLA, UNITA, FNLA, they were all crazy guerillas more interested in rape, torture, murder and looting than political affiliations. The Cubans were Soviet surrogates and fighting for money that Castro needed badly."

"An historian, too." CIA sought out Fluffy and returned her eyes to Tommy.

"None of them were up to human standards." Tommy casually looked around for any kind of advantage. Nothing. Maybe he could flip the chair over his head at one. But that Linda, she was going to be quick. He'd get one chance—if that. He eyed the white fur ball of a dog that was busy sniffing everything in the room.

Suzie Q continued mercilessly. "Directly you popped up in a hellish motorcycle gang in southern Arizona under the moniker of The Vicar." She didn't look away from him.

"Why are you telling me this?"

"Apparently you accounted for dozens of mules and human traffickers. That comes from a classified diary of an INS supervisor."

They had great intel on him. Could there be a sleeper agent in the group nowadays? Or earlier. Should he try to contact the Bear to warn him? Maybe not, the informer could be the bartender Phil. Phil was a decent guy regardless. Besides, Tommy had his own problems now.

The dog kept trotting over to the three humans, sniffing, and returning to elsewhere in the condo. Each time he got closer to Tommy.

Tommy shook his head angrily. "First of all, those men were multiple rapists and murderers of the worse sort. Second, I ain't admitting anything. Third, where the fuck was your precious federal government? And fourth, you probably noticed by now that I don't like rapists."

Suzie smiled thinly. "We could tell from the immediate demise of the rapist and the judge who let the rapist off over in

Tampa."

"I dunno what you're talking about."

"Let me continue, Mr. Atkins or whatever your name is. After that we have you as a real hitman in Tampa and elsewhere for a mob guy Santana and a couple of other capos. Nobody knows exactly what you did there, but our people interviewed a retired police lieutenant who surmises you took out maybe twenty, including the aforementioned judge."

"One, you can't prove anything. Two, was that old Delmar Rios?"

"It was."

"How's he doing?"

"Retired and fishing all the time. Said he's glad to be shut of you."

"Decent guy for a cop. He never could count right."

"Next it's off to prison."

"They can't get you on one thing; they'll trump up charges on another. You can't fight the man."

Suzie went on as if he hadn't interrupted. "The warden couldn't prove it, but he suspects you of killing three or four men there."

"I keep saying, you can't prove it. You can't prove any of this. You're trying to hold it over my head for some reason, some leverage. I point out that you gotta protect yourself in the slam. You can't give one damn inch and, if you do that thing, you make enemies. They pretty much left me alone. Finally, if you get a certain reputation, lots of things get blamed on you which you didn't do."

CIA was relentless. "Lately, we have a rumor of half a dozen dead 13 soldiers, proof of another five or so in San Antonio. Maybe six more outside of Nogales. Toss in one crime boss in Vegas."

These people had undercover agents everywhere. The dog was sniffing toward him.

"You can't prove any of this and they ought to learn not to fuck with me."

"Suddenly now, you've turned noble. All your energies expended on behalf of Mrs. García."

"You mean María Elena?" he asked casually and snatched up Fluffy to pitch the dog underhanded at them.

But Linda Landover was too quick for him. "I'll put three rounds through Fluffy into you."

Tommy knew what she said would occur.

Suzie Q stepped closer to him than she should have, but he knew she still commanded the situation. "Put him down, Mr. Atkins, or I will kill you."

"I believe you would."

"She would, quick, too," said Linda. "Believe me."

Tommy pitched the dog onto a nearby couch. "I don't hide behind dogs anyway."

Suzie Q glanced at Linda L. "Did you see how fast he moved? Fluffy was on the floor and instantly Atkins had the poor thing."

Linda nodded. "Suze, we should just kill him now. He's too dangerous to let go and, if we do, he'll fuck everything up pursuing his own agenda."

"Say again?"

"He's one of the few who will change the situation—"

"Maybe it needs changing?"

"It does, but not to his specs, but to ours. I'm telling you." Linda began pacing.

"We can squeeze him and then trade him to the marshals."

"For what? Afterward, they wouldn't pay off anyway."

Was she trying to intimidate him? Did they want something from him? If they did, there was something bad wrong between 13 de enero and JTF 13. Tommy could almost guess what it was. His eyes followed Linda. The other, Quantrell, was highly dangerous, but she was cerebral and would work out solutions. FBI would take the shortest, most efficient path: kill him.

Suzie Q, irritated, said, "I know Linda is beautiful; your eyes follow her, they won't leave her. Quit it."

"That's not why he's watching me, Suze."

"No?"

"Ask him."

Tommy said, "She's right, ma'am."

"What the hell's going on here?"

"Well, CIA, it's not her sexy fuck-me eyes, but the stuff under that layer. She's one of the three or so most beautiful women I've ever seen in person. I am paying attention to her not because of that, but because she is one of the most dangerous people I have ever seen. Believe me, I know. Most professionals can tell." Tommy grinned suddenly. "Not counting a certain late Cuban commander who I tracked through jungle and dusty hills from Zaire well into Angola. He was tough and tricky."

"I'll be damned," said Suzie Q. "Complimentary, ain't he?"

"And not counting some old sergeants, SEALS, Special Force guys on duty across the world that nobody's heard of."

Linda stopped pacing. "Okay, Atkins, so who are the others?"

"One is a Mexican, the late Juan Pablo from Sonora."

CIA and FBI glanced at each other. "We heard he was dead."

"That's so."

"Who killed him?" Linda wanted to know.

"The other of the three."

"That would be?" asked Susan Quantrell.

He didn't answer.

"It's obvious," said Linda. "He did it."

"Aw shucks," said Tommy, wondering why he was banging his own drum. Was he subconsciously trying to impress FBI?

"Between the two of you, this place is full of—oh, yeah, modesty." CIA shook her head.

Tommy's eyes went back to FBI.

She faced him, legs apart, hips thrust out. "Thank you for the compliment." Then she grinned. "You oughta see me on PMS. Anyway, you flatter me." She turned to Suzie Q. "He's buttering me up, trying to set me up."

"Wasn't a compliment, merely the truth," Tommy said. "One thing though?"

"And that is?" She cocked her head.

"You gotta quit smoking, sweetheart. Your enemy is gonna

know your habits. All they have to do is wait outside for you to take a smoke break. As attractive as you are, they still gonna off you—no matter the terrible waste."

FBI smiled widely. "Fuck that. I'll take my chances."

Tommy grinned. "You know, under different circumstances I could really like you."

"Well, thank you, Mr. Atkins."

"But it's you and CIA here, isn't it?"

"You guessed?"

"No, I figured. The protective way you work together. The way you look at each other. Little tell tales. It's another weak spot."

FBI relaxed. "You got it half right. I'm bi-. And I'll tell you what, if we break up or anything happens to her, I'll come look you up."

"My pleasure—if you don't kill me off. That is, if a certain lady dumps me and I don't eat my gun because of it, or she doesn't make it through—"

Quantrell interrupted. "That answers a ton of questions."

"Ain't love grand," said Linda simultaneously.

"—this and you're available," Tommy finished.

FBI gave him an enigmatic smile. Which told Tommy that she hadn't decided whether to kill him or not. "If I don't kill you now, I might later, if anything happens to Suze."

Women, go figure. "First: no you ain't. Second, I never killed any women—that I know of—and I ain't gonna start now. Anyway, not going to happen on my account, you and me, for my heart is taken by another. I came here to rescue her and she's not here."

CIA perked up. "Rescue? We're talking María Elena García?"

Tommy hesitated, and then nodded. "We went to her father's lawyer's house. Quinones. He was María Elena's godfather. He took her in a cabin cruiser out into the bay down in Miami this morning."

Brow furrowed, CIA asked, "What do you mean 'took her?' What exactly is going on? Why did you and she go on the run? I mean besides you being an escaped prisoner and all."

Tommy saw she had her own suspicions, but the smart ones always wanted your information to work on regardless of what they already knew. He decided he had little choice but to level with them, for he needed them to be either on his side or neutral. "María Elena discovered her husband was cooking the books and getting rich off donations to 13; not only that, but he was charging people to bring them out of Cuba and maybe running drugs and spitting on the sidewalk, too."

"When you paint by the numbers and the blocks fill, pretty soon the real picture begins to emerge." CIA dropped her weapon to her side. But Linda still had hers trained on Tommy. Doubtless, he thought, that was plenty.

"So now you're backing a bad hand," Tommy ventured. If they were in on it, he'd just gotten himself killed and doomed María Elena.

"How'd you get mixed up in this?" asked Landover.

"I stumbled upon García killing the old man and turning his men loose on María Elena."

The two looked at each other. "You'd swear to that in court?"

"Sure. But I ain't going to court and you know it."

Quantrell nodded and Linda said, "You bet your ass you ain't."

It was obvious that JTF 13 had no control now and they'd be guilty by association. They were in a pickle, too. Whatever, he might have just turned the corner with these two.

Quantrell continued. "So you interfered, grabbed the girl, and ran. And you and Ms. García have been on the run ever since."

Tommy shrugged and sat back to telegraph to FBI he was no longer a danger to them; not true, but that's what he wanted them to think.

She didn't buy it for she remained as she was, with the weapon trained on him.

"Why did you stay together?" asked the CIA agent.

"You ask too many questions, CIA. It just happened."

"Stockholm Syndrome?" asked Linda.

Suzie Q shook her head. "Methinks the opposite of the Stockholm Syndrome, as you speculated earlier. He said he was in love with her."

"No I didn't," said Tommy, feeling like he should cut off an ear.

"In so many words." CIA went to a side board and brought over a laptop computer. "So García has his wife back. What's he going to do now?"

"Kill her," said Tommy and Linda at the same time.

"When you want to know the answer, ask a professional," Suzie said.

"Will you help me?" Tommy asked. A question he had never, ever asked anyone, anytime, anywhere.

"I don't know," said CIA.

"What's in it for us?" asked FBI.

Tommy snorted. "Look, you might be recording this whole thing, it occurs to me too late. So you are not going to agree to money or me swearing to kill García. So how about this, suppose I help you with your problem?"

"Our problem being?" asked Quantrell. She knew the answer, but wanted to hear if he'd figured it out far enough.

"A rogue militia unit. Murder cover-up. Misuse of federal funds, or downright theft. Association with human trafficking. And maybe drugs. JTF 13 is in trouble and the man will whack the whole task force if this comes out. Not to mention you all getting canned. And that's just a start."

"It's nothing we can't handle," said FBI.

"And haven't already handled institutionally before," added CIA.

Tommy shrugged, jingling the cuffs in front of him. "Go ahead, then."

Neither answered him.

Tommy glanced around the room. They'd been looking for evidence or some specific piece of information, he couldn't guess which.

"So where's Diego García?" he asked casually.

The two looked at each other. Quantrell said quietly, "We don't know. And we would like to know."

Tommy cursed silently. He believed this woman. They needed to take García out any way they could and the sooner the better. Especially since they'd learned of the María Elena kidnapping.

"I'll open with a couple of cards," said CIA. "He could be anywhere. He's not here and there are no signs of a quick and final exit to a country with no extradition treaties with Uncle Sam." She paused to think. "Given what you told us, I suspect he was fairly comfortable here and in his role until this morning when he obviously learned of your and Ms. García's presence. That would trigger him to find out what she knows so he can evaluate his own personal safety. So he needs to be collocated with her and, at the same time, have the ability for a quick getaway."

"What was the name of the boat she was taken on?" asked FBI.

"CUBAN BEAUTY," said Tommy.

Linda pulled a cell phone out and hit a quick dial preset. "Sandy? Listen, we need an immediate BOLO on a boat called *CUBAN BEAUTY*, slap a national security priority on it." She listened. "I dunno, just a sec." She looked at Tommy. "Describe it."

He did.

"All right, thanks, you can look it up in the data bases, too." Landover closed her phone.

"Good, that cabin cruiser will be parked somewhere around, even down in south Florida where it can run up a channel or two inland." Suzie Q reached for her laptop. "And if García makes a run for it, it's likely he'll use that boat for his getaway."

"Maybe you-all could see your way into releasing me and letting me go after them," Tommy said hopefully.

CIA shook her head. "No can do. I don't trust you. Your goals and ours are not the same. You might also screw things up for us. You'll stay with us so we can control the situation."

Tommy's voice became harsh. "Let me go and I will solve your problem. Period."

"You might solve *your* problem by taking us out," Quantrell pointed out.

Actually, Tommy was thinking about doing that in order to escape. "I told you I don't kill women."

"We are going to keep you honest in that endeavor, Mr. Atkins. You might well prove useful to us later on."

Tommy fumed.

CIA fiddled with her laptop. FBI watched Tommy closely, her weapon maintaining its target.

"This is where they have to be," Quantrell said, pointing to the screen. Tommy looked and only later wondered if she wasn't just priming him and aiming him at the problem. But he didn't care now or then, he simply had to get going. The sun was almost down now and time was elapsing. He might have a slight margin because it would take time for García to move from one location to wherever they were holding María Elena, or it would take a lot of time if they went down through the keys around into Florida Bay and lose themselves in the 'Glades or one of the thousands of islands dotting the coast around to Naples. He wondered if they'd take her to the training area they were using when they originally killed the old man and he'd interfered. García might also be hesitant to kill María Elena because of Tommy's warning; likely he now knew about Tommy burning down the house as a message and might be heeding that message: use María Elena as bait. And he needed her healthy to bait the trap. Might being the operable word. For all Tommy knew, Diego García might well just kill her right away and lure Tommy in any way.

CIA found a south Florida map and called it up. "Likely they'll repair to their own headquarters and their training ground over by the border of Dade County and the Cypress National Preserve." She played with the touch pad. "See, you can drive to it and you can moor a boat anywhere and drive right to it."

Tommy tried to memorize landmarks, but she kept getting her shapely hip in the way.

Linda was looking at the screen, too. "That's got to be it, Suze. The permanent cadre there are not the original 13 members; they have to be Don Diego's men. The old guard all have jobs and families. So anyone on that base would be sworn to García."

CIA scrolled and clicked. A topographical map came up. "We leased them a ton of acreage for a dollar, way back in the day when the cold war was hot and we needed them to distract Castro and his Soviet bosses."

"I've never been there," said Linda.

Suzie Q expanded the map point. "I have. A few thousand acres in the middle of nowhere. They even have a landing strip for choppers and cargo planes. We landed there once in an executive jet. Over here are the headquarters area and storage and supply buildings. This one, if I remember, is some kind of barracks. Farther along, this is the actual headquarters building where they run things and where the senior officers live." She was using her finger to touch the screen, a habit Tommy hated. But he was paying close attention. He still didn't know exactly where it was. Far to the west of Miami; he thought he recognized the Tamiami Trail. He thought only in passing that they were playing a game here to feed him info. It didn't matter as long as they had him under guard and handcuffed. Maybe the blonde was priming him in case he in fact did escape or they turned him loose. On the final hand, perhaps she was simply thinking and planning aloud.

"It's beginning to make sense to me, Suze," said the brunette. "If you're going to make a quick getaway, go where you got a stash of cash and documents for emergency. Go to an isolated location that you know well and have set up for such a purpose; García must have an escape plan and it's only logical that he escapes from territory he controls. It makes it so much easier."

"Or it is the best location in which to fight your enemies: on ground you have trained upon," said Quantrell quietly. "We can prove that somewhat if we search his home here. If we turn up nothing, that would mean his escape kit, documents, money, whatever is elsewhere in a place where he controls everything."

"Let us finish tossing the place then," said FBI.

CIA pointed at Tommy. "Secure him somewhere. I don't trust him loose."

Tommy's mind worked quickly. He was going to miss his opportunity. Not that Linda Landover had given him that opportunity, not even half of one.

The drapes around the window smelled of cigar smoke. García at least had good taste in cigars, he thought. Cuban and the finest, Tommy decided.

CIA's cell phone rang and she clicked it on. She listened for a moment. "The same name? *CUBAN BEAUTY?*" The blonde turned to look at Tommy. "Wow. You don't fuck around." She listened another moment. "Okay, thanks Sandy. Stay in touch." She pocketed the phone and shook her head at him.

"What?" asked Landover.

"Mr. Atkins," said the blonde, "perchance did you shoot up an exclusive neighborhood this morning?"

"Not exactly."

"And while you were not exactly shooting up the place with automatic weapons did you pause in your efforts to burn down a multi-million dollar mansion?"

"You bet, sweetie." He nailed her with his eyes. He was tired of sparring with these women. It wasn't getting him anywhere and María Elena was no closer to being rescued.

Quantrell observed him for a moment. She turned to Linda. "I can only guess that when they took the girl this morning, that Mr. Atkins over-reacted and drove all over this highly secure gated community with guns ablaze and, out of spite, torched a large mansion."

"*C'est la vie,*" said Tommy.

"Wow," said FBI and Tommy wondered if he'd detected a small dose of awe and jealousy. This thought comforted him: the feds were not all cookies and cream and bureaucrats and paper pushers. FBI was one who realized stuff needed to be done and went ahead and did that stuff.

CIA went on. "Secure him somewhere out of the way. Then let's finish tossing the place and get going."

"What do you want to do with him?" Linda asked.

"We have to decide if it's safe to take him with us, or should we get a SWAT team and an armored paddy wagon to cart him out of here."

FBI stepped toward him and inched the gun upwards a couple of times.

Tommy stood and she motioned him to go ahead of her toward the patio.

"Outside," she said.

He nodded and slid a pair of sliders aside and stepped onto the patio. The early night was warm and lights were coming on up and down the beach. He looked down at the beach and saw only small waves lapping ashore. Late afternoon was the best chance for thunderstorms, but not tonight.

FBI urged him toward the waist-high railing. He stood next to it. She tossed him a handcuff key. "You know what I want."

He removed one handcuff and threaded it around the top rail and resecured it. He held the key out to her awkwardly, not able to reach far because of the handcuffs restraining him to the railing.

She shook her head and nodded to the floor.

Tommy dropped the key and kicked it over to her. She scooted it farther from him, past the reach of his feet and legs, and, bending over, retrieved it. Of course, his eyes cued to her cleavage as the dress dropped away from her body. When she straightened, he just shook his head. Her eyes flashed acknowledgement and she turned and went inside. He watched her as she went to the table with the laptop and set her automatic down. Then she began a professional job of opening and closing drawers, searching behind furniture and shelves.

Tommy leaned on the rail. The design of the condo units were such that it would be highly dangerous for him to try to drop to the patio of the unit beneath him. And the other towers were too far to jump between. The construction of the outside walls contained no fancy decorations he could use for climbing. Five floors below him was the Olympic pool. It looked almost as if you could jump off this patio and land in the water, at the diving end. But he knew this to be an optical illusion. You'd need a boost like a trampoline or a spring board to reach out far enough to land in the water.

There was no way he was jumping off that balcony anyway. He did know that he had zero chance of making it through the condo with the two feds alert as they were.

But he had no choice. While leaning over the railing and appearing to be watching the pool below and the flight of pelicans winging over the Atlantic, he manipulated his necklace cross and the hidden handcuff key popped into his hand. Quickly, while blocking any view of his activities with his body, he uncuffed himself and slid the cuffs inside his jacket pocket. As he tried to formulate a plan, he reaffixed the key back into the cross design.

He decided to attract FBI out on the patio to take her and then deal with CIA after.

He glanced over his shoulder to place the two women inside.

But Linda Landover apparently had ESP and knew something was wrong, for her head was craning around toward him. She was alongside the wall leading from the patio searching an entertainment center. Her gun was still on the far table.

She must have smelled something; the good ones can do that. She dropped what she was doing and ran toward him. The two sliders were still open, so she had to jump slightly to miss the threshold and the slider tracks.

That was her undoing.

Tommy stayed as he was until the last second. When she was airborne for that second, he made his move. Likely he could beat her hand to hand, but that would take too long and it was not a guarantee. He could kill her while she was vulnerable. But he respected her and didn't kill women. No, there was only one choice. He kept his hands at the patio rail, seemingly still handcuffed to the cross piece.

As Linda lunged forward, Tommy ducked and grabbed her by the perfect curve of her ass and under her shoulder and, harnessing her forward motion, threw her high up over his head and the railing.

As she sailed over him, her eyes smoldered with the urge to kill him.

"Suze!" she shouted. She wasn't hollering for help, Tommy knew, but to warn the other woman.

FBI arced up and out. Tommy knew exactly what she was thinking. Her hand darted under her dress to her thigh. He watched the thoughts process through her eyes. She had a hideout gun, no doubt. A lightweight belly gun likely, one well rounded and sleek so as to draw quickly and not snag on clothing. She could take the time to draw and kill him or she could take the time to orient herself for any possible chance of survival. Surely she knew of the pool below? He also thought she'd want to shoot him in order to protect Quantrell from him. He saw all these thoughts process through her in a micro second, just as they would have through him were the situation reversed. He saw her decide that since he hadn't killed her outright, he likely wouldn't kill Suzie Q unless it was absolutely necessary. He saw her conclude that their best chance was for her to survive the fall.

She discontinued the attempt to draw her hideout weapon and at the apex of her forward arc, she swiveled her head to locate herself in relation to the building and the ground below. Without a moment's pause, FBI rolled her body into a perfect swan position for the fall toward the pool.

Tommy knew this was a mistake, and he saw the realization on her face, too. As she started her fall, she jackknifed her body to a feet first orientation. As her fall accelerated, that wonderful yellow sun dress flared up like a storm of butterfly wings and exposed her lower body. What an ass, he thought. A thong revealed a whole lot. But he also saw that on one thigh, she had strapped a hideout gun, likely a snub nose, something light, smooth, and sleek, as he's speculated, easy to draw and not get hung up on clothing. Maybe a five shot revolver, but probably a six since FBI obviously liked firepower.

On her other thigh, some kind of knife was snuggled in by a black strap.

Fascinated, he watched as she flew down faster and faster. He wondered if he'd tossed her far enough to clear the pool deck and land in the deep end. She certainly had a chance.

The yellow dress billowed and she stretched her arms over her head, a good move, so that she could bring them down and brake her out-of-control knifing into the pool water.

And she cleared the pool deck and lip of the pool and cut into the water like a dolphin. Her dress captured water and tugged her to a stop as she flayed her arms to keep herself from slamming into the floor of the pool. In seconds, she popped up and stroked for the side of the pool. She levered herself up and her eyes searched above until she saw him leaning over the railing watching her. If her eyes were lasers, they would have struck him dead.

Tommy Atkins gave Linda Landover a friendly wave and smile. At least one thing had gone right today. Then he cursed himself, for he'd been witnessing the drama and should have been moving. CIA could well be standing behind him fixing to shoot him.

He whirled and didn't see her anywhere in the living area. He hurried inside and grabbed FBI's gun and strode quickly to the master bedroom. A circular bed made him angry and he didn't know why for a second.

"Goddamn it," he said, realizing the source of his anger. García and María Elena had likely shared that bed. "Goddamn it," he said again. An ameliorating thought struck him: García might have bought this condominium after the two had separated. Somehow that thought helped a little.

He heard a toilet flush and flattened himself against a wall. Then he heard water running into a basin. It stopped and in ten seconds Suzie Quantrell walked into the master bedroom oblivious. It was almost anti-climatic.

Tommy put the barrel of the automatic up against CIA's head. "Do exactly what I say. We are in a hurry. Into the living room."

She looked at him fearless. Her gray eyes pierced into him. "Where is Linda?"

"She went for a swim. If you hurry, I won't have to shoot her when she returns. She's gonna be hot enough to fuck."

Suzie Q processed this information and, probably since she'd heard no gunfire, nodded acquiescence.

Tommy produced the handcuffs. "Put these on one wrist."

She did so as they moved quickly into the living room. He maneuvered them to the sideboard and retrieved his two weapons. He dropped FBI's automatic on the sideboard. No need to steal her gun.

"Where is she?" CIA demanded.

"She went for a swim."

Quantrell's eyes told him she'd extrapolated what happened. Her expression turned to fury.

He ignored her and hustled her down the hall and into the lobby. FBI would be coming up here soon, mad as a swarm of pissed off wasps.

He thought about using CIA as a hostage for when FBI came boiling up to this landing. Likely that wouldn't work, not with a professional like Landover. She might sacrifice a co-worker. But considering the vibes between the two, the bisexual business, and the obvious comfort level they had with one another, they had to be a couple. Like everything else lately, there were no easy answers. The best plan was to separate himself from them, quick and total.

In front of them was the only elevator. Off to the right was a fire exit, obviously stairs. On the left wall was another exit, a bit farther. He had to guess which access FBI would use. And whichever, she'd come through it on fire with her finger already tugging of the trigger,

What would he do? That's it. He'd take the elevator up knowing that the enemy is likely standing there waiting for you.

But he'd go to the sixth floor and maybe walk down one of the stairways. He could just push five and come flying out at the last second gun ablaze, but that wasn't the best percentage move. That's it, take the elevator to six, push five and rush down a stairway to burst out of the landing when the elevator hit five and opened, drawing his attention.

Okay, which stairwell? The nearest or farthest? The nearest, it had to be, since she might figure the farthest stairwell would take too long and not allow her to beat the elevator to five.

Tommy urged Suzie Q to the nearest stairwell and snapped the remaining cuff on the door handle. Let Landover deal with that. Just in case, he went to stand next to the farthest stairway exit up against the wall. That way he covered all possibilities.

The elevator pinged and the numbers began climbing. That had to be FBI. Tommy didn't want a firefight here; there'd be no winners. The look on her face as she went over the rail and then climbed out of the pool told him she would be on fire.

CIA was moving stealthily, looking to open the door she was chained to.

He pointed his gun at her and wagged it.

Linda was very sharp. Were it him, he'd think it through by now and do the unexpected. She had to bank on the fact that he had CIA captured. If it was the other way around, she had no problem—except how to take her anger out on him.

She would figure the problem just as he had; and then she would know he'd think the same thoughts and defend for that specific approach.

Goddamn it!

Instantly, he ran back inside the condo. The elevator was climbing quickly.

He dashed into the kitchen and tore through two cabinets near the stove.

"There you are," he said, relieved. He grabbed the large bottle of olive oil and ran back out.

Pocketing his automatic, he wrenched the cap off the bottle.

Quantrell was pushing into the stairwell, her arm still tethered to the door handle. Her intention had to be to warn Linda if she wound up coming down that way.

But Tommy now knew what Landover would do. He looked at the elevator floor indicator and it read "6".

Against the elevator door, he heard the ping of the door closing above.

She was going to fake him out and come back down on the elevator, a move he ostensibly wouldn't suspect.

He poured olive oil all over the tiles in front of the elevator. He tossed the bottle aside and saw Quantrell watching him through the almost closed exit door.

Tommy grinned at her and waved once. He ran to the farthest exit door and opened it quietly. He heard nothing, meaning there was no pissed off killer FBI agent breathing fire scrambling down the stairs.

He turned and pulled the door almost closed. He saw the elevator door open and nothing happened. He counted five slowly and the elevator doors started to close and Linda Landover dived out, snub nose revolver swinging back and forth.

Suddenly, her feet lost purchase and her legs bicycled trying to stay upright. Her feet slammed out from under her and she went down hard on her butt and slid across the oily floor.

Tommy didn't see where she ended up, for he'd pulled the door closed and took the stairs down three at a time. He thought he ought to have some small satisfaction for at least one battle won, but such was not the case. He was angry at the delay.

On the first floor, he came out of the stairwell behind the security guard. The man was standing, phone to his ear, his eyes glued to the rotating screens in front of him. Tommy saw one shot of Linda coming out of the condo, probably not looking for him as Suzie would have told her he was gone, but likely bringing the handcuff key. Even though the CCTV images were black and white and a bit grainy, he could tell her dress was still plastered to her hips and breasts. Whether from the pool water or the olive oil, he didn't know, nor was it important. Still, the clinging material was sensual.

Tommy ripped the phone from the desk guard. He checked and the man had no weapon.

Tommy stuck his automatic into the man's ear. "Go to the men's room and don't come out for ten minutes."

The guy's Adam's apple bobbed worriedly. "Yes, sir." Maybe Elmer's story about the madman shooter and arsonist had made it this far.

As the rent-a-cop headed down a corridor, Tommy went out the front door and through the parking lot and into the night.

CHAPTER TWENTY-NINE: HER

"Why is it then, Eduardo, that you treat me this way? You say you wish to atone, yet you are delivering me to Don Diego, to a certain death. Why, Eduardo, why?"

He shook his head and walked to the companionway. "I don't know," he mumbled, anguish on his leathered face.

"Is it because Diego will kill you if you don't cooperate?"

He shrugged. "Kill me he would, yet somehow that does not bother me."

"Then why?"

He looked at her sadly. "I do not know exactly; perhaps it is because I have lived a lie for so long? I don't know. I do know that I would continue as I am. You belong to Diego García, legally and more so in our culture. Perhaps it is because I no longer wish a constant reminder of your mother and my perfidy, my complicity in her torture and death. Perhaps I would wish to continue living a lie rather than going to prison or being assassinated. Perhaps I have no choice, do you not see?" He went up the companionway. In a few seconds he returned. "Also? Perhaps it is the mountains of money involved now." He flashed a crazy look and went back up.

María Elena was disgusted with her world. It had shattered in the swamps and now she found it would never return.

CUBAN BEAUTY moved for hours. Sometimes she could tell they were at sea, other times they were in calm waters. It could be they were just cruising until dark. She had no way of guessing.

They let her go to the head and drink and eat. Then they strapped duct tape around her once again.

It was night now. Eduardo came down into the cabin. "It is time to go, my dear."

"It goes without saying you're taking me to *him*?"

"I am."

"Thereby condemning me to death?"

He avoided her eyes. "Not necessarily."

"Where?"

"The headquarters," he said. Then his voice hardened. "You do not know, but your compadre, the mad man, killed my trusted servant. He also torched my wonderful house and there is nothing left except some block wall and smoldering embers."

She straightened. "Gee, thanks for cheering me up." She thought it through. Tommy did not act out of anger—not much anyway. He wouldn't have taken the time. She knew he'd fired the AR-15 at the retreating boat which in turn would draw the police. So he had a reason for burning the mansion. It would certainly generate attention. So he was sending a message. Certainly not a message that said "Look at me, I'm coming." No, it was more subtle since he preferred to operate under the radar and anonymously. Nor would he warn his enemy. She was well versed in his mindset. No, he was telling somebody something. That somebody would only be Don Diego. It was the first shot of the battle between the two. A tricky first chess move. Suddenly, María Elena had no fear. Come hell or high water, Tommy was coming for her. Period. Only the details remained to be sorted out.

In blood.

The boat was slowing in shallow water and soon she felt the soft thud of protective bumpers during the docking. They took her out on deck and she found they were an enclosed boathouse. Diego had resources.

A crewman pasted a strip of duct tape across her mouth and they marched her to a

Chevy van waiting inside the covered dock. She recognized it as one of the small fleet of vehicles at 13 headquarters. They had vans, SUV's, pickups, and Hummers. Not to mention a small fleet of ATV's which she thoroughly enjoyed driving through the swamps and the dry plains; there were a couple of airboats, too, and troop carriers.

Eduardo and one of his crew got in along with two uniformed 13 soldiers. Two more crew members were refueling the boat and obviously preparing it for an immediate departure.

Soon they were driving off. It was some out of the way location, obviously, because she didn't recognize it. Homestead? She didn't think it was as far as Flamingo, but if so they could hit 27 and be at the base in a matter of hours and avoid all the Miami-Dade traffic and policed roads. Did that mean they feared law enforcement was after them? Anything was possible.

She was sitting on a bench seat in the back.

Eduardo told his crewman, "I want her down. A cop may notice us driving with a bound woman."

The man dragged her down and she lay on the carpeted floor. After that she saw nothing else. Finally, the motion of the van turning and driving put her to sleep.

A loud challenge woke her and she opened her eyes and struggled to sit up. Without help, she leveraged herself up onto the bench seat. The soldier and boat crewman watched her contortions with interest. She glared at them, telling them they'd never touch a woman such as her.

She recognized the sentry point on the incoming shell road to headquarters and the training base. Spotlights glared and flashlights probed inside. This was unusual, for seldom did they have more than one guard in place, and that only to keep lost tourists and unwanted visitors out. Now there were several armed guards.

The security gate arm went up and the soldier driving accelerated. They wound along the crunching road for almost a mile. The entire base was a training area. There were thousands of acres involved in the 13 base: approximately four thousand acres of dedicated land, and another five thousand that the government let them use. Of course, lately there had been too many environmental constraints placed on 13. You could no longer run your tanks and Jeeps over just any ground and destroy flora and fauna and od Indian hammocks at will. She shook her head to clear it and get back to the present.

Through her limited vision from the back of the van, she watched as they threaded their way through a couple of out buildings, the larger aluminum warehouse supply buildings, and then the Quonset huts of troop barracks. They passed the access to the airdrome, which consisted of a small unoccupied control tower more like a forest ranger station than a control tower, and a long, slender paved runway. The runway lights were off, of course.

The driver swung into a parking slot in front of headquarters. A couple of pickups and a Humvee sat there crowding each other. She was surprised by the nighttime activity. Upon reflection, she guessed that Diego had gathered his loyalists, those he had recruited, around him for protection. As soon as Eduardo had informed him of her arrival and Diego had learned of the mess on the islet, then he'd decided to consolidate his strength and protect himself until it could all be sorted out.

The soldier hustled her out the rear of the van and up the stairs into the headquarters. The first floor consisted of offices, a kitchen, a small conference room, a large open area lounge they used for general meetings, training classes, commander's addresses. Upstairs were a few bedrooms and bathrooms for Diego, her father, and VIP's. She used to have her own bedroom assigned, but then...

They escorted her up the stairs into the building and past two alert sentries. Her father never posted sentries at headquarters. Tonight all were dressed in official 13 jungle fatigues.

Don Diego was in the lounge, standing at a long table, packing two large canvas bags. He looked up as they brought her in and zipped the top of one of the bags closed. He was always handsome, a rugged male handsomeness she'd thought, which had ameliorated her reluctance at the marriage. Her eighteen year old self found it a boost to her ego that he was attractive—and not pretty boy young attractive, either. Diego García stood maybe six feet tall and had a well maintained goatee which fit his character very well.

Laid out on a long table in front of him was a scattered array of weapons. Diego was finishing loading a shotgun. She could see many weapons, an Uzi, a MAC-11, a real nice MGP-15 submachine gun, maybe a MAC-10, a Desert Eagle .50 caliber handgun, a couple of M-16's. Was he preparing for a war?

María Elena extrapolated that he was preparing armament for a getaway—if he thought it necessary. He was gathering magazines for the various weapons and taping them together for like weapons. The other duffel probably had his escape kit, or maybe more weapons. She continued to extrapolate. You aren't going to take all those weapons on an aircraft; and the only other way to escape would be on the sea. So, perhaps it followed he was going to take *CUBAN BEAUTY* to make a run for it if things went from bad to worse.

Momentarily, she paused as they entered and he looked over at her. María Elena remembered the first years, those years of promise and dedication, years before, where they really thought they were making a difference against the Castros. It was an exciting time for 13 de enero, a renewal as Diego moved into leadership presaging change and renewed energy, plans with real scope, a vision which he readily shared of freedom for their people on the island. After years of failure to make major inroads, 13 had reclaimed hope. Alas, change was not for the better, not for 13 de enero. Oh, the window dressing was there, and that was about it. This aspect was not readily apparent; it was something which took years to develop and come forth openly. Their marriage paralleled the fortunes of 13. At eighteen, she was an easily influenced young lady. The arranged marriage was against what she wanted, yet she was steeped in the culture where she must obey, and that wasn't necessarily an earth-shaking event; her upbringing did not make her arranged marriage as easy as one in other lands where such was the norm, not the exception. So, married they were. And at first, Diego had treated her pretty well. And he was attentive and charming.

And it was all so new to her, a different life from growing up as her father's daughter. Gradually, she found the marriage was becoming one of convenience to him. He was losing interest in her; she knew he was with other women—she might have been young, but she wasn't stupid. At the time, she attributed that to her reluctance against an arranged marriage. Grudgingly, she admitted it had been one hell of a learning situation; and she knew well that she had grown up quickly in a few short years. Maturity was forced upon her long before it was due. Wistfully, she wondered what had happened to that young girl.

Now here she was, back where it had all started, already blooded herself, and holding her emotions in check while evaluating everything, calculating what would help her, what situation she could turn to her advantage. It seemed that she had learned a great deal from Tommy.

His two troopers each held an arm and urged her into the room through an open double door. Her feet began to drag and they lifted her.

"No, no," Diego motioned. "Remove the tape, please. She can walk on her own, too."

Soon she was free and rubbing her mouth and wrists. She shook her hair out angrily and stared at him.

"You are always more beautiful when you are angry," Diego said.

Quinones came in behind her. The guards went back into the hall and waited along with the previous two sentries posted at the door.

Eduardo sank thankfully into a metal folding chair. "I see you are packing, Diego. Perhaps you are embarking upon a long trip?"

Diego nodded. "I am. It's time for a lengthy trip to my ranch in Mexico. I will run 13 de enero long distance by cell phone and Internet."

"And this is a result of?" asked Eduardo.

"Events seem to be going from bad to worse here, in large part, I might add, due to your mismanagement of these events and your inability to control things better."

Eduardo shrugged. "The way things are going, doubtless you are correct. However, I was not the one killing people and hiding it."

Diego shrugged. "A good leader does what needs to be done and does it swiftly and decisively." He frowned at Eduardo and looked at María Elena. "At this moment, who did what to whom matters not; there are federals all over Miami I am given to understand. In addition, I believe JTF 13 is now taking an active role, and doing so on the ground in South Florida."

"I read it the same," said Eduardo.

"I do not have an aircraft available right now," Diego shook his head regretfully, "so of a necessity, I must take *CUBAN BEAUTY.*"

"It is called commandeering," Eduardo pointed out. "That was obvious when my crew took the boat all the way through the keys and docked southwest; it is a straight shot to Mexico from there."

"When I am done with it, I will send it back to you."

"Will you, Diego? Am I to be left here the sacrificial goat?"

"It is your choice, patrón."

"I doubt that." Eduardo sat up straight and the chair scooted backwards a bit.

"Your keen mind," said Diego, "continues."

María Elena wondered what this was all about. They were dancing, verbally, with one another. Both seemed resigned to something, and were working together to reach that point.

Eduardo sat there and said nothing.

"It occurs to me," Diego went on, "that if things are falling apart as they appear to be, then one person knows the most about the operation, about history, about monies, about who, what, when, and where."

"I am that man," said Eduardo.

Diego nodded. "You are. At your age they will peel you like a banana."

"Have I a choice?" Eduardo asked. "Shall I die by your hand this night? Or shall I accompany you to Mexico?"

Diego raised his hands. "I have not yet decided. On one hand you know all there is and cannot be allowed to talk; on the other hand, you know all there is, a valuable commodity, and you know where the bodies are buried, which is a major asset to me, and leverage if necessary. Not coincidentally, have I forgotten our original goal of participation in a post-Castro government. I can still do that, yet my position would be strengthened with your assistance and your contacts. Networking is important."

"I am grateful you have realized that," Eduardo said. "I feared I would have had to lay all that out for you."

"A good case you make, my friend. I also do not ignore the fact that I am rich and powerful and here because of you, patrón."

María Elena interrupted. "None of that means anything, Eduardo, for he will kill you in a heartbeat if it will help him."

Eduardo sighed. "This I know, Alejandrina. Unfortunately, I know this."

Diego moved to his other canvas bag. "You see why our marriage had problems, Eduardo? She was intrusive with her opinions, loudly and vocally so. She intruded where no woman belonged in our business. Her father should have brought her up with more respect."

"Nonetheless, Diego, we're now back where we started."

"There is that."

"What is your intention to do with Alejandrina?"

Diego looked at him speculatively. "She knows too much, now, and she is the one who uncovered all the irregularities. She must die."

"Right now?"

"Not at all. We have problems, patrón, with the man who burned down your fine home. And maybe some others, I do not yet know. We might need a hostage to get through this. Also? If she is dead, this man who is with her now is known to be one of those who will follow you forever and kill you mercilessly. Frankly, it is why I am not yet running for the boat. I need to deal with this man. If he is dead, it will be much to our advantage later on in our lives. In order to bring him to us, I find I need María Elena alive and well. I do not know about the well part, but it would likely be better if she were not yet harmed. We might have to, ah, harm her in order to bend this killer man to or will."

Don Diego was one cold hearted son of a bitch, thought María Elena. But it did occur to her that Tommy had sent his message and that message had its desired effect: her temporary safety.

She leaned against a table. "Don't trust him, Eduardo. See those two bags? I'd bet the rent that one of them contains all the cash he could scare up in the last couple of days plus whatever he had on hand here." Maybe payroll cash, maybe illegal activity cash, cash he had not yet laundered, and more than likely cash he had been withholding for circumstances such as this. Escape cash. She continued, "The other bag? A variety of those weapons and perhaps identity documents and passports with current stamped visas for many countries south of here."

Eduardo looked accusingly at Diego.

Diego said, "You expected otherwise?"

Eduardo said, "I guess not. I take it you are prepared for the advent of this man—Atkins?"

"Guards are posted everywhere, especially at the gate, and roving patrols, and all are my men, not candy-ass weekend warriors." He grinned and walked over to the doorway. "If either of these two within attempt to leave, hurt them badly, and disable them, but keep them alive."

As Diego walked out of the room, María Elena's heart soared. Could it be? Was it possible in any universe?

And then Diego García turned around. He took two sets of handcuffs from one of the guards. He brought them over and snapped one half on Eduardo's right hand and the other cuff on María Elena's left. Then he dragged both of their chairs to the side wall and snapped the second pair in a loop between their handcuff chain and a thick PVC pipe lifting from the floor to the ceiling and the floor above. He flashed a smile. "You understand, don't you?" He left once again.

Now here she was prisoner.

Where was Tommy?

If she knew anything, she knew he was on the way. But he would be walking into a trap. Once again she had failed and gotten herself into a situation in which she needed his help to stay alive.

But this time they were prepared for him.

On the other hand, they had little idea with whom they were dealing.

CHAPTER THIRTY: HIM

Tommy went to a 7-11 and a Wal-Mart to get maps and a *Florida Atlas & Gazetteer*. He sped back to Weston and went to their hotel room where they'd left their gear.

He spread the maps and used his laptop to locate the 13 de enero home ground. It matched what that woman from Washington said. It did not escape his notice that it was possible that she was aiming him right at this Don Diego. It did not matter, for he was going in one way or the other.

The major acreage was suitable for 13's training purposes and a place to store and maintain equipment and vehicles and so on. It was also located with a more or less direct route to the Caribbean and the Gulf of Mexico. And that cabin cruiser, *THE CUBAN LADY*, was just right for running across the Gulf or to go anywhere in the Caribbean. He could easily find the training ground and the headquarters, but it would be impossible to locate the boat without help. Doubtless, María Elena was long gone from the boat anyway.

He recalled the description of the grounds that CIA had given, and he went to Google Earth to confirm the info and refresh his mind. He also went to other maps to insure he wasn't missing anything. Apparently, there was only one real way in if he didn't want to wade across country or take an airboat or walk through acres of sharp sawgrass.

He put his laptop in a backpack and stuffed the rest of their cash and documents into the remaining pockets. He dressed in jeans to protect his legs and wore long sleeves and a vest to help hold all the ammunition and magazines he was carrying. He carried two pistols and a knife with the sawed-off shotgun tied to a tether around his neck and dropped down the back of his shirt. He pulled his new leather jacket over the shirt and vest and stuck a pistol in one of the many pockets and the rest of his ammunition and magazines went into other pockets.

He hoped that if a cop stopped him, it wouldn't be a rookie, because he wouldn't know what to do and Tommy wouldn't be able to count on him to make the right decisions.

He filled a duffle with a few of his clothes and many of María Elena's. That woman had accumulated some clothes. Not to mention several pairs of shoes he couldn't fit in. Reluctantly, he left his books out, and then decided otherwise. He took the Kipling and put it in one of the side saddle pockets on the motor-cycle. He felt stiff and ungainly, burdened with all the weaponry and ammunition he'd stuffed in his clothing.

He felt an inordinate sense of urgency. He had to get there. Knowing the swamps and scrublands of south Florida, Tommy knew it would be difficult, if not impossible, to navigate off the road, on foot or on the Harley, in the dark. But he could arrive and be infiltrating by dawn.

After all these hours, María Elena would either be already dead or still alive. Most of the time the smart guys would keep their hostages alive as possible trade bait. Tommy fully expected this might happen, and he was equally determined for it not to happen. He wanted to control events, make his entry on his own terms. Though, he noted, he'd sent his message to them telling them he was coming, to expect him.

He drove away from Weston already tired. He hadn't slept any that night; and the night before, while memorable with María Elena, had been long, but short on sleep. He grinned to himself; it had been worth the trade off for sleep.

13 headquarters was so remote, it took him almost an hour and a half to reach the coral access road. The Harley's tires offered up a grinding hum from the rough and mined coral. He kept the sun visor down and it became splattered with mosquito

pulp. When he saw what had to be a lighted and guarded entry into the grounds, he veered to the edge of the road and tossed the duffel of clothes and his laptop backpack behind a pine tree.

He slowed as he approached the entrance. He saw it had a two man guard shack in the middle of the road. More spotlights were on than you'd ordinarily expect. A security gate arm was down across the road and two men stepped out expectantly. They carried rifles, probably surplus M-16's he guessed from this far. He decreased his speed much more and idled up to them.

No, AK-47's, he corrected himself. No surplus this. He scanned alongside the road as he approached the two sentries. He thought he caught a movement behind the underbrush lining the narrow road.

He slowed to a stop and kicked the motorcycle into neutral.

He decided to play on the fact that the Autolinx carrier was designed for carrying a golf bag and assorted clubs therein. In fact its appearance was of a golf bag and clubs.

The two sentries moved toward him.

He raised his visor. "Shit, this don't look like Plantation Country Club Golf Course."

"What do you want?" asked the guy with a couple of chevrons.

"We got an early tee time and I wanted to hit the driving range early to get the kinks out." Tommy was assessing the situation. He was now certain that there were others, how many he didn't know, in the brush, hidden and covering him.

The guy was suspicious.

"They don't usually got guns at golf courses," Tommy said wonderingly. "This ain't Plantation, is it?"

"No, sir, maybe you tell us who you are." The guy's AK-47 was no longer across his body; it was now casually held in one hand, muzzle pointing toward the roadbed at Tommy's feet.

"Jesus," Tommy said, "is this some secret government installation? I'll kill that son of a bitch who trick-fucked me into coming here. Shit. I'm gonna send him a telegram his mother died." Tommy looked around behind him to set up the fact he was going to turn around.

The chevron guy thought this was funny.

"Hell, I'm sorry," said Tommy. "Lemme go someplace and find out where Plantation really is." He cranked the wheel over and engaged first gear.

The chevron guard held up his hand and said, "I must check with operations. Do not leave."

Tommy engaged the clutch and revved the engine and shrugged at the man telling him he didn't understand. He reengaged first gear and slowly went forward, turning to the left.

They were startled. He gave a friendly wave and accelerated. He couldn't outrun any bullets, so he had to gut it out. He went slowly and started to increase his speed as if normal. While it was still dark, he took a chance and snaked the machine slightly from one side to another. If they had a sharpshooter, he might escape the first shot or the first burst. He kept the RPM's down so they wouldn't miss the noise when he killed the engine.

He continued on past the turn where he'd dumped his gear earlier. He killed the light and turned around. He coasted a hundred yards and got off and pushed the bike to the pines where his gear was hidden. He pushed the Harley out of sight and walked quickly down the road back toward the guard shack.

He never prayed, but he did now; bringing María Elena's clothes: would that jinx him. Was it too much to expect?

He shook his head to clear it and dislodged a few mosquitoes. He'd looked hard for evidence of night vision, or infrared, goggles or glasses or whatever they might have. He'd seen nothing to indicate they had any.

Once he could see the guard shack, he walked off the road next to the brush and trees lining the road. A quarter mile out, he merged into the jungle. He had to go farther wide than the hidden shooters would be ensconced. Some of the ground was soft and wet forcing him to walk more carefully. He had to decide whether to bypass the security check point altogether or go in and kill them all. The problem was that he was on one side of the road. Likely he could take out those in waiting on this side and then the two out in the open in the sentry shack. But that left any possible troops on the far side that would automatically open fire; if he lived through that, the noise would be a warning to Diego García and a whole lot more troops. Hardcore, well trained troops, not family guys with day jobs. No, he'd better continue on and not start the fight here and handicap himself by warning the whole camp.

He swung wider and the edge of the swamp became deeper. He was up over his ankles by an inch and thankful he'd laced his boots high and tight. There was a minimum of moonlight, perhaps a quarter, and plenty of stars. While this helped him navigate his way, he'd have preferred rain. Rain would offer much better cover and allow him to move quicker.

Mosquitoes swarmed around him, but they were attacking a man who'd lived in these conditions for many years, a man who'd walked all over Zaire and Angola under worse conditions. Those mosquitoes had given him malaria. There were worse diseases to be caught over there and he was thankful that malaria was his only one.

He slung the AR-15 he was carrying over his shoulder and pulled out a pistol with a sound suppressor already attached. Dawn would be here soon and he knew he had to hurry for darkness was his best friend right now. He went as far as he thought necessary and then turned back to the approach road. The quarter moon was gone now and he found it easier to walk alongside the road. When he saw a flicker of lights through the trees and jungle growth, he moved to the cut-back brush maybe ten feet off the road and paralleled the road.

In a few minutes, his internal night-movement guidance system told him to get away from the road and go through the woods. He did so and found a barely discernable sawgrass patch. He didn't mind sloshing through ankle deep water and muck because by its nature it precluded most booby-traps and early warning devices. He doubted they had any of those things. After all, they had no ostensible enemies in south Florida, just in Cuba, and this place was merely a training ground with no external threats. However, Tommy believed in the Boy Scout motto: Be Prepared.

He came out of the water behind a Melaleuca tree, an invasive species from Australia or nearby environs. He ducked under a branch and went around the trunk.

Dirt and sand made up the ground around the lip of the camp.

Tommy saw lights on everywhere. Something was going on, obviously. He spotted a jeep slowly cruising the perimeter with a spotlight illuminating the brush. He hurried back to the Melaleuca and stood quietly behind it.

He was acutely aware that as soon as he was discovered, even if he avoided capture or won a firefight, his mission was over. All García had to do was call out for him to come in by threatening to kill María Elena. The bastard might even bring her out and have her assaulted in the open to draw him in. Don Diego had nothing to lose. Except Tommy was bound and determined the man would lose his life.

So his plan boiled down to infiltrate silently and, once discovered, make a frenzied attack on the target, keeping them off-balance and on the defensive so they couldn't use María Elena against him. However, he knew that no plan goes off without a hitch, and he'd have to be prepared to deal with whatever came along.

He fixed the locations of buildings in his mind; he certainly didn't want to end up around the barracks and be discovered there. And there was no reason not to hold María Elena at the headquarters building—if they indeed had her here. Now that was his secret fear: that she was not prisoner here, or had not yet arrived. He shrugged it off, for he had no choice.

The eastern horizon was showing light as Tommy Atkins began his assault. After the roving patrol had passed, he made his way silently into the compound. He headed obliquely toward what would charitably be called the motor pool: an open Quonset hut with a couple of vehicles inside and several outside. No one was about. He moved through the yard to the other side, grateful for the cover.

He had little fear of dogs, for to maintain dogs they had to have a permanent cadre. And as watch dogs, out in the swamps and scrublands, there were too many animals which would trigger all-night barking. And no one wants to be awake all night with their dogs barking at rabbits, raccoons, possums, gators, and a thousand other sounds and movements and smells in the night.

Before he moved past a troop carrier, he surveyed the area. All spotlights were on, pushing back the night. Occasional soldiers passed between buildings and he identified at least two more roving patrols. They were expecting a war?

Well, they were going to get one.

Tommy slung the AR-15 over his shoulder displacing a dozen mosquitoes. He drew his silenced pistol.

He hurried into the repair building and searched around quickly. He found a pack of Pall Malls and a pack of matches which suited him fine. Behind the maintenance building he located the gasoline supply. It was a five hundred or so gallon tank. With a nearby wrench, he loosened the sump drain and gasoline began to flow. He took the demand hose and sprayed gasoline all over the tank itself and around the perimeter. He hoped the acrid smell wouldn't attract unwanted attention. He filled a bucket with gasoline and poured a trail on the sand and dirt into the building itself. He splashed an area well with the liquid and sat the bucket down. He put two metal folding chairs facing each other in the center of the spilled gasoline. He spread a sheet of the *Miami Herald* between the two, anchoring each side with a couple of wrenches so that the newspaper page stretched between the two chairs.

He went away from that area and lighted a Pall Mall. He inserted the unlighted end into the pack of matches and closed the pack. Mentally crossing his fingers, he walked carefully to the chairs and set the matchbook and burning cigarette gently on the newspaper.

He moved quickly after that, not trusting his homemade bomb to work as he'd designed. He left the motor pool in a hurry. His time was now limited.

As he prepared to snake his way forward, he scanned his recent memory for anything he'd forgotten. He imagined there was something, but couldn't come up with it.

He slithered through the shadows the lighting made between buildings. His breathing was slow and paced. One smaller outbuilding and then he'd be close to headquarters. He hustled to that building and looked around the side of that Quonset toward headquarters. Headquarters was a real building, likely block and siding construction was his guess. He cautioned himself to watch his aim should he engage in a firefight: he didn't want to shoot through the building and hit María Elena.

He was conscious of the passage of time. He imagined the Pall Mall burning down swiftly. He did know that if you weren't dragging on the smoke, it took longer to burn down. Oddly, he wondered what brand of cigarettes Linda Landover smoked. He'd bet the rent money it was an unfiltered brand like Lucky Strikes.

In front of the headquarters was an open plaza where troops gathered for formal ceremonies and briefings. An empty flag-pole stood alone at the top of the parade grounds. Several vehicles slotted into parking in front of the building, and it was well lighted. A soldier left through the front door and nodded to the guards. Tommy wondered about a back door. He figured he barely had time to reconnoiter and turned to go back and around the headquarters to find out. Perhaps a stealth entry would be easier back there instead of out here in the well lighted and very open central plaza.

He imagined the Pall Mall was now reaching the match heads in the pack and beginning to blaze, sulfur flaring up.

He turned to retrace his way around this Quonset and saw three soldiers approaching quietly. They were just as surprised as he was that he'd turned and discovered them.

His silencer spat six times and they went down, the last raising his AK-47. Tommy reloaded quickly.

They'd known where he was. How?

They were wearing ubiquitous headsets. So they'd been

directed specifically to his location. Again, how? Night vision goggles or equipment wasn't necessary in the spillover light here.

The whoop whoop whoop intruder alert of a siren cut through the air. Somebody was watching him.

What was it that he'd missed?

He stood up straight and invested the time to look around. He was pretty well covered by the smaller Quonset and if he could see nobody, they couldn't see him.

So he looked up and around.

Over there. A couple of hundred yards. Toward the end of the asphalt paved landing strip. The "control tower." It wasn't much, just a series of stairs leading to an enclosed platform. Likely used for monitoring military maneuvers. One man with a good pair of binoculars could survey the entire compound comfortably.

The old Black Hawk squatted comfortably near the mobile control tower. Tommy thought that chopper might well be on stand-by to carry Diego García and his upper cadre away. Tommy shook his head, he had no time to backtrack and disable the chopper. Too much to do, too little time.

Troops were beginning to stumble out of the barracks units and the guards on the front of the headquarters stepped to the edge of the landing, weapons at ready.

Tommy shook his head knowing his mistake might well have killed him and damned María Elena.

His attempt at a diversion must have failed, for surely by now the pack of matches had burned through the page of newspaper and fallen, sparks and flames, onto the gasoline soaked ground. The spread of flames to the mother gasoline tank would be immediate. But how long would it take for the thing to explode? If it would, that is, for it takes oxygen to mix with the petrol for an explosion to occur.

That left only one thing to do: he had to attack before they got their act together. Keep them off balance. He reloaded and pocketed his handgun and brought the AR-15 to the ready position.

A round was already jacked into the chamber and replaced in the magazine. He flipped the safety off and took off. He wanted to be at a full run before they spied him. He kept low and zeroed in on a van between him and the entrance to headquarters.

A shout alerted him to the fact that he'd been spotted and he saw more soldiers come out the front. One man pointed at him and raised his rifle to shoot at Tommy. Tommy fired two three-round bursts at the group hoping for a hit, but not counting on it since he was running hard. His shots were closer than he'd thought and the soldiers scattered and dropped. Tommy wished he had some grenades. Next time.

He slammed into the van and scurried around to the front, leaning quickly over the stubby hood and raking the front landing with a withering fire. He changed magazines quickly and continued. They were beginning to return his fire and several soldiers were gathered somewhere behind him had opened fire raggedly at him.

Tommy berated himself. One mistake, now he was in an untenable position, caught in a cross fire in between enemy troops. He spared a couple of bursts at the soldiers emerging onto the plaza.

He took a deep breath preparing to launch a frontal attack when the entire camp lighted up, all darkness swept away in a single giant explosion. Tommy felt the heat as the blast wave swam past him.

He knew he had only seconds of grace and he sprinted toward the headquarters building, maybe fifty yards ahead. He sprayed the landing with another volley of fire. Someone was paying attention, for an AK-47 opened up and automatic fire crackled the night around him. They were too used to thinking that more is better. If you depend on automatic you sacrifice aim, not to mention your magazine runs dry immediately. It's why Tommy always used maximum of three round bursts.

Another weapon opened up and Tommy felt a stinging sensation along his left forearm. He thought it was a good thing he was right handed. He zigzagged forward and reached the steps to the landing. The glow of the explosion was dying and soldiers were regaining their senses. Tommy fired two bursts and ran out of ammunition. He threw the AR-15 at a camouflaged figure aiming at him. The rifle bounced off the floor and hit the man in the hip.

By then Tommy had an automatic out and began shooting shooters. Soon there were no more. He swarmed up the stairs and flattened himself against the wall alongside the front doors. Two outer screen doors were closed. The inner wooden double doors were wide open for the night breeze.

A round clanged off the landing. They were homing in on him. He hoped they thought to be careful, for likely there were more of them inside. Nobody wants to be killed by your fellow soldiers.

Suddenly, a cackling static came across the camp.

"Atkins!"

The public address system. He guessed the speaker was Diego García.

Another fire flared off in the distance. And, he noted, dawn had exploded and night was no longer an issue to figure in.

Tommy risked a glance inside and down the hallway. Nothing. Surely once he made his entrance, the place would fill with gunfire. He had no choice. It was about the only thing he could do. They'd expect him to charge right in.

So he grabbed an AK-47 from a dead 13 soldier on the landing, and hosed off all remaining ammunition in the banana magazine across the plaza where he thought the majority of the enemy were. Then he slammed the butt of the AK-47 through the screen and tossed the rifle down the corridor. It drew immediate fire.

That's what they expected, and he didn't want to disappoint them.

He whirled, ran, and leaped off the landing, and raced along the side of the headquarters building. A couple of rounds came close, but it was obvious they didn't want to fire into the headquarters, after all that's where leadership was.

Sliding to a stop, he peeked around the corner. One sentry, his rifle at his shoulder, scanning all approaches. Tommy shot him before the man could register his presence.

He scrambled up the back steps and slammed through the screen door there. One more soldier ran out into the hallway from a side room and Tommy put him down.

The PA system squelched again. "Atkins, thirty seconds and she dies."

Tommy was beginning to hate that voice.

He said nothing, hoping that they'd not know if the attacker was in fact him. That possibility might give García pause.

A mosquito sank her nose into his throat and he absently smashed it.

Tommy ran down the long corridor. It looked like it might go all the way through the building to the front end he'd just evacuated.

Then some bright son of a bitch tossed a metal folding chair into the hallway and he tripped over it and went sprawling. He tried a paratrooper shoulder roll, but the corridor was too narrow and he slammed against a wall. He regained his feet and shot into the room from whence came the chair. Then he stopped as María Elena might be in there. He was stymied. He didn't have time to check every room.

"Out of time, Atkins," the grating voice said over the PA. "If you shoot now, you will kill her."

María Elena stumbled out between a set of doors down the hall on the left. Immediately following her came another, seemingly attached to her. He tripped and almost dragged María Elena down with him.

It finally registered on Tommy that the two were handcuffed together.

Tommy raised his weapon to kill the next man to come out of that same room.

No longer on the PA system, the same voice said, "Atkins, surrender now or I will kill them."

María Elena smiled at him wistfully. Frantically she looked

around for somewhere to run to.

"Kill him, Tommy!" she shouted.

"Too late, Atkins," the voice yelled.

Tommy started toward the two in the hallway and the man was on his knees now and a shot reverberated in the close confines and half of his head exploded. María Elena stared in horror.

She turned to him. "Run, Tommy," she said matter-of-factly, telling him to save himself.

He grinned at her. "Hell no, Pocahontas. I wouldn't leave you for the world." He dropped his handgun. "García? I threw down my gun."

García stepped out into the corridor. He was immaculate, freshly showered, dark hair still wet and slick, goatee dark and ominous. He aimed his automatic at Tommy. "Yet I'll wager you are still armed."

"Of course."

"I guess it won't matter in a few seconds."

"I guess not," Tommy replied. "I have no choice, but I do expect you to keep your unspoken agreement."

"You'll never know," said García.

"Diego, no!" begged María Elena.

"No?" García asked.

"I beg you. If I ever meant anything to you."

"Pocahontas? Do not beg, he's going to kill me anyway. Save your breath."

"I'd do anything for you, Tommy. Even to this fucking pig."

García spoke to her. "Your friend is correct, my dear. He knows I am going to kill him. He's asking man to man for me to not kill you, too. It was his bargain for surrendering to me."

"I know that. Do you still think I am a stupid young girl?"

"I never thought so," García said sadly. "Why, did you think I was never in love with you? I was older and could not express myself in your terms. And look what you've done to me." He spat. "And you never gave me an heir." He paused. "A boy."

María Elena froze and was staring at him. She ignored the

fact she was handcuffed to the body of Eduardo Quinones. Tommy recognized the man, what was left of his face, from the quick view he'd caught at the mansion on the bay.

"What do you mean what I've done to you?" María Elena demanded.

García lifted his shoulders and wagged his handgun at Tommy. "We remain husband and wife. You have cuckolded me."

She stood still, staring at him.

"Let me say it differently, María Elena. You are fucking a man who is not your husband."

She continued to stare at him.

"It is not that you fuck so very well at any rate, my dear. Yet you are doing it to him."

"No, Diego, I…"

"Do not deny it. It is intuitively obvious, my good wife. Look at Atkins, he is not denying it. Think you he'd go through this if it were not for love?"

"It doesn't matter," María Elena said.

Tommy was inching his hand toward the pocket with the silenced handgun in it.

Diego was watching him. "Don't. Well, Mr. Atkins, I certainly hope she has treated you better than she treated me. If she does it well these days, do not forget I taught her how to fuck." His voice turned vicious, angry. "I used to think it was great to deflower a virgin, but she was the exception to the rule." He was hammering Tommy to get at María Elena. "Look at that mouth on her, Mr. Atkins. A beautiful thing, no? Made to give a man a blow job. Perfect lips. Any man's dream. Could I persuade her to do a little oral sex? No, sir. I never even found out if she would swallow or not. I hope you had better luck." García was working himself up now, more angry after each word. "When she finally left me, I refused to give her a divorce, for I became vindictive. I had her watched. If she had a man friend, my associates would discourage his attentions." He grinned at his own machinations.

It occurred to Tommy that García had really been in love with María Elena and was bitter that his affection was not returned. Tommy absently scratched at the mosquito bite, but García was watching him closely. Tommy regretted wearing the leather jacket for it prevented him from making a quick draw. And most of his weapons were underneath in the vest or in his waistband. Or down his back.

"He's a nasty son of a bitch, isn't he?" Tommy asked María Elena.

"Now he is," she nodded. "At one time that was not the case."

"And is she not the most beautiful creature you have ever seen?" García continued.

"She is," said Tommy. "But you wanted a trophy, arm candy, a woman to enhance your reputation, a free ticket to run 13 de enero." Tommy was thinking to make him angry enough that he'd make a mistake. Tommy could see the same thought on María Elena's face. If he could distract García enough, maybe María Elena could incapacitate him long enough for Tommy to get over there.

"I wanted her to suck me off like mine was the last dick on Earth," García continued.

"It pleases me greatly I never fulfilled your wishes," said María Elena."

"At first, I was thinking love conquers all," García said. "Soon you disabused me of that quaint notion." He laughed. He nodded at Tommy. "That is why I gave her to my men. Somebody sure needed to enjoy that thing. I did not, not for very long anyway. Soon she became just a warm place to jack off in. Did you not find it so also, Mr. Atkins?"

"María Elena?"

"Yes, Tommy?"

"We need to change your last name as soon as possible."

"Yes, Tommy." Her eyes grew wide. "Yes, Tommy!"

García stared. "Well, that's not going to happen. She's crazy and cold, Atkins. You want nothing to do with her." He shook his head as if trying to remove memories. "I wanted her; I married her, because she was so beautiful—if young. And it took marriage to get into her pants."

"Frankly, García, I found her to be someone to love and cherish. That's all it takes. Not someone to use. Look, I understand you're trying to hurt me, us, because of perceived wrongs. Can we stop making like teenagers?"

"So it is that you wish me to kill you right now instead of putting it off for a few minutes?"

"No. You need to escape. You've fucked this all up pretty much. I know some things you need to know to escape. My bargain is that you keep us alive, and I will tell you what you need to know to get out of this alive."

"You bargain with no chips, Atkins." He shook his head and waved his automatic at Tommy.

"I will put them on the table. You need to know what the feds know, where they are, and their intentions."

García thought for a moment, stroking his goatee. "And you know this information how?"

"Yesterday late, early evening, I spent some quality time with JTF 13 and we had a very fruitful discussion."

"Your proof?"

"Nothing in black and white and you know it, García. The names Susan Quantrell and Linda Landover. How's that?"

"Not bad, what else have you got?"

Tommy shrugged his shoulders and scratched the mosquito bite on his throat again. "I am betting our lives on it."

García thought for a moment. "Very good, Mr. Atkins. Shall we talk?"

The sound of a jet engine throttling down came into the quiet building.

Tommy had no clue. Perhaps García had gotten an aircraft for his escape. But then the look on García's face told him otherwise.

Tommy took advantage of the situation. "I'm not going to talk like this. Release María Elena from that dead man first."

García was distracted as they all heard the aircraft land and the engines die. He spoke into the room, quick Spanish that Tommy didn't understand. Two men came out and dragged Quinones' body into the room, effectively pulling María Elena behind him.

García kept Tommy covered. "Inside the room, too."

Tommy appeared to accept his fate and walked quickly toward García. But the man was a pro and stepped far aside, motioning Tommy into the room.

Tommy smiled professionally at the man and turned into the lounge. His anger was cold and deadly. He knew that the words García had spoken meant little, but the man had said those words to hurt María Elena and Tommy.

Two camo clad soldiers were affixing another set of handcuffs to the one strung between María Elena and the late Eduardo Quinones. Then they wrapped the chain around a PVC pipe and clipped the other cuff to the chain. She was chained to the PVC while remaining cuffed to Quinones. The men stepped back and under García's direction, came over to Tommy and stripped the jacket and vest off of him. They searched him well and removed all his weapons, including his knife and the short shotgun down his back. Finished, they stepped away.

"Cuff him," said García.

"In a minute," Tommy said with determination. He walked toward María Elena.

"Atkins, stop or I'll kill you."

"Go ahead, García. You'll never find out what I know." He kept walking. "She's bleeding and I want to check it out." He massaged the mosquito bite again angrily.

María Elena had been forced to sit on the floor alongside Quinones. The blood Tommy referred to was most likely from the attorney.

He bent over her rubbing his throat.

Her eyes went to García and did not react as if the man was lining up a shot at Tommy.

"Are you okay?" he asked, his eyes flickering downward to his chest as his fingers went from rubbing his throat to dragging out his crucifix.

"I...I don't know," she said, picking up on the gambit and playing for time.

"You have to learn to not pay attention to what an angry husband spews; it is all anger and no sense."

The chain swung free and the crucifix hung right in front of her face.

"Well, he never talked like that when we got married," she responded and reached up with her lovely mouth and bit through two links in the chain. The chain snaked loose and landed on her lap. She jiggled a leg and the chain slid to the floor.

He stared into her eyes and saw an age-old understanding.

He smiled encouragement. She nodded agreeably like everything was going to be okay. She leaned her forehead against his and closed her eyes for a moment.

Tommy didn't look at García or his goons; they either saw the exchange or his body sufficiently concealed the exchange. "I think that's not your blood," he said, standing upright. "Too bad for Quinones."

She nodded at him, the crucifix lodged successfully in her mouth, tucked behind her teeth into the left cheek.

Tommy turned to García. "If you'd treated her right, she'd have made you a good wife."

García was on his cell phone. "What do they want?" He listened. "For Christ's sake, don't bring them here. I have the situation under control, but we need to clean up bodies and blood and evidence of a massive gun battle." García's voice indicated strain, but his eyes were watchful. He motioned with his automatic.

One of the men came over and handcuffed Tommy with plastic tri-fold disposable restraints. He ratcheted the plastic on tightly. "Sit against the wall," the man directed. Tommy saw a bored indifference on his face.

Diego García snapped his cell phone closed. "It seems as if we have visitors. And they do not appear hostile. Perhaps, Atkins, you lose your bargaining chip."

"Who is it?" Tommy was curious.

"That is none of your affair." García motioned to two men. "Guard them well. If they make any noise, kill them. If they try to escape, kill them."

"Aye, Commandante."

CHAPTER THIRTY-ONE: THEM

They sat on patio lounge chairs on Diego García's patio. The evening was late. Suzie Quantrell was still wearing her slacks and blouse; Linda Landover wore a very short beach robe, courtesy of Diego García's closet. Apparently, he kept extra clothing for female guests. Linda's clothes were currently spinning in García's dryer back in his laundry room after having been washed twice to get the chlorine and vegetable oil out of her sun dress.

Suzie sipped her martini, thankful for García's good liquor selection. Her eyes went from Linda's long, exposed legs to the magnificent view of the Atlantic. Lights flowed across the horizon, mostly south to north as ships used the Gulfstream to assist their transport.

Linda raised her martini glass and took a sip. "This is the life. How is it the bad guys get all the bennies in life?"

"Maybe they're simply lucky," said Suzie.

"I don't believe that, and if it's true, it ain't right." Linda took another small drink. "I could get to like this, but I don't want to have many more if García will walk in that door any minute."

"He's not, Linda. The place feels abandoned. While we've found personal items, they're not necessary. No papers, no money, no jewelry, nothing of consequence. Nothing on the computer. He's a goner."

"Our hotel does not compare to this place. If we rack out here tonight, we can wait for him to show, if he does."

"We will, hon. Listen, it's time we went pro-active."

"Pro-active didn't work so well with Atkins."

"For you, maybe," grinned Suzie. "For us? Time will tell."

Linda stuck her tongue out at Suzie. "Thus your info dump into his brain about the 13 training grounds. You aimed him like a torpedo. It appears you were thinking the whole time of releasing him."

"That was part of a possible scenario; it would work both ways. Look, Linda, we have a major problem. Our, your and my asset, JTF's asset, one 13 de enero, one Don Diego García has gone rogue on us. Here we are holding the proverbial bag."

Linda poured another martini. "This ain't bad right now."

"It will be if we don't turn a miracle trick."

"And what would that be?"

"I do not know yet. But it's outcome based. The outcome is that García needs to be dead, methinks. That way we can blame the girl's father for poor judgment in management hiring. Then we claim credit for discovering the problems and crimes. Just doing our job, we'll say. Congress cut funding and thus limited our oversight ability; implied will be that the powers above us failed to fight harder to maintain our funding and therefore keep us on our mission. That leads to them sharing some guilt and therefore they won't push it too hard in order to keep their own asses clean. We'll look good by taking corrective action."

Linda patted Suzie's leg. "You're brilliant."

"I prefer 'results oriented,' if you please."

"How about Machiavellian?"

"Whatever." She shook her head. "I still strongly believe that when we drop the economic boycott on Cuba, that bone yard economy will be just ripe for us. We have to stay in the game."

Fluffy wandered out onto the patio, sniffed around and wandered back inside.

"I can jump to conclusions." Linda rested her head on the back of the lounge. "It means to me that we must personally be on the spot when some of this goes down, so we can manage, or make that 'perform damage control' as you always put it."

"Yep." Suzie stood and walked to the railing. "We need to invite ourselves to the after party party." The pool below was lighted by underwater spotlights. "You really dove from here?"

"Feet first, it was safer. And please, don't remind me?"

Suzie turned and smiled at Linda. "My bet is that you would like to go another round with our Mr. Atkins."

Linda shrugged self consciously. "It's at the top of my bucket list."

"Maybe we can arrange that thing sooner rather than later."

"Suze, I can see formulae and possibilities and schemes scrolling through your wonderful eyes. I can see where you've aimed Atkins in a direction you wanted him to go and it well could be that he is performing the task of softening up the enemy for us."

"Yes, dear. I wouldn't be surprised if Mr. Atkins isn't wreaking havoc out there in the boondocks pretty soon."

A muted ring emanated from Suzie's pocket. She removed her cell and clicked it on speaker. "Go ahead, Sandy. You're on speaker and Linda's listening."

"Just as you suspected, Ms. Quantrell. I'd be grinning if we were on Skype or something."

"At what?" Suzie sat down on Linda's lounge and pushed her shapely legs aside to make room. She set the phone on Linda's lap.

"The Attorney General? He sort of followed the Janet Reno model. State's attorney, then became the Federal Attorney out of Miami-Dade. Picked from that position as a third choice by the president."

"And?"

"That's the thing. The state's attorney part. In Florida, district attorney's are called state's attorneys. Political connections, you run for office from that platform or you get appointed higher. This AG got appointed from Tampa to Miami, a state job, to the federal job."

"A lot of mention of Tampa," Linda pointed out.

"Yes, ma'am. It was a convoluted trail to work out, but the

info is there if you dig hard enough. When the AG was up and coming, he had a mentor. A certain judge. The AG became state's attorney right after his mentor was shot down. Lots of rumors about mob connections, none proved. The prime suspect eventually came down to our Mr. Atkins. But with no evidence, they grabbed him on racketeering. The reason he was in state custody so long was that the state's attorney put a hold on him trying to get him for murder. But before he did, the prisoner escaped." Sandy cleared her throat. "Some years later, that same state's attorney became the federal attorney and then when this president took office, a couple of appointments fell through for various reasons, and finally he picked the Miami federal attorney for the AG post. Fast forward and here we are."

"Good work, Sandy," Linda said. She raised her almost empty glass to Suzie Q. "And your instincts reign supreme."

"Bad news for us," Suzie said, her hand rubbing Linda's leg above the knee. "That can only mean that the AG's toy-boys are around and active. That bald headed marshal is one sharp cookie and he's been around long enough he can smell smoke before it becomes smoke."

"You're saying we now have a sense of urgency?"

"You bet. Sandy? I'm putting you on hold for just a second."

"Yes, ma'am."

Suzie hit the button. She continued to stroke Linda's leg. "Listen, Linda. We got a major problem. That marshal's going to ferret out what's going on. It wouldn't surprise me that he'd show up any time."

"We don't want him to find out how fucked up things are?"

"No we don't, hon. The way bureaucracies work, it isn't going to be good. If another agency becomes involved then we're back to being held accountable. They can't keep it in-house for us; they sell us down the river to insure their own survival, even if it is not our fault. Even if we're pure as the driven snow and were simply doing a great job to serve and protect our country. They'd still hang our ass."

Linda grinned. "I'd love to say you were in charge and I was just a worker bee, but that ain't the case. I'm the FBI rep."

Suzie pouted at her. "You wouldn't jump ship on me."

Linda took Suzie's hand. "Not in a million years."

"We gotta get this thing fixed right away. We're out of time." Suzie picked up the phone and clicked it off hold. "Sandy?"

"I'm here."

"Look up the coordinates of the official 13 training location. It's out by the Dade County line. There's a landing strip on it, I've been there before. Call our pilot and have him ready to go before dawn. He'll complain, but the landing strip is long enough for the jet." She'd been through this previously; pilots were a safety conscious bunch. She knew a Cessna 560 Citation Encore, the model they'd flown down here in, could land in less than 2,800 feet and take off short of 3,400 feet. Those numbers were what the aircraft was rated for, but any good pilot could take a chunk out of that.

"Got it."

Suzie clicked off. She ran her hands over Linda's legs some more. "We can get a few hours of sleep here and head straight to the airport."

"I thought you'd never ask." Linda stood and pulled Suzie up. "I do see more than sex in your eyes."

Suzie gave a sweet smile. "You bet. Think about this. This aforementioned judge that our Mr. Atkins offed?"

"And?" Linda led the way inside.

"If he was crooked and linked to the mob, how does our fine AG fit into that equation?"

"Doubtless he's clean, Suze. Or they wouldn't have vetted him to be AG."

"Sure. But we could raise so much smoke about it that the AG would rather play ball with us than let those nasty ole marshals take us down." She smiled brightly. "We just got us a get-out-of-jail-free card, my dear."

They sat opposite each other as the two engine jet banked and leveled and banked again. Suzie could hear the pilots grousing through the accordion door. She scratched Fluffy behind the ears and watched Linda clean her weapons.

"Pool water doesn't help your gun," Linda said.

"Nor apparently, your disposition," Suzie said. "That gleam in your eyes spells revenge to me."

Linda looked up at Suzie expectantly.

"Getting even should not interfere with our mission."

"Yes, ma'am."

"It shouldn't be on the menu."

"Yes, ma'am."

"It shouldn't cloud your judgment."

"Yes, ma'am."

The aircraft banked again. The copilot slid the accordion door aside. "Look out the port window. A giant plume of smoke. Be advised that's our target."

Both women turned to stare. Dawn had washed over the Everglades and the area looked bleak. The Cessna made a high level pass and Suzie saw oil smoke churning into the sky from amongst the buildings of the base.

"It's clear to land," Suzie told the copilot.

"Your wish is our command." The copilot slid back and the door closed.

"Smart ass," said Suzie.

Linda was still staring out the window as the aircraft banked again into a short turn and lined up on the runway. "Looks like the party's already started."

"Tommy this, and Tommy that, I think Tommy shoots and Tommy explodes stuff," said Suzie.

"This is liable to be dicey, Suze." Linda finished cleaning and put the kit under her seat. She reloaded all her guns. "Suze?"

"Yes, dear?"

"Don't over think this thing now, okay?"

"Yes, ma'am."

"It appears to me that we're past the machination stage, we're to the shooting stage."

"Yes, ma'am. If necessary."

"And I doubt if we have any allies here, Suze. We're on our own."

"Yes, ma'am. I have confidence in you."

Linda gave Suzie a knowing smile.

The government Cessna 560 Citation Encore touched down right at the end of the skinny runway and soon bumped to a stop. The pilot swung the aircraft around and taxied to a parking slot at the base of the make-shift tower.

The copilot opened the door on the left side behind the cockpit.

As they jumped to the asphalt, Suzie told him, "Wait for us. And keep the dog with you, okay."

"You're the boss."

"You got my cell number, I just checked and I have bars. And keep your head down, there might be some gunfire." She paused. "Never mind what you hear going on, we need you here to exfiltrate us immediately if necessary." Obviously so the two crew were not part of things and wouldn't be witness. The two JTF 13 agents had to continue to cover their ass.

He nodded at her absently as he watched Linda's rear end and legs shown through her yellow sun dress. Not perfect clothing, but they hadn't made it back to the hotel to change.

Suzie shook her head.

"This crew's all right; we flew into worse down in Columbia a couple of years ago."

"Well, his eyes were stuck on your tits and your ass."

"He's a puppy dog."

They walked toward the combat tower. A hundred yards from the tower sat an elderly Black Hawk helicopter. In a minute a jeep came around a building and headed for them.

The smoke was still pouring from ahead. Dawn mosquitoes swarmed and Suzie swatted at an errant cloud of them. "This is disgusting."

"City girl," Linda accused.

"Bet your ass, sweetie."

Linda's eyes never stopped roving.

The jeep pulled up alongside them. A man with captain's bars got out.

"Who are you? What is it you want?" He stuffed a cell phone into his breast pocket.

Suzie fixed him with a glare. "Who are you, captain?"

He stiffened at the command in her voice.

"I am the executive officer." He stood straighter. He was clean shaven and Suzie could tell he thought he was a real ladies' man. He eyed the two women.

"We came to see García," said Suzie.

"What about?"

"We'll take that up with him." Her voice took on a tone of anger.

The exec looked over his shoulder back at the camp as if he'd just come from a firefight. Maybe he had. "Commandante García is not available right now. I will tell him you came."

Linda stepped forward and flashed an ID. "JTF 13. Take us to García."

The captain stared at her and her out of place yellow sun dress. "But—I cannot."

Linda shook her head and her demeanor changed.

"Is Mrs. García here, too?"

The executive officer looked worried. "You'll have to ask the Commandante. My orders are to put you back on your jet and see you off."

"On that jet?" asked Linda, pointing.

He glanced over at the aircraft. When he returned his gaze, Linda's automatic was staring him in the eye.

"You drive, we'll ride."

Linda sat behind the driver's seat with her weapon to the back of the captain's head. Suzie Q rode in the passenger seat.

"Just a minute," said Linda. She nudged the captain's head with her gun. "Head over to that chopper."

"But—"

"Do it."

In a minute he pulled the Jeep alongside the Black Hawk.

Linda jumped out, her dress billowing. "Watch him, Suze." She stepped into the open door of the chopper and disappeared.

Suzie Q kept her weapon on the captain.

In two minutes, Linda hopped out of the craft and climbed back into the rear of the Jeep. "Let's go."

The captain looked at Linda strangely and put the vehicle into gear.

Suzie glanced at Linda and she smiled widely. Suzie now understood. Linda had somehow booby-trapped the chopper to prevent someone, probably García, from using it to escape.

They wound through the base and approaching headquarters, Suzie could tell some kind of firefight had occurred. She exchanged a confirmation glance with Linda.

The devastation around the motor pool was extraordinary. "What happened here?" she asked. She smelled burned fuel.

The captain kept driving and ignored her.

Shortly, they pulled up in front of headquarters. The captain hit the horn once and Linda ground the muzzle of her weapon into the back of his head. He climbed out with her right behind.

She withdrew her gun as they walked to the entrance and started climbing the stairs. Warning flags flew to her; bullet holes and splintered wood stared at them.

Immediately, Diego García appeared and came through the double doors. "Captain, did you not tell them we were unavailable?"

"I did, Commandante. They insisted with weapons."

"Ah, I begin to understand. If I do not already have enough trouble with women today."

Suzie stopped. "García? What's happening here? Mutiny?" She figured well what was going on, she needed to give him something to grasp.

Linda was beginning to feel like they were in an untenable position.

"Not at all, Ms. Quantrell, isn't it?"

Suzie nodded.

"Suze!" Linda's warning was too late.

"Kill them," García said loudly and dived back inside.

Linda shot the executive officer in the back of his head and his head exploded spraying blood and gray matter forward.

Suzie had her weapon out as several soldiers ran around a corner shooting.

Suzie dropped to a knee to present less of a target and began firing.

Linda fired, dove and rolled in the dirt and came up shooting. The three went down almost immediately.

Another soldier stepped out of the front door with his M-16 on full auto and a line of rounds etched through the gravel and coral and dirt of the parking area and across Suzan Quantrell.

Linda fired and that soldier's left eye disappeared.

Suzie spun as if hit by a car and went down limp, blood beginning to stain her white blouse under her jacket.

Linda fired through the open doorway and her gun ran out of ammo. She pulled her hideout from under her dress and hunted for a target as she scrambled to Suzie.

"Suzie, goddamnit, talk to me."

Linda saw movement in an upstairs window and fired two rounds through it at waist height so as to not over correct for the acute upward angle. No further movement right away, so she opted to get them out of the line of fire out in the open instead of reloading.

That was her mistake. She had to make a judgment call and she did so.

She was already on high adrenaline. She grabbed Suzie under her arm and dragged her along the porch of the headquarters. She heard movement hurrying toward them from somewhere offset of the front and the jeep which had brought them.

Linda got Suzie against the wall near the corner when incoming fire stopped her. Gray painted concrete block chipped and shards flew stinging her shoulder. She stood quickly, her hideout revolver ready. She spotted the shooter hiding behind a Humvee and snapped a quick shot at him with no results. Another three or four men ran across the parade ground toward them, rifles at ready. She fired her last couple of rounds at them. She bent and dug out two magazines from Suzie's jacket pocket. She stepped back and retrieved Suzie's automatic, dropped the magazine and replaced it with a full one.

More fire came her way, and she went to fire Suzie's weapon and nothing happened.

"Damn." A quick glance told her the 9 millimeter had been grazed by one of the M-16 rounds. She dropped it and dug in her pocket and came up with more .38 rounds, her last, for the revolver. She dropped to one knee dumping the empties and feeding the last rounds into the gun.

A very large man, bigger than Atkins, saw her trouble and swaggered around the corner with a wide grin. He had sergeant stripes on his BDU's. He looked down Linda's cleavage and his grin widened. Linda shot upwards, the round entering his mouth and traveling all the way through his head on an upward trajectory.

More shooting sounded and she shot the man behind the Humvee, this time hitting him as he aimed. His surprised look faded as he sank to the ground, head lolling.

A MAC-10 or a MAC-11 opened up and Linda knew she and Suzie were goners. Likely a thirty-two round magazine. She decided it was probably a MAC-10 as the rounds sounded more like 9mm than .380 rounds—although M-10's could fire .45's. The incongruity of the very non-military weapons did not escape her. The first pass went above her head and she took her revolver in both hands in the approved manner, and locked in on the machine gun's location. He was firing over the hood of a pickup. Linda was at a bad angle but fired two rounds. The windshield of the pickup starred and the shooter ducked, but that was it. Two shots left. She fired one through the pickup's window to scare the shooter into an exposed position. He took the bait and popped out over the hood once again, finger on the trigger and another line of fire raced toward her.

Linda Lavender stood determined over the top of Susan Quantrell's unmoving body with one shot remaining. She ignored the chattering fire and pounding noise screaming towards them and calmly fired her last round and watched as the shooter's head disappeared in an explosion of flesh.

More incoming fire traced its way toward her. In case she'd miscounted, she triggered her revolver once again and again, with only dry, lifeless clicks to reward her.

The enemy seemed to realize her predicament and one by one, a half dozen jungle BDU dressed soldiers stood and began walking toward her.

Linda threw her weapon at the lead soldier who laughed and ducked it easily. He stepped onto the landing as Linda stood over Suzie, protecting her to the bitter end.

The soldier laughed again as he came forward and died with the grin on his face as Linda snatched her hideout knife from its position on her upper leg under her blood-stained yellow sun dress. Blood sheeted from the soldier's throat and he simply folded to the ground.

Three other soldiers cursed and jumped upon the landing, rifles lifting to end it all.

Linda looked down at Suzie and said, "Fuck it." She dove at the lead soldier who was too close and not expecting Linda to continue the fight. The knife ripped into his neck and severed an artery. She used her momentum to fling his body at the other two and they scrambled aside. She followed through, the knife arcing and slicing into another's thigh, eliciting a scream of pain and that man fell back, wounded but not dead. However, the knife had lodged into his flesh and likely gotten lodged against his hipbone and his frantic retreat tore the knife from her hand.

She continued the movement and her foot swept around aiming at number three's throat. Her momentum sufficiently slowed, he easily stepped aside. So she tumbled into a roll and knocked the last man off his feet. Her lancing hand crushed his Adam's apple and she came up with his M-16 ready to fire.

The entire enemy contingent had fallen into a stunned silence.

Linda saw a couple of men squatting behind a Jeep and she fired under it, hoping to take cut off their legs.

That action renewed fire against her once again. She stood to her full height and raised the weapon to her cheek and clicked on single fire. She didn't know how many rounds she had left. But she did know her position was untenable. She saw movement and fired once. She spun and leapt back upon the landing and grabbed Suzie with a quick ducking move and stood with an effort, Suzie slung over one shoulder. More rounds came their way and she skipped aside.

But something was wrong. She couldn't stand. Her left leg crumbled and she sank down, Suzie still hanging from her shoulder, bleeding all over her favorite yellow sun dress.

Linda held the M-16 at waist level as she sat awkwardly against the wall of 13's headquarters building. She shifted her body so that Suzie slid mostly behind her, protecting Suzie with her own body.

Linda looked dumbly at blood welling from her thigh.

A shadow flickered in her peripheral vision and she snapped a shot that way, rewarded by a cry.

More incoming fire tracked to them. Linda wondered just how much of an army they had here.

She fired the M-16 a couple of more times until it, too, ran out of ammunition.

"Well, shit, Suze," Linda Landover said conversationally, "I always knew it would end, but not this way, not in a last stand." She leaned back against Suzie Quantrell and waited as more rounds inched their way across the landing.

CHAPTER THIRTY-TWO: HIM

García was gone and Tommy knew they had little time. He stood eying the two soldiers guarding them. One motioned with his M-16 telling Tommy to move against the wall. Tommy could see the man thinking: he'd been instructed to secure María Elena to the wall, but García had been distracted before he'd given similar orders concerning Atkins. Before the man could decide, Tommy stepped as far away from María Elena as he could and came to a stop against the wall, closer, he noted, to the table where García had weapons and a couple of intriguing duffle bags.

The first soldier saw Tommy looking at the table and finally made the connection; he started walking toward Tommy, his weapon straight ahead of him pointing right at Tommy. Tommy tried to use his peripheral vision to see if María Elena was working on her handcuffs, but didn't because he couldn't turn his head that way in case it gave the guards a tipoff. He continued to survey the table. A couple of handguns sat alongside a large, open duffle. Inside the canvas bag, Tommy could see the stocks of a couple other weapons, and maybe the folded stock of a submachine gun of some type. This led him to believe that the bag was full of handguns and automatic weapons. The duffle was certainly large enough to accommodate even the length of M-16s and other similar weapons. A getaway stash in case García had to go on the run? Likely. That well could have been what García's intentions were anyway.

The sentry was almost to him.

Tommy turned his head and coughed violently, risking a glance at María Elena. She was calmly watching the choreography of Tommy and the two sentries. But Tommy noticed muscles in her lower arms working, and her hands were partially covered. Because this was their one best chance to escape, Tommy continued with his plan. He coughed some more and began to wretch. The dry heave caused the soldier to step back. Number two sentry was watching expectantly.

Tommy stepped forward, still gagging and the guard stepped back. Tommy wanted the two guards in each other's way to impede any movement they might make.

The guard waved the muzzle of his M-16, warning Tommy to go back. Tommy ignored him and wretched again, this time infusing spittle and phlegm from his throat into the movement. The spray with attendant globs flew from his mouth and the guard retreated quickly.

While he had his chance, Tommy struck with a booted foot, catching the man in the right thigh, spinning him backwards and the two guards slumped together for a second before they could untangle their weapons.

That was all that Tommy needed. He followed up with a powerful kick to the back of the first sentry's knee, the crack of breaking bone audible across the room. The man screamed as he went down grabbing his knee from the front.

The other guard danced backwards but hit a wall himself and Tommy kicked a metal folding chair at him as he swung the barrel of his weapon toward Tommy. The man ducked and Tommy swarmed in as the chair banged to the floor. It was difficult with his hands cuffed behind him. He slammed into the guard, preferring to operate inside the radius of the rifle. Stupidly, the guard wouldn't let go of his M-16 to get himself out of trouble. The man was pinned against the wall and Tommy kneed him in the groin. The sentry screamed and folded over, puking. Tommy dodged aside and kicked him in the left kidney hard. The guard screamed and went white and writhed on the floor. To make sure, Tommy kicked him in the temple and the ugly sound put an end to any movement or noise from the man.

Tommy spun, looking for the guard with the broken knee. Never leave an enemy any chance.

María Elena was swinging another metal folding chair and it collided with that sentry's forehead with a sickening whack. Blood and bile leaked from the man's open mouth hanging there. He would no longer offer a problem.

María Elena rushed to the table where Tommy had been disarmed, retrieved his knife and came and sawed off the plastic restraints on his wrists.

Tommy shot a thankful look at her and rubbed his wrists as he hurried to the table and started to rearm himself. He kept the sawed-off shotgun in the crook of his arm at ready. No one here was their friend, so he needn't worry about where the shot pattern went.

"Once again you done good, Pocahontas. Find yourself something to shoot with, preferably more than one thing with ammo. We're gonna have to shoot our way out of this."

"Yes, dear." She took a Glock off the dead guard she'd killed and pulled a couple of magazines off his belt.

"María Elena? I'm not inclined to run out of this just yet. I think we need to finish it."

"Me, too."

"I don't suppose I can convince you to hide out while I take care of business?"

"Not a chance." She ejected the magazine from the Glock, checked it, and slapped it back into the gun. She went over to the duffle. "A treasure trove of weaponry."

Tommy joined her, keeping an eye on the entryway. He dug through the duffle. He pulled out a small .32 revolver. "Here, this is just right. Stick it under your waistline at the small of your back.

A fusillade of shots came from out front of the building. In a second, he could hear return fire. It died then started again.

"One hell of a firefight out there," he said. "So who…?"

"Beats me?"

"I need to find out. Keep your head down. Can you shoot a MAC-10?"

"You betcha." She smiled at him.

He was glad she could smile. Not a lot of people can think straight with dead guys lying around and bullets flying all about.

He retrieved the submachine gun from the duffle and handed it to her. "I'll see what's going on. Sit over there in the corner where you won't be seen immediately if someone comes in the room. Kill them if they're not friendly. I'll call ahead when I come back."

"Yes. Don't take any chances."

"Life's one big chance, sweetheart. Sometimes it's worth it." He patted her on the ass and turned to go.

"Tommy? Before you go?"

"What?"

"Just in case." She grabbed his head and pulled him down to her. The kiss was brief but singular and full of heat and promise. She stepped back. "For the record, yes, I will marry you."

He gave her a big wide smile and turned and bent over to pick up an errant M-16 lying unused on the floor. He went to the other dead sentry and took the spare magazines on the man's web belt. He slipped on his vest and pocketed the magazines. Then he went out.

CHAPTER THIRTY-THREE: THEM

Linda Landover was sitting there on the sprawling front landing of the 13 headquarters. Automatic weapons fire was searching them out. She casually looked out over the battlefield, a strange mix of parade ground, parking area; gravel, grass, dirt, hardpan, crushed coral, battle damaged vehicles. She wondered about life. She regretted some things she'd never done; but she was honest with herself, actually she'd done about all she really wanted to. She regretted most of all not being able to save Suzie. She didn't really care about herself, which was why she was such an effective combatant. She never, ever gave up.

But right now Linda was tired, oh so tired.

She watched the morning sun peep above a line of palm trees to the east and kind of liked the sight. She'd never been into sunrises and sunsets. She could get to like them. Maybe a cold martini in one hand and a good Lucky Strike in the other. Unfiltered Lucky Strike, of course. She breathed deeply, imagining she was inhaling. Absently, she checked the pocket of her favorite yellow sun dress and found no smokes. Maybe she'd left them on the Cessna.

Suzie's warm body stuffed behind her gave Linda pause. Somebody needed to see to her funeral, it was only fitting that that person be her. Suzie's body was still warm, so she could well be alive. If so, it was likely the poor woman wouldn't live out the hour, much less the day.

What was that thought she'd just had? Linda scoured her

mind, knowing it was important. A round clipped the top of her shoulder. Another skinned through her favorite yellow sun dress and tore a hole in the damn thing.

The thought? What the fuck was it? Goddamn! That was it. Never, ever give up. Then why the fuck was she sitting here like at a goddamn Sunday picnic looking out over some stupid fucking lake with ducks and geese and shit like that?

"Awright, goddamnit, gimme a fuckin' minute here." She was talking to her smarter, survival self. She hiked her dress and observed her wound. Deep blood welled out of her thigh, but it wasn't spurting or pumping. She wondered if her leg still worked. It had folded beneath her earlier. She shook her head to clear it. "Stay on task, dammit."

Linda ripped a strip off her favorite yellow sundress where the MAC-10 round had torn a path. She hiked her dress, took a deep breath, and lifted her leg. It worked! Quickly, she tied a temporary tourniquet above the wound. The blood stopped welling.

"Well, shit," she said aloud, "nothing to it when you know how."

Incoming fire intensified as if the enemy out there saw what she was doing and finally figured out she was not dead or dying. She started pushing herself up with no plan in mind when another flurry of fire concentrated on them.

Something hit her head with a glancing blow and she fell. Feeling the incoming fire targeting them finally, she crawled to Suzie and threw her body over that of the CIA agent.

"We've been through this before, Suze. It doesn't look good again."

Incoming fire intensified and she felt impacts tracing along the front of the building racing for them.

Out of the corner of her eye, she saw the front doors slam open and a big man stride out carrying two M-16s, one in each hand. He opened fire with three round bursts, calmly picking his targets. When one M-16 emptied, he tossed it aside and fired with the other. That one ran out of ammo and he dropped the magazine and slapped in another and began firing once again. This time he fired on full auto as he strode toward Linda and Suzie.

Linda recognized he was forcing the 13 soldiers to take cover.

Again he switched magazines and again he emptied the M-16. Now there was no return fire, the fierceness of his attack sending the enemy into hiding. Acrid gunsmoke drifted about and then faded.

He dropped the rifle and Linda felt a strong arm lifting her. "Suzie, get Suzie."

Atkins tucked her under one arm and lifted Suzie with his other. He turned and strode quickly to the front doors, stepped over the late executive officer and moved swiftly inside.

He continued down the hall and turned into a doorway. "Pocahontas, it's me," he said aloud. He went through the double doors and headed to a couch. He sat Linda down on one end and lay Suzie down alongside her on the remainder of the couch.

"Is she dead?" asked Linda, voice raw.

CHAPTER THIRTY-FOUR: HIM

"Let's find out," Tommy said.

He turned Susan Quantrell face up and ripped open her blouse. The jacket was in the way, so he peeled that aside.

Linda Lavender levered herself over Suzie.

"Don't get in the way, FBI. María Elena, we got a couple of short minutes before they stick their head up again. Help me here."

He felt CIA's throat for a pulse then saw the woman breathing shallowly and discontinued the pulse check.

María Elena came over.

"Keep an eye and an ear on the door," Tommy told her. "Do you know where the first aid kit or medical supplies are?"

"In the orderly room adjoining the barracks." She pointed. "A hundred and fifty yards or so that way."

"Well, we got to stop this bleeding. She doesn't look so good."

Linda scrambled up and limped around Atkins and María Elena. She reached down and pushed Suzie's jacket aside. She tugged out a fanny pack from beneath her friend, zipped it open, and dug inside. She came out with several feminine hygiene pads and tampons. She ripped the paper off two.

"Here. Strip the tampon and push it into the wound. Then slap the pad over the top of that. The wings and edges are sticky and should hold."

Tommy was already doing that thing. The cotton mix in the tampon was very absorbent, of course, and staunched the blood flow immediately. There were two wounds adjacent to each other and they'd become one large wound. The tampon fit perfectly. He applied the pad and stretched the wings and smoothed them down. "As good as we can do."

Linda leaned over Suzie and propped open an eyelid. She looked up at Tommy who spread his hands in a question. "I've no idea, but doctors do that in the movies." She stood upright and wobbled.

Tommy moved swiftly behind her and grabbed her. He sat her down on the couch in her previous seat. He knelt before her and pulled up her yellow sun dress.

"Apparently, you ain't bullet proof," he observed. He untied the yellow dress strip tourniquet and said to María Elena. "Give me a couple of those pads."

María Elena did so, and said, "These are panty liners."

"I don't need to know this shit," Tommy said. "But she carries a lot of supplies."

Linda's head was leaning against the back of the couch. "It's for both of us. Our periods are due any time."

"Us?"

"Synchronized," Linda said.

"I don't need to know this shit," Tommy said again.

"It happens when women are together a lot," María Elena said, "like in a military unit."

"I really don't need to know this shit."

"Atkins? You owe us nothing. But thanks for the assist anyway."

"Sure thing, FBI. We might need help busting out of here and I pick you for our team."

She smiled gratefully.

He rose and went swiftly to a table at the far side of the room upon which sat the requisite coffee pot extant in every military day room in the world. He snatched a dispenser of sugar and brought it back with him.

"María Elena, if you don't know, this here's FBI, a tough lady named Linda Landover." He nodded over at Suzie. "And

Miss CIA, Susan Quantrell." He knelt in front of FBI and sprinkled sugar over her wound. At her questioning glance, he said, "Bacteria can't grow in a sugar environment." He nodded at CIA. "He wounds are too severe for me to try this trick." He finished putting the panty liner on Linda's thigh. "A shame to mar such fine legs." He shrugged. "But it'll heal with a tiny puckered scar. It'll show character."

Linda snorted.

"JTF 13," said María Elena.

"In person, but not functioning very well right now," said Linda.

María Elena said, "I've been engaged for only about twenty minutes and already my fiancé has his hand up a beautiful woman's dress."

"I knew it was you," said Linda. "And smokin' hot, too. Congratulations."

"There's a small matter of making me a widow first, but Tommy's going to take care of that."

"Lucky guy. You're absolutely beautiful."

"So, too, are you," María Elena replied.

"Disregarding all the blood?" Linda tried to grin.

"You bet," said María Elena honestly.

"Next time," said Tommy uncomfortably, "one of those Velcro straps on your thighs would make a good tourniquet." He needed them to change the subject.

Surprise etched on Linda's face. "Damn, I wasn't thinking. Hell, I thought I was dying." She paused. "And I ruined my favorite yellow sun dress."

"It still looks good on you," said Tommy. The dress was sprayed with blood from her and somebody not her, and had been ripped and shot through several times.

Linda smoothed her sun dress back over her legs. She looked over at Suzie with concern. "I'm worried."

"Anybody have a cell phone? We might call for the cavalry."

Linda leaned over and searched Suzie's pockets. She found it in another jacket pocket, but it was smashed from all the falling and tumbling.

Tommy thought that might not be a bad thing. He didn't need a bunch of feds running around asking questions and taking names. On the other hand, they were surrounded by bad guys with lethality on their minds.

"We do have two pilots over at the landing strip," said Linda. "Their orders are to remain aboard. I don't know what they'll do having heard a small war over here."

María Elena went to a small table by the door and picked up a landline telephone. "No signal, the distribution box is over by the motor pool, so somebody's disabled it."

"Or blew it up," said Tommy. "Fire a couple of rounds down the hall and out the front doors, will you please?" he told María Elena.

She picked up a sentry's Glock and triggered two rounds from behind the doorframe.

"I guess we'll have to do this the hard way," said Tommy.

Linda stood uncertainly. "The sooner we clean out this nest of vipers, the sooner we can get Suzie some help."

"Can you walk?" asked Tommy.

"I guess I'll have to." She limped tentatively across the floor.

"Good," said Tommy, "let us go forth and kill some of those Saracens."

"No," said Linda, "let us go out and kill all them mother-fuckers."

María Elena said, "Count me in."

"I was kind of hoping somebody would stay with Suzie," said Linda.

"She's your buddy," said María Elena, "you stay."

They both looked at Tommy.

"Don't get me involved."

María Elena looked down at Suzie Quantrell. "Um, I'm thinking you both are the professionals. I fold. I'd only slow you two down."

Linda nodded. "That's fact." She shot Tommy a knowing look. "And here I thought it would be me against you, not us against them."

Tommy said, "The longer we talk, the more organized they're going to become."

Linda limped back to the couch. She bent over Suzie and smoothed her hair out. She skimmed her lips over Suzie's cheek. "We'll get you out of here soon, hon. Hang on, okay?" Linda straightened abruptly and headed for the table and weapons. "Let us proceed to kill those who badly need it."

Tommy was checking the load in his handguns and poking around in the giant duffle.

María Elena came over and examined his left forearm.

"Didn't penetrate much, just a scratch."

"We've another panty liner," she said.

"Not even upon the threat of death." The bleeding had pretty well stopped.

Linda had checked her weapons and pulled an ammo pouch over her shoulder. She filled it with magazines.

Tommy carried mostly his own weapons. He had the AR-15 at ready on a sling. The sawed off double-barreled shotgun swung from its strap over his shoulder. He carried an M-16 and he had a .38 and a couple of 9 mm automatics stuffed about his clothing. The vest was weighed down with ammunition. He found his knife and returned it to his boot, noting the jealous look FBI gave him. Well, that explained the artful spray of blood across the front of her yellow sun dress.

When they were ready, Tommy saw Linda Landover loaded with weaponry much as he was.

"I'll go out the front," he told her. "That will draw their fire and their attention. You slip out the back." He thought about the building layout. "Move clockwise and I'll move counterclockwise and we'll meet in the middle." There wasn't much likelihood of the enemy being on the south side. But you never know and certainly don't count on it. "Try not to shoot me when we get close."

Linda nodded. "If you're waiting on me, you're already late." She limped into the hallway, smiled weakly at them. Her voice was strong. "And swiftly comes the scythe." She turned right, headed for the back.

Tommy nodded to María Elena.

A major but muted explosion rolled over the buildings. The vibration shook the headquarters Quonset.

Linda stopped halfway down the corridor and turned. Her grin was genuine. "Ahem. That chopper is no longer operational." Answering his unspoken question, she said, "They shouldn't leave incendiary grenades lying around."

"Maybe it took out García making a run for it," said Tommy.

"We can only hope," said Linda. She continued her journey down the hallway.

María Elena stepped close to him.

"No melodrama, okay, Pocahontas?" Her faint animal cinnamon scent hit him with emotion.

"Yes, dear. Just come back to me."

"Sure thing, María Elena. Wouldn't miss it for the world." He took her hand. "Keep a good watch and have your weapons ready."

"Yes, dear." She squeezed his hand.

And he was gone, swift and silent.

He paused at the front doors, reviewed the terrain immediately outside. No use to show himself quickly to see if he'd draw fire: then they'd be ready. He burst through the double doors, M-16 in his right hand targeting where he thought would be the best concealed place they'd be waiting. He hit a three round burst and dodged right, rolling off the landing to the clockwise side, weapon at ready. One man stood surprised and Tommy put him down with a single round. No use leaving your rear open.

He turned around and peeked out. No fire. They were either intimidated or somebody cagey, probably an old sergeant, was directing their resistance.

He went back to the body of the soldier he'd just killed. Tommy picked the man up by the back of his uniform even though the bullet had drilled right through his center chest and out the back. He began running to the corner with the body held in front of him. One step, two, three and several weapons opened up.

They had been biding their time. It sounded like a bunch of kids banging on pans.

He tossed the body to his left, toward the front of headquarters. Incoming fire tracked the body as Tommy sprinted right and ahead, trying to get to a troop carrier for cover. He hoped he'd taken their attention sufficiently for Landover to make it out without notice. He shook his head. Yellow sun dresses were not the best of stealth cover. However, he knew she'd make up for that by her burning anger over CIA. He shook his head. Women.

Though he had to admit, they'd probably used him, played him like a fiddle.

He snaked under the double rear wheels careful not to hang up the shotgun and trigger it into his torso.

CIA and FBI, JTF 13, had to have set him up to attack this base. He suspected it was Quantrell, she was the spymaster. FBI didn't usually play those games. Although there was no way they could have programmed his hideout handcuff key and his throwing FBI off that balcony.

Tommy saw two pairs of legs double-timing it toward the front of headquarters. Maybe they figured they could go in now. He gunned them down and watched them flop around on the ground. He didn't finish them: Let the enemy waste energy and manpower taking care of their wounded. If they had that kind of fellow concern, he amended.

He scrambled backwards out from under the vehicle and stepped around behind it. A slight shift in the body warned him as he felt more than saw a Glock appear over the tailgate. He reached up and grabbed the hand, twirled a 360 and heard bones crunch followed by a wailing scream. He stuck his M-16 up there and hosed off the rest of the magazine. Quickly he stuck his head inside and looked. Two more down. He popped the magazine onto the ground and dug another from his ammo pouch.

Realizing he was more exposed here than he wanted to be, he zigzagged across the parade ground, trying to keep the flagpole and a Humvee between himself and the majority of the vehicles in the parking lot where the enemy had to be hiding. Several shots followed him.

He made it to a Quonset hut he didn't know the purpose of and edged around the far side. They knew where he was. If he could draw their attention, then FBI could take them out from behind.

He caught his breath and stopped to even out his breathing. Out of control breathing is not conducive to accurate shooting and good judgment.

If the two women hadn't intended to send him to this 13 training base, it had worked out better for all of them—unless you count CIA taking a big hit. At any rate, given a few hours, he'd have figured it out himself. He would have had to find somebody in the know and rip the information about this base from them. And that would have cost him too much time.

Tommy snaked around behind the Quonset. Nobody. He kicked in the screen door, his rifle ready. Nothing. A storage building, folding metal chairs, tables, refrigerators, tents.

Automatic fire opened up, but it wasn't near him. Landover.

He went out and peered around the other side. A line of automatic fire chipped aluminum next to his head and dented it and snagged ragged holes where his head had been. He was on the ground rolling back. He came to his feet at a dead run and zigzagged to another Quonset. A quick glance told him that it was a mess hall. Though they look different almost everywhere, there was a sameness about military eating facilities. Any GI anywhere can invariably go right to the closest one.

If Quantrell and Landover had in fact set him up, were they on his and María Elena's side? For a while, they'd been assisting Diego García. Or somebody had. Maybe they'd had a change of heart. Maybe a change of plans? If so, why?

The best answer was that García had gone off the reservation and was too high profile to cover up his transgressions. Things like that domino, especially when the government gets involved. There are no secrets. Just check with the officers' wives' clubs.

Suddenly, it made sense. JTF 13 needed somebody unsanctioned to take out García, somebody not connected to them. And he fit the bill nicely. He grinned. "Glad to oblige," he said aloud. He did admit that García had screwed even that up by attacking the women. They should have stayed away and awaited the outcome of Tommy's one man assault.

The mess hall was empty. He began to wonder if they hadn't killed so many that the rest had decided to cut and run. He moved to go around the mess hall and turn back to his clockwise movement. He skirted the now non-existent-but-still-smoking motor pool.

Quantrell's plan had been highly Machiavellian. She was someone whose tactics manipulate everyone involved to affect her strategy. He had underestimated the two women before and determined not to do so again.

He smelled burnt fuel. Two men were sneaking away from the firefight and he let them go. They never saw him.

He heard not-so distant gunfire. FBI was still in the fight.

Whether they'd aimed him at García and this base didn't really matter, for it facilitated his search for María Elena. And he would take García out. If that's the way it all worked out, he'd be more than glad to oblige them.

He moved quietly forward, hearing gunshots off to the front and the right. FBI was getting involved.

All his speculation aside, he still wondered about Quantrell and Landover. Both were super bright and deadly. FBI was as good as anyone at this game. And CIA had the equivalent of a supercomputer in her brain. Not to mention a stupid fucking dog.

An automatic weapons burst smashed into his M-16 and he dropped it like it was on fire. His hand was numb and he dropped to the side and rolled against an errant smoking tire.

He'd been too busy thinking. Three soldiers ran to him, their rifles spitting bullets. It's hard to run and shoot accurately, he thought, and swung his shotgun. He triggered both barrels and they went down like pins in a bowling alley.

He leapt to his feet and ran forward between two buildings. He'd been gone too long. They had too much opportunity to attack headquarters. He wished CIA was still operational. He came upon a half dozen crawling like they were at basic training on an obstacle course. They were headed directly for the landing of headquarters. He saw them become bold when they received no fire. Someone was shooting into the building to give them cover.

Tommy flattened against the troop barracks, glanced in a screen door and saw no one. Everybody had to be outside and involved in the battle. He did give them credit, for strong resistance. But these were García's men, maybe drug runners, gang members, cartel shooters masquerading as militia soldiers. Tommy couldn't tell where the sniper was, so he brought up the AR-15 and began firing into the six men. He hit three before they reacted and began returning his fire. Tommy calmly shot them all and felt bad about it. They were soldiers, allegedly, and aware of the risks. It was as if García had sent them out to be killed. Good loyalty on their part, stupid judgment. He spotted the lone gunman dodging behind the first Quonset Tommy had vacated. Tommy stepped out into the open to draw his fire. He dodged back and nothing happened.

Tommy ran more to the south of the headquarters building digging up gouts of dirt behind him. The gunman stepped out and drew down on him and a shot rang out and the man folded into himself.

Landover.

He edged to the side and whispered, "FBI?"

"Atkins."

He found her leaning against a fatigue green trailer. He saw a trail of blood leaking down her leg, pain etched on her face.

"Is your side clear?" he asked.

"Pretty much. And the rest discouraged."

"Mine, too, though they have a lot of places to hole up I didn't have a chance to check out." Tommy saw a flash and grabbed Linda and dragged her down. Two rounds clanged into and off of the trailers side wall.

"Where is he?" she asked.

"That makeshift tower over by the landing strip."

"A long way for an M-16 to shoot accurately," she said.

He held up his AR-15. "This should do the trick."

"Gimme."

He handed her the weapon and she squirmed around and rested the barrel across his upper back.

"More elevation," she said.

He lifted his shoulders and rested on his forearms.

"Come on, show yourself," Linda said conversationally.

"Ah."

Tommy could do nothing about his ears. His head was ducked as far as possible when the rifle went off and he could hear nothing after that. He felt her withdraw the weapon and knew she'd gotten the target.

He shook his head and his hearing started to return.

"I think the organized resistance is gone," Linda was saying and he read her lips until the sound penetrated.

"Concur," he said, knowing his voice was too loud. He tried to pitch it lower. "I'm concerned. No García, and not much happening any longer. I'm not sure María Elena and CIA are safe."

"Me, neither," she said.

"I saw no signs of García."

"Me, neither," she said. "Not a creature is stirring, not ever a mouse."

"Good work."

"Although, I will admit several of them ran past as if some devil was on their ass. You must have been effective. They were quitting being combatants, so I let 'em go." She grinned at him and eased her leg. "On the other hand, there aren't many combatants left anywhere I can tell."

"I don't want to perform a sweep of all these buildings to find

García," said Tommy.

Landover shook her head. "That would take forever. I need to get Suzie help."

"He's got to be somewhere. His getaway kit is still sitting in the headquarters lounge." Tommy kept his eyes roving. "And you're bleeding again. You need help, too." He paused. "So maybe that's where he will return to?"

Just then, as if to fulfill his prediction, a Humvee slewed around a corner and sped to the front of the headquarters building. Gravel and dirt flew from the four-wheel slide as it came to a stop. Six men leaped out.

"García," Linda gasped.

"We gotta go now, before they get set," said Tommy.

"Or kill our folks."

One man ran inside, the other five deployed in front of headquarters' landing and behind the Humvee.

Tommy took off heading left. The soldiers were just now finding their positions. One opened up before the others and a shot from over Tommy's shoulder spun the man around. He screamed and his four fellow soldiers looked at him in horror. While he had a shot, Tommy fired a long burst into the bunched up men and two more went down.

He continued to run trying to keep the Humvee between himself and the soldiers. A couple of shots came his way, but nothing serious yet. He zigzagged, head low, presenting as small a target as he could.

Glancing over his shoulder, he saw Linda in her horribly ruined and bloody yellow sun dress limping gamely around to the right. Her position was more exposed because of the way the men deployed themselves.

Because of this, Tommy changed his angle of attack and sped toward the men, holding the Humvee between them. More fire came his way.

In some faraway pocket of his mind, he heard the sounds of another jet, two engines, just like the Cessna. What could it be? Reinforcements? John Law? If so, he and María Elena were sunk, especially him. Perhaps it was more likely to be an escape vehicle for Diego García. Regardless, he still had to continue his attack.

Deadly fire was arcing toward Linda. She couldn't move fast enough to avoid good targeting, nor could she zigzag like he could. Tommy finished off his magazine shooting on the run, trying to pin them down and prevent them from shooting. It worked only slightly, as one of the weapons turned on him. His glance told him the two remaining soldiers taking aim at FBI and him, and another wounded soldier lying on the landing preparing to shoot from the prone position. These were real fighters, he had to give them credit. He hadn't been in a shootout like this since Angola and Zaire.

The wounded guy shooting prone squeezed off a single shot and Linda went down without a sound.

"Goddamnit!" Tommy said aloud. In his peripheral vision he did see her tuck her shoulder and hit the ground rolling.

Tommy had only seconds. He was almost to the Humvee, so he faked the logical move and decoyed the final leg of his run to the left, to appear to go around the rear of the Humvee where it would be safer for him. Once to the vehicle, he ducked farther and ran right. His rifle was empty, so he had drawn two automatic pistols, both with rounds chambered and ready.

He burst around the hood of the Hummer and surprised them. The two upright troopers were watching and waiting for him to run around the rear as he'd decoyed, and the wounded soldier was staring at him in horror. Tommy shot him immediately. Then as the other two realized their mistake, he held out both of his pistols in front of himself and triggered all the remaining rounds.

Both soldiers went down, one getting off a final shot into the ceiling of the landing's overhang. Tommy didn't take the time to reload his weapons, he simply dropped them and grabbed his shotgun; his longtime companion felt comfortable in his hands. He snapped it open to double check that he'd reloaded.

He should probably go to FBI's aid, but García was inside

with María Elena and a dead or incapacitated CIA.

Tommy slammed into the doors and, since they opened outward, burst them off their hinges. He ran to the entry to the lounge and skidded inside. His breathing was not in control and he didn't think it was because of the physical exertion.

He froze at the tableau he saw. María Elena was sitting on the couch in front of Susan Quantrell as if to protect her.

Don Diego García stood in front of them, his Glock held in front of him, squeezing the trigger.

If Tommy shot him, then the shot pattern would hit María Elena and Suzie Q also. He lifted the sawed-off shotgun anyway.

CHAPTER THIRTY-FIVE: HER

María Elena watched uncomfortably as Tommy and Linda ran out.

It wasn't long before she was hearing the sounds of running battle. Soon she could distinguish two separate on-going fire-fights. As the shooting continued, it waned at times and started again with renewed vigor.

María Elena walked over to the hallway and checked outside. Nothing.

She went to the weapons' duffle and pawed through what remained. MAC-10, MAC-11, some kind of Uzi, a folded AK-47. She grouped a few of the weapons and laid out their spare magazines.

She went and checked the other duffle, over behind the table. "Wow," she said.

Inside was an envelope and stacks of banded cash. Mostly dollars she saw, but a lot of Mexican pesos. She ripped the envelope open and inside was a sheaf of personal ID and documents, all showing Diego García with different names and professions.

Outside, firing had died momentarily.

She heard a discordant sound and finally placed it coming from the couch. She hurried over.

Susan Quantrell's eyes were fluttering. She croaked.

Linda hurried over to a water bottle and drew some in a cone cup. She brought it back to the couch and touched it to Suzie's lips.

The CIA agent's tongue flicked out and lapped a little water.

María Elena tipped the cup into her mouth and the woman drank greedily. María Elena hoped this wasn't going to adversely affect her wound. But that wasn't intestinal, so it was likely okay.

She withdrew the cup and the woman's piercing gray eyes locked onto her own.

"Linda?" she croaked, voice still dry and low.

"She's okay."

"Where?"

"She and Tommy are out killing Diego's soldiers."

Suzie Q seemed to sink back into herself.

"We've stopped your bleeding. But we don't have a land line or a working cell to call for medivac. We have to wait until Tommy and Linda to, um, finish."

Suzie eyelids fluttered.

María Elena didn't know whether that meant Suzie understood or she was falling unconscious again. María Elena tried to find a pulse, but her own heart was racing and she couldn't tell the difference. She licked the top of her hand and held it under the CIA agent's nose and felt a slight stirring,

She went to the double doors again and checked the hall. She stole down the empty hallway, automatic in hand. She found a window which had been nearly destroyed with gunfire and peered out around the frame. She saw nothing, could tell nothing. More firing erupted off to the northeast corner toward the motor pool.

Where was Diego García? He'd simply run out.

Suddenly, it occurred to her that no one had checked upstairs. Diego could be concealed and waiting his opportunity to pounce when Tommy returned. She crossed her mental fingers and amended, when, not if, he returned.

She went back down the corridor to the stairs and mounted them swiftly and silently. Not that silence was important with a couple of firefights raging in the distance.

She scoured the upstairs of the headquarters building quickly, feeling more confident with each empty room. Diego's room showed evidence that he'd slept here some in the last day or so. It was in disarray and she saw a leather bag sitting packed and waiting on the bed. Thinking of that bed, she shook memories out of her head and gripped her pistol with resolve.

Becoming concerned again with Suzan Quantrell, she hurried back downstairs, silently, still careful. Nobody was around and she peeked into the lounge to make sure no one had come in since she'd left.

Nobody.

María Elena stepped to the couch and bent over Suzie. She seemed grayer, if that was possible. From the lack of blood? María Elena checked the feminine hygiene bandages and blood had leaked out, but not much. Maybe the woman had bled out? María Elena chose to think that the bandages, tampons as it were, had plugged the bleeding.

Suzie's eyes flicked open in a horror rictus, bulged and snapped closed. Her back arched and she gagged, spittle edging from her dry mouth. Her entire body trembled. Then she trembled, fell back, and ceased any movement, turning flaccid.

"Oh, my God," said María Elena.

Suzie's mouth froze open.

María Elena dropped her gun and fell to her knees.

"Not on my watch," she told Suzie and ripped what little was left of her blouse out of the way. She linked her hands together in the approved fashion, took a breath, and placed them on Suzie's chest. She rose from her knees and pushed hard against the agent's chest. She rolled back onto her knees, rose again and slammed into the woman. She did this over and over until she became dizzy from panic and worry and still she continued, this time with more control over her own breathing. She found a rhythm and counted to herself.

She stopped counting and started talking. "It's almost over, you can't go. Linda would never forgive you leaving her." Pump, pump, pump. "Linda and Tommy are out there right now shooting the hell out of all of them." Pump, pump, pump. "You just have to hang in there."

Her focus gave her only a slight awareness of the jet engine noise. She barely gave it a passing thought. "Just stay with us, okay? Me and Tommy have been through a lot. Too much for you to bail on us now. Hear?"

She continued to perform CPR.

Suzie's right eyelid flickered. She suddenly inhaled a small breath, then a larger one. Both eyes popped open.

María Elena stopped the hard pressure of her CPR. She was afraid to immediately quit, so she decreased the force of her heart manipulations. Soon she dropped her arms.

María Elena became aware that a new spate of shooting had begun, this time right outside.

Suzie's eyes focused and somehow María Elena could tell the woman knew exactly what had just occurred. She felt Suzie's hand on her arm. A small squeeze of acknowledgement.

María Elena sank onto the couch next to Suzie and pushed some of the blond hair off her forehead. "You're one tough lady."

She heard a noise, feet sliding. She twisted on the couch.

Diego García was standing there with fire in his eyes. And his Glock out and aimed at her.

María Elena moved slightly to put her body more in front of Suzie to protect the wounded woman.

Diego nodded at her. "Well, my dear. You have exceeded my expectations. Would that you had shown this character when we married."

"You should have looked for it," she told him.

He ignored her. "Strangely, María Elena, I find that now I admire you, so much more than all those years ago."

"Then you turn around and leave right now," she said calmly.

He shrugged. "You know me better than that. Take my admiration to your grave, my dear. If I cannot kill your lover, than I shall take from him what he took from me."

María Elena felt a tug at the back of her shirt.

"All right, Diego. Show the world what a man you are, kill a woman. Mucho hombre. What machismo. You'll be proud."

Another tug and the .32 muzzle scraped her back as it pulled out of her waistband.

Diego gave her a sad smile. "Sorry. This is the way it is." His arm tensed and he centered the sight on her.

Just then Tommy slid into the room trying to stop himself and orient his body so that he could interfere. He was bringing up his shotgun for a last chance shot.

Suzie's hand wormed around María Elena's waist.

The little .32 banged weakly compared to all the shooting which had been ongoing.

Diego's eyes opened wide. He looked down and his knee blossomed blood.

It would no longer hold him and he fell to the floor.

María Elena was closer than Tommy and she lunged for him and his gun.

He brought the Glock around, triggering a shot which went into the wall.

María Elena pounced on his gun hand and the force of her body landing on his wrist forced his hand open to release the automatic. She knocked it away.

Then Tommy was there, lifting her to her feet.

He jammed his shotgun into Diego's throat. "Stand aside, María Elena, the shot will ricochet."

She knew what she was going to do.

"No," she said simply.

"No?"

"No. Move, Tommy." She pushed him away.

Diego's eyes followed her with hope now.

"Pocahontas, goddamnit. If…"

"Do. Not. Kill. Him."

"Why not?"

She stepped back to the couch and pulled the .32 out of Suzie's weak hand. The agent's eyes followed her and seemed to understand.

María Elena went back to stand in front of Don Diego García. He was lying flat on the floor and then raised his smashed knee, grasped it with both of his hands and moaned in pain.

María Elena shot his other knee.

He screamed and spasmed on the floor.

She lifted the little gun for another shot.

His eyes pleaded with her.

She smiled crookedly and shot him on the right side of his chest, just nicking his lung, she hoped.

"That one's for 13 de enero," she said.

He fell back eyes open wider than any human had any right to do. She was ignoring Tommy's training: kill clean and quick.

She could see waves of pain cross his face.

"Jesus," said Tommy.

"This one's for Poppá." She shot him in the other lung. The sound of the .32 came across flat compared to all the other gunfire of this day.

Shock supplanted fear on his face. Quickly horror replaced fear.

Blood began welling from the right lung shot. And almost immediately, the left began bubbling blood.

"Very shortly," she told him flatly, "you will begin to gasp for breath. And you won't be able to get enough air. Oxygen starvation. It's a miserable way to die."

Tommy was watching with awe.

Even Susan Quantrell was staring at her.

"And this one's for me," said María Elena, and calmly shot Diego García in the center of the forehead. The result was a final sounding thunk.

She felt nothing. Diego looked as if his forehead had been pushed in and dark lines ran from the bullet's impact point. Only a bit of maroon eked out of the wound.

His eyes slowly closed as the life drained out of him.

María Elena dropped the gun and walked to Tommy Atkins. It was finally over.

Wasn't it?

"Where's Linda?" croaked Suzie Q.

"Uh, oh," said Tommy. He snatched up García's Glock and

handed it to María Elena. "Follow me."

They ran out to the landing.

"Stay here," he said. "Cover me."

He jumped off the landing and sprinted to a crumpled pile of yellow out in the parking lot.

María Elena scanned all around and saw the absolute carnage. "Mother Mary." She mentally crossed herself. Yet she continued to move her eyes, Glock following where she was looking.

Tommy bent and carefully lifted Linda in his arms. He glanced around, taking time to assess his situation.

"Hurry," María Elena urged him.

Tommy rushed up the stairs carrying Linda Landover and went into the building.

María Elena backed through the ruined doorway, weapon still roaming. Then she followed Tommy in.

Tommy went into the lounge and sat Linda down on the couch next to Suzie Q's head. María rushed over to help.

"FBI? Can you hear me?"

Her head lolled and her eyes fluttered, then opened. Then they scanned the room, stopping on Diego García's body. "Good move," she whispered.

Tommy was moving her around a bit and checking her body. She was soaked in so much blood it was difficult to separate hers from unfortunate 13 soldiers.

"Here," said María Elena, bending over Linda. She parted the woman's long, brunette hair and exposed a bleeding furrow. It had soaked the whole side of her head, but it was difficult to see immediately because of her long hair.

Tommy stood and scrutinized the wound. "Head wounds bleed notoriously. The bleeding has almost stopped. She's just very weak from loss of blood."

María said, "They need medical help badly. I'm going to try to find a cell phone."

She had already checked all the bodies. Maybe outside? "Be right back," she told Tommy.

She went down the hall and through the ruined double doors

and stepped out on the landing. She walked right into the muzzle of a government 9 mm automatic. The gun gestured her back and she stepped back.

The three marshals from the fake fire in the Sarasota condominium stood there. Another man with a bad comb-over of his brown hair waited at the foot of the stairs.

María Elena took a quick breath to shout a warning to Tommy and the center marshal slapped his hand over her mouth. The other two grabbed her to restrain her.

Comb-over said with a whiny voice, "Eisenberg, what are you doing? Remember you're a sworn officer of the law."

"Don't want her to warn Atkins, Dr. Henderson. She was preparing to do that."

Henderson shook his head. "This is pure massacre. You'd best watch every step, Marshal."

"Yes, sir." Eisenberg's voice was a bit surly and María Elena saw Dr. Henderson take note with raised eyebrows.

Eisenberg flipped María Elena around and pushed her in front of him. "You are strikingly familiar, sweetheart. Where do I know you from?"

Of course, she couldn't respond as his left hand was clamped over her mouth. They walked quietly down the hall and María Elena kicked out at the men holding her. She went into a frenzy of movement, trying anything, trying to make noise to get Tommy's attention.

The two men holding her merely lifted her off her feet and moved away from her. She bit down on Eisenberg's hand and he grunted in surprise and pain. He let go in automatic reflex and she tried to yell but was out of breath and the sound only came out a croak. By then they were to the doors of the lounge and the three had seen inside and it was too late.

Still, she tried again with a quick breath. "Tommy!"

As they moved into the room, she saw Tommy was still holding Linda upright with one arm and dabbing at her head with a wet cloth, probably from the water bottle against the wall.

Three U.S. Marshal's weapons lined up on Tommy. His look

to her showed concern as they let her go and pushed her into the room ahead of them. Henderson followed a few feet behind.

"Mr. Atkins, I presume?" said Eisenberg. "I've been hunting you for a long time."

Tommy fixed María Elena with his eyes and smiled. "It ain't been our day, has it?"

Anger built within her. It was different from the smoldering hate for Diego. This was red and getting hotter. It wasn't fair. They'd overcome so many obstacles today and won a war. Damn it!

Henderson walked into the room as if he were in charge.

Eisenberg motioned his weapon at Tommy. "Get up, Atkins."

Tommy looked at Linda's bloody head and back to the three marshals. "I'm kind of busy here."

"Do it now."

"I don't think so," said Tommy. "Your superiors won't like it you stopped lifesaving attention to an FBI agent—not to mention a CIA agent, too."

María Elena thought this was an exaggeration, but Tommy was trying to increase the odds of their escape. Or even survival.

Henderson turned to Eisenberg. His whiny voice gained an octave. "Marshal, you just hold your horses." He walked to the couch. "Let me look."

Eisenberg said, "You're an assistant attorney general, what are you gonna do?" It was more of a challenge.

"Any more guff from you, Eisenberg, and you better call Human Resources because your pension is in jeopardy." He knelt next to Tommy.

Linda's eyes were open now. "You're a professor doctor."

"You bet your hot ass, sweetheart," Henderson said. "And I was a medic in the Army Reserve. Spent a tour in Iraq; I know trauma wounds. I wanted to be a medical doctor but never had time to pursue that." He nudged Tommy aside. "Gimme a report on both of them."

Tommy showed him Linda's head wound, then flipped up her dress and showed him the leg wounds. He then moved to

Suzie and pulled her tattered blouse apart again. "Two wounds adjacent, lots of bleeding, but no bubbles so maybe they missed the lungs."

Henderson pried the feminine liners and pushed at Suzie's skin to see how well the tampons were stopping blood flow. He turned his head. "I need a medical kit, first aid, anygoddamnthing."

"There used to be one over by the barracks," said María Elena.

"Well, run then, girl. Quickly now."

She spun and Eisenberg pointed at one of the other marshals. "Go."

María Elena sped out the door, down the entry corridor, and out on the landing. She jumped to the ground and ran around a pickup and a Jeep in the parking lot. They seemed to be the only vehicles which hadn't been damaged in the gunfight. She ran quickly, but still saw bodies almost everywhere. The motor pool was completely gone, a smoking ruin with a couple of small fires still burning, and everything else residually smoking. She ran into the Quonset they used for many things including an infirmary. She glanced at the barracks to insure no 13 soldier would pop up and open fire. There were two large deployment medical boxes. She pointed at one and picked up the other. "Hurry."

The marshal cooperated. She could tell he was in awe of the battlefield.

"What in the world happened here?" he asked as they threaded their way back to the headquarters building. "A butcher's been through here with a scythe."

María Elena wasn't going to help the marshals in any fashion. "I think it means you better not screw with Tommy Atkins," she said flippantly before she realized she might be incriminating him.

He looked at her strangely.

One of the camo-clad bodies tried to sit up. She ignored him.

When they got back, Henderson was still ministering to Linda and Suzie. They brought the kits over to him and set them on the floor and popped them open for him.

"Excellent," he said, fishing around inside. "They need immediate attention."

"Their government jet is sitting on the landing strip with two mighty curious pilots," said Eisenberg. "Let's load 'em up or put 'em in our jet and go."

Henderson shook his head. "No way." He nodded at Suzie. "Only professionals should move her with professional EMT equipment. She needs IV fluids badly. If she's moved, the wounds might open and then we are in big time trouble." He shook his head. "Nope." Then he said to himself, "Ah."

Tommy was standing against the wall and Eisenberg and the third marshal had him covered. María Elena knew how tired she was, and Tommy had to be a lot worse off.

Henderson pulled out a fancy smart phone and punched a quick dial number. "This is Doctor Henderson, gimme FBI command center." Almost immediately, he said, "Good. This is Doctor Henderson. Here's my code, authenticate. Urgent and immediate." He spoke a series of numbers and letters. "Can you lock onto my signal and get the coordinates? It's a landing strip out in the goddamn swamps and scrublands east of Miami some damn place. Here's what I want. I want the closest best medivac team you can dig up and I want them here fifteen minutes ago. We have agents down. Alert the nearest trauma center that we have incoming. And from the looks of things, I might need a SWAT team to mop up. I don't know what's gone on here, but they got bodies all over the damn place." He listened. "That's right, and stop wasting time. Agents are dying." He winked at everybody and shrugged. He clicked off and pocketed the unit.

Linda was awake and aware now. María Elena brought her a cone of water and she drank appreciatively.

María Elena held another cup of water to Suzie's lips and spoke to Henderson. "Fifteen, twenty minutes ago, her heart stopped and I gave her CPR until she revived and breathed on her own."

Suzie coughed and spit. "Thanks." Her voice was weak and

fading.

Eisenberg went to Tommy and put his gun against Tommy's neck. "How do you like it?" While he did so marshal number three went behind Tommy and snapped on a pair of handcuffs. Then the officer frisked him.

Tommy looked at María Elena and shrugged.

She smiled encouragement.

"I want the woman, too," Eisenberg said.

Henderson looked up. "I might need her for an assistant."

"I'll wait."

"What's she done to you, Marshal?" Henderson said.

"Aiding and abetting."

"Won't hold up," said Henderson. "But I don't care."

Suzie Q looked at Linda and mouthed words María Elena couldn't make out, even though she was close. Linda leaned toward Henderson.

María Elena could make out only a few of Linda's whispered words. "Attorney General....Tampa....judge...."

Henderson nodded. "Well, I think we'll all wait until the FBI gets here and straightens things out. I saw a whole lot of bodies outside. A war zone as it were. They'll take over and handle the prisoners."

"No, sir. Atkins is *my* prisoner," said Eisenberg rubbing his almost bald head. "They can have the woman."

Henderson shrugged. "You do what you think you have to, deputy marshal, but surely the FBI can take care of things. They should be on their way."

Linda spoke lowly again.

Henderson said, "Not my problem. That's the best I can do for you."

Eisenberg looked at his men, seemed to come to a decision, and said, "Doctor Henderson has everything here under control. We need to get this dangerous prisoner to more secure confinement and debrief him." The two other marshals looked uncomfortable but nodded.

They started to leave, pushing Tommy ahead of them.

Henderson said, "Leave me one man. We might need security here. Too much unexplained killing."

Eisenberg said, "All right, Doctor." He pointed at number three. "Stay." He motioned to number two. "Go. Now." He grinned nastily. "Now I can retire."

"You'd have to since doubtless everybody knows how embarrassed you were in Sarasota." Tommy was replying to the marshal's nastiness.

"Wait," María Elena shouted. She ran to Tommy. She wiped her mouth and molded her body to him. She threw her arms around his neck and folded him down to her. Quickly she arranged Tommy's handcuff key that she'd had pocketed to the front of her mouth. Their kiss was short and interrupted by her moving the handcuff key from her mouth to his. He grunted his satisfaction.

The marshals dragged them apart and pushed Tommy out of the room. She heard them go down the hallway and out the door. The Jeep started up and backed out. She followed the sound of it as it went into gear and drove off toward the landing strip.

María Elena knew full well that Tommy was in big trouble. He needed time when he wasn't under surveillance to escape; and the fact they'd handcuffed his hands behind his back would make the trick most difficult if not impossible.

She sank against the wall, miserable.

Henderson was working on Susan Quantrell again.

Linda looked at María Elena urgently and María Elena went over to see what the problem was.

Linda's voice was a harsh whisper. "If they get him away from here, you'll never see him again. Never." Linda was fighting exhaustion and blood loss. "No amelioration. No time served. He will disappear forever."

María Elena stood taller, panic settling in. "No," she whispered. "No."

"They will watch him like a hawk. That key won't help, not much."

Nothing escaped Linda.

"Whatever it is, you have to do it now," Linda urged. Her shoulders slumped. "I can't help. Suze can't help. It's up to you."

The plan sprang into her mind fully formed.

María Elena whirled and strode over to the table, elbowing the remaining marshal aside.

He dodged, wary of her anger, but not threatened.

She went to the duffle on the table and came up with a .38, spun around and jammed it into the marshal's ear. "Over to the wall. Now." Her voice was commanding. He moved, but slowly.

She stuck the revolver between his legs and fired a round into the wall. He jumped a foot and moved quickly.

"Down." María Elena motioned. "On your stomach, hands behind your back."

As he was kneeling, she glanced at Henderson to see if he would take action. He was watching intently without any indication of interfering. Linda was nodding approval.

María Elena ground the gun into the back of his head. "I don't want to add another corpse to the count, but I will if I have to."

He dropped onto his stomach a complete believer. Next to him lay the handcuffs which had contained her to Eduardo and to the wall. Quickly, she cuffed his hands to each other and then that to the same PVC running up the wall. Then she searched him and took his weapon and handcuff key.

She jumped to her feet and ran back to the table. She started pawing through the contents once again. Then she stopped and grabbed the whole bag and swept some of the magazines and weapons she'd separated earlier into it. She slung the heavy bag over her shoulder and shot Linda a thank you look. Then she turned and ran through the door, down the hallway, through the double doors and down the stairs and to the remaining whole vehicle.

She threw the bag into the bed of the pickup, jumped in and found the key where it belonged: under the sun visor. She cranked the engine and it ran ragged. Without looking she knew it had taken a round or two and she hadn't seen the damage on her run through the parking lot.

She slammed the shifter into reverse and backed out quickly. Then into first, popping the clutch and spinning the tires which in turn spewed gravel and dirt in a rooster tail behind her. She wound it up past the redline on the tach and popped the shifter into second, foot floored on the accelerator. She kept it in second because it was easier to control. She slewed between Quonsets and over a smoldering something next to the motor pool.

They'd been through so much today; there was no way she was going to give up, going to let them take Tommy. She worried that if he managed to free himself from the handcuffs, he'd wreck the plane or it would crash in the following melee.

The pickup's engine screamed in protest and she pushed the accelerator farther into the floor. She did a four-wheel slide onto the access road to the landing strip and the Ford pickup took off. She went far into the red on the tachometer and finally slammed into third gear, double clutching it. She was pushing seventy when she emerged onto the ramp. The makeshift control tower was near the north end.

One jet sat there, ready, with two pilots sitting on the ground under a wing. The old chopper sat, burned hulk still smoking.

The other was taxiing to the far, south end of the runway. She wrestled the steering wheel to the right, almost rolled it, and downshifted to second to slow it enough to keep from rolling and ruining Tommy's only chance.

She finally got it slowed and straightened out and floored it again. The tach went past the redline again, and another thousand RPM's when the engine blew and she lost all power. She punched in the clutch and shifted to neutral to keep going. But something had happened to the transmission too. It wouldn't go into neutral and the clutch wouldn't work. The truck slowed immediately. She slewed it sideways and stomped on the brake. Maybe if she blocked the runway they couldn't take off. She looked left and right, judging the distance. She was perhaps one third of the way down the landing strip. That gave them two thirds to operate. If she remembered correctly, probably about three thousand feet, maybe a shade more. She hoped the pilot would see reason and abort his take off. If he did, she wasn't altogether certain what she'd do, but she was determined to do something.

The sound of two jet engines going to one hundred percent grabbed her attention.

"Oh, shit."

The aircraft began to move toward her.

She slammed the door open and vaulted into the bed of the pickup. She grabbed the duffle with all its weapons inside and set it on the roof of the truck's cab. She picked and grabbed for a moment and laid out a few weapons and magazines on the roof of the cab. She grabbed an M-16 since it had longer range and threw it to her shoulder, jacking a shell into the chamber. She took aim at the onrushing jet, lowered her sights to its wheels and tires and opened fire. She didn't particularly want to hit anything, just get them to stop.

The aircraft kept coming, picking up speed. She emptied the entire magazine.

"That pilot is a damn fool," she told no one.

She lifted the Uzi and fired until it was empty, not long at all on full auto.

The Cessna continued on its takeoff roll.

In her mind's eye, María Elena could see Eisenberg standing behind the pilots urging them on, refusing to let them throttle back.

She dug out another weapon, the MAC-11 and opened fire, full auto, the damn thing bucking in her hand. She didn't have much control over the accuracy so she simply sprayed bullets onto the asphalt.

The magazine died and she tossed another empty weapon into the bed of the pickup. She plucked one of the remaining weapons, a rougher MAC-10 and began firing it. Empty shells flew and she realized she'd been peppered by hot empty shells much of the time shooting, though some empties littered the runway beneath her and the bed of the pickup.

They weren't going to stop. Her ears were pounding from the noise of the guns. She reloaded another magazine into the MAC-10, in essence a machine pistol and famously inaccurate unless you're in close confines. She hosed off that magazine and tossed it aside. Selecting the next weapon, she saw the two waiting pilots standing and watching her with awe.

The sleek Cessna continued accelerating. She guessed it to be used for CIA drops where they didn't want to advertise whose corporate jet it was, just like the other one behind her on the ramp.

She knew little about jets or any aircraft, but she did know that there had to be a point of no return on takeoff.

She knew this was almost her last chance and Tommy's final shot at freedom. It might even be too late, for if the jet crashed, then he'd be in that crash and in real danger. You just don't crash airplanes and walk away.

She snatched the AR-15, insured a shell was in the chamber, and wrapped the sling around her forearm for a more stable firing platform.

The scream of the jet engines sent hackles up the back of her neck. She shook her head to clear it. She aimed at the tires and fired two three round bursts, just as Tommy had taught her. She thought she'd gotten a hit, but the aircraft continued to scream toward her.

She was now in jeopardy herself. She recognized now that the aircraft had to lift to clear her and the truck or simply crash into it. She did not think any further.

One final attempt and she aimed for the onrushing jet's windscreen. She didn't want to kill the pilots since they needed to control the aircraft, but she had to frighten them.

"Now or never," she said aloud. She fixed the moving target in her mind and down the barrel of the AR-15 and the trajectory it would take. She squeezed the trigger once and tracked the aircraft blazing toward her and fired again. The right top of the windscreen above the copilot's seat starred and cracks lanced across the whole thing.

The aircraft continued to scream toward her and she watched it come over the barrel of the AR-15 in fascination. If something didn't happen in the next few seconds, they'd all be dead.

As if by her mental command, the jet engines stopped screaming and some kind of airbrakes came out. Then the sound of thrust reversers began. She didn't know what the Cessna employed to stop it besides the brakes, but it was happening. Some kind of air brakes or flaps widened. Yet the damn thing was still screaming toward her, and there was no way it could miss her.

Then a tire blew and she knew that she had hit it or grazed it enough to matter.

The Cessna jerked to the right and smoke seared off its brakes. It kept skidding sideways heading toward her and she saw the pilot desperately working controls. The engines advanced quickly and the small jet lunged forward and missed her and the truck. But the passing engine blast knocked María Elena off her feet and out of the pickup. She smashed into the runway, trying to perform a shoulder roll like Tommy had taught her, and failed, but not completely. She ended up on her back suffering a lot of pain.

"Not my left shoulder again," she complained, scrambling to her feet.

She watched the jet slide off the runway, tires smoking and stinking, into the scrub alongside the strip. The tail end of the plane slewed farther around and the damn thing spun a couple of three sixties. Then it went farther into the scrub and into the muck and was going slowly enough for the landing gear and wheels to sink and get hung up. It did so and slammed to a stop. The engines died or the aircrew killed them.

María Elena knew she didn't have long. She leaped back onto the bed of the Ford pickup and snatched the .38, stuck it in her waist. She dug around and found a .44 Desert Eagle, eight shot mag and powerful. She jumped back down onto the ramp. She ran toward the smoking Cessna, sunk up to the middle of its wheels in swamp muck. She checked the load in the Desert

Eagle, and it was good. She should have used this to stop the jet; hell it would stop a buffalo or so the PR said.

She favored her left shoulder but continued to run.

The whole place was strangely silent. No more screaming jet engines, no more automatic weapons fire. She wondered if her hearing would ever be the same.

Tire smoke hung listlessly in the morning sun and it stank worse than the disturbed muck.

María Elena knew that she was in big trouble now. You don't just shoot down a government airplane full of U.S. marshals and their prisoner and aircrew. And you don't just try to effect said prisoner's escape.

She hoped Tommy was all right. Or at least not injured badly. Her feet began sinking in the mud and she lifted them to take longer strides.

She didn't care if she went to jail for a long time, she wasn't going to let them take Tommy without a fight.

Water was now atop the mud and she waded forward.

The door on the left side of the Cessna swung open toward the cockpit, the boarding ladder fell into place and she cocked the Desert Eagle and lunged ahead.

Baldy stood in the doorway, one hand holding on to the frame and the other bringing his automatic to line up on her.

As she lifted the heavy Desert Eagle to shoot, Baldy suddenly flew out of the door, tried to right himself while airborne, and hit in the water and muck face down. He splashed swamp water all around him and immediately pushed himself to his knees coughing and sputtering. A second man appeared in the doorway, the other marshal, and he raised his hands in surrender, looked over his shoulder, and jumped.

Then Tommy stood there smiling at her. He gave her a thumb up and she saw a handcuff swinging from his wrist. He disappeared back inside and then the pilot and copilot jumped out. Their flight suits became immediately soaked. The three stood beside Baldy in the shallows of the swamp.

Disturbed mosquitoes swarmed angrily around them all.

Tommy stepped out. He waded toward her. "Each time I see you I am glad to be alive, just to look at you. This time more than most. Thank you, Pocahontas."

"Yes, dear. Me, too." She dimpled at him and handed him the Desert Eagle.

Baldy sat up and sputtered, completely covered in muck. He gagged and spat.

Tommy tucked the Desert Eagle under his arm and finished unlocking the other handcuff. He waded back to the aircrew and marshals. Mosquitoes flew into the air. He climbed back into the dead Cessna and came out with two more sets of handcuffs. He cuffed all four together and then to a strut on the left landing gear. "Shouldn't be too long," he said amiably. "Gotta be a thousand feds on the way."

Baldy coughed and started to shout, looked around, and stopped abruptly. His shoulders sunk.

Tommy and María Elena waded to the hardpan and stomped off their feet. Tommy kept looking admirably at her and shaking his head. "I ain't ever getting on your bad side."

She stuck her tongue out at him.

They walked past the late Ford pickup and back toward the mobile tower. When they neared the other Cessna, the two aircrew were standing staring at them. It was obvious they didn't know what to do. One spoke to the other, he nodded, and they turned and ran toward the short tower.

Tommy fired a round from the Desert Eagle and it knocked a barrel over in their path and ricocheted off into the distance.

Both stopped on a dime.

Tommy motioned to them. "Over here. We don't need any loose ends."

They came hesitantly.

"We're out of handcuffs," said María Elena. She pointed to the Jeep. "Get in and drive." The copilot sat in the driver's seat and she gestured the pilot into the passenger seat. She and Tommy climbed into the back, thankful that the cover was down.

The pilot looked over his shoulder in awe. "I've never seen

anything like that. Jesus, lady, you're crazy."

"Then you need to do what I tell you."

She directed them to the headquarters building. As they threaded through the compound, the extent of carnage was highly visible. A couple of burned buildings still smoldered and bodies sprawled everywhere, in various positions.

The parking area immediately in front of the headquarters building appeared as a vacated battle zone, with dead soldiers and shot up vehicles sitting askew. One wounded 13 soldier moaned and his arm flopped on the ground.

The pilot said, "Jesus," and shook his head.

They avoided bodies and buckets of blood on the landing as they climbed the stairs and stepped gingerly on the surface.

They all trooped inside, the aircrew first.

Susan Quantrell saw them first, her eyes going wide. She was still limp on the couch, and Doctor Henderson had her feminine hygiene bandages off and was applying some kind of solution around the wound.

Linda Lavender had not moved. Her head was lying back against the top of the couch. She popped an eye open. "God, now what?"

Suzie waved them over.

Tommy pointed to a pair of metal chairs and the aircrew went and sat obediently.

She and Tommy went to stand next to the couch.

Her voice was difficult to make out, but María Elena watched her intelligent eyes and they were clear.

"We came here to investigate rumors of mutiny and were ambushed by whom we don't know yet. Some citizens and other JTF 13 'assests' assisted us in the firefight. Those citizens and assets left abruptly."

"Fine by us," Tommy said immediately. "We're glad to be out of here, thank you very much."

Not that they had any choice, thought María Elena. She and Tommy were the only ones left standing. She looked at Linda. "You okay with this?"

Linda smiled wanly and nodded. "It's been fun."

Tommy pointed his Desert Eagle at Henderson. "And the doc?"

The man nodded, his comb over still in place. "I, ah, concur. We've had a discussion and my boss will buy off on it."

The Attorney General.

Susan Quantrell grinned as if this were her greatest accomplishment.

Linda held up a card. María Elena took it. It had a symbol with a 13 and JTF on it with a phone number and email address. She pocketed the card.

Voice failing, Suzie said, "We need assets in the new and coming Cuba. If you're available when normalization comes, it could be you both."

María Elena cocked her head.

The agent fell silent and Linda Landover took over. She nodded at the pilots across the room. "They will take you to a secret landing strip in Costa Rica and somebody will meet you and take you to a safe house until we can make arrangements."

María Elena looked at Tommy and he shrugged.

The FBI agent pointed at the two pilots and waved them over. "Remember the landing strip we went into two years ago February, down in Costa Rica?"

The pilot nodded. "In the jungle, maybe as long as this one." He pointed.

Linda said with a finality, "Take them there. Now."

The pilot opened his eyes wide.

"You know nothing, you just did as you were told," Linda said. "And you stay down there until the smoke clears. We'll pick up the Cessna later. Got it."

The pilot fidgeted. "I dunno."

"Gordo?" whispered Suzie Q.

He shifted from foot to foot. "I guess orders are orders."

Suzie Q gasped the words, "Your orders are to fly these agents to Costa Rica so they can undergo, ah, training and language prep, and prepare for later insertion into Cuba." She coughed lightly.

"Yes, ma'am, that ought to cover us." The pilot shrugged; obviously he was grateful they'd have legitimate reasons for flying across the Gulf and half the Caribbean. "Good thing we have the gravel runway kit installed," he grumbled.

María Elena turned to look at Tommy once again. His eyes were guarded.

Should they trust the women and the pilots? There were a lot of holes in this plan. On the other hand they were in jeopardy here right now, big time jeopardy.

"Whatever, let's just get the hell out of here." Tommy's voice was decisive.

The pilots went out back to the jeep and María Elena and Tommy began to follow.

"Hey," whispered Linda. "Good luck."

Tommy nodded. "Watch your step, FBI, the floor's slippery." He ameliorated the joke with a wink.

"Christ, I need a smoke," said Linda.

María Elena gave her a smile. Her eyes picked up the table recently vacated of weapons.

"I forgot a bag," she said.

Quickly she retrieved Diego García's other duffle full of dollars and pesos. She stepped over his body to get to the doorway and didn't give him a second look.

A final glance over her shoulder showed Linda watching closely. She understood without knowing. A faint smile crossed her face. María Elena shrugged as if to say, "I am his widow, his only heir. Therefore, this belongs to me." María Elena went out the door.

The pilot drove them back to the runway and to their Cessna.

Tommy tapped him on the shoulder and pointed. "The pickup."

The pilot nodded understanding and raced over to the carcass of the Ford in the middle of the runway. He put the Jeep's bumper on the rear bumper of the pickup and pushed it off the runway.

It ended up on the coral base toward the crashed U. S.

Marshal's aircraft. The four men there stood and watched.

María Elena worried about that but there was nothing she could do. She could only hope that the power of the Attorney General would keep the lid on this whole thing. Otherwise, she and Tommy once again would be hunted.

Back at the JTF jet, they boarded and soon the pilots had run their checklist. Tommy went forward and slid the accordion door closed. "Don't bother us until we get there. Okay?"

"Yes, sir," said the pilot with a bit of trepidation. After María Elena had faced them down in the middle of their takeoff roll, they were believers.

"I'll be doggoned," said María Elena as Fluffy jumped off a seat and trotted over to her. She scooped him up and scratched his head.

"What do you think, college girl?"

"I dunno, Tommy. It was short and quick and it's full of holes."

He nodded. "I give them credit for helping. They didn't have to do that thing."

"I suspect it was politically expedient," she replied. "The best outcome would have been for us to become casualties. That would make things so much cleaner."

"It was the best they could do short of killing us," he said, fiddling with his seatbelt. The inside of the small jet wasn't luxurious, but it wasn't anything like flying tourist. There were eight seats configured four to a group, two facing each other. "Nice ride," he said. He kicked at the duffle María Elena had brought along. He looked inside for the second time.

"Nice doggy," María Elena said.

"He belongs to them, the two agents."

"A strange pair."

"Not one you want to cross," said Tommy enigmatically.

María Elena cocked an eye at him.

The aircraft continued to taxi south to the far end of the runway.

"The thing is, with this deal, we are not in charge of ourselves, not much anyway."

"No," said María Elena. "I've been worried about that."

"And we'd be in a foreign country. Stand out bad." He scratched his head with the muzzle of the Desert Eagle.

"I could get along. But you are distinctive," María Elena said.

"Well, I should hope so." He looked out the small window near him. "There's an old Bantu proverb: 'The road doesn't enlighten the traveler as to what he may find at his destination.'"

She shook her head. "The famous Cuban writer, Jose Marti said, 'A grain of poetry suffices to season a century.'"

He grinned at her. "I'll try to tone it down, Pocahontas."

"On the other hand, Tommy, that's part of your charm."

The Cessna 560 Encore was at the very end of the runway and beginning to swing around.

María Elena sensed a growing concern in Tommy. They simply had not had enough time to think this through, to plan.

"Given a few days," she said, "I think I could find the *CUBAN BEAUTY*. It's a nice time of year to take a cabin cruiser around the Gulf of Mexico and the Caribbean."

"We'd have to change her name," Tommy pointed out as the engines came up to 100 per cent and take off form.

"Right after we change my name," she said. "I'm a widow, you know."

He popped off his seat belt. "Well, we still have a motel room over in Weston."

"Done, Tommy."

Tommy stepped to the accordion door and pulled it aside a bit. "Hey! Throttle back." He waved the Desert Eagle vaguely.

The pilot did so. "Now what?"

Tommy said, "The dog needs to walk for a minute. Or you clean it up."

"All right, all right."

Tommy went to pull the door closed again, then stopped. "Like I said, we don't want to be interrupted. She's gonna walk the dog and when she gets back on I'll close the door and you go ahead and take off. Got it?" Tommy scratched his temple with the sight at the tip end of the Desert Eagle.

"Yes, sir."

"You can wake us when we land in Costa."

He nodded and Tommy closed the door.

He turned to María Elena. "Run forward so you don't get caught up in the jet intake. Let the dog do its thing and make sure you bend over and show them a fine show."

"And you?"

"You'll see."

Tommy grabbed the handle and opened the forward entry door. The ladder fell into place. He helped María Elena down and she ducked and carried Fluffy away from the aircraft. She bent over and set the dog down. Fluffy must have been full, for he peed like a racehorse. María Elena shook her head. She thought she should have peed herself before they left. She bent over the dog and purposefully let her shirt ride up her torso.

She glanced back at the aircraft and saw Tommy scrambling under the low fuselage toward the rear, carrying the duffle. He ran to the edge of the runway and tossed the bag into the brush. Then he ran back.

María Elena scooped up the dog and hurried back to the Cessna. The pilots were watching her closely.

She set the dog back inside and Tommy motioned her under the aircraft to exit as he'd done. She did so, knowing that the pilot likely couldn't see her since the access door opened toward the cockpit.

He spoke into her ear. "Keep low and insure the fuselage stays between you and the marshals up the landing strip. We don't need witnesses."

When she was safely away, Tommy folded the boarding ladder up into place, slammed the door and locked it from the outside. He ducked quickly under the fuselage and ran toward María Elena. The aircraft's engines gained power and Tommy dodged aside at the last minute.

They knelt together in a clump of two and three foot tall torpedo grass watching the jet roll down the runway faster and faster, go airborne, and then dwindle into the distance. They kept their heads down so the marshals far up the runway couldn't see them.

"It's maybe a thirty minute walk through the woods and we have a motorcycle to ride to the hotel."

"I know where there's a nice bar for sale," she said. "After we spend some of Diego's money."

"I don't know," he replied. "I'm thinking of retiring. After our boat trip, that is." He grinned at her. "I got a few hundred grand and in that duffel bag your, ahem, dowry, is maybe ten times that."

"Whatever, but I need a shower worse than anything right now."

"Me, too. Let's."

ABOUT THE AUTHOR

JAMES B. JOHNSON has written seven novels: *Trekmaster*, *Habu*, *Mindhopper*, *A World Lost*, *Daystar and Shadow*, *Counterclockwise*, and *When the Pirate Prays*, all of which are being published by The Borgo Press. *Mindhopper* was optioned twice for a movie, and three of his books were translated into French and German. He has also penned numerous short stories and articles. Jim has sold advertising, worked for the Post Office for fifteen years, and spent eleven years in the Air Force. He lives in Sarasota, Florida, with his wife Beverly.

www.ingramcontent.com/pod-product-compliance
Lightning Source LLC
Chambersburg PA
CBHW051551250626
47157CB00001B/269